DYING EMBERS

An unputdownable psychological thriller
full of breathtaking twists

MARGARET MURPHY

JOFFE
BOOKS

Revised edition 2021
Joffe Books, London
www.joffebooks.com

First published in Great Britain in 2000

ISBN: 978-1-78931-646-9

For Sue Mortimer, friend and mentor.

1

Monday morning. The clamour had already started. Catching up on the weekend's gossip: who'd got off with who; who'd scored — girls, footie, drugs, it didn't matter, it was all news. The broad corridors of St Michael's were already crowded with children and the polished linoleum was strewn with sports bags, art folders and square-sided wicker baskets.

Geri Simpson grimaced. She felt cheated, having missed the still, serene twenty minutes before the slow drift of children through the school gate became an onslaught.

'Miss — Miss Simpson!'

Geri sighed, checked her watch. She had a call to make to a parent before registration, and she was already late for the staff briefing. 'Yes, Dean?'

'Miss,' Dean said, 'can I go into class?'

She looked down at him. He looked like he had fallen out of bed five minutes earlier. Small, skinny, with mouse-coloured hair that never sat flat on his head, Dean was as unlike his brother, Ryan, as it was possible for two brothers to be. Aware of her scrutiny, he made an effort to tuck his shirt in, and even raked his fingers through his hair.

'What d'you want to go into class for?'

'Finish my homework.' He mumbled this, frowning.

Geri was buffeted by a sports bag, carried at shoulder height. She hooked a thumb round the strap and dragged it down. The boy carrying it spun round, scowling, then seeing her, apologized.

'Set an example, eh?'

'Miss.' He wandered off, absently swinging his bag back onto his shoulder halfway down the corridor.

She shook her head, deciding it wasn't worth the hassle of calling him back — besides she was now very late. She turned back to Dean. 'You had the weekend to do your homework.' He bit his lip. 'Homework is work you do at home.'

The set of his face changed from embarrassment to resentment. She didn't have time for explanations about health and safety, reasons for setting homework, the application of rules to all, so she told Dean she would see him at registration, and he stamped off, muttering.

Geri carried on towards the staffroom, hurrying, dodging dawdling clusters of girls and admonishing boys for slouching along with their hands in their pockets. Sometimes a look was enough, at others a direct request was necessary, keeping the tone of her voice low and strong, in order to make any impact over the babble of scores of voices. Despite her small stature and slight build, the children minded Miss Simpson. New pupils sometimes mistook her for a sixth-former — they never made the mistake twice.

Geri eased through the door, shutting it against the noise that by now had almost reached its peak. The staff briefing had already begun. She saw Coral Jackson immediately; the gold, green and red colours of her woollen dress seemed to glow against the rich dark colour of her skin. Her hair was newly braided and beaded, and she stood erect and attentive with her back to the staff pigeon-holes. Geri found a spot next to her, reassessing her own choice of grey skirt and maroon sweater as dowdy and unadventurous.

'The children should be properly prepared for Sergeant Beresford's visit . . . especially in the light of Friday's incident.

Year Nine form tutors please take note.' Geri had yet to see a quiet week as a Year Nine form tutor — thirteen- and fourteen-year-olds were traditionally the most difficult. 'As of today, liquid paper is banned,' the headmaster went on, 'Confiscated containers to the school secretary, please.' He referred to his notes. 'Year Seven are on first lunch this week . . .'

Geri whispered to Coral, 'When's he due in?' Sergeant Vince Beresford had been appointed as drugs liaison officer shortly after his arrival in the area from London. His visits were a regular feature, an essential part of the Personal and Social Education lessons, and he had been expected for the past fortnight, his visit postponed twice.

'Five and six,' Coral whispered, referring to the lesson slots. 'Question is, who's advising who?' Geri raised her eyebrows in question, and she chuckled. 'The ban on liquid paper? Boys from 9G caught sniffing it at Friday afternoon break.'

'No wonder they're comatose,' Geri said. Coral nudged her and nodded in the direction of the headmaster. Mr Ratchford finished his list of notices.

'Interim reports are due in by Wednesday.'

Geri groaned. Alan Morgan wandered past muttering, 'Here a tick, there a tick . . .'

Geri made a note of the time of the drugs liaison officer's visit. She had to catch a couple of members of staff before they went off to registration: messages that had come through on Friday concerning her form — home problems, pleas for help in getting homework instructions down, a request to encourage one of the girls to use her new spectacles. On the way out of the staffroom, she checked the noticeboard. She was down for a double cover. Amy Wilcox was off sick — again.

Coral Jackson looked over her shoulder, checking the cover list. She stood head and shoulders taller than Geri. 'Good weekend?'

Geri's shoulders sagged.

'Hm. Nick?'

Geri answered her with a look.

'Say no more.' Coral had been Geri's mentor in her first year of teaching and had never quite dropped the habit of care. She followed Geri out of the staffroom in silence, and Geri was grateful that she didn't probe further. At a T-junction, where the main corridor ran to right and left, Coral said, 'This is my turn-off — and believe me, I mean what I'm saying.'

Geri shot her a questioning look.

'Amy Wilcox's form for registration,' she added. Coral was pastoral tutor for the whole of Year Nine and volunteered for registration duty whenever one of her team was absent. She shrugged. 'It keeps me in touch with what the little darlings are up to.' She turned and strode off, breasting the tide of incoming children like a great black figurehead on the prow of a ship.

The bell sounded for registration. Geri would have to skip assembly and make that call. Mrs Davies worked a ten-two shift as a cleaner in the hospital, then put in an evening pulling pints at the Firkin and Trotter. Her son, Jay, was giving cause for concern: homework not done; inattentive in class — he had even fallen asleep in an art lesson. His interim reports were likely to be less than fulsome in their praise.

Job completed, Geri unlocked her classroom. She still got a little rush of pleasure, looking at the gleaming new double desks paid for by the parents' association. For the first two years of her tenure, she'd had to put up with graffiti-scored tables with the Formica nibbled away and the chipboard temptingly exposed.

She called the register as exercise books shuffled left and right to the centre, then up to the front of the class to the collector's piles. Orange for geography, green for science, red for maths. Precious textbooks had been sent home for the physics homework and a second monitor ticked off the number designated to each pupil as they came in.

Her own work started arriving as she gave out the form notices; she asked the children to make a note that their PSE lessons would be in the hall for today, while skimming down the list to see whose social commitments had caused them to neglect their academic obligations. She was aware of Dean sulking at the back of the room, but she had to get through all the messages before assembly started. Someone threw a book from the back of the class. It skittered across the top of the geography stack and landed on the floor.

'Don't throw!' Geri boomed.

'*You* do, Miss.'

'I do *not* miss. That's why I'm allowed, and you aren't.'

The culprit laughed. 'Nice one, Miss. You should be on telly.' Geri fixed him with a deadpan stare, waiting for the punchline. 'Next to me mum's plaster poodle.' That raised more laughter, and Geri allowed herself a smile.

She checked the lists before asking the monitors to take the homework away. Dean got as far as the door at the end of registration before she saw him and called him back. He looked washed out, almost ill with tiredness. 'You haven't handed in any work?' Often the indirect question got a less aggressive response.

He shrugged. 'Mum's gonna phone.'

She regarded him thoughtfully. She wouldn't get anything out of him the mood he was in. She would try again at afternoon registration. 'All right. But I want you to see all the teachers concerned and apologize, okay?' Another shrug. He wouldn't meet her eye.

'All right, Dean,' she said, quietly, and touched him lightly on the shoulder. He stiffened and for a moment she thought he would burst into tears, then he turned and almost ran out of the classroom and down the corridor.

* * *

The Drax congregated in the narrow galley kitchen area next to the coffee bar; they were six in number — five tall, slightly dishevelled boys wearing long grey-green woollen overcoats that fell almost to their ankles, and one thin, sickly looking girl. She wore a long, black jersey dress over lace-up boots. All of the gang had the same vampiric look of anaemia that had earned them their nickname. Baz called them to order and they huddled closer.

'So, where is he?'

A ripple of shrugs went around the group. Siân looked into their faces. Ryan was her boyfriend and since he had failed to phone her on Sunday night, fear had wormed in the pit of her stomach until it sickened her. 'Who saw him last?'

The boys shuffled a bit and she sensed an unwillingness to look at Baz. 'John? Frankie?'

'Didn't he get on the bus with you, Baz?' Frank Traynor said this, clearing his throat first to stop his voice wavering too much. He didn't look up, but he could feel Baz's eyes on him.

Baz didn't answer immediately, he waited until Frank was visibly sweating, then said, 'He got off at Derby Street. Said he was going home.' He had a way of talking softly, so that you had to look at him to make out the words, and when you looked at him . . . Well, nobody crossed Baz. Some said it was because he was hard, and he had been notorious as a scrapper lower down the school — he even had a scar along his jawline to prove it. But it was mostly that look. It wasn't mad or wild or anything, it was cool, a bit distant, like he was seeing you — not picturing, actually *seeing* you — after something bad had happened to you, and he was enjoying the spectacle. Maybe he was capable of doing the bad thing, and maybe not, but few people ever pushed it far enough to find out.

'When?' Siân asked. Baz continued staring at Frank and Siân repeated her question more urgently. 'When, Baz? What time?'

'Time is relative,' Baz said, still looking at Frank.

'Bullshit!' Siân grabbed his sleeve and pulled him round to face her. 'Ryan's missing, Baz. Do you know where he is?'

Baz narrowed his eyes. This kind of outburst damaged his cool image. He gazed at Siân with rapt concentration.

'Oh, my God,' she murmured. 'Did you give him something? Did you, Baz?'

He closed his hand over hers and prised it away from his arm, then slowly tightened his grip until she winced at the pressure. 'Keep your voice *down,*' he breathed.

'Did you spike his drink, Baz?' She went on, because her fear of what Baz might do wasn't yet greater than her fear of what might have happened to Ryan. 'D'you know how cold it was yesterday? He could be lying somewhere freezing to *death*!'

Barry was fast. Siân flinched, but he had tight hold of her. He slowed the movement of his free hand from a threatened slap to a single raised finger. It came to rest so close to her eye that she could feel her eyelashes bat against it when she blinked. He smiled, but his eyes were cold and hard. He touched his finger to his lips.

Frank moved closer, risked one look into Baz's face and shook his head. Baz let go of Siân's hand and, still in that quiet, reasonable tone that could send shivers up your spine, he said, 'He was fine when I left him. Just a bit high.'

'I thought you said *he* left *you*.'

Baz watched Siân thoughtfully. His eyelids flickered slightly. 'Whatever,' he said.

* * *

Dean was sent home ill after morning break, so Geri didn't get a chance to speak to him. She sat in on Sergeant Beresford's talk; he managed the Year Nines well, seemed to have the knack of informing without patronizing. Since taking up the post of liaison officer, he had even shown up at the school youth club on occasions. He had come to the north from Thames Valley, promoted to sergeant — returning to uniform after a spell as a DC with a Vice unit.

She paused to speak to the policeman as the children filed out of the hall at the end of the lesson. 'Sorry, Vince, I can't stop,' she said. 'Sixth-Form lesson — General Studies.'

'Okay. But I need to talk to you.' Vince looked around at the mass of boys and girls. 'Maybe after work?'

A couple of girls caught each other's eye and burst out laughing.

'You've got mucky minds, the two of you,' Geri said, and the girls left, blushing and giggling. Truth to tell, they had a crush on Sergeant Beresford — along with the majority of Year Nine girls. Catholic school or no, hormones were apt to rule the heads, hearts and emotions of girls at thirteen and fourteen years of age. Geri didn't blame them: she could easily fancy the sergeant herself, with his thick, nut-brown hair and blue-grey eyes. 'I'll call you when I get home,' she added, surprised that Vince seemed embarrassed by the girls' attention.

The Lower Sixth were in restless mood when she arrived. They seemed irritable and ill-at-ease, anxious to get the lesson over with and get out of school.

Ryan's desk was empty. Ryan was never absent, and he never bunked off lessons — even General Studies lessons. 'Where's Ryan?' she asked.

'He's dead.' It was a common enough response, it passed as a joke among the lads and even raised a laugh on occasions, but this time, all the joker got was a few venomous looks from the rest of the group.

'Probably hung over,' Baz suggested.

Geri stared at him. She often wondered what the others saw in him; no more than average height, with mud-coloured eyes and slightly pock-marked skin, he excelled in nothing, as far as she knew, but they seemed to look up to him as a leader. 'It's the middle of the afternoon, Barry,' she said. 'Does *anyone* know where Ryan is? Siân?'

Siân jumped up, scraping her chair back. 'Ask them,' she shouted, holding back tears. 'Ask them!' She ran out, and Geri turned to face the rest of the class.

'Well?' she said, her eyes drawn to Baz Mandel.

'Well what?' he said, on the defensive. 'Why ask me?' She waited. 'How'm I supposed to know? We're mates, not lovers.'

That raised a laugh, then one of the girls came in with, 'He's probably roosting in a dark cave.'

Geri ignored the comment. 'So no one knows what's wrong with him.' The joker at the back of the class looked like he was going to come up with a list, but Geri silenced him with a glance. A few outside of Baz's magic circle looked genuinely nonplussed, but the rest were unwilling to meet her eye. She thought again about Dean, sent home at morning break time; perhaps there was a bug going around the family, that's all. Then she happened to glance over at Barry again. He was seated near the back, out of the range of vision of most of the class, but his eyes moved from one person to the next, resting on the back of their heads, and although she told herself it was fanciful, she could swear each of them tensed at Barry's scrutiny.

* * *

Vince Beresford cornered DS Garvey by the soft drinks machine. He had returned from St Michael's to find out that Garvey had taken one of his officers, without proper sanction, to take part in an ill-planned set-up which might have ended with serious injury — or worse. He had just come from a debrief with the WPC involved, and he'd had to send her home.

'Next time you want officers from my team to do your dirty work, ask me first,' he said.

Garvey picked up his can of orange from the slot and turned to face Vince. His face was exactly the same shade of red as his lips.

'What's the matter, Beresford — frightened they're not up to the job?'

'I know they are,' Vince said. 'It's you I'm worried about.'

Garvey opened his mouth to come back at him, but Vince didn't give him the chance. 'I've worked CID, Garvey. I know the types. You're the sloppy type. The type who'll get out of anything dirty or strenuous or dangerous — usually by getting some poor mug to do it for you.'

'She was glad of the chance to do some real police work,' Garvey said.

'She's inexperienced,' Vince lowered his voice as a couple of constables in uniform walked past. 'She felt under pressure to agree to your hare-brained scheme.'

'Is that what she's saying?'

'She doesn't have to.'

'Come on, Vince,' Garvey sneered. 'She bottled out. They weren't gonna do anything to her.'

'You know that, do you?'

Garvey smiled and cracked open the can. It took all of Vince's self-control to keep from trying to ram it down Garvey's throat as he took a greedy swallow.

Vince leaned in closer. 'She was surrounded. Trapped in a cellar with four villains — one of whom was carrying a knife.'

'"One of whom"?' Garvey said. 'Lovely grammar. The fact is, she started screaming blue murder and bollocksed up the entire operation.'

'She felt under threat.'

'We lost Stanfield as a result of her *feeling under threat*. He's gone to ground. And the lorry-load of booze he nicked could be anywhere by now.'

'That's not my concern. You put an inexperienced officer under cover, insufficiently prepared, and with inadequate backup.' He'd phrased this to sound official, and Garvey responded to the implied threat.

'That what you're putting in your report, is it?' The sneer on his face barely masked Garvey's anxiety.

Vince returned his stare with cold contempt. 'That isn't even the half of it,' he said.

2

It was cold. Cold enough for ice already to have formed in milky patches in the gutters and in the depressions of cracked paving stones. Geri dug her free hand deep into her coat pocket. She had left her gloves at home in her hurry to get out that morning, away from Nick.

She could have waited for the bus, but at the end of the school day the last thing she felt like doing was supervising children — and she knew that she was incapable of ignoring rowdy behaviour from St Michael's pupils, even out of school hours.

Anyway, the traffic would be building in the approach to rush hour, and the January sales hadn't quite finished, which would add to the congestion in the city centre, so it would be faster walking.

Geri lived half a mile from the centre, but on the western side of the city, the shops and offices acting as a buffer-zone between home and school. When she passed the twin towers of NorthWest Assurance, she felt the school day was over.

At first, when her family had moved to the north just short of her tenth birthday, she had felt oppressed by the narrow streets of red-brick terraces and the imposing Victorian gothic architecture of the civic buildings. Now, she derived comfort from the solidity of the houses, the sandstone facades of the museum and art gallery, the lovingly planned and maintained patchwork of parks and gardens squares within walking distance of even the most built-up areas of the city. This was home to her in a way that the succession of pretty suburban houses her parents had taken on short leases had never been. This was the place where, for the first time in her life, she felt settled. Her father had worked as a sales rep — anything from double glazing to greetings cards — and when one job fell through, as it invariably did because of his heavy drinking — they moved to another. In her first nine years of life, Geri had lived on the fringes of no fewer than eight towns and cities from the midlands to the north of England.

She walked quickly, trying to keep warm, and now that the distractions and responsibilities of the school day had ended, she found herself unable to suppress the events of the morning.

It had started well, with Nick volunteering to get up and have breakfast with her. By the time she had showered and trotted down to the kitchen, Nick had opened the blind, and silvery winter sunshine gleamed on the stainless-steel cookware, hung on rails next to the cooking range. His short towelling dressing gown showed a tempting length of thigh. Pumping all that iron had certainly built up his quads and glutes to flattering effect.

His dark hair was so fetchingly tousled, his chin so newly shaven that she almost suspected him of orchestrating some kind of dramatic moment. Nick did that sometimes, usually after they had had one of their more acrimonious rows, but although Sunday evening had brought a routine outburst of bickering, it was nothing too strenuous or bitter, so she couldn't see a reason for this surge of apparently motiveless charm.

Nick was determinedly cheerful, pouring cereal, brewing coffee and toasting bread as if they were things he did every day.

Geri asked him about his plans — he had the day off — and he told her he had decided to do some work on his bike. Nick had found work at a horticultural research station after three years of short-term contracts in unskilled and poorly paid jobs. After a pause that was just too long to be comfortable, he asked her about her timetable; he had a vague understanding that there were good days and bad days but could never remember which they were.

'Not bad,' she said. 'Double Year Nine lessons five and six, but I've a couple of frees this morning and the Sixth Form last two.' Which reminded her that she had a stack of exam questions to hand back to them.

Nick was saying something, but she interrupted him. 'Sorry — I've got to do this before I forget.'

She ran upstairs to get the papers she had marked in bed and returned, stuffing them into her briefcase before picking up a slice of toast and sitting at the table again.

'How far on are you on with the bike?' she asked.

The Triumph Bonneville had been in pieces in the wooden shack at the side of the house for six months. Too large to be described as a shed, and too small for a garage, Nick called it his workshop.

He looked at her but didn't reply.

'Nick?'

'Sorry,' he said, 'Were you talking to me?'

Geri felt a familiar gnawing pang of unease. His mouth had taken on that down-turned look of sneering petulance that preceded one of his nastier outbursts.

'Nick, what's the matter with you?' At first, he didn't answer, but she could see he was working himself up to a response.

'Nick?' she repeated.

'I'm in mid-bloody-sentence and she just ups and walks out,' he said to an unseen third person.

'I'm getting ready for work. I can't go in unprepared.'

'Still,' he carried on, ignoring what she had said, 'What could I possibly be saying that was of any *fucking* interest or importance?'

'Why d'you have to do this?' she said. 'Why d'you have to start a row just as I'm going out of the door?'

'I didn't start it, *you* did.'

She held her hands up. 'No,' she said. 'No, I'm not getting into this.' She picked up her briefcase and headed for the hall. Nick followed her.

'Should I make an appointment, or what? When are you free this week, with your parents' evenings and your youth club and your eternal bloody play rehearsals?' His dark eyes glittered angrily.

Geri dragged her coat from the hook and felt something catch and tear.

'It's my job, Nick. It pays the mortgage.'

'Right, throw that in my face. Maybe we should make it official — you could make me up a nice little blue rent book, like Lauren's.'

'I wasn't — I didn't mean . . .' He always managed to make it look like she was bitching.

'Yeah? What *did* you mean?'

She shook her head. 'I can't talk to you when you're like this. You won't listen. You take everything I say and twist it.'

'Okay.' He folded his arms. 'Go ahead. I'm listening.'

'I haven't got *time*, Nick!'

'That's the trouble,' he said, following her to the door, yelling after her, 'You've *never* got the bloody time!'

Geri heard the door slam behind her.

'Fuck,' she muttered. 'Fuck you, Nick.' When she realized she hadn't taken her car keys from the hallstand, she decided to walk. It wasn't much over a mile to school, and the exercise might improve her mood.

She hadn't thought about Nick all day, but now, slithering along the glistening pavements on her way home, the anger and frustration she had felt that morning returned as if it had never left her.

'Miss — Miss Simpson — hiya!'

Geri turned, still glowering, and saw a girl, dressed in a long green waterproof jacket and tracksuit bottoms. Her fair hair hung loose over her shoulders and she wore a woollen hat pulled low over her forehead. She smiled shyly.

It took a moment, but then the name came to her. 'Adèle!' Geri exclaimed. 'Sorry, I was . . .' Adèle hopped from one foot to the other, her *Big Issue* magazines clutched to her narrow chest, as if for protection from the cold. 'You must be freezing,' she sympathized.

'Spent most of the day in the library. Thought I'd sell a few before . . .' She gave a self-deprecating little shrug, and Geri realized she was about to say, 'Before trying to find somewhere to sleep.'

'How's the hostel?' Geri asked. The last time she had seen her, Adèle told her she was trying out hostel life.

She looked embarrassed. 'Didn't take to it.'

Geri regarded her for a moment or two. 'You're not there anymore?'

'Not as such . . .' She looked ready to cry; her teeth were chattering, and her face was mottled with cold. It was after five p.m., but although she had work to do Geri was in no hurry to go back to one of Nick's simmering silences. The punishing looks and impatient sighs were more than she was equal to right now.

'Have you got time for a coffee?' she asked.

Adèle checked the time on the digital clock over the funeral parlour — a not very subtle reminder, Geri always thought, that you never know the hour . . .

'Fifteen minutes, the rush'll be over.'

'Okay, I'll meet you at the caff — Let's have one of those, will you? It'll give me something to do while I'm waiting.' She dug into her briefcase and retrieved her purse.

'Second down, four to go,' Adèle said, handing over a copy of the magazine.

* * *

Adèle arrived as Geri was ordering her second coffee. Daphna's coffee shop faced the squat oblong of St Cecilia's church in a side street cluttered with wine bars and restaurants. Daphna stayed open until seven most nights, thus catching some of the theatregoers who didn't have time for a restaurant meal before the performance, but who were too hungry to wait to eat afterwards.

Geri added a sandwich and a large latte for Adèle and bought two outrageously huge Danish pastries to go with them.

'You didn't like the hostel, then?' Geri asked.

Adèle stared into her coffee. 'There's some bad people in them places,' she said, darkly.

She didn't elaborate, but Geri knew what she meant. Some of the characters Adèle must have had to deal with at close quarters in hostels were the same men that Geri would cross the street — even walk down a *different* street — to avoid. Drunks, drug addicts, the mad and the mean — predators who were always alert to vulnerability.

'Can't Paul get you into an all-woman hostel?' Paul was the manager of the local office of the *Big Issue*.

'There's not that many about, and I don't want to move out of the area.'

'Even so . . .' Geri bit her lower lip: Adèle was no longer her pupil, she was a young woman who had lived through the degradation of drug addiction and homelessness. There were no easy solutions for Adèle, no quick fixes, but that didn't stop Geri worrying.

Adèle tore a strip from her pastry while she thought about how to explain. 'Difference is, on the street, you can get away from them, hide, if you need to. In the hostel, they know where to find you.'

'They?'

She frowned, suddenly angry, as if Geri's gentle probing for an explanation could force her back to a place where she didn't want to go. She took a breath and spoke in a rush. 'You've got two types of blokes in hostels, right?' She thrust one hand forward and then the other, palm up: 'Them that want to buy, and them that want to sell. I can do without scum like that messing me up, giving me a hard time.' She blushed, realizing that she had raised her voice, and took a sip of coffee before going on. 'I know I'm no saint, but I'm trying to get straight.'

'I know,' Geri said, 'I know you are.' Adèle had told her that she was saving to get set up in a flat. Paul had put her name down for a housing trust property. She had tried once before and failed, but she was more in control of her drug habit, now, and she was keeping more aloof from her street buddies. 'Have you heard anything yet?' she asked.

Adèle turned down the corners of her mouth. 'Long list,' she said. She didn't need much encouragement to talk about her plans. Once she'd got a flat and made it the way she liked it, she would try for a job, hairdressing, maybe, so she could be earning while she was training. Maybe she'd do a night-school class in beauty therapy as well.

'You'd be good,' Geri said. 'You've got the looks and you could talk for Britain.'

Adèle laughed. 'I was always getting in trouble for gabbing in your lessons, wasn't I?'

Geri laughed with her, but added, 'I meant as a compliment — you're good with people.'

Adèle grinned. 'D'you really mean it, Miss?'

'Geri,' she said, wincing. 'Call me Geri.'

'Okay, Geri.' Adèle giggled. 'Sounds like I'm being cheeky, though.'

Her face was flushed after the coffee and food, and Geri saw her again as the girl she had taught two, perhaps three years before. 'Just let me know which salon,' she said, 'and I'll be your first customer.'

'Client,' Adèle corrected her. 'They call them clients nowadays.'

'Client,' she repeated.

'Sounds more professional.' Adèle traced a swirl in the coffee ring left by her mug. 'Yeah, if I can just get straight.'

'D'you want to talk about that?'

Adèle winced, and seemed to withdraw, and Geri began to apologize.

'No,' Adèle said, her eyes widening. 'It's okay. I will — some day — but . . .' She trailed off.

'You're not ready, yet.'

She relaxed, her shoulders dropping two inches. 'I knew you'd understand, Miss.'

Geri sipped her coffee and Adèle finished her sandwich.

Suddenly Adèle reached across and squeezed her hand. She looked up, surprised and touched.

'Are you all right, Miss — Geri?' Adèle asked.

'Why do you ask?'

'Well, before, you looked kind of stressed. And just now . . .' She frowned, trying to assess accurately the emotion she had seen. 'Sad.' She said it with a hint of an inflection, so that Geri could interpret it as a question.

Geri raised her eyebrows. She hadn't realized she was so easy to read. What to tell her? The first bit, about Nick and his infantile tantrums? It seemed so trivial having listened to Adèle, to her hopes and dreams. Or should she tell her about Ryan? What was there to say? That a seventeen-year-old boy didn't turn up for a lesson and she was worried about him? She smiled.

'Nothing,' she said. 'Bad day.' But she kept seeing Dean's face, pale and sick-looking, the shadows under his eyes like he hadn't slept, and the casual comment Aidan had meant as a joke when she'd asked where Ryan was.

He's dead.

* * *

He sat in his car for a few blissful moments, the engine turning over quietly, warming himself after the fearful cold of the derelict cottages. He closed his eyes, dizzy and exhilarated. They had spent most of the day together, him and Ryan. He liked to think of it this way, of them *spending time* together — what he felt for Ryan wasn't sordid. Nevertheless, he reeked of sweat and sex. He would have to go home to shower and change, which meant leaving Ryan sooner than he would have liked.

He fretted; Ryan was safely bedded down, but he wanted to be with him, keeping him warm, touching his body, kissing him, exploring . . . He groaned. It was tempting to turn the engine off and go back inside, but he was expected — there was no sense in drawing attention to himself by his absence. And nothing to stop him dropping in on the lad whenever he felt the need for human comfort. Nothing to stop him doing whatever the hell he liked.

3

It was after seven o'clock by the time Geri turned the corner of Gresford Avenue and started the steady climb home. Frost glistened on the pavements, gleaming in the moonlight, making a fine lace on the brickwork of the garden walls.

After leaving Adèle, she had taken the long way home, walking three sides of a square instead of cutting diagonally across, through the warren of side streets. She could no longer feel her fingers, and only knew she still had hold of her briefcase because it clunked against her leg every couple of strides. Her face was numb, her cheeks like slabs of marble.

She realized she had been putting off her return, hoping that if she delayed long enough, Nick would have given up on her and gone out for a drink. With any luck she would be asleep by the time he got back.

The security lamp came on as she walked up the front path. The hall light was a soft glimmer behind the fleur-de-lis pattern of the stained-glass panelling in the front door.

Geri took a breath and fished in her coat pocket for her keys. 'Be pleasant,' she told herself. 'Stay calm.' She put down her briefcase, consciously willing her fingers to uncurl from the handle, and searched in the other pocket of her coat.

‘Shit.’ She unfastened the clasp on her briefcase and rooted around inside. No keys. The security light clicked off and she was left with only the dim incandescence from the hallway, promising warmth.

‘Damn and bugger.’ She resigned herself to the inevitability of Nick’s ridicule and rang the doorbell. Its shrill, brassy ring echoed through the house, but there was no response; no lights as doors opened, no rapid pounding of footsteps on the stairs. The house was empty.

‘Bloody hell!’ She turned away from the door, then turned back, thinking she had heard something — a noise inside the house. She waited a few moments longer, but no one came, and she kicked the door, cursing, then went down the front steps. It was too damned cold to be out on a night like this. She could walk back into town and find a restaurant to eat, but there would be no guarantee he would be home when she got back. Then she remembered that the library closed at seven on Mondays; Lauren would be home soon. Best wait for her. But what if she’d decided to go out straight from work? Hell. Geri stood at the end of the drive, stamping her feet and looking up and down the road for signs of rescue.

Geri had inherited the house on the death of her mother, five years previously. She was nineteen, alone in the world, unable to face the prospect of selling up and losing the last ties she had with her past, and unable to afford what was left of the mortgage after her mother died. And the upkeep of a large Edwardian property was a scary prospect at the time.

Lauren, ten years her senior, had been supportive without being patronizing, she paid her rent on time and was scrupulously fair about making contributions to her share of the food and the quarterly bills. It was a huge relief to Geri and, until recently they had managed well.

She didn’t want to think about the reasons why she had started slipping into debt and after a couple of minutes, she became restless, and tried Nick’s workshop. It was locked. She opened the side gate and walked down the narrow path at the side of the house. The moonlight cast blocks of deep shadow onto the lawn, but the paved area at the back of the house and the path down to the vegetable garden and the shed were well lit, the moss between the herringbone pattern of bricks embossed in black. Geri set down her briefcase and blew on her fingers as she sized up the flimsy hasp and tiny padlock that secured the shed door. 'Lever,' she murmured, casting about for something that might do the job. There was nothing. Not so much as a garden trowel.

'Bloody hell!' she mouthed, her breath making two white puffs of moisture, rising rapidly into the freezing air. 'God, I've got to get out of this cold!'

She reached for one of the decorative stones that edged the path. It was frozen in place and her fingers slipped off it, the cold cutting to the bone.

'Shit!' She tucked hands under her arms and worked at the stone with her heel. Eventually it loosened and she picked it up, juggling it from hand to hand, as she carried it along the path to the shed, then used it to take a couple of swings at the padlock.

As she raised her arm a third time, a high-pitched, frightened voice called out, 'I've rung the police. You'd better get out of here right now!'

Geri dropped the stone. 'Lauren? It's all right. It's me.'

Lauren came around the corner of the house, a tall, thin woman, bundled up against the cold, holding a couple of books up in front of her, as barriers or weapons, Geri couldn't decide which.

'What the hell are you doing?' Lauren demanded. 'You scared me half to death!'

'Forgot my keys,' Geri said, feeling foolish.

'Oh, well — that explains everything.'

'Tell me you've got yours,' Geri said, lifting one foot off the ground away from the penetrating cold.

Lauren held up her key ring and jingled the keys, and Geri gave a yell of relief — Lauren often got up so late that she left her keys in the house in her rush to get to work on time.

'I heard you leave this morning,' she said. 'I thought I might be needing them.'

Geri winced. 'Sorry.' She crunched back down the path and retrieved her briefcase, hurrying Lauren ahead of her. 'You were on duty last night, weren't you?' Lauren did voluntary work for the Samaritans, and Sunday had been one of her regular overnight stints.

'I got in at half seven. I was just nodding off when Armageddon erupted.'

Geri mouthed 'sorry' again, at her back.

Lauren let them in. The house was warm and, flinging her briefcase aside, Geri rushed to a radiator and hugged it.

'You'll get chilblains,' Lauren warned.

'It'll be worth it.'

Lauren set the two books down on the window ledge. She had a superb profile: delicate bone structure, a finely chiselled nose. Her hair was feathered onto her face, emphasising her elfin features. She took off her coat and scarf and hung them up, seemed to debate about removing her cardigan, then decided to keep it on.

How can she look elegant in flat heels and two layers of woollies? Geri wondered.

'What are you looking at?' Geri demanded, and Geri realized she'd been staring.

She shifted her gaze to squint at the book titles beside her friend. '*Quilting Magic* and *Fun with Soft Furnishings*. If it'd been a real burglar, you could always have bored him to death with those.'

Lauren shot her a withering look. 'I'll brew up, and leave you to commune with the central heating system, shall I?'

After a hot mug of tea, a hotter microwave chicken korma and a couple of glasses of wine, Geri felt more mellow. 'I really am sorry you lost your beauty sleep,' she said. 'Nick can be such a pig sometimes.'

'It wouldn't have been so bad, except he kept flouncing about the house after you'd gone, rattling tins and slamming doors till I gave up and came downstairs.'

'Wait till I see him.'

'Get the murderous gleam out of your eye. He was apologetic. Said he thought I was out — he'd forgotten I was on the afternoon shift.'

'Sure he wasn't just hoping for a sympathetic ear?'

'I'd've told him to call back during office hours.'

Geri had to smile. Lauren was a sucker for a sob story, but she couldn't bear to be thought a soft touch. 'Still, you do look all-in.'

'That's my bad side.' Lauren turned her face a little and lifted her chin.

'Here—'

'Maybe in a dark corner with subdued lighting . . .'

'Honesty is a grossly overrated virtue,' Lauren said with a sniff.

Geri laughed. 'My mum called it the eighth deadly sin.'

They sat for a few minutes, listening to Alison Moyet singing that she might as well give up the fight, because he'd always convince her he's right.

Geri snorted. 'Not much chance of that, cock,' she muttered into her wine glass.

Lauren glanced up from her book on quilting. 'Can I ask you something?' she said.

'Anything.'

'What the hell *were* you doing, attacking the shed with a rock? His bike, I could understand, but the shed . . .'

'It's freezing out there. I was looking for shelter.'

Lauren laughed. 'You're cracked.'

'Unlike you, I don't wear several layers of thermals.'

'Unlike me, you don't feel the cold.'

'I bloody did tonight . . .' Geri took a slurp of wine, aware that she was drinking too quickly, mutinously telling herself she had a right to the odd night off from marking books. 'How do they do it?'

'How do who do what?'

'Homeless people. In weather like this.'

'We had a few calls last night,' Lauren said. 'People desperate for an emergency shelter.'

'Did you find somewhere for them?'

'Places to try, at least . . .'

They fell silent. Geri was thinking of Adèle, who didn't like such places, and would rather sleep rough than use them.

'I almost bought a pair of boots in the sales. I was that cold,' Geri said.

'Almost? Too tight?'

Geri shook her head. 'One was missing — who the hell nicks one boot?'

Lauren laughed suddenly. 'You don't know?'

'Go on then,' Geri said, eager for something to make her smile, something to take her mind off Dean's uncharacteristic behaviour and Ryan's mysterious non-appearance at school that day.

'Guess,' Lauren challenged.

'I don't know — one-legged shoplifters?'

'Foot fetishists.'

Geri pulled a face. 'You're winding me up.'

Laughing, Lauren explained. 'They hang around shoe shops, waiting for women to try on shoes, then they pick them up and sniff them.'

'And if they take a particular fancy to them, they smuggle them out of the shop and take them home? Yuk! I don't think I'll ever shift that image. Every time I try on a pair of shoes . . .' She thought about it for a moment. 'What would you do with a caller who told you something like that?'

Lauren shrugged. 'Advise him to seek help. Give him a couple of numbers to ring.' She caught Geri's expression. 'Not like *that*! Counsellors, that sort of thing.'

'Oh,' Geri said solemnly.

Lauren arched an eyebrow. 'So, what would you do?'

'How should I know . . . Suggest retraining as a chiropodist, I suppose.'

Lauren collapsed, giggling and threw a cushion at Geri, who caught it and lobbed it back.

The front door slammed and they both froze momentarily, then Geri crossed her eyes and Lauren roared with laughter, covering her face with the cushion to stifle the noise.

Nick opened the door of the sitting room and looked at the two of them. The slight glazing of his eyes, and the way he held on to the doorknob told Geri that he'd had a few more than his usual two or three pints. For an instant, Geri saw her father. It was her tenth birthday, and he was drunk, wearing the suit he had left for work in three days previously. He had stood in the doorway just as Nick did now, shamefaced yet defiant, and Geri had no trouble getting her laughter under control.

'Enjoying yourselves?' he asked.

'Talking shop,' Geri answered.

'What's for dinner?'

'Whatever's in the freezer.'

He stood for some moments as if undecided about whether to say more, then he muttered something about a takeaway and blundered out.

'Glad I'm wearing my thermals,' Lauren said.

'Yeah, well, he pisses me off.' There was a silence, then Geri stood up. 'I've a couple of calls to make,' she said. 'Might as well do a bit of marking while I'm at it.' Suddenly marking 7A's attempts at poetry seemed an attractive option after all.

'In that case,' Lauren said, gingerly placing the cushion on the sofa beside her, and uncurling herself from her reclining position, 'I might just get an early night.'

Geri knew Nick wouldn't disturb her in her study; she wasn't yet ready to speak to him, especially with a few pints pickling his brain cells — besides, it wouldn't be fair to put Lauren through another sleepless night.

She telephoned Dean's mother first, feeling guilty that she hadn't done it earlier. She kept the home phone numbers of all the members of her form in her teachers' planner. The school secretary had told her that when Mrs Connelly came to pick Dean up, she looked pretty rough herself. The phone was answered on the first ring.

'Ryan?'

For a moment Geri was confused. Mrs Connelly sounded distressed, almost desperate. 'Mrs Connelly, it's Miss Simpson, Dean's form tutor.' She heard a sound at the other end, like a muffled sob. 'I heard he was sent home,' Geri went on. 'Is he okay?'

Another sob, and then a few whispered words of explanation to someone else in the room. 'He's . . . well he's not so good, love. None of us is. You see . . .'

'Is it Ryan?' Geri asked, filling the gap. 'Is he all right?'

'We don't know, love,' Mrs Connelly said, trying to keep control of her voice. 'We just don't know. He's not . . . He didn't come home yesterday.'

'Have you called the police?'

'They say they'll look into it, but all they've done is go around to his aunties and uncles, asking stupid bloody questions. If they want to know anything, I can tell them. I'm his mother—'

Geri heard a man's voice in the background. 'Aye,' Mrs Connelly said. Then, with a sigh, 'Aye, all right, I'll ask her.'

'Anything,' Geri said, eager to help.

'That police sergeant. The one that comes into school. Could you have a word with him? Only our Ryan wouldn't stop out like this. Everyone's out looking for him — his dad's only just got back — but it's not the same, we need help.'

'Of course,' Geri stuttered. 'I'll talk to him — I'll do what I can.'

As she keyed in Vince Beresford's number, her fingers trembling, she wondered if the sergeant's request that she phone him had anything to do with Ryan's disappearance.

She was ready to give up when he answered. 'Sorry,' he said. 'I was in the shower. I wanted to ask you about—'

'Ryan.'

'You've heard.'

'His mother just told me. Vince, he's not the sort to go off without telling someone.'

'That's what I thought.'

'His mother's distraught. Can't you—'

'We're doing all we can,' he said before she could finish. 'First we check with relatives and friends — he was last seen on a bus heading out of town on Saturday night, but he got off early.'

'On his own?'

'So his mate says.'

'Who was it?'

'The mate? Baz something.'

'Barry Mandel.'

'You don't like him.'

'It shows, does it? Why can't you search the area where he got off the bus?'

'Money, Geri.' It was said gently, apologetically. 'Under normal circumstances, a missing person case stays with uniform for thirty-six hours; after that, it's passed on to CID. They might organise a search, but something like that is very labour-intensive; you have to be able to justify it to the management.'

'Justify it! Tell the management to talk to his mother — she'll give them justification!'

'We don't *enjoy* penny-pinching, Geri.'

'I know,' Geri said, tiredly. 'I know, Vince, but it seems harsh, weighing a boy's life against a balance sheet.'

'He'll probably show up at home tonight, the worse for wear, feeling sorry for himself.'

In the pause that followed, Geri had an awful premonition that Ryan wasn't ever going to come home.

Vince spoke again. 'I've asked the patrols to keep an eye open, and I phoned round or dropped in at all the likely places myself, before I came to the school this afternoon.'

'Likely places?'

'Nicks, hospitals, bus depots, the city-centre stations, arcades, a few caffs known to be hang-outs for teenagers — I've even tried the emergency shelters . . . No one answering Ryan's description.'

Geri looked out over the garden. It was well below freezing outside, and no prospect of a let-up in the icy weather.

The trees had accumulated a crystalline fuzz of hoar frost; it dusted the branches and twigs and bearded the edges of the evergreen leaves. What if Ryan was hurt? At these temperatures he wouldn't stand a chance.

* * *

Adèle was looking forward to getting back to her place. She wouldn't call it home, she'd reserved that name for her flat, when she finally got one, a proper place, fit for the word, where she could put her name over the bell-push, her plants and knick-knacks in the kitchen and hall and bedroom. Hot water on tap. Locks on the door. Maybe a radio — telly gave her a headache.

She smiled, thinking about Miss Simpson — she was so nice. One day, she would tell her — not just the good bits, the things she wanted for the future — but what it had been like for her on the streets. It wouldn't be like talking to the social services, or the GP Paul fixed her up with. Bastard treated her like she was some kind of leper — or an idiot. Both.

Miss Simpson listened in the way that Paul did. You felt like you were telling him facts, things that happened to you, things you'd done. It wasn't like you had to apologize — you didn't have to tell him you were sorry or ashamed. He knew how hard it was just to live through the night on the street, and he knew you did things you weren't proud of, but you could tell him, so he'd know which was the best way to go, the pitfalls to look out for.

In her rucksack she had a bottle of mineral water — for making hot coffee — fresh milk, a loaf of bread, butter (the real thing, spreadable, on offer at LoCost) and a packet of chocolate biscuits. She didn't usually splash out, but on a cold night you needed something to get you through. Anyway, a couple of people had given her a quid and not wanted a magazine, so she was feeling flush.

The office buildings stopped suddenly, as if a line had been drawn at the edge of the map and the planners had decided that next to the commercial centre, they would build the slums. It was striking the way the city ended and the tenements began, five-high blocks of dreary grey, with stone steps to each landing and no lifts, and emanating from each dark stairway the overpowering reek of urine. Built in the fifties as shining new symbols of hope, replacements for the back-to-backs flattened during the Blitz, now empty and falling down, they acted as a firebreak between the city-centre shops and the disused warehouses near the ship canal.

She hurried on, past the sullen frontages, with their blank windows and ruined walls, and the stench of decay. Overshadowing the doomed tenements, the warehouses loomed, massive haunted relicts of a more prosperous age. Their gleaming red brickwork had long been tarnished by soot and exhaust fumes and they took on the colour of dried blood, but after several days of frosting, the walls glittered as with a billion flecks of mica or steel, and the water gushing from pipes and gutters had frozen, sculpted into weird and breathtaking statuary.

She stopped, alert. It was dark in the shadow of the warehouses, the cold intense. The sky was no more than a thin murky strip overhead. She waited a full five minutes until she was sure no one was watching her, and then she dodged down a passage at the side of one of the buildings. The entrance was barred with a wire-mesh gate, but the padlock had perished long ago. Halfway down the passage, past a sodden piece of old carpet, now frozen solid and strangely ornate in its new incarnation, she found her way in. An iron door stood part-way open, enough to admit someone relatively slight, the darkness beyond a deterrent to all but the boldest or the most desperate.

It had been a grain store until the 1970s, but had lain idle, gently decomposing for nearly thirty years. The upper floors were drenched with rainwater which leaked down from gaping holes in the roof. The basement and ground floor were sodden with rising damp, but the first floor wasn't too bad if you took care on the stairs and she had found a dark dry corner, away from the windows.

She'd been in the warehouse for nearly two weeks now, and it was getting to feel familiar, less scary, but Adèle had only survived on the street because she was careful. And she knew that you couldn't lower your guard, even for a minute, because when you did . . .

She tried to shut out the memory of what had happened to Andy. He had been careful too, until New Year's Eve, when optimism and exuberance had taken him onto the street to celebrate the new millennium. Maybe he had drunk too much, maybe he had failed to sense when things were turning ugly. His biggest mistake was going alone.

They had found him in the doorway of C&A. Kicked to death. As a final mark of contempt, the killers — revellers with a sense of humour — had stuffed a party squeaker into the bloody pulp that had been his mouth. Adèle swallowed hard and wiped her nose with the heel of her hand. If you got to dwelling on things like that, you lost your nerve, and when you're stuck on the street, there's nowhere else to go but out of your mind.

She slithered across a large milky patch of ice, ready to bolt at any sign of human occupation, and tiptoed up the sagging wooden staircase, still listening, watching her step on the calcified slime that had built up from thirty years' run-off, finishing up at the furthest corner of the vast floor space of the first floor.

She'd been careful, bringing all the bits together for her bivvy, moving stuff in piece by piece when it was dark, so she didn't attract attention. Some of it was already there, like the panels that looked like they'd been pinboards in a previous life. She had stood them opposite each other — they had little feet, like upside-down saucers, and only one was broken — and used a piece of plywood for the back, then covered the lot with two layers of corrugated card for insulation. The roof was card as well, a nice long piece — packing off a sofa which was now on display in Gorton's on Dean Street. Lifted it straight off the skip five minutes after they threw it in, so it was clean and fresh.

A night like this, you appreciated corrugated card. No matter how many layers you had on, the cold got through. If you weren't careful, it sank in, till it felt like it was coming from your insides out — a solid core of it high up under your rib cage sending shivery waves to your skin, seeping into your bones, till you couldn't move, and didn't care if you died.

Although her shelter was lopsided, she viewed it with satisfaction. She had found a big sheet of plastic on a skip only the week before and was using it as a ground sheet. A blanket on top served as a carpet, and extra pieces closed off the front of the three-sided cubicle.

In ten minutes, she had her primus lit and her bedroll out, and she was snuggled into her sleeping bag. She tried not to notice the skitterings and high squeals of the rats, but she dragged one of her boots closer, just in case one of them got greedy — some were as long as your arm and scared of nothing.

She felt a small throb of excitement, the kind she remembered dimly from a school trip, a week in Colomendy. Somewhere in Wales — she knew that now — but then it seemed foreign, exotic. She didn't allow herself to question her excitement. It had the high, hysterical quality of a child screaming with laughter as the swing goes *higher! higher!* She gave herself this degree of leeway because the alternative, too awful to entertain, was despair.

4

The bus stopped at Derby Street, its air brakes hissing and throwing Siân forward so that she almost lost her balance.

'Nearly missed it there, love,' the driver said.

'Sorry, I wasn't sure this was it.' She was ready to step off, but he kept the doors closed.

'And you are now?' He peered into the darkness. 'You meeting someone?'

'No, I—' She looked nervously back down the bus. There were two other passengers, both men, and they eyed her curiously. 'Look, can you open the door?' she asked.

'Sure, but you want to be careful around here. It's not the sort of place for a nice girl like you to be wandering about alone.'

'I can take care of myself.'

The driver smiled as if to say he doubted it. 'You're sure you don't want to change your mind? I turn around and come back the same way at the end of the route. I could have you back in town in forty minutes.'

Siân felt her resolve begin to crumble and, impatient with herself as much as with the driver, shouted, 'Open the bloody door, will you?'

‘Okay, okay . . .’ He reached for the lever and the doors folded back with a slight squeak. As she stepped out into the darkness, he called after her, ‘Don’t say I didn’t warn you.’

She walked away fast, to prevent herself from turning around and beating on the doors to be allowed back in. She didn’t know where she was going, but she that knew this was the last place Ryan had been seen. She felt she would be able to sense his presence if he was close by, and she had an image in her mind of Ryan lying injured, somewhere inside one of the houses — perhaps he had gone to sleep off whatever it was Baz had given him — maybe he had fallen, hurt himself, and needed help.

The cold was pitiless; it glazed the gutters and pierced her woollen jacket and dress, chilling her to the bone within minutes. She hurried along the side of the gaunt empty building that overshadowed the bus stop, looking for a way in, but it was secure: steel plates on the doors and windows. She walked down one of the narrow side streets, letting her instincts take her to where she felt sure she would find Ryan.

Ten minutes of wandering brought her to a wretched three-high dwelling. Just looking at the gaping darkness of the entrance to the tenement block set her heart racing. She waited for her pulse to steady. In her imagination rats, cockroaches, spiders lurked in the dark corners of the rotting flats. She shook her head. *I can’t think like this or I’ll never go in!* She took a deep breath and heard her pulse throbbing in her throat. Reaching into her bag, she took out a torch.

‘For Ryan,’ she whispered, clicking on the light and walking slowly forward.

Even with the damp frozen solid by the icy weather, the place stank of decay and stale urine. She trod carefully up the steps, trying the doors on each landing. Some had been smashed open and looking inside she saw that the fittings: cupboards; bathroom and kitchenware had been ripped out — even the copper piping had been stolen. Florid growths of fungus bloomed on the walls like ink on blotting paper, some encased in sheets of ice. Glass crunched underfoot, and in some of the flats, the floorboards had been torn up and used as firewood. At first she thought it must be kids — arsonists — but the charred areas were contained, small, and with a quickening of breath she realized the fires could easily have been set by squatters.

Her lips trembling, she moved on, trying each door; sometimes — to give herself courage — softly calling out Ryan's name.

On the third floor she thought she heard a sound. A rat, maybe. She was about to retreat, when the stupidity of her cowardice came home to her: it could be Ryan. *If he's hurt, he may be too weak to call out.* The idea made her hurry, and she went to the source of the sound, a flat with its door still on its hinges. She turned the handle and pushed hard; something was blocking it, and she saw with dazzling clarity, Ryan, lying behind the door, dazed, injured. But as she shone her torch downwards, she saw only a rolled-up piece of carpet, which had been acting as a draught excluder. Gingerly, she moved it out of her way with the tip of her toe and stepped inside.

Something moved in a far corner of the room and she turned the beam in that direction. 'Ryan?' she called.

A shadow, a blur, it leapt at her, seized hold of her. It was a man in a dirty black coat. She saw his teeth, bared as if to bite, his beard, yellow and matted. She screamed — then his hand was on her neck, the overpowering reek of urine and unwashed hair assailed her. He breathed into her face and she gagged at the foul stench of him, at his filthy yellowing nails digging into her flesh. She screamed again and lashed out with the torch.

'Whadda you want!' the man shrieked. 'Whadda you want?'

She was so overwhelmed by her own terror that she didn't hear the fear in his voice. Screaming again and again she hit out, flailing with the torch, kicking backwards, using the heel of her boots, her nails, her head, anything to make him let go of her.

He threw her away from him and she fell, grazing her knees and hands on the floor, dropping the torch. It was pitch-dark, but she could smell him, coming at her again. She scrambled towards the draught of cold from the open doorway, hauled herself through it, getting to a crouch before he lunged and grabbed her ankle. She pulled herself up, using the balcony for support, kicking back again, making contact with his face, screaming madly as she ran for the stairs. She stumbled and fell, scratching her face on the brickwork, getting to her feet again, feeling nothing, running, running headlong, hardly knowing where she ran, back through the silent, ruined streets. She found the main road and ran, flinging a backward glance over her shoulder, into the path of a bus.

As the driver pulled up she turned a horrified face to him and placed her hands on the windscreen, leaving two bloody palm-prints on the glass.

* * *

A sharp jab of pain shot from Geri's shoulder to the base of her skull. She reached awkwardly with her left hand and fumbled the receiver from the cradle, trying to straighten up. Her arm was heavy and numb, and the spasm tensed her muscles agonisingly.

'Yes?' she mumbled, forcing herself awake.

'Miss Simpson, *please*! You've got to help me!' The voice was raised, hysterical.

Geri sat bolt upright, grunting as pain ripped again through her back and neck.

'I thought it was Ryan . . . He tried to grab me.'

'Siân? Where are you? Who tried to grab you?'

'I just wanted to find him.' She broke down, sobbing.

'Siân!' Geri said sharply, in an effort to break through the girl's panic. 'Tell me where you are.'

There was another choked cry, then silence.

'Siân!' Geri called again, becoming frantic.

An exchange of words, then: 'She's with me.' A man's voice.

Geri felt suddenly cold. 'What do you *mean* she's with you? Who are you?'

'I'm a bus driver,' the man said, pronouncing it 'buzz'. 'The lass ran out in front of me.'

'My God!' Geri exclaimed. 'Is she hurt? Have you called an ambulance?'

'I didn't *hit* her,' he said, evidently offended by the implied slur on his driving ability. 'But she's shook up. She won't let me call the police and she won't go to hospital.'

'Tell me where you are,' Geri said, hugely relieved. 'I'll come and fetch her.'

* * *

Siân sipped hot tea with shaking hands. She shuddered as Geri put one hand on her shoulder. Her cheek was raw: parallel welts beaded with blood marred her pale, tear-streaked face.

'I tried to clean her up a bit,' the man said, 'but she's in shock, like. Not herself.'

Geri crouched next to Siân and touched her knee. She winced and drew back but carried on sipping the tea compulsively. They were in a small, nicotine-yellowed canteen at the far end of the oily garage that housed forty or fifty buses, parked for the night, nose-to-tail and eerily quiet, like soulless corpses without their passengers. The high, corrugated-steel roof was rusted and light from the sodium lamps in the street pierced the darkness with fuzzy coronas of orange radiance.

The man shuffled a little. 'It's knocking-off time for me, now.' Embarrassed to be rushing them, but anxious to get home.

'I'm sorry,' Geri said, standing to shake his hand. 'Thank you. Thank you very much.'

He coloured slightly. 'Best get her home to her mam, eh?' he suggested, lowering his voice.

'I'll do that,' Geri answered.

Siân shivered slightly but appeared not to hear. She stared into her cup until the click of the man's shoes was no more than a faint *tick* in the distance, then she looked up at Geri. 'I'm not going home,' she said. 'Mam'll kill me. I'm not supposed to be out — school nights, I'm not allowed.'

'I'll go with you,' Geri soothed, remembering Mrs Walsh's unforgiving face from parents' evenings, during which Geri had found herself defending Siân's barely average performance in her studies. 'Your mum'll just be glad to see you're all right.'

Siân gave her a tiny shake. 'He's there — I know he's there. But that man . . .' She hunched her shoulders, cringing at the memory. 'I've got to go back. If he's hurt—'

Geri considered: if Ryan *was* lying injured somewhere, she would never forgive herself if she didn't go out and check. But Siân was in shock — nearly hysterical — she should be at home.

'We'll talk about it in the car,' she said, easing Siân to her feet. 'You can tell me where to look and I'll go and see if I can find anything.'

Siân was about to protest, then she wrenched free of Geri and stumbled past her. Geri turned.

'Frank!' She was looking into Frank Traynor's anxious face.

'I phoned him,' Siân explained. 'After I called you.' She turned to her friend. 'You'll come with me, won't you, Frank?'

Frank looked from Siân to Geri, then sighed and looked at his shoes.

'All right,' Siân said, limping to the door. 'I'll go on my own.'

It was Geri's turn to sigh. 'We'll use my car,' she said. 'I know I'll regret this.' She was regretting it already, but she wasn't going to leave Siân wandering around that part of town on her own at nearly midnight.

Siân led them straight to the tenement.

'He's here!' she insisted. 'I know he is. But what if that man—' She shrank back against Geri, trembling.

'All right,' Geri murmured, gently passing her over to Frank. 'We'll soon see.' She left them below and climbed to the second floor.

Her nostrils flared at the pungent smell of urine. There was a faint glow from the landing, and Geri's breath caught as she heard a faint scuffing sound.

She paused at the turn in the concrete staircase, gathering strength, willing her quivering limbs to take her the last few steps. Bracing herself against the crumbling balustrade, she ran onto the landing at a crouch, immediately falling back with a cry of dismay.

'Miss Simpson?' Frank's voice sounded thin and frightened.

Geri's breath made white puffs of condensation on the freezing air. She felt winded by the shock.

'*Miss?*'

She knelt by the body. 'Fetch an ambulance.' The first time she said it, no sound came out, and she had to take a breath and try again, instructing Frank to use Siân's mobile.

Steeling herself, she lifted his wrist to search for a pulse. The flickering light from Siân's damaged torch animated his face grotesquely. It was covered with blood; it matted his beard and stained the front of his coat. He reeked of urine and worse. His pulse was rapid but strong.

'It's an elderly man,' she called to Frank, trying to keep her tone even and controlled. 'Tell them he's in shock. Hypothermic. I think he's taken a beating.'

She tried to ease him onto his side, listening to be sure that Frank had done as she instructed. The man was bulky and difficult to move in the narrow confines of the landing. Breathing through her mouth to avoid the smell, she leaned across him, intending to pull his left hand across the front of his body and lever him into the recovery position.

Suddenly his free hand snapped out and gripped her with surprising force. 'Get away from me!' he croaked. 'Leave me be!'

His teeth were stained with blood, almost black in the failing torchlight.

‘It’s all right.’ Geri’s voice was a breathless squeak. ‘Try to stay calm.’ She felt near to panic herself. Abruptly his grip slackened, and his eyes glazed, and Geri escaped, standing clear of him and hugging herself, her teeth chattering. She stayed near him until the ambulance came, but she couldn’t bring herself to touch him again.

Siân could not be persuaded to come and see the old man’s pitiful bolthole for herself until he had been safely removed from the landing. Piles of newspaper and card occupied one corner of the room, layer upon layer, twisted and shaped and stamped down, so that it looked like a giant nest. A couple of filthy blankets lay on the floor, as if discarded in haste.

‘He’s just a harmless drunk,’ Geri said.

‘He went for me!’

‘You frightened him. He was defending his home.’

Siân insisted on searching every room before she would be satisfied. ‘I thought—’ She bowed her head and sagged against Frank.

Frank shot Geri a worried look. Geri gently brushed a tear from Siân’s face. ‘We’ll go home now,’ she said.

‘But the police—’

‘You can give your statement tomorrow. I’ll talk to them after I’ve dropped you off.’

Siân was silent and passive until they reached the bottom of the stairway and stepped onto the roadside. Without warning, she shoved Frank away and began screaming, calling Ryan’s name over and over again.

* * *

Less than half a mile away, Ryan heard the ambulance klaxon and stirred briefly from his stupor. He should be afraid. He knew, in theory, what he should feel, but instead he felt nothing. No pain, no fear — fear was too abstract a concept to hold on to. He was drifting. Floating effortlessly.

He exerted himself, trying to experience the outrage, the anger, the burning humiliation he should feel, but there was no answering emotion. He understood what was happening to him, but it didn't matter. Nothing mattered.

Later — how much later? Minutes? Hours? There was no time in his drowsing state — cries ripped through the night: the screams of a vixen, scavenging the city boundaries. But it seemed in his daze that the coughing barks called his name over and over. Ryan! Ryan! Ryan!

5

It was just after four when Geri got home on Tuesday. Nick was on the early shift, and she wanted to give them both a chance to make up after the argument on Monday. Exhaustion was also a factor: after dropping Frank and Siân home, she had given her statement to the police, not arriving home herself until after three a.m.

During a few hours of troubled sleep, she slipped into a recurring loop in which she lost the school party she had taken to see *Romeo and Juliet*. She searched frantically backstage, finally losing herself in a labyrinthine system of corridors and dressing rooms and returning to school to face anxious parents who demanded to know where their children were.

It was a relief to wake up to face the real difficulties of the day, despite her tiredness and Nick's back turned coldly to her in bed.

Now, after struggling through a day in which her pupils seemed more quarrelsome and fractious than normal, she was at home again. Tired but unable to sit still, she marked a few books, made herself a sandwich and tidied up the mess Nick had left in the kitchen; apparently, he had been home and gone out again. She couldn't get the events of the previous night out of her head. Siân seemed so certain that something terrible had happened to Ryan, and the feeling was contagious. She kept imagining him in one of the empty properties in the old trading area, unable to help himself — Siân was sure Barry had slipped something in Ryan's drink in the pub on Saturday night, and although Siân hadn't been there, Frank had, and he seemed very shifty when Siân questioned him about it on the journey home from the tenements.

She went through to the hall and telephoned the hospital. The telephonist couldn't tell her anything about the old man they had admitted on Monday night.

'He was an emergency admission,' Geri said. 'It must have been around midnight.'

'Haven't you got a name?'

'No,' Geri said, 'but I do know he was taken to casualty. Can't you check with them?'

'One moment.' The line clicked abruptly, and Geri was left on hold for several minutes. The hall was freezing, and she struggled into her coat, making the hole in the lining bigger.

The next she heard from the switchboard was, 'Royal Infirmary, how may I help you?'

It seemed that the telephonist had forgotten her. 'I was waiting for word of a man admitted to casualty—'

'Just one moment,' the woman interrupted. 'I'll try to connect you.'

Geri opened her mouth to protest, but it was too late. The line was ringing, and she had to explain again, this time to a charge nurse in the A & E department.

'Les? The tramp?' He paused. 'Are you a relative?'

'I found him,' Geri said.

'Well you saved his life. He'd have died of hypothermia if he'd been out much longer.'

'Will he be all right?'

'Depends what you mean by "all right". He'll be his old self in a couple of days . . .'

The implication was clear, and Geri felt an urge to explain or defend the way the old man lived. But she said nothing.

'He'll be all right, love,' the nurse said, relenting a little. 'Most of the blood was from a nose-bleed. It wasn't the injuries made him pass out, it was the booze.'

Geri thanked him and hung up. At least that would be one less thing for Siân to worry about. She tapped the phone receiver with her index finger, undecided for a moment. Siân's mother hadn't been exactly friendly the previous night. But she decided that not to phone would be the coward's way out, and quickly looked up the number, punching it in on the keypad before she could change her mind.

Mrs Walsh was not openly hostile, but her reception was distinctly frosty. 'What do you want?' she asked.

'I was wondering how Siân is.'

'How d'you think she is, after what she's been through?'

'Could I speak to her?'

'She's in bed.' Evidently, she was unwilling to disturb her daughter.

'Perhaps you could tell her that the old man is all right. I telephoned the hospital—'

'He wants locking up!' Mrs Walsh interrupted. 'It's a pity she didn't hit him harder. Bloody animal!'

'Siân was worried,' Geri tried again. 'When she realized—'

'Realized what? That he lives like vermin, among vermin? She should never have been in that godforsaken hole — and you should've known better than to take her!'

'Mrs Walsh, I didn't—' But the line was dead.

Geri paced. It seemed suddenly hot, despite the cold of the hall. A pile of books on the window ledge caught her eye, but she knew she wouldn't be able to settle to marking homework and, pausing only to drop a discarded newspaper on top of them, she grabbed her keys and went out.

Adèle had already left her usual pitch near the funeral parlour. Geri was disappointed: she had hoped to enlist her help, but she pushed on. Arcades, cafés, and the railway station Vince had said — all places where runaways might be found. Ryan wasn't a runaway; she knew it in her heart. He would never stay away from home, worrying his parents and girlfriend — not if he had a choice in the matter.

That thought gave Geri's search greater urgency. She ducked into perhaps twenty cafés and half a dozen arcades. Sometimes it was difficult to get a response from the kids, and it was hard to say how much the glazed look of the arcade junkies was down to over exposure on the machines and how much to chemical stimulants.

How many of them went to school? she wondered. And what excuses they would give for homework not done — not that homework would take high priority for these boys. She thought she recognized a face in one of the arcades, but he melted into the shadows and was gone before she had the chance to talk to him.

At the station, a gang loitered by the drinks machine. They looked around as Geri approached and one or two jeers went up. She braced herself, her heart thudding — these boys did not know her; she couldn't call upon her school reputation to demand their respect.

'Want a drink, love?' a tall, weasel-faced youth asked. 'Giz the money, I'll get it for you.' The other lads laughed gleefully.

Geri ignored him and looked at the other four. 'I'm looking for a boy who's gone missing, she said. 'He's seventeen, he's got dark brown hair, and he's about six foot tall.'

'Sounds like he could look after himself,' one boy commented.

'You his mam?' A stocky, dark-eyed boy with a skinhead cut asked the question.

The weasel gave him a shove. 'Dickhead — she's not that old!'

The stocky boy squared up to him. 'Fuck off!'

Weasel backed down immediately, looking away, but he repeated. 'I'm just saying she's not old enough.'

'Fancy her, do you?'

This provoked uncouth laughter. 'Have any of you seen him?' Geri persisted.

‘Might’ve.’ It was the weasel again.

Geri held her breath. This was the first possible sighting she’d had all evening. ‘Where?’ she asked, unable to hide her eagerness.

‘How much?’

‘Depends how sure you are,’ Geri said, holding on to the five-pound note in her jacket pocket.

The boy moved away from the machine. ‘Tall lad, well built,’ he said. ‘Brown hair. Looked older than seventeen, though.’

Geri held out the note, almost grateful to this cruel-faced boy. ‘That’s Ryan,’ she said. The boy took the money while the others watched expectantly.

He screwed up his face in concentration, clutching the note tightly in his fist. ‘Nah!’ he exclaimed. ‘Haven’t seen him.’

Then they were off and running, jostling Geri out of the way, whooping and shouting, darting through the crowds on the concourse, like a pack of hounds.

Geri regained her balance and watched them go, feeling foolish and angry, but more than anything bitterly, bitterly disappointed.

She returned to her car, defeated, but something made her rebel against the failure of the night, and she drove out towards Derby Street. Barry Mandel had seen Ryan get off the bus here and, like Siân, Geri had an irrational notion, only half-formed, that simply being near the place would give her some insight into what had happened to him. The cobblestones of the side streets popped like bubble-wrap under her tyres, and she drove in exaggerated swerves to avoid the many potholes. How could Adèle ever find safe haven in its empty, rotting landscape?

It was almost a relief to find the buildings secure. It wasn’t until the fourth or fifth that her resolve was tested: the wood of a door had perished entirely and the lock had fallen away on one side.

Geri pushed the door; it opened. She checked over her shoulder, but there was nobody about, and she flicked on her torch and shone it into the interior. The floor was piled with splintered beams and dirt from a roof fall; the building reeked of burnt wood. She took a deep breath and stepped inside, letting the door swing to gently. The place had been lived in, and recently.

She heard a faint shuffling coming from outside. At first, she thought it was a rat. It came again, louder this time — a footfall. Heavy, booted.

Geri cast about, the torch bobbing wildly. The building was no more than a shell: flat, empty, featureless. The door creaked.

Oh God! Nowhere to hide.

She killed the light and felt her way to a corner of the floor. Perhaps it was just a drunk, looking for somewhere to sleep. Whoever it was, he was bound to leave when he saw the ruinous state of the place.

Had he heard her? Her heart hammered painfully in her chest and she had to put a hand to her mouth to stop a whimper.

A strong beam of light probed the space, picking out the empty beer cans, a yellow polystyrene burger carton, slate and broken bricks. It swept the area methodically, getting dangerously close.

Geri crouched lower and lower, hardly knowing how her knees supported her. Then the beam was in her face. She sprang forward.

'Stay away from me!' she yelled, raising the torch over her head. Her voice was harsh, barely recognizable, even to her own ears. 'Stay away!'

The beam played over her face a moment longer, and she braced herself, gripping the torch tighter.

'Geri?'

Relief flooded through her. She knew that voice.

'Geri?' it repeated. 'What the hell are you doing here?'

'Joe!' She flung herself at him, sobbing and laughing. For a moment, he was too stunned to react, then, slowly, he put his arms around her and comforted her.

'This isn't the way to find him, pet,' he said, when she was calmer. 'You'll not find him like this.'

Joe Langley was a security guard and this building was on his rounds. Joe helped out at the youth club; always reliable, always cheerful, Joe had kept the club going when otherwise it would have shut through lack of adult support.

Geri refused his offer of a lift home, but he insisted on following her in his security firm's van as far as Derby Street. By the time she got home she was ready to drop. At the gate, she noticed something fluttering on the door post, next to the bell. She peered at it as she went up the path, digging in her pocket for her keys. Then the security light came on, and she saw it clearly: A scrap of paper torn from a pocket notebook. It was pinned to the door frame by a syringe. The syringe was half full of blood. Trembling, Geri glanced about her. She was alone. On the top step she stopped, her keys still in her hand, her breath making ragged bursts of mist in the air.

Three Hints for Healthy Living

1. Get plenty of sleep.

2. Eat five portions of fruit every day.

3. Keep your long fucking teachers nose out of other peoples business.

A cool, objective part of Geri's personality noted the lack of apostrophes: one of her sayings, frequently quoted back at her by the kids was, 'If in doubt, leave it out.' Had one of her pupils sent this? Her hands were shaking so badly that she couldn't get the key in the door and had to ring the bell.

Nick answered the doorbell. He was about to turn away then, catching the expression on her face, he stepped outside and took her arm.

'What . . . ?' he asked. She nodded at the note, pinned to the door frame next to him. He reached up, but she grabbed his arm.

'There's blood in the syringe.'

'Sick fucks,' he muttered, then, with remarkable gentleness he helped her inside. 'You go and sit down,' he said. 'I'll take care of it.'

'Leave it,' she said, clenching her teeth to stop them chattering. 'I want Vince to see it.'

* * *

Ryan sat opposite. His eyes, falsely animated by the flames of the fire, were ocean blue. He wanted to kiss those long-lashed eyelids closed.

He stood, and Ryan looked up groggily. He felt his heart rate surge, looking down at him kneeling there, stupefied, helpless. His erection was almost painful. He sat next to Ryan and put his arm around him, groping gently at first, then with more urgency; nuzzling at his neck, his hand on the boy's thigh, moving to his crotch. Ryan struggled, tried to pull away.

He pulled the Ryan's hands behind his back and pushed him towards the fire. His own face, pressed close to Ryan's ear, felt the searing heat, and his skin seemed to shrink from the flames.

'Relax,' he said. 'You'll enjoy it more.'

Ryan pushed back, but he was disorientated and weakened by the cocktail of drugs.

'Oh, God,' he said. 'Please . . .' The hot air must have caught in his throat and he began to choke.

'Do as you're told, and I'll let you up.'

Ryan whimpered and he was assured of the boy's co-operation. He planted a kiss on Ryan's cheek, satisfied, rather than offended by the lad's shudder of revulsion. He sat back on his haunches, holding the boy to him while he decided what he wanted Ryan to do for him.

His breathing quickened, and he felt the blood rush to his face. Was it the anticipation of sex? Or the knowledge that Ryan was going to die? He stood before the boy, holding him gently — just enough pressure on the back of his neck to keep him from pulling free, urging him on, gripping his ears at the climax, and even as the euphoria of ejaculation faded, planning how it would be. He would be gentle, reverent. He wouldn't leave a mark on him.

He looked down at Ryan, retching and sobbing on the floor, and said, 'We're gonna party.'

6

'Once more, on pain of death, all men depart.'

Liam finished his speech with a flourish.

'Good,' Geri said. 'Now before we move on to poor, love-sick Romeo' — she got the expected groan at this — 'Who can tell me what the last speech was about?'

She was feeling better than she had right to, after last night. Vince had come straight round and had taken the note away with him. He told her she had probably upset one of the suppliers with all her questions on the street — the police had got wind of her inquiries even before she had moved on from the cafés to the railway station — and he seemed to think that, as long as she stopped trying to play amateur detective, they would leave her alone.

'But why would my questions upset them?' she demanded.

'Punters might think you're police — The pushers worry that you'll arouse police interest in the places where they do business. It's unsettling. Affects their profit margins.'

'How did he know where I live?'

'You told some of the boys you were a teacher. Maybe someone recognized you—'

'Jay!' Vince looked at her, questioningly. 'It must have been him. One of my pupils,' she explained. I saw him in the arcade in Mill Street.'

Vince made a note of the name and left her to Nick's ministrations. He was less solicitous than he had been prior to Vince's arrival, and Geri thought she detected a whiff of jealousy, but at least they had remained on speaking terms.

* * *

A sharp rap at the classroom door announced Mrs Golding. All eyes turned to the plump, grey-haired woman in the doorway. The look on her face was enough: she had come for Dean. He was slouched across his desk, one arm flung out to the side, his head resting on it. When he saw Mrs Golding he sat upright, watching her as if she were a snake about to strike.

'Miss,' he said, watching the deputy head, but talking to Geri. 'He's telling them off.'

'Dean . . .' Mrs Golding said. She had a sharp, business-like manner, but she knew when to be gentle.

''Cos they're always at it, fighting and that, bickering back and forth.' The urgency in his voice turned to desperation. 'Miss—'

'Dean—'

'The lads wanna prove they're hard, so they're always looking for a ruck, taking offence — say it's a nice day, they'll ask if you're being funny.'

Geri and Mrs Golding exchanged a dismayed glance.

'And the old ones wanna prove they aren't past it. It's just . . . mad.'

He carried on with furious concentration, gritting his teeth and hunching his shoulders, talking faster and faster. 'So, he's telling them they've had it this time. It's their last chance. Anyone else gets caught at it, they're dead.' He flinched at this word, and went on, as if trying to take it back: 'When I say dead, I mean they're in big trouble, 'cos it's not safe to walk the streets, with them sword-fighting and—'

Geri walked over to him and placed one hand on his shoulder. He fell silent and looked at her as if she had done him a mortal injury.

'It's all right, Dean,' she said. 'Mrs Golding will look after you.'

Dean walked to the front of the class, watched in silence by the others. He looked incredibly small and fragile. His breathing rasped in the silence, and he turned back to Geri as if expecting her to rescue him. He shuddered as Mrs Golding touched his arm. She looked over at Geri. Whatever had happened, it was worse, much worse than she had imagined. She understood his reluctance to leave. While he remained in class, while he remained ignorant, he could imagine anything at all — that Ryan was off somewhere enjoying himself, oblivious to the concern he was causing. Going with Mrs Golding would change all that. Instead he would be presented with the unavoidable, irrevocable truth.

'Thank you, Nine S,' Mrs Golding said, retreating into brisk formality. 'You can carry on now.'

Geri stared at the anxious faces of her form and they stared back. *No*, thought. *We can't*. A line kept running through her head, "Oh where is Romeo? — saw you him today?"

'D'you think it's Ryan, Miss? D'you think they've found him?'

'I don't know, Mari.' She collected herself and tried to pick up the threads of the lesson, but she was exhausted after the forays of Monday and Tuesday night, and her thought processes were slow and muzzy.

'Perhaps we should—' she began.

'Three days, he's been gone.'

'Four, if you count Sunday,' Jay chipped in, turning around to evaluate the others' reaction. 'Did you see the look on her face?'

The concern was fake, but blonde hair and an open expression are gifts to a compulsive liar, and Jay Davies was becoming just that. Geri suspected him of trying to hijack the lesson in order to avoid homework — he had failed to hand any in that morning, and it was far from the first time — but the distress on the other children's faces was genuine. What should she do? Ignore it, just so that Jay didn't get away with putting one over on her?

Bloody hell, Geri thought. How could she go on with the lesson? She, too, had seen the look on Mrs Golding's face. She wasn't bringing good news for Dean.

'All right,' Geri said. 'If you want to talk about this, we'll talk about it.' She didn't want to encourage rumourmongering or fire up hysteria, but she could see that some of the girls were already close to tears — she couldn't just ignore what had happened. 'It could be bad news — we don't know that yet, but it could be — Just remember that whatever happens, Dean's going to need our help and support.'

At the end of the lesson Geri went directly to find Mrs Golding, but she wasn't in her office. Geri hurried down to the staffroom. Coral Jackson was talking to two other staff at one of the clusters of chairs near the centre of the room. Alan Morgan stood at the edge of the group, waiting to put in a word. Short and neat, he always wore a brown suit, tan shirt and a green or brown tie. His skin was the colour and texture of a russet apple, and he had the dry, used-up look of a man who had spent too long in one school and felt thwarted by the limitations of his horizons.

Coral glanced up as Geri approached and said, 'It's bad.' She took Geri's hand and pulled her to a seat.

'Play with fire, expect to get your fingers burned,' Alan Morgan chipped in.

Geri looked around. 'What?'

His lips quivered, but he said nothing.

'Alan, for God's sake!' Coral intervened, and Geri turned back to face her. 'They've found Ryan,' Coral told her. 'A body,' she added, before Geri could get her hopes up.

'A b—?' She shook her head. This couldn't be.

'He was identified by his signet ring.'

Geri couldn't take this in. 'What do you mean?' she asked 'I don't—'

'There wasn't much left bar a bit of pork scratchings,' Morgan said.

Geri stared, horrified into Coral's face. 'Are you saying he was burned?' she demanded. 'Are you telling me Ryan was burned to death and he's making a joke of it?' She jumped to her feet and Morgan backed away.

'It looks like it was a terrible accident. Some kind of drugs experiment,' Coral went on.

Morgan moved to the kitchen area and began spooning coffee into a mug.

Geri heard what Coral was saying but focused on Morgan. 'And you think that's funny, do you, Alan? Is it one huge belly-laugh that some poor lad's got himself burned to death?'

Morgan threw his spoon into the mug and leaned across the kitchen work top towards her. 'No,' he said. 'It's not funny — it's bloody tragic. Don't get me wrong. I don't give a shite about some gluey who's so doped up he can't even feel his skin turning to crackling. What's tragic is this used to be a good Catholic school with sound ideals and church-going families.'

'It still is,' Coral said.

Morgan snorted. 'Don't make me laugh! They only send their kids here because they've got just enough idea of right and wrong to hope we'll look out for their moral welfare. Else they're just too damn lazy to send them up the road to the comp.'

'We've got good kids and bad kids, like any school.'

'Ah,' he said, raising a finger, jabbing it at her, 'but it isn't, is it? It isn't like any school. We're supposed to be a Roman Catholic high school, with a value placed on moral and religious development. And what do they get? What do we give them?'

Geri suddenly saw where this was leading.

'Right,' he said, reading her pained expression. 'We give them Personal and Social Education. Not religious instruction. Forget the Gospels — the teachings of Our Lord. Give them PSE — how to get contraceptives and what to say when your best friend tells you he's gay. And what did we have only on Monday? Lessons on drugs.'

'Lessons against the use of drugs!' Geri exclaimed, outraged.

'If they weren't bombarded with information on how to use them, they mightn't be so gung-ho about trying them.'

'And you'd know all about that, wouldn't you, Alan?'

'I know he was in a derelict building, empty butane refills, tubes of Bostik, plastic bags — I know he set fire to himself and didn't feel a thing. You don't have to be Einstein to work it out.'

Geri opened her mouth to speak, but Morgan hadn't finished.

'Don't you ever wonder what they get up to, when they're out of your sight, these nice lads who say please and thank you and push their chairs in before they leave your classroom? D'you think they go home and study, help their mums peel the spuds for dinner?' He snorted. 'They're more likely hanging about on street corners, terrorizing the neighbourhood, or thieving to feed their drugs habit.'

'What the hell are you doing here, if you hate them so much?' Geri asked.

'I'm a realist, girl. A realist.' He picked up his coffee and swept out of the room.

Geri wondered at a reality that made monsters out of ordinary children — children whom she knew to be as kind-hearted, as cruel, as amenable, as difficult, as pleasant and as truculent as any adult she had ever met. They were people after all.

'Don't let him get to you,' Coral said. 'He's a disappointed man.'

'I don't understand, Coral,' she said, feeling suddenly weak and confused, unsure of her ground. 'The kids here aren't bad, are they?'

'St Michael's has fewer discipline problems than most urban schools.'

'I thought Ryan was one of his star students — a grade A historian.'

'Like I said, he's disappointed.'

'Is it true, what he said? About Ryan, I mean?'

Coral looked away. 'The essentials, yes.'

'He burned to death?'

Coral nodded. 'And there were empty tins — lighter fuel, that sort of thing.'

For a moment, Geri was too stunned to speak. Suddenly, she blurted out, 'But that doesn't mean—'

'I know. But' — Coral tilted her head apologetically — 'you have to admit, it doesn't look good.'

'What the hell does he know about kids?' she demanded, furious that Morgan so easily discounted Ryan's good name. 'He bullies and blusters and calls it discipline. He's never in his narrow life tried to imagine what it's like for these kids — constantly faced with temptation—'

'It's all right,' Coral soothed. 'You don't have to convince me.'

Geri paced, too agitated to accept her friend's counsel to sit and talk it through. She wanted to go after Morgan, to exact and apology — to make him take back what he had said. But she had to acknowledge the wretched truth that part of her outrage was at her own misgivings: no matter what Morgan said to pacify her, he could never make her unthink the doubts he had sown in her mind. Remembering all of Ryan's good qualities: his generous spirit, his kindness, his boundless energy and enthusiasm, Geri saw her own easy capitulation as a form of treachery.

Geri returned to her seat and was silent for a few moments, then recalling why she had come looking for Coral, she asked, 'What about Dean? Mrs Golding came to fetch him, but I can't find her now.'

'She took him and his mum home.'

'Is he all right?' As pastoral head of the lower school, Coral would have been present when his mother broke the news. Geri shook her head. 'Stupid question. I mean, how did he take it?'

‘I don’t know . . .’ Coral frowned. ‘He didn’t say anything. No reaction, nothing. He wanted to go back to class. I guess it’s shock.’

* * *

It wasn’t true that Dean didn’t react. When Mrs Golding took him down to her office, he knew what she would say. He knew his mum would be there, sitting in the yellow armchair, waiting for him.

They took him inside and sat him on the matching chair, and his mum looked at him, so that he had to close his eyes to shut her out. He recited in his head, with the same fierce conviction that Liam had used, ‘On pain of death, depart.’ but she was still there when he dared to look, still telling him that Ryan was dead.

He asked could he go back to class because if he did, he had a confused notion that everything would go back to normal; they would go on with the play and he’d try hard, offer it up for Ryan. He should have been doing that since Sunday, since he knew Ryan hadn’t come home, but first of all, he had felt smug, because Ryan almost never got into trouble and this time he was in deep. Then he had worried and fretted, but that wasn’t enough. God wouldn’t settle for that. He wanted blood, pain, sacrifice.

His mum told him again, her face wet with tears, ‘Dean, love. D’you understand me? It’s our Ryan. He’s dead.’

He couldn’t help it. It came into his head without him wanting it to. He thought, *I suppose now I’ll get the bedroom to myself.* All the time hating Ryan for not being there, hating Mrs Golding for fetching him, hating Miss Simpson for letting him go, hating his mum for telling him. But mostly hating hating hating himself.

He bit down hard — so hard that his back molar chipped and he could feel the enamel, gritty and sharp, working its way to the back of his mouth. He swallowed. Now he had something to offer up for Ryan. A penance.

7

DS Garvey arrived late, puffing with the exertion of hurrying the few steps from his car, his face florid, despite the biting wind blowing off the ship canal. He wore a grubby, bile-coloured windcheater, but his suit jacket hung below it, a grey frill beneath the stretched elastic of the weatherproof.

'Brass monkey weather,' he remarked to WPC Dhar, ignoring Sergeant Beresford. 'Who's the supervising officer, love?'

Vince Beresford waited while Dhar pointed out that her supervising officer was standing three paces away from him.

The SOCOs had already packed up and gone, but Garvey nodded at a woman picking her way through the debris that spilled from the front door of the end house. Her white overalls seemed to glow in the oppressive gloom. 'What's forensics doing here? I thought it was just some gluey set fire to himself.'

'We don't know that till the PM,' Vince said.

Garvey smiled, mouthing the words silently in a mocking imitation. 'You'll never make a detective, lad.' He sniffed, wiping a pendulous drop from his nose with the back of his hand. 'Who sanctioned it?'

'DCI Thomas is the SIO.'

Garvey's reaction was unreadable. DCI Thomas was regarded as a thorough and fair senior investigating officer.

Garvey looked up at the row of tiny terraced houses. 'Nice,' he said.

'They were, once,' Vince said, glancing up at the first-floor windows. The glass had blown out in the heat of the fire and the frames were blackened and cracked. The air stank of burnt wood, overlaid by a sickeningly sweet smell which made his stomach roil. 'Artisans' cottages,' he added. 'The last in the city.'

Garvey eyed him with amused disdain. 'How d'you know that?'

Vince shrugged, embarrassed.

'I mean, me, I've lived here all me life and I never knew that.'

'It's local history, Garvey,' Vince replied, rallying to the attack. 'Part of your local heritage.'

Garvey snorted. 'Not mine, mate. I grew up on a nineteen-sixties' housing estate, me.'

Vince shrugged, already bored with the exchange.

'Who's the pathologist?' Garvey asked, showing no eagerness to enter the ruin of fallen plaster and ceiling laths.

'Drayton.' Vince left it until Garvey, surrendering to the inevitable, started up the slippery pathway to the door into the dark and dripping house.

'Been and gone,' he said to Garvey's back. 'So's the body.'

Garvey turned, raising his eyebrows, brightening visibly. 'Looks like I've missed all the fun,' he said.

* * *

It hadn't been much fun for Ryan. The lighter fuel had made him sick, very sick. Inhaling, vomiting, inhaling again the fumes of his own ignited vomit. The volatile gases bloated his stomach until his mouth filled with saliva and he fell to his hands and knees trembling, retching like a dog.

And all the time, that insistent voice, persuasive, unrelenting: *'Gooo-on, lad. Soonest begun, soonest done.'*

He wanted to scream *Enough! Please, no more!* But his brain had ceased to function properly, he had forgotten the words, and as the second wave hit him — hot fumes from the dancing flames, he forgot who he was and what had brought him to this. Gradually, as the butane displaced the oxygen in his lungs, he began to lose consciousness, then the toxins slowly paralysed his autonomic nervous system, and his heart failed.

* * *

The youth-club doors were already open when Geri arrived. Joe Langley, probably. Monday to Thursday he was there, from six thirty to nine thirty, even though his night shift started at ten p.m. Geri only came once a week, as a rule, on Thursday, but tonight she thought it would be unfair to leave Joe on his own to deal with the fallout resulting from Ryan's death. It was difficult because she wasn't sure how she felt herself, beyond being numbed by the news. Ryan had been a popular figure at school, a good all-round athlete, and area record holder for several track and field events — he had even been scheduled for a trial at Man U at the end of February. He was also a regular helper at the youth club, organising events and competitions and assisting Joe with football training, so getting through the first night without him was going to be tough.

Their customers were thirteen- to fifteen-year-olds in the main, mostly kids from the part of the estate which backed on to the school playing fields. The brick-built hall had originally been used as a store for mowers and other equipment by the grounds staff. After grass-cutting and grounds maintenance was franchised to a big company serving all the schools in the diocese, the store fell into disuse and became a target for vandals. When the local council offered to refurbish it as a community hall, the school governors had jumped at the chance. The council had stipulated that its use must be non-denominational, but it was St Michael's pupils who attended regularly.

The club was housed in an L-shaped building, with the entrance in the centre of the long edge of the L, pool and table-tennis tables to the left of the door, table football to the right, and bar and coffee-making facilities on the back wall, opposite the door. A jukebox, donated by parents, was sited in the foot of the L, along with four circular tables in the area the kids called the café.

There was only half the usual number for a Wednesday night. It seemed that news of Ryan's death had hit hard. The few who were present sat at the bar, or around the tables on the far side of the hall, talking in whispers.

Geri shrugged off her overcoat and hung it on the stand next to the bar. She had been too busy to repair the frayed hole where she had caught it on the coat hook on Monday, so she folded it inwards to hide the tear in the lining.

Joe was often hard to pick out from a crowd of the older lads. She found him standing in a group of four, puzzling over some problem with the jukebox. He'd had his hair done in a spiky urchin cut, a style that suited him and made him even more difficult to distinguish from the others; he looked no more than eighteen, although he must be in his mid-twenties.

Occasionally, when he felt the need to assert his seniority, or when he went for his job interview as a security guard, and wanted to put on a few years, he would grow a thin bar of close-clipped beard down the centre of his chin, and a carefully shaped moustache. The boys called it his George Michael look.

Geri walked over to Joe, who was now replacing a fuse in the plug for the jukebox.

'Glad you could make it,' Joe said and his soft Durham accent was instant balm. 'I could do with a bit of moral support tonight.' He finished the repair and plugged the machine in. 'I doubt they'll be having much use for that.'

She smiled. 'How've they been?'

'Quiet,' Joe said. 'How about you? I mean after last night, like.'

Geri grimaced. 'There was a note waiting for me when I got home,' she said quietly. 'Blood-filled syringe, and a note.'

'You're joking me!'

She shrugged. 'Vince thinks I upset some of the local heavies.'

'So you're not bothered, like?'

She smiled wanly. 'Bothered enough to keep my "long effing teacher's nose out"? I'd say so.'

Joe nodded, apparently relieved.

'Vince is looking into it,' she went on. 'But it seems all the more sinister, taken next to Ryan's . . .' She couldn't finish, and Joe gave her elbow a discreet squeeze.

'They will've thought of that,' he said. 'Don't worry.'

Geri nodded, still fighting tears. 'You've got your hands full,' she remarked, trying to distract herself from thinking about Ryan.

'Actually, I'm surprised so many turned up.'

Geri shrugged. 'Curiosity, maybe . . . Or maybe the need to talk about what's happened.'

A movement over by the door caught her eye. Barry Mandel had come in. He went directly to a group of boys and girls sitting in the cafeteria area, to the right of the door, walking past Joe and Geri without a glance. Geri recognized the children as Year Nines — thirteen- and fourteen-year-olds, though they were not from her form.

'Hell,' Geri muttered. 'What's he doing here?' Barry stood over the group in the café area, talking in a murmur. They looked tense, unsettled by his presence, and he seemed to revel in the control he exerted over them.

Joe followed her line of sight. 'Count Dracula? Beats me, but if he's brought that streak of urine as his heavy, he'll be wanting a couple of lumps of lead in his pockets as ballast.'

Frank Traynor stood behind Barry, looking miserable. Geri was never quite sure why Joe disliked Frank. He was a gentle soul — the trench coat and death's-head badge on his lapel were a poor disguise — he tried to hide behind people like Baz, but nobody was fooled. He was always willing to help out, and he was good with the younger kids. He saw Geri and Joe looking at him and glanced away, embarrassed.

Barry seemed to sense their scrutiny and looked across. 'Miss Simpson,' Barry said, smiling, smooth, and Geri had a sudden picture of him in two or three years' time, tidier, suited, hair slicked back — an oily businessman, patronizing his clientele, the untrustworthy gleam in his eye betraying his need to put one over on them.

Geri looked past him, taking a couple of steps towards the cluster of circular tables nearby. 'Everything all right, Frank?' She wanted to ask him if he had seen Siân.

Frank blushed.

Barry thrust both hands into the deep pockets of his heavy overcoat then flung his arms open, flashing the rich, dark red silk lining. 'Thought you might appreciate some help tonight,' he said, barely raising his voice. 'It's hit some of these kids hard.' He placed a hand on the shoulder of the boy seated in front of him. There was something in the slow, insinuating movement that made Geri shudder. The boy, obviously feeling it, too, flinched.

'Kind of you to think of us,' she said. 'But we'll manage.'

Barry looked into her face with a disconcertingly bland, meaningless smile.

'Well,' he said in his implacable murmur. 'We've said all we have to say on the subject.' The children around the table shifted uncomfortably and he glanced away from Geri, scanning the others slowly, deliberately.

Geri stood at the edge of the group of tables, watching him as he moved towards the door. He seemed to take her steady examination as a challenge and, changing course so that he had to pass close by her, he eased past, so close she could feel his breath on her cheek.

'We're two of a kind, you and me,' he said. 'Just helping kids kill time.'

Geri turned angrily to face him, but he moved quickly on. Frank followed him, taking the longer route. None of the others looked up, so they missed the exchange. She glanced across to Joe, who shook his head in disbelief at the cheek of the lad.

The tame way Frank trotted obediently after Barry made Geri suddenly furious. 'Not staying with us tonight, Frank?' she called out.

Frank shot her a panicky look.

Barry turned his attention first to Geri, then to Frank. It was gratifying to see quickly covered surprise in his face.

'Frank, mate,' he said, 'you should've said. I didn't know this was a regular gig.'

'Sorry, Miss,' he muttered. 'Only I'm a bit busy tonight.'

'Oh, yeah,' Barry said, and although he hadn't raised his voice at all, the silence in the club was so intense that they heard every word. 'Life's just one big social whirl, isn't it, Frankie boy?'

There was a collective sigh of released tension as the door closed behind them. Geri continued watching the door as if her anger could follow Barry into the night. Then Joe dropped a coin in the jukebox and Shania Twain's 'That Don't Impress Me Much' broke the silence.

Geri looked over at him and he laughed. 'Flash bastard. Did you see the lining of his coat? Suits his nickname, doesn't he?'

'He gives me the creeps, I know that.'

'Don't worry about him. He'll get his come-uppance. Lads like him always do. Throw your weight around like he does, you've got to be able to back it up.'

'He's known as a tough nut at school,' Geri said doubtfully.

Joe gave her a slow, ironic smile. 'Aye. At school . . .'

* * *

They were short on takers for the table tennis, so Joe and Geri had to make up the numbers.

Now she sat on a bench by the table-tennis tables with a group of thirteen- and fourteen-year-olds, sitting or standing by her, drinking a glass of lemonade after winning her game, trying to get them to talk.

'He's landed us all in it, hasn't he?' Jay ran a hand through his mass of blond curls.

'He's landed himself in it,' Carl replied. Carl was a little older than the others, a tall, pale boy, with a long, solemn face. His family were strongly religious, and although he wasn't shy of expressing an opinion, he rarely spoke about his beliefs.

'Yeah, well *he* won't have to take the consequences.'

Carl looked astonished. 'Don't you reckon? I mean I don't see him here tonight.'

'Well, yeah, if you look at it that way, but I mean he won't have to deal with the fallout.'

'Pretty extreme way of getting out of a ticking-off, wouldn't you say?'

One or two others muttered encouragement to Carl.

'*You* haven't had your dad going on, have you?' Jay said.

'How would you know?' Carl demanded, leaning forward to make eye contact with Jay at the other end of the bench.

This was turning into a personal confrontation, and Geri was about to intervene when Mari spoke up, blushing as the others looked at her: she lacked the confidence and sophistication of the other girls; her brown hair was coarse and badly cut, as though she had tried to trim the fringe herself, using nail scissors. She had a broad, rather flat face and heavy eyebrows, which nobody had shown her how to shape.

'Miss, d'you think—' Mari broke off. Her face was puckered with distress.

'What, Mari?'

'D'you think . . .' She looked at the boys and girls around her, as if she were afraid that they would laugh at her. 'It's just — me mum said he'll go to hell.'

Geri frowned.

'D'you think he will, miss?'

The reaction of the others surprised Geri. They didn't have Mari's naivety; they were poised, knowledgeable, and mostly they affected a sneering contempt for the accepted doctrine. But now, they all as one looked at her, their toughness for the moment sloughed off, and they were only children, afraid of the dark, of death and an unforgiving God.

'No.' She took a moment to clear her throat and take a breath. When she spoke, her voice, though quiet, was surprisingly firm. 'No, I don't think he'll go to hell.' The truth was she didn't believe in hell or damnation, or life everlasting. But that wasn't the sort of thing to bandy about if you were a Catholic teacher with ambition in a Roman Catholic high school.

'Will he go to purgatory, then?' Mari asked, her eyes full of horror.

Geri made room on the bench, pulled Mari onto the seat next to her and put her arm around the girl.

'I'll tell you what I think,' she said. 'I think Ryan is where no one can hurt him, where he feels no pain and he isn't afraid.'

Mari's relief was palpable. 'D'you think so? Honest?'

'Honest,' Geri said.

'Oh, man . . .' Jay groaned. He was eyeing the table-football teams nervously.

'What?' Geri asked.

'Officer Dibble's in.'

Vince Beresford was talking to members of the teams who were waiting their turn. He was in his civvies, but at six foot four he was an imposing presence in or out of uniform.

'So what?' she said. 'Vince has come in before. It's no big deal.'

'All the same, I think I'll be popping off.' Jay got up from the bench and pulled on his jacket.

'There's no need for you to go . . .' But it was no use. Jay left, and shortly after him, the group that Barry Mandel had been talking to earlier.

‘Something I said?’ Vince wondered, sitting down next to Geri.

Joe joined them. ‘Why didn’t you come in your jam butty car with the lights blazin’ and the siren on?’ he asked.

The children looked agog.

‘Look, Joe, I just thought the kids might want to talk — ask questions — whatever. I’m making myself available, that’s all.’

Joe didn’t look convinced. Geri sent the next team of four to start their game, shooing them away from an argument she felt they shouldn’t witness.

‘Come on, you two . . .’ she said.

Vince ignored her. ‘I’m not even on the case, right? It’s out of uniform division’s hands now.’

‘Stop giving him a hard time, Joe,’ Geri intervened. ‘It was good of you to spare the time, Vince.’

‘I wouldn’t worry too much about his bank balance,’ Joe said. ‘Just ’cos he’s out of uniform, doesn’t mean he’s not clocking up the hours.’

‘Joe!’ He shrugged and went off to adjudicate what was left of the table-football tournament. Geri turned back to Vince. ‘Sorry,’ she said. ‘He’s been a bit tense tonight.’

‘It’s all right,’ Vince said. ‘You get it from time to time — frustrated coppers resent the real thing more than villains do.’

‘I don’t think that’s fair, Vince, things’re just difficult at the moment.’

Joe had said in the past that he thought Vince scared off some of their clientele — the lads most likely to be out getting into bother if they weren’t kept occupied. He thought the positive benefits of contact with a sympathetic policeman were far outweighed by the negative effects, but Geri couldn’t tell Vince that.

He regarded her steadily, then nodded, apparently deciding it wasn’t worth arguing over.

It turned out that the few who had remained after Sergeant Beresford’s arrival did want to ask questions and

Vince was busy for the rest of the night. Why were the police still interviewing Ryan's friends? Were they going to arrest anyone? What would happen to the body? There were a few more detailed questions about the state of the body, which Vince fielded well, bringing the discussion back to the possibility that Ryan had been experimenting with drugs, and the sad conclusion that even once is enough for things to go drastically wrong.

The club emptied early, and they had cleared up and wiped down by nine o'clock. As Vince helped Geri cover the pool table, she became aware of his quiet interest and looked up and caught him watching her.

'What?' she asked.

'You tell me.'

She took a breath, then shook her head. 'I don't want to land someone in the shit just because I don't like them.' She pulled a ruck out of the dust sheet and glanced again at Vince.

He was observing her with that same patient look in his smoky blue eyes.

'If you find out someone else is implicated, will you prosecute?' She raised her hand to stop him and added, 'Not the stock answer, please, Vince. Tell me the truth.'

'It's like I told the kids — it really does depend on the circumstances, but if others are at risk, their parents should be told.'

Joe's mobile trilled. He put down the brush he was using and dipped into his inside pocket, wandering over to the café area for privacy. A couple of minutes later he came over.

'Can you manage the rest? Bit of an emergency at work. Someone's not turned up for an important job.'

'Sure,' Geri said. 'No problem.'

Vince helped her finish brushing up, then she switched off the jukebox and unhooked her coat from the stand and she and Vince walked to the door.

'I know you can't give me details,' Geri tried again, 'but you do know the people who are investigating . . .'

‘’Course I know them. We work out of the same nick.’ He flicked off the light switches.

Geri debated with herself a moment. The brief exchange with Barry had shaken her. What had he meant by ‘killing time’?

‘Did you say you’d interviewed Barry Mandel?’ she asked.

Vince frowned, concentrating. ‘Scruffy-looking, longish hair, hard-faced, calls himself Baz — you don’t like him.’

‘Right,’ Geri said. ‘Which is why I’m not sure if I should tell you this. I might be letting my dislike of him colour my feelings.’

Vince waited.

‘He was the last person to see Ryan, wasn’t he?’

‘The last we know about. Ryan got off the bus in Derby Street — I told you this.’ He held her coat for her.

‘But you only have Barry’s word for it.’

‘He went straight to the Gryphon — it’s a pub on the edge of the main university campus, a bit of a hang-out for student-types. A few of his mates’ve corroborated his story.’

‘They would, wouldn’t they?’

‘Because . . . ?’

Geri sighed, closing the club door and locking the mortise. Vince helped her to slide an extra bar through stays welded to the metal door and she clamped a padlock to each end of it.

‘I don’t know, Vince. I just don’t like the effect he has on some of the kids. It’s like he’s got them scared, or at least he has some hold over them. I don’t want to get him into trouble he doesn’t deserve, but if he had something to do with Ryan’s—’ She was unable to go on, suddenly choked with emotion. ‘Oh, hell!’ She fished in her handbag for a tissue and blew her nose.

‘Come on,’ Vince said, taking her arm through his. ‘I’ll drive you home. And I’ll pass on what you’ve said to DCI Thomas — he’s in charge of the investigation.’ They walked to his car, the only one on the car park, and he unlocked the passenger door before walking around to the driver's side. 'If this Barry, or Baz, or whatever he calls himself, had anything to do with Ryan's death, Neil Thomas will ferret it out.'

That Geri felt so much better having told Vince her concerns, she put down to the legacy of her Catholic upbringing. She hadn't been to confession in over five years — not since the death of her mother — but she still felt the need to purge herself occasionally.

Vince dropped her at her front gate, refusing the offer of a drink and appearing suddenly awkward. 'Well,' Geri said, giving him a quick peck on the cheek, 'thanks again.'

He waited until she was through the front door before driving off. Geri made herself a strong coffee and, taking her briefcase from the foot of the stairs, climbed to the first floor. Hers and Nick's bedroom was on the same landing as her study, but the heating had switched itself off — an economy measure, since their last gas bill — and it was cold enough for a mist to rise from her coffee mug. After a brief deliberation, she decided it would be warmer marking her Sixth-Form homework in bed.

The door was open a crack, and warm lamplight spilled onto the carpet. She elbowed the door open and saw Nick propped up in bed, reading.

'Hi,' he said. Since Monday they had called an uneasy truce, and Nick was chastened, almost apologetic.

'You're in bed early,' Geri said. It was barely nine thirty, and Nick generally sat up to watch the late film.

'Nothing on telly. And anyway, it's freezing downstairs.'

'You could've turned the heating back on.'

He didn't answer this, but the wounded silence that followed made her think he was implying that he didn't really feel he had the right. Perhaps she was being over-sensitive. She undressed and slipped into bed beside him, sipping her coffee while she marked the scripts. The previous week she had asked the class to find a newspaper article on geology or palaeontology and write an essay on the subject. Most showed scant research and a distinct lack of commitment. She had handed back the scrappier work on Monday to be redone, with a stern warning that they were to incorporate properly referenced additional material. Given the turmoil of the last few days, it was to their credit — or perhaps a measure of her fierceness during Monday's lesson — that the majority had made the Wednesday-morning deadline.

Barry Mandel's was better than the rest — he had a good command of English and he had evidently looked up one or two references in his biology text books since his first desultory attempt. Siân's was carefully presented, but still lacked insight. Poor Siân. If Geri had known when she handed the work back on Monday that she had spent Sunday worrying about Ryan's whereabouts, she would never have asked her to do the work again. It was typical of the girl's conscientiousness that, despite her ordeal on Monday night, she had somehow found the self-control to sit down and write the essay out again. Siân hadn't been in school on Tuesday or today, Wednesday, but she had got the work in via a friend. Aidan's work was marred as always by exclamation marks, triple question marks and overuse of capitalization. The name at the top of the next script gave her a jolt. Ryan Connelly. She had stuffed the resubmitted scripts in the same folder as the marked papers. She read the opening paragraph.

In the sands and gravels beneath the centre of London, palaeontologists have found evidence that rhinoceroses, elephants and other tropical creatures roamed the south of England during a warm interglacial period, 125 000 years ago. Does this explain the origins of the quaintly named Piccadilly Circus and Oxford Circus?

Geri smiled. Humour was a relief when you had twenty or more thousand-word essays to mark. She read it through again to the end. It was well argued; Ryan had done his background research and given proper attribution. She had given it a B grade.

She must have sighed, because Nick put down his book and asked, 'You okay?'

Geri closed her eyes and pressed with her forefinger and thumb on the eyelids. She had a headache coming on. 'No,' she said. 'Not really.'

'I heard about that lad from your school. It was on the radio.'

She held up the two closely written sheets. 'This is his.'

'You're marking a dead lad's work?'

'Yes,' she said, on the defensive. 'I suppose that's what I'm doing.' But while she was reading the script it had seemed that he wasn't dead: she could almost hear Ryan speaking, heavily accented, but articulate and urgent in his delivery as he made each point.

Nick covered her hand with his. 'I'm sorry,' he said. 'I'm just not sure if . . .'

'Me neither.'

Nick slipped one hand behind her head, drawing her closer. She responded but drew back when she heard the crackle of scripts, crushed between her body and his. 'Papers,' she murmured distractedly. He grabbed a handful and bundled them onto his bedside table. They made love, and afterwards she wept for the tenderness he had shown her, and for the aching loss she felt.

She listened to Nick's heartbeat as he stroked her hair and soothed her; gradually his hand slowed and stilled, and he began snoring gently.

Her reading on drug abuse, and everything Vince had told her, gave glue-sniffing as a group event. It didn't make sense him being alone. Had Ryan's friends pushed him into it? Coerced him into doing something he despised? Ryan was well on the road to becoming a professional footballer — why would he jeopardize all of that for a short-term high? She saw him sitting in a circle, nervous, maybe trying to bluff his way out. Doing it, just to get it over with. But if he was with friends, how did he end up unconscious, unable to save himself as his clothes caught fire? Why didn't the others help him?

She could not reconcile Ryan's stance on drugs with his taking part in a 'drugs experiment'. Which left another possibility — one which she had skirted around all day, avoiding it, yet catching it, like a glimpse of movement in the shadows on a solitary walk.

Ryan had been forced.

She remembered how Siân had rushed out of her lesson on Monday. *'Ask them!'* she had said. *'Ask them!'* They knew something, she was sure of it, just as she was sure that Barry Mandel was mixed up in it.

Finally, exhausted, but unable to sleep, she crept out of bed, pulled on her dressing gown and went downstairs.

As she passed the sitting room, she heard Lauren's voice, a low monotone: she was talking on the phone. She went to the kitchen, her toes curling at the icy cold of the tiles, and made coffee for both of them, then she tiptoed back to the sitting room. The air in the hallway was freezing, and beyond the front door the night seemed unnaturally bright — it was snowing. Geri listened at the door. All was quiet. She tapped and went in.

'Am I disturbing you?' she asked.

Lauren shook her head. 'I've finished.' She had dragged the two-seater sofa close to the gas fire and was curled up on it, the phone in her lap.

Geri handed her one of the coffee mugs and Lauren sniffed it. 'Anything in this?' she asked.

'No, but that's soon remedied.' Geri set down her own mug and went to the big glass-fronted cupboard that served as a bookcase and drinks cabinet. She held up the Irish whiskey and a bottle of Tia Maria. Lauren opted for the Tia Maria. Geri gave herself a generous tot of whiskey, and as she topped up Lauren's coffee, she asked, 'Want to talk about it?'

Lauren took a sip of her drink, then made room for Geri on the sofa next to her. 'Probationer,' she said.

'Your baby Samaritan?' Lauren was supervisor to a new member of the team, and as such was expected to act as mentor as well. 'You weren't on duty last night, were you?'

Lauren shook her head. Sunday was her evening on the switchboard. She sipped her coffee thoughtfully for a few minutes, and Geri realized that she would not discuss the call any further.

'What about you?' Lauren asked, at length.

Geri's eyes widened. 'Me?'

'It's after midnight and you're prowling around as if you've lost something.'

Geri placed her cup carefully on the arm of the chair. 'I suppose, in a way I have.'

Geri looked up to Lauren. She admired her long-term commitment to the Samaritans, her level-headedness, the way in which she handled the conflicting demands of her voluntary work: the requisites of concern with emotional detachment. She wished she had even a small measure of Lauren's cool objectivity.

Her reaction to Ryan's death was complicated by her memories of losing her mother. Six years on, she still felt the need for reassurance.

'Sadness can be so isolating . . .' Lauren said, voicing Geri's own feelings.

Geri nodded unhappily. She felt the need to tell someone who would gather her up and kiss her forehead, take away the hurt.

Like a child, Geri thought. *Like a child in need of comfort.*

8

For hours Geri watched from her study window as large, soft snowflakes fell, hesitantly at first, but later in a steadier drift, slowly but inexorably covering the lawn and path, blanketing the borders and draping bushes and trees.

Its fall seemed gentle, almost solicitous, whispering a message of tranquillity and acceptance.

Geri rebelled against its hypnotic persuasion. She could not, *would not,* accept what had happened to Ryan. His life had been stolen from him, and with it all the hopes, dreams, possibilities of his future. How could she ever accept that?

At four thirty she crept into bed, cold and shivering, comforted by Nick's warmth and his sleepy reassurances. For perhaps two hours she slept, dreaming of heat and flames, woken by the sound of screams.

Confused, she sat up, peering into the darkness of the room. Nick stirred and groaned.

'Turn the bloody thing off!' he grumbled.

The alarm clock! She reached across and snapped the switch.

For a few minutes she lay listening to the silence. The streetlamps reflected from the snow created a false dawn; it peeped through the curtains, giving an eerie tint to the room.

There was a breathless expectancy in the stillness and Geri felt a pleasurable spurt of excitement, but a jolt as solid as a punch hit her as she remembered Ryan and she wished fervently that she still had her faith. Plain truths, simple views of right and wrong, the promise of life everlasting.

Geri sat up, impatient with herself and with the religion that had so confused her throughout her life: it was, after all, those same beliefs that had led Mari to ask if Ryan would go to hell. What sort of God was it that frightened children, and for whom salvation or damnation were so negligently meted out?

Fighting exhaustion, she dragged herself to school, depressed at the thought that there were still two more days of work to face, driving with elaborate care through the snow. Attendance had been up since Ryan's disappearance: parents were being more conscientious about checking their children's whereabouts. But she was surprised to see so many in so early.

A few of the younger children were building a snowman on the tennis courts. More were throwing snowballs or rolling with enviable energy and exuberance in the snow.

Geri skipped the morning briefing and went in search of Frank. If anyone could tell her what had really happened to Ryan, Frank would. He had followed Ryan everywhere ever since they had palled up in Year Ten. Geri was damned if she would accept the official explanation for Ryan's death. Ryan did not do drugs — would never have done drugs — and she would prove it.

Frank was in the computer suite, surfing the Net. Many of the rooms, with their leaky steel-framed windows, were freezing, and Geri had come to school wearing woollen trousers and a polo neck, but she still needed a cardigan over her sweater. The computer room was the warmest in the school, its windows welded shut, denying draughts as well as burglars access. The quiet exhalation of the computer fans was strangely soothing. The suite was situated on the second floor, next to the lecture theatre, out of sight and sound of the turmoil of the school playground.

Geri stood beside him. He was aware of her but refused to acknowledge her presence. 'Can I have a word?'

Frank shrugged, clicking at random and causing an electronic bleep followed by a synthesised musical chord.

'Frank—' There were others in the room, and she didn't want to embarrass him. 'My room? Five minutes.'

He was there in three. They stood at the back of the class, next to the bookshelves and pinboards full of children's work displayed on primary-coloured backing paper, out of sight of members of Geri's form who might want to escape the snowballing and the cold outside.

'Have you seen Siân?' she asked.

'Her mum won't let me near her.' A shadow of emotion flitted across his face.

'But you've spoken to her.'

He bit his lower lip. 'She can't stop crying.'

Geri reached out to touch him, but he moved slightly out of range. 'Are *you* all right?' she asked. 'I mean are you coping all right?'

Frank looked sick. During the last week he had lost weight he could ill-afford to lose, and his skin had taken on the chalk-pale translucence of a convalescent.

'Frank?'

He jerked as if she had shouted. 'Fine,' he said, without conviction. 'I'm fine.'

'Ryan was a good friend to you,' she said gently.

'He stuck up for me when I first came here — when I was too little and too scared to stick up for myself.' Geri remembered with a jolt how small and vulnerable Frank had been when he came to St Michael's at the age of fourteen. 'He was a good mate.' He spoke in a rush, angrily, as if Geri had challenged him to defend their friendship. 'He taught me footie skills, helped me with homework, explained things—' He stopped, his Adam's apple jerking convulsively as he swallowed, fighting the emotion that threatened to choke him.

'And Baz?' Geri asked. 'Does he stick up for you?'

Frank closed in on himself, shutting her out, resentful of the question.

'You don't need Baz,' Geri went on. 'You don't need his sort.'

He glanced at her, making fleeting eye contact. She read annoyance, perhaps even scorn in his expression.

'You think bullying stops in the Sixth Form?'

Geri blinked. The question had winded her. Was this awful event down to bullying? Was what had happened to Ryan some sort of sadistic punishment?

'Was Ryan being bullied?'

Frank laughed, a high, cracked sound, near to tears. '*Ryan?*'

She took a breath, silently berating herself for having misread the situation so badly. How could she have been so blind?

'*You're* being bullied?'

He looked away. 'No.'

'Because if you are—'

'No! I told you — no.' There was a pause, which he eventually broke. 'Hang around with Baz, nobody messes with you,' he muttered.

'Is that why you're protecting him? Quid pro quo?' Seeing his puzzled look, she added, 'You scratch my back . . .'

He shrugged, his face sulky, his manner truculent.

'I got a threatening note,' she said. 'Fixed to my door with a syringe.'

His eyes widened, and she thought she saw a fleeting terror, then he closed down again, shutting her out.

He exasperated her with his self-absorption and his sullen refusal to communicate. 'I thought you cared about Ryan!' she exclaimed.

Frank frowned — she had hit the mark.

'He looked out for you, Frank. Why can't you return the favour?'

He glanced at her, his eyes darting nervously away as she tried to make him see her frustration. 'Something happened — while you were all together. I know it did.'

He shook his head. Tears stood in his eyes and he bit his lower lip as if afraid he might otherwise let out his secret.

'You don't care about Ryan,' Geri said, unable to conceal her contempt. 'All you care about is yourself.'

His hurt was so profound that Geri responded to it with an uprush of feeling. She swallowed hard.

'I'm sorry,' she said. 'I shouldn't have said that. I want to help you, Frank, really I do.'

She felt the same frantic desperation she had experienced watching her mother die — seeing her go through months of agony, until she couldn't tell which limb was which, because her entire body was one screaming mass of pain. And knowing that her concern, even her love, were worse than useless.

Frank looked into her eyes, and what she saw made her heart shrink.

'No, Frank,' she whispered. 'No.'

She saw in his face what she had seen too often in her mother's: the unspoken words, *I want to die. I just want to die.*

* * *

There was a snowball fight at lunch time. Snowballing had, of course, been banned at assembly, and Mr Ratchford threatened dire consequences to anyone caught flouting his edict, but the temptation was too great. Classes had been kept in during break time, due to a further fall of snow, which undid all the hard work of the maintenance staff who had cleared the paths before the start of school. The children resented the cancelling of their break and the snowflakes whirling outside the classroom windows had increased their pent-up excitement.

Amy Wilcox, having returned after a remarkably speedy recovery from 'flu, was on yard duty with Geri. As the snowballing grew from a few cheeky flurries to a frenzy that smacked of feuds and old scores being settled, Amy was hit in the back of the head with a snowball and stormed inside, leaving Geri to cope on her own. Geri sent a sixth-former to summon backup, and then surrounded herself with a posse of the bigger Upper Sixth lads until help arrived. It took the combined efforts of seven teachers to break up the fight, and the nucleus of nine or ten who had started the trouble were rounded up and marched down to Mr Ratchford.

The afternoon seemed interminable. Her classes were inattentive, watching for signs of further snowfall, and Geri herself was preoccupied. She sought out Coral in her office at afternoon break. Her visits to Coral's sunny room, lush with plants and decorated with watercolours and prints, always cheered her up.

Coral was talking to three Year Nine boys. Coral rarely raised her voice; today was one of the few exceptions. She dismissed the boys, warning them to return to her at the end of lessons, and scarcely had the control to wait for the door to close behind them before exclaiming, 'I don't believe it! Look at this!' She opened her hand to reveal a few small tubes of kit-making glue. 'Stolen from the art department. Mr Burnley caught them red-handed.' She threw the tubes onto her desk. 'After all that's happened!'

Geri prodded the tubes. 'Bloody idiots . . .'

'God almighty!' Coral growled under her breath. 'Do they *want* to die?'

'No, Coral, they just think they're immortal.'

Coral shook her head, rattling the beads in her braids. 'Live fast and die young, eh?' She sucked her teeth. 'I don't know how to get through to them on this, I really don't.'

'Vince was doing his bit down at the youth club last night.' Which reminded Geri that a two of the boys Coral had been addressing were in the group Barry Mandel singled out the previous night. She opened her mouth to say something, then Vince's words came back to her: if Barry was mixed up in Ryan's death, DCI Thomas would find out.

'What?' Coral said.

'Nothing. Well, yes there *was* something. I want to go and see the Connellys. Would that be all right?'

Coral gave Geri one of her narrow-eyed looks. 'Depends what for.'

'To offer my condolences. To let them know I'm thinking about them. To see how Dean is.' She shrugged. 'That's it.'

'You sure now?'

Geri gave her an up-from-under look. 'You're always trying to find ulterior motives. Take it at face value, Coral.'

Coral gave one of her fruity laughs. 'Not in me nature, girl.' She considered for a moment. 'Maybe you could . . .' Thinking out loud. 'I have got to see those fools after school. And there's a pastoral meeting at four thirty . . . It would be nice to get home before seven for once . . .' She made up her mind. 'I was going to take this myself, but if you want to go — it'll give you an excuse for turning up on their doorstep uninvited.' She took an envelope from the top of her out-tray and handed it to Geri. 'On behalf of the school,' she explained.

Geri groaned, taking the envelope between finger and thumb. 'A mass card!'

'Now don't start with your heathen ways.' Coral treated Geri's lapsed faith as a temporary aberration, a difficult phase she would grow out of. 'It's not going to burn you.' She stopped and gave her head a little shake as if she couldn't believe what she had just said. 'It'll make Mr and Mrs Connelly feel a whole lot better knowing the Carmelite sisters are praying for their son.'

Geri looked at the card, addressed in Coral's bold copperplate. 'All right,' she said. 'I'll do it.'

The grim determination in her voice made Coral laugh again. 'I know you're up to the job,' she said, letting Geri out of the room, but then calling her back before she had got two paces. 'Tell them they're in my prayers,' she said, all trace of laughter gone.

'I will,' Geri said.

'You be sure and tell them,' Coral called after her, just before Geri was swallowed up by the press of children making their way to the last two lessons of the day.

* * *

Garvey was looking remarkably cheerful for a man who had received a stiff reprimand from his boss only the day before. He finished his call and hung up, rapping out a drum-roll on his desk.

'That your bookie, was it, Sarge?' DC Winters asked. It was a relief to see him smiling.

'No, but my luck's in all right. Fancy a pint?'

Winters checked his watch. It was after six. 'Go on then.'

Winters was as fair-skinned as Garvey was florid. He wore his hair close-cropped and he was lean and fit. He sat across from Garvey in the pub, assessing the older man, thinking that the paunch and the high colour was a sure sign of blood pressure. He took a pull on his pint and silently vowed never to let himself get so out of shape.

Garvey outlined the content of his telephone call: he had spoken to a mate who had moved to the Met eighteen months previously. 'It seems Vince Holier-than-thou Beresford left under mysterious circumstances.'

'What was it?' Winters urged. 'Death in custody?'

Garvey shrugged, slurping a couple of swallows of beer and licking his lips before answering. 'Haven't got the details yet, but he moved out of Vice, then put in for a transfer up north a couple of months later.'

'He did all right out of it,' Winters said, meaning Beresford's promotion.

'If you can call a move back into uniform "all right".' Garvey mauled a handful of peanuts from the packet on the table and began munching. 'Beresford likes to think he's a man of mystery. Well, there's mysterious and there's cagey. You mark my words — he's hiding something.'

9

The Connellys lived in a red-brick terrace two miles from school. Officially, they were just over the boundary of the catchment area, but the parish priest had put in a good word when Mrs Connelly had first applied for a place for Ryan. Their status as regular churchgoers and Mrs Connelly's reputation as an excellent PTA member and fund-raiser for her sons' primary school had clinched it. And once Ryan was safely installed at St Michael's, the process had been easier for Dean.

The houses opened directly onto the pavement, and snow and slush were banked up against the door sills. Geri glanced over at the house as she locked the car. The curtains upstairs and down were pulled tight and no light escaped into the night. It looked as if the house was empty.

She trudged over the rutted slush in the roadway, wishing she had thought to change out of her school shoes into her boots; the temperature was tumbling and a crusting of ice was already forming on the ridges of the tyre tracks. She rang the doorbell and immediately heard a distant thump, like a soft implosion as a door was opened with some force inside the house.

Three long strides — she heard their booted thud in the hallway — and the front door was dragged open and a fierce, square face was thrust into hers.

'What do you want!' the man yelled. 'Just what do you want from us?'

Geri could see, even in the uncertain light of a stuttering streetlamp, that his eyes glittered with anger or tears.

She took a step back. 'Mr Connelly? I'm from St Michael's. Miss Simpson?'

He straightened up and passed a hand over his face. It came away wet. 'Oh,' he said. 'Sorry . . . Sorry, love. Come in. Come inside.' He stepped aside, then looked up and down the street before closing the door after them.

'Reporters,' he explained. 'They won't let us be.'

He leaned with his back to the door for a moment, as if trying to overcome a dizzy spell, then dragged his hand over his face again. 'Sorry, love,' he repeated. 'Go through. We're in the back.'

Geri walked down the hall and into the kitchen. It was a large room, taking up the full width of the house, and it looked newly decorated. In the centre of the pale parquet floor was a pine table. Mrs Connelly sat at one end and another woman — her sister, judging by the resemblance — sat adjacent to her. They both looked up as she came in, and Geri got the feeling she had interrupted something, some angry exchange between the two women.

Geri had met Mrs Connelly before, at parents' evenings. She was in her late thirties and wore her dark hair long, in a mass of curls. Her sister looked older and was grey-haired, but she had the same ruddy colouring and small, slightly flattened nose. Mrs Connelly pushed her hair from her eyes and for a moment she looked lost, bewildered by the appearance of a stranger at her door.

'Miss Simpson,' Geri said. 'Geri.'

'Aye, I remember.' Mrs Connelly glanced at the older woman. 'This is the lady I told you about. Dean's teacher. Sit down, love, I'll make you a cuppa.' She stood with such an effort, it seemed that gravity almost defeated her. There was tension beneath the good manners, and Geri saw her struggle with a spasm of distress that looked almost like physical pain.

Geri glanced in alarm at the older woman, but she merely shook her head. Mr Connelly leaned against the wall, his arms folded and his head on his chest as if he had forgotten there was anyone else in the room.

'Una,' the woman said. 'I'm Theresa's sister.'

Mrs Connelly smiled apologetically. 'Aye, I'm forgetting my . . .' Her voice trailed into silence and Geri shot Una a concerned look. Una shook her head again and continued talking, her voice louder than the size of the room warranted.

'You've come about Dean have you, Miss Simpson? Worried about him missing school?'

'We're all concerned about Dean, of course,' Geri said. 'But you mustn't rush him into coming back.'

'Never had a day off sick in his life,' Mrs Connelly said. 'Him or our Ryan.' She looked around as if she might catch Ryan in some childish prank, hiding from her in a corner of the room.

'I came to offer my condolences,' Geri said, feeling awkward, insensitive for intruding on their grief.

'Good of you,' Mrs Connelly murmured, as if reciting a well-rehearsed line. It was said without feeling, and with that same air of distraction that was so heartrending.

'Mrs Jackson asked me to tell you that she's praying for you.'

'She what? . . . Oh, aye . . .'

The kettle clicked off, claiming her full attention for the moment.

'We said prayers for Ryan at assembly, as well.' Geri suddenly remembered the mass card and took it out of her handbag. 'And there's this.'

Mrs Connelly stared at the card without taking it. 'It's not true, you know,' she said.

'What?' Geri looked from Mrs Connelly to Una for clarification.

'Our Ryan. He wouldn't . . . He said drugs was for pin-heads, didn't he, John?'

Geri had forgotten Mr Connelly. His head jerked up off his chest and he gave his wife a harried look. 'Don't, Theresa,' he said. 'It won't do any good.'

'So, I'm to put up with the lies the papers are telling about him? A druggy, they're saying. Glue-sniffer. My Ryan!' Her silence required an answer, a defence of her son.

'Have you spoken to his friends — to Siân?' Geri asked.

'Poor lass is shattered. She doesn't believe the trash the papers are printing any more than I do.'

Geri noticed the 'I', and the sudden stiffening of Una's shoulders.

'We're not saying—'

'Not saying he's a gluey?' Mrs Connelly interrupted. 'Maybe. But you're not saying owt to defend him, are you?'

'Did they have any idea why he might've got off the bus at that end of town?' Geri butted in, anxious to deflect a return to a row that she sensed had been raging for some time.

'There was none of them with him, only Barry,' Una said.

Mrs Connelly snorted contemptuously. 'Well, they're not going to *admit* to being with him, are they?' she said. 'Not if it'll get them in trouble.'

'The police have questioned them, Theresa,' Una said tiredly.

'They don't know those kids. They don't know when they're lying. You want answers to your questions, Miss Simpson, you ask Frank Traynor. He knows a lot more than he's saying.'

'I spoke to him today,' Geri said.

Mrs Connelly stared at her. 'Well?' she demanded.

'You're right. He is hiding something or protecting someone. I'm not sure which.'

Mrs Connelly shot her sister a triumphant look. 'See?'

'Ryan always told the younger children to stay away from drugs,' Geri went on. 'Kids take drugs to experiment, to get high, to escape — or because of peer pressure.' She looked from Una to Mrs Connelly. The sister's mouth was drawn into a thin line, but Mrs Connelly seemed curious. 'Ryan wasn't interested in experimenting,' Geri went on. 'He didn't need drugs to get high, and he certainly didn't need them to escape. He loved life!' She stopped, embarrassed at her outburst. 'I don't need to tell you that,' she apologized. 'As for peer pressure, the kids followed his example. Ryan was a leader, not a follower.'

She saw a look exchanged between Mr Connelly and Una. She had gone too far. Una spoke up, 'You're not helping her, you know.'

'I'm sorry,' Geri replied, 'But I can't believe that Ryan—'

'None of us can,' Una broke in angrily. 'But we're going to have to come to terms with it.'

'Yes . . .' Geri said, 'I'm—'

'Don't apologize, love,' Mrs Connelly said. 'Don't you be sorry for believing in him more than his own father does!'

'Theresa!' Una exclaimed, appalled.

Mr Connelly opened his mouth to speak, but the words would not come and a soft moan escaped from his lips. He grappled for the door handle and stumbled out into the hall.

'They don't even know if he had drugs inside him, yet, and his own father has condemned him!' Mrs Connelly shouted after him.

Geri got up to leave, offering an apology, but Una spoke over her:

'Just get out, will you?'

'If there's drugs in my Ryan, somebody forced them on him,' Mrs Connelly muttered, her eyes ablaze.

Geri hurried into the hall, in time to see Mr Connelly blunder up the stairs. She opened the front door and stepped outside into the bitter cold. The snow was packed hard on the pavement and she almost fell backwards but managed to regain her balance and pull the door to before returning to her car.

For several minutes she sat behind the wheel, shaking uncontrollably, her teeth chattering. 'Ryan did *not* do drugs,' she said aloud, just to hear if she sounded convinced. 'He bloody didn't!' She banged her fist on the wheel.

Mrs Connelly's final words rang in her ears: *'Somebody forced them on him.'* But who among Ryan's friends would do such a thing?

She started the engine and pulled out, her tyres cracking the crust of ice that had formed like a thin layer of icing over the slush in the short time she had been indoors.

The end of the road had been polished to a smooth sheet by children sliding on the surface, and Geri felt the car slip sideways as she braked. Cars were parked either side of her and she held her breath, pumping the brakes until she stopped, slightly askew, just beyond the T-junction.

She waited until the thudding of her heart was less painful, then checked left and right. Behind her a flare of light warned of an approaching vehicle. The driver was likely to have the same trouble as she'd had, and she quickly glanced in her rear mirror to gauge how much time she had to turn the corner. At that moment she saw a figure hurry across the road, the woman's dark hair unmistakable in the headlights of the following car. Geri eased her Renault around the corner and pulled up gently; the rear end drifted a little, and the tyres bumped the kerb. The woman was alongside her by this time, and she looked anxiously through the passenger window. It was Mrs Connelly.

Geri leaned across and opened the door. 'Where are you headed?' she asked. 'I'll give you a lift.'

'Erskine Street. I can get a bus.'

'There's no need. It's on my way.'

Mrs Connelly hesitated a moment longer, then ducked inside, just as the following car hit the patch of ice and slewed to a halt after bouncing off the opposite kerb. The driver, a man, crunched the gears angrily and then sped off, fishtailing down the road. Geri waited until he was out of sight, then eased away from the kerb and drove for a few minutes without speaking, concentrating hard on her driving until they had reached the relative safety of the gritted main roads.

'Is Mr Connelly all right?' she asked. 'I didn't mean to upset anyone.'

'To hell with them.'

Geri glanced at Mrs Connelly. Her face showed grim determination.

'If his own family won't stick up for him . . .' She sighed. The rest of the journey was conducted in an uncomfortable silence. Within minutes they were in Erskine Street.

'Where shall I drop you?' Geri asked.

'Anywhere here'll do.'

Geri found a large gap in the line of parked cars and glided to a stop. 'Thanks, love,' Mrs Connelly said. 'And thanks again for what you said.'

'Are you sure you'll be all right?' Geri asked. 'How will you get home?'

'Taxi,' Mrs Connelly said, evidently anxious to be rid of her. 'I'll hop a taxi.'

Geri watched her slip and slither down the street and then disappear through a gate in a set of high railings. She was too far down the road to see the building. Geri braced herself for the tricky manoeuvre of getting out into the centre of the road again, and after waiting for several cars to pass, managed it without a hitch. This road was clearer than most side roads, mainly because of the volume of traffic using it. She noticed that two of the cars that had passed her had parked opposite the railings and the occupants had used the same gate as Mrs Connelly.

She slowed from a crawl to a virtual stop at the entrance. The front of the building had a tall window either side of a double door; both windows were protected by iron grilles. The building was large, a plain oblong of greyish brick, the only concession to architectural design being an ugly concrete awning over the door. A sign over the awning read

SPIR TUALIST C URCH

A banner, made from an old sheet, had been strung from hooks in the concrete awning and tied off at the bottom to the metal grilles on the windows:

Service Tonite
6 — 8 p.m.
We are privileged to announce
our visiting medium is the renowned
Agnes Hepple.

Wincing at the spelling of 'tonight', Geri went through the gate and mounted the shallow steps to the double doors. They were locked. She retraced her steps, then followed the path that had been cleared and gritted; it led down a narrow passageway to the right, running between the building and the perimeter wall. The wall was topped with broken glass which stuck up through the snow like jagged teeth.

She followed the path towards a faint light. The only sound was the occasional swish of cars on the road. The passage came to a dead end; on her left was a door, leading into the building. She tried it and found it open. It gave onto a corridor that smelled of mouldy paper and damp carpet — a dark brown runner, worn to the hessian backing in places.

A noise came from further down the corridor, something like a collective clearing of throats, then silence. Geri walked towards the sound and stopped at a door which was helpfully labelled 'ENTRANCE'. A high, fluty voice beyond the door was saying something indistinguishable; this time the response, heard only as a cough at the far end of the building, was a clear 'Amen'.

Then came the unmistakable wheeze of a church organ and voices were raised in song.

Geri edged in at the back of the hall as the congregation, reading from a hymn sheet, sang to the tune of 'How Great Thou Art':

'Oh, Spirit World, when I in awesome wonder
Consider all the hope you can convey
I hope you will allow communication
With all our friends on the Spirit Plane today . . .'

Geri stood in the back row of straight-backed dining chairs. Behind her, a trestle table had been set up on which cups and saucers were placed. The decor was circa 1950: beige roses twisted on a trellis in a repeating pattern. The floor was plain boards, grown splintered and pulpy with the damp that seemed to pervade the building, despite the ferocious heat thrown out from radiators on either side of the hall.

The service was conducted from a stage at the front by a small, silver-haired woman with a benign face. She dispensed with the use of the hardboard lectern, because she could not be seen behind it.

'Friends,' she said, as the organ gasped reluctantly to a halt. 'Friends old and new, welcome. Before we enter into the business of the evening, can we pause for a moment, to send out our healing to the world. It doesn't take long and remember that the healing that you send out today will return to you a hundredfold.' She smiled, spreading her arms wide to encompass her audience. 'Send out your healing. Your gift to the world.'

In the silence that followed the only sounds were the frantic rush of water in the heating pipes and the gentle creak of shoe leather. Geri looked around at the congregation. A man of no more than thirty sat at the end of a row near the front; his face avid, he stared to the right of the elderly woman who led the prayers and hymns, his gaze fixed on a woman who sat in the shadows at the back of the stage, her head bent, her hands clasped in front of her.

Sitting in the row behind him, Mrs Connelly held herself with tense dignity. Geri wondered how she was reconciling her Catholic faith with what she was doing now. It certainly explained the atmosphere in the house when she visited. Spiritualism was only one step removed from voodooism in the eyes of many in the Catholic church.

The silence ended and the elderly woman spoke again. 'Tonight,' she said, in the delighted tones of an indulgent granny imparting news of a special treat, 'we are privileged to have with us a very exceptional lady.' She stole a glance over her shoulder and the shadowy figure nodded graciously. 'Miss Agnes Hepple has been called the new Doris Stokes,' she went on, with due reverence to the great name. 'Well, maybe we shouldn't make comparisons, but whichever way you look at it, she's a very great lady, and she's battled with the elements so as not to disappoint us this evening.'

Didn't she know the weather was going to be bad? Geri thought, irritated with the woman before she'd even opened her mouth. Someone tapped her on the shoulder, and she gasped; she hadn't seen anyone in the area behind her, and she certainly hadn't heard them approach. She turned to face a woman with a frizzy perm and badly fitting dentures.

'It's ticket only,' the woman hissed.

Geri reached for her purse. 'How much?' she whispered.

'Five pounds.' She must have read the surprise on Geri's face, because she added, 'She's very famous.'

'She's also very expensive,' Geri muttered, handing over the money.

The woman gave her a ticket and told her to hang on to it: it gave her a chance in the raffle at the end of the evening.

She settled back just as the woman seated in the shadows stood up and walked to the lectern. She was about forty, medium height and build, with brown hair.

'I blushed a little at your introduction,' Agnes Hepple began, smiling at the silver-haired woman. 'The privilege is mine entirely.' There were one or two murmurs of approval and people turned to each other and smiled, then they started to applaud — raggedly at first, but then with real warmth.

Agnes tilted her head in a shy gesture and waited for silence. 'You're here to make contact,' she said at last. Her voice was sweet and rather girlish, despite her age, her accent northern, but not strongly so, and she had a halting, rather nervy delivery that reminded Geri of the actress Harriet Walter. She knew how to work her audience: a pause for dramatic effect here, a touch of humour there, and constantly moving on, never delving too deep, never allowing her audience to become restless or bored.

She stood at the lectern for most of the session, but from time to time she would stride out to the front of the stage and stare fiercely out at the rows of people.

'I have a Doreen,' she would say — or a Martha, or a Jack — and half a dozen hands would go up.

'I'll take that!' was an expression all the regulars used.

Miss Hepple would elaborate: 'He's come to me in uniform. It's . . .' For a moment her gaze would become unfocused, distant. 'It's blue . . . air-force blue.'

A woman in the third row was nodding enthusiastically. Geri wondered how much her act relied on non-verbal signals. 'He's asking me do you remember the dance? Does that make sense to you?' She smiled beatifically, and the woman gave a joyful sob.

They were mostly in that vein. 'You did look lovely in that frock . . . He says to say hello to the children.' Each encounter would end with a message. 'Can you understand that?' And if they couldn't, if it made no sense to them that the visitor was pointing to a house, or an ornate bureau, or thorny roses, then it was a symbol, a warning or advice for the future.

Geri watched the grateful acknowledgements and listened to the sighs, the broken laughter, and became increasingly uneasy. Her anxiety turned to bafflement, and finally frustration.

Miss Hepple's voice broke into her thoughts: 'I'm going to come to the lady on the second row.' There was a rustle of interest. So far, Miss Hepple hadn't singled out any individual, preferring to cast her net wide and wait to see what it trawled in. 'The lady with the dark hair and the brown coat.'

Geri paid attention. She had settled on Mrs Connelly. 'I'm getting a lot of pain,' she said, tucking her hair behind her ears in a quick nervous movement. 'It's a recent loss.'

Mrs Connelly nodded, and Miss Hepple pressed her hand between her breasts as if to ease some hurt. She swayed for a moment, then seemed to come to. 'He's telling me something.' She leaned back, listening. 'I can't quite . . . His voice is hoarse.'

Mrs Connelly put her hand to her mouth and gave a choked cry.

'He's telling me you've no need to feel ashamed.'

'I'm not!' Mrs Connelly jumped to her feet. 'I'm not, Ryan! I love you, son!'

God, no! Geri thought. *Don't do this to yourself.* She got up and made her way down the centre aisle.

'Tell him,' Mrs Connelly said through tears. 'Tell Ryan I love him.'

'He knows.' Miss Hepple replied, gently, pityingly. 'He can hear every word.'

Mrs Connelly collapsed back into her seat, and the medium went on, 'He says to tell you he's happy where he is.' She gave a sudden, girlish laugh. This was cruel — what could possibly be funny?

'All right,' Miss Hepple said, 'I'll tell her.' As Geri reached Mrs Connelly the medium said, 'He says they've got footie teams here — d'you understand that? Does it mean something?'

'Oh, it does — thank you! Thank you!'

Geri put her arm around Mrs Connelly, and she turned and buried her face in her shoulder. She helped her to her feet, and they edged along the front of the hall, past the organist then to the back of the hall and into the corridor. As they walked, Mrs Connelly grew calmer, and by the time they had emerged into the icy cold night, she was able to say, 'Did you hear? She knew . . . He said I'm not to be ashamed. I've no cause to be ashamed.'

Geri wondered if the *Evening News* had carried the story of Ryan's death. 'I heard,' she soothed.

'You don't believe her.' Mrs Connelly pushed away from Geri, slithering on the ice that had reformed on the gritted path at the side of the building. 'You think she's heard it in the news — read about him in the paper. Well, I heard him. She couldn't fake that.'

'Heard him?' Geri echoed faintly.

'Guess what, Mum,' he said. 'They've got footie teams here.'

'No . . .' Geri said.

'Trust our Ryan, eh? Him and his football.' She laughed a little wildly and began searching in her handbag for tissues.

'Mrs Connelly — Theresa — that wasn't Ryan. Miss Hepple does a good turn, but that's all it was—'

Mrs Connelly seized Geri by the shoulders, her fingers biting into the flesh, despite the thick overcoat she wore. 'It was Ryan,' she said fiercely. 'My Ryan.'

* * *

Miss Hepple was still talking. Theresa Connelly found her way to an empty seat near the back. She wanted to get closer, but she didn't like to distract her from her work.

The woman had a glow about her. Perhaps that's what they meant by an aura. Mrs Connelly had always thought all that about lights and colours was rubbish, but it was like a light came off her, a healing, golden light, like the halos on the plaster saints in church.

Mrs Connelly waited, singing along with the songs that weren't quite hymns, feeling uneasy that what she was doing was blasphemous; she was here against her husband's wishes, and in the face of her sister's disapproval. If Father O'Connor knew where she was— But how could it be blasphemy to sing the praises of God's children?

It comforted her to think of Ryan as God's little child — as chosen.

The organist packed up and tea was served. Biscuits were offered round and still Mrs Connelly waited. Listening to the childlike voice of Agnes Hepple, a strange calm had drifted over her, as soft and light as a communion veil. She kept watch, in case the medium should suddenly decide to leave, but she felt shy of intruding on her conversations with others.

She waited until it was almost too late. Most of the congregation had sipped their tea and left via the side door; the main doors remained locked and bolted. Miss Hepple touched the elderly woman who had led the service lightly on the arm and said something before turning to leave.

'Miss Hepple,' Mrs Connelly called. 'Miss Hepple!'

Miss Hepple looked round and Mrs Connelly hurried forward. 'You were right,' she said.

The clairvoyant seemed puzzled.

'About my Ryan. He's a football fiend.'

Miss Hepple crinkled around the eyes, but she did not speak, and Mrs Connelly was grateful for the clairvoyant's patience in waiting for her to decide what she wanted to say, and giving her the time to summon the courage to say it.

'Nobody believes me,' Mrs Connelly said in a low voice. 'My Ryan wouldn't do . . . what they said.' She looked over her shoulder, afraid that someone would overhear.

Miss Hepple fixed her with her intensely blue eyes and said slowly and clearly, as if to emphasise the importance of her words, 'It doesn't matter what anyone else believes.'

Mrs Connelly sighed with gratitude and had to fight back tears. Miss Hepple seemed untroubled by her emotional state but continued to hold her with her steady gaze.

'Would you like to talk to him again?' she asked.

Mrs Connelly's eyes flew wide open and she stared imploringly at the clairvoyant. 'Can you? I mean, is it possible?'

Miss Hepple smiled. 'In the spirit world, anything is possible.' She offered her hand and Mrs Connelly felt she would like to kiss it. As they shook hands, Mrs Connelly felt a small but definite shock; a tingling sensation in her hand which became a shimmering tremor of warmth that ran through her entire body. She looked upwards, thinking that someone must have turned on the overhead lights, for it seemed suddenly brighter in the hall. She squeezed Miss Hepple's hand and the clairvoyant, in return, placed her free hand over both of theirs and once more gave her that warm, reassuring smile.

* * *

Thursday was Geri's night at the youth club, and Joe would be expecting her. She knew Joe would most likely be running it single-handed if she didn't turn up. Coral would often show her face after her pastoral meeting, but it depended how long the meeting went on. Occasionally other teachers would put in an appearance, but in weather like this, people preferred to be at home in front of the telly, or working up an alcoholic glow in the pub.

She paced up and down outside the spiritualist church, unsure if she should simply leave or if she should wait for Mrs Connelly. It wouldn't be right to leave her alone, after seeing her so upset. She decided to go in and wait; at least she wouldn't freeze to death.

With all the congregation gone, the heating system was finally having an effect: the hall felt muggy and smelled of hot dust, soggy biscuits and the faintly doggy smell of damp wool. Mrs Connelly was talking to Agnes Hepple. She still looked distressed, but there was also a glimmer of hope as she spoke to the medium.

Miss Hepple seemed absorbed in her communication with Mrs Connelly. Communication, Geri reflected was the best word to describe it: it could hardly be called a conversation, since Miss Hepple barely spoke, but she *was* communicating with that penetrating look. Then she took Mrs Connelly's hand and Geri saw a shudder, barely perceptible, but unmistakable, shake Mrs Connelly's tired frame.

Then Miss Hepple handed Mrs Connelly a small card. Mrs Connelly turned and hurried down the aisle, her eyes fixed on the card as if it carried a living image of her beloved son. She almost bumped into Geri, and as she hastily slipped the card into her coat pocket, Geri caught a glimpse of a crescent moon and stars etched in silver.

'I will take that offer of a lift home, if it's still on,' Mrs Connelly said a little stiffly.

'Of course!' Geri took her arm and drew it through hers; Mrs Connelly looked suddenly exhausted to the point of collapse.

They drove back in silence. Mrs Connelly turned to Geri as she pulled up opposite the house. 'I'd ask you in, only . . .'

Geri gave her a rueful glance. 'I don't think I'd be very welcome,' she said.

'Oh, no, love!' Mrs Connelly exclaimed, distressed that any guest in her house should feel unwelcome. 'Normally, like . . .'

Geri smiled. 'I know.' These weren't normal circumstances, and it was hard to imagine how life for the Connellys could ever be normal again.

By the time Geri arrived at the youth club, Joe had already started clearing up.

'I'm sorry,' she said. 'I got sidetracked. Did nobody else turn up?'

Joe threw her a withering look and said, 'That streak of piss showed up for a bit.'

He meant Frank. 'You're not being very fair to him, Joe.'

Joe grunted. 'He's about as much use as a chocolate teapot.'

'He's a good lad.'

'He's flamin' wet!'

'He's quiet, and he may not be too bright, but he does his best. And he is reliable.'

'If you say so.' Joe handed her a tea towel and she began drying glasses.

'Anyway, I'm sorry you had to deal with it alone.'

'Gives them an outlet. If it hadn't been for the youth club when I was a kid, I'd've got into all kinds of trouble.'

'Still, it must be exhausting, doing this, three times a week and then going on to your job.'

Joe shrugged. 'It's only a couple of hours. Anyway, it isn't exactly demanding, what I do.' Joe's regular shift ran from ten p.m. until six a.m.

'What *does* it involve?' she asked, curious.

'Rattling padlocks and shining my torch into dark alleyways, mostly. I'm what you might call a visible deterrent. Catching the buggers at it isn't so easy, 'specially when you've got twenty-odd sites to cover.'

'I thought you were based in one place?'

'What made you think that? I do the railway station occasionally, but that kind of job can drive you quietly bonkers. Anyway, I like being mobile — you can feel trapped working the same site all night.'

Nick had felt the same way when he did a stint as a security guard. Once he had told her he liked working nights, roaming the city in the dark and the silence, while others slept.

'So,' Joe asked. 'Where were you in my hour of need?'

Geri sighed. 'The Connellys'.'

There was an awkward pause. Finally, he asked, 'Are they . . . okay, like?'

'As okay as you can be in these circumstances.' She paused. 'Mrs Connelly doesn't think it was an accident.'

'What else could it be?'

'She thinks the solvents were forced on him.'

In the silence that followed, Geri got a sense of Joe wondering whether he should ask the next question. 'What makes her say that?' he asked, at last.

'You knew Ryan, Joe. He wasn't the type. It just wasn't like him.'

Joe took his hands out of the soapy water and flicked the suds off them. 'There *is* no type, Geri. *You* should know that.'

'Not Ryan,' she said. 'You heard him talk about drugs, Joe.'

'I seem to remember River Phoenix was dead set against them an' all, but when he collapsed and died, there was enough shit in his bloodstream to keep half of Hollywood high for a month.'

Geri felt a hot surge of anger. Ryan always stood up for people, getting them out of holes they had dug for themselves. It didn't seem fair to make assumptions about what had happened to him when there was no one to fight his corner.

'If he did try it just the once — and I'm not saying her did — where were his friends?' she demanded. 'He wouldn't just go off and do it alone.'

'Looks like he did though.' Joe wiped down the bar. 'Unless his "friends" are lying.'

10

Adèle was dreading sleeping in the warehouse again. It was even colder tonight, the sort of cold that hot coffee and digestive biscuits couldn't keep at bay. She had put off going back, had gone into the city centre and wandered the shops, taking advantage of Thursday late night opening. She was so depressed that she swiped a box of chocs from Birtle's. First time in ages. Seeing all that stuff, people spending thirty and forty quid on perfume and make-up, when she had earned the grand total of £6.50 all day, got her down.

Lifting the chocolates made her feel like she'd got her own back. Only the feeling didn't last long. She started worrying about how she might have got caught — it wasn't like she was invisible in her green weatherproof. After all her hard work, she could end up with a fine that would take every penny she'd saved.

She was so disgusted with herself that she almost chucked the chocolates in the next bin. Almost: it was daft to take the risk and not get the benefits. As she walked out of the city centre, into the slowly crumbling remnant of tenements and warehouses, she began fantasising about pinching a drop of something to go with the chocs. But the offies usually kept the spirits behind the counter, and chocolates and wine didn't really go together. She put it out of her mind: it was too easy to slip back into thieving, too temptingly easy.

She climbed the stairs, dumped her stuff inside her tent of plastic and corrugated card and crawled through the opening. It was freezing. The moisture in the blankets and her sleeping bag had frozen and they were stiff and uninviting.

'Shit!' Adèle felt tears prick at the back of her eyes. When would this fucking cold go away?

She reached inside one of her carrier bags and fumbled with the matches, trying to get them to light. After the fourth try, one caught, and she held it to her primus stove and turned the knob to release the gas.

An explosive puff, and then the flame lit and settled to a purr. She warmed her hands for a minute or two, hypnotised by the blue light and the low buzz of the flame, enjoying the feel of its warmth on her face. Then she put a billy can on the ring and added some mineral water.

Abruptly, the purr became a low growl, the stove popped and coughed, and the flame went out.

'Oh, Jeez, oh, fuck, oh, please, no! Not *now*!' She hadn't realized just how much she had used the stove over the last few days, and she had been so glad when daylight had come and she could be up and out again, able to find somewhere warm to sit, that she had forgotten to check the level of the gas in the canister.

For a while Adèle sat and wept, but it got so cold that she had to move, so she packed a few things in a carrier bag and thought about what to do next. It was a toss-up which was worse, emergency shelters or hostels, but right now she would be grateful for anything. The hostels would all be full in this weather anyway, and it was too late for them anyroad. At least an emergency shelter would only be for a few days, until the thaw. There *had* to be a thaw soon — this pigging weather couldn't go on for ever.

She started taking apart the ramshackle tent. If she had to leave her stuff here for a few days, she could at least make it look like it wasn't worth robbing. She wasn't about to risk taking her primus and sleeping bag to a shelter — they were full of knockoffs and Shylocks.

She layered the cardboard and plastic over the blue pinboards and hid her valuables under the lot. It looked like a pile of rubbish — stuff kids might use for a bonfire.

* * *

Samaritans. Call logged at 11.05 p.m., Thursday. Male. 15 +? No name given. Seemed very distressed. 'It wasn't an accident. What happened to Ryan Connelly.' The caller broke down. Then he repeated, 'It wasn't an accident' and hung up. Call ended 11.09 p.m.

The Samaritan who took the call asked for advice from the duty manager. No further action was taken.

11

Coral called Geri in to her office at break time on Friday morning. She seated Geri opposite her, while she sat behind her desk, so Geri knew it was official.

'What in the world happened yesterday?' she demanded, without preamble.

'Happened?'

'We've had a complaint from Mr Connelly.'

Geri flushed. 'I knew he was upset, but I was really just a bystander caught in the middle of a family row.'

'That's not his interpretation.'

'I did say I couldn't believe that Ryan—'

Coral raised a hand to interrupt. 'The police have told us that there was no sign of assault — physical or sexual.'

'I know,' Geri said. 'I know all that.'

'And there's nothing to suggest that anyone else was involved.'

'Yes, I know . . .'

'So why are you obsessed with the idea he was coerced?'

'Because I know Ryan.' Geri caught herself, closing her eyes for a moment and taking a couple of calming breaths. It was still so hard to get the tenses right. 'I . . . *knew* Ryan.'

'We all did,' Coral said, softening a little. 'He was a good lad. He'd've most likely been made Head Boy next year. But we all make mistakes.'

'You only saw Ryan in school,' Geri said stubbornly. 'I saw him in situations where he could let his hair down.'

'The youth club . . .'

'Yes!' Geri replied, indignant at Coral's dismissive tone. 'Ryan never even got drunk, as far as I know.'

'As far as you know,' Coral repeated oppressively. 'But you can't be sure. Look . . .' She seemed to be deliberating, wondering if Geri could be trusted, then she nodded to herself and went on. 'Melvin — my youngest — he was caught at a rave with Ecstasy on him, two years ago now. I had *no* idea. He said, "Everyone does it. They think you're weird if you don't." You think you knew Ryan?' She clicked her tongue. 'Think how I felt, my own son! He lives in my *house* and I don't know what he's up to.'

'You didn't hear Ryan at the youth club, talking to the other kids about it.'

'I'm not saying he was a regular user. You've seen the leaflets, Geri. One fifth of glue-sniffing deaths are first-time users.'

'They haven't even got the toxicology reports back yet! They're basing their assumptions on a few pots of glue — aerosol cans . . .' She was too angry to go on, but she *knew* that Ryan wouldn't have been in that squalid place out of choice; knew it with an obdurate assurance born more of loyalty than reason.

Coral exhaled loudly and slapped the table with the palms of her hands. ''Fess up, girl, you just don't want to admit he did this to himself.'

Geri tried to be honest. 'I was relieved when they said he hadn't been assaulted, but okay, I admit that a part of me was disappointed in him.'

Coral sat back. 'You see?'

'But Coral, I'd prefer to believe it *was* an accident. That way, I wouldn't have to think about who was with him when he died. Did they hurt him; did he die afraid — in pain?' The air seemed suddenly thin and she had difficulty breathing.

'You'll drive yourself crazy, thinking like that. Look at the facts.' Coral counted the points off on one hand: 'He was acting strangely the night he died. His friends thought he had taken something. He disappeared off on his own — *on his own*,' she stressed. 'And he was found with no signs of violence on his body, with solvents in his blood, and with glue-sniffing gear nearby.'

'And the literature also says that glue-sniffing isn't a solitary pastime, it's a group event. And it's usually younger kids, not lads Ryan's age! I can't help the way I feel, Coral. I don't believe he was alone, and neither does Mrs Connelly.' If she sounded defiant, she didn't care. 'I don't regret what I said.'

'Geri!' Coral launched the full force of one of her disappointed looks at her.

'Ryan always stood up for the kids who didn't have the nerve to speak up for themselves.' Geri shrugged. 'He deserves a bit more . . .' She wasn't sure what.

'Loyalty?' Coral offered. 'Blind loyalty can be destructive, Geri,' she said gently.

'Like blind faith,' Geri said, bitterly, before she could catch the words and stop them.

Coral stood up, towering over Geri. 'You were supposed to ask after Dean, deliver a mass card and leave.'

'I *did*!'

Coral leaned across the table towards her, resting her weight on her broad forearms. 'So how did you end up attending a spiritualist meeting with Mrs Connelly?'

'Oh.' Geri was hoping that Mrs Connelly would keep that to herself.

'Well?'

'She was distraught, Coral. I was worried about her. I gave her a lift, that's all.'

Coral's brown eyes searched hers. At last she seemed satisfied that Geri wasn't hiding anything from her, and she sat down again with a sigh. 'Ill-advised,' she said.

'Maybe, but would you have left her in those circumstances?'

'I might've tried to persuade her against it. I might even have suggested she talk to her parish priest.' The reproach in her tone was a criticism, not only of Geri's actions the previous night, but a sad reflection on her lack of faith. As if to ram her point home, Coral added, 'Anyway, I thought you didn't believe in all that.'

'I don't,' Geri answered. 'And I didn't know where she was going, otherwise—'

'You drove her there, for heaven's sake! How can you say you didn't know?'

Geri pushed a hand through her hair and tried to think how to explain herself. As she opened her mouth to begin, Coral spoke again.

'Never mind. I don't want to hear it. I thought you had a bit more sense — a bit more *sensitivity*.' She sighed and shook her head, and her beads clicked disapprovingly. 'A bit more respect.'

Geri was dismayed. She liked Coral. It hurt her to think she could have such a bad opinion of her. Did she think Geri had some mischievous aim in taking Mrs Connelly to the meeting?

'Coral . . .' she began.

'No,' Coral said, raising a hand to silence her. 'Don't bother trying to justify what you did. Just stay away from that family, now, you hear me? Take time to think about it over the weekend. But keep away from the Connellys.'

* * *

Garvey took his tray and carried it over to where Vince was sitting. Ian Winters was with him. They had spent a fruitless day checking out lockups near the docks — a tip-off from a snout that had come eight hours too late. If the stuff was ever there, Stanfield had moved it elsewhere. The WPC's attack of nerves had cost him dearly. *Still*, he thought, *I got one useful bit of information today.*

He started a conversation about football, but Vince didn't seem interested in joining in. 'Who d'you support, then?' he asked.

'I'm not all that keen on football,' Vince replied. 'But if I'm pushed to it, Man United.'

Garvey laughed. 'That why you came up north is it — the football?'

'That and the warmth of the northern welcome,' Vince said.

The irony was lost on Garvey. 'So, you're not escaping a broken love affair?'

Vince shot him a sharp glance. 'How come you're so interested all of a sudden?'

'Well, for some people, it isn't what they're coming to that's important, it's what they're leaving behind. Love affairs, family problems, a balls-up at work.'

Vince looked away, and Garvey knew he had scored a hit.

'You know, once you get a bad rep, it's a bastard to shake it.'

'Yeah,' Vince said. 'You should know.'

Garvey had expected that. He grinned. 'He's hysterical, isn't he?'

Winters smiled, but he couldn't see where Garvey was taking this.

'No,' Garvey went on, 'go on, mate. Tell us what made you give up the Met. I mean, people move south — better career prospects and all that, but there's not many move north from London.'

'It's the chance of working with pros like you.'

Garvey could see Vince was trying hard to stay cool, but he had him on the run.

'I can see that would be an attraction, but what made you take the leap of faith?' He shot Winters a droll glance. 'What pushed you over the edge?'

The colour drained from Vince's face. He cleared his plates and muttered that he had work to do.

'Haven't hurt your feelings have I, mate?' Garvey said.

Winters looked in askance at Garvey, but he waited for Vince to leave, watching his back, willing him to turn, so he could smile or drop him a wink.

'What the hell was all that about?' Winters demanded.

Garvey tilted his head. 'I got a result on that bit of digging, and I've turned up some very juicy bones, Ian.'

'Go on then.'

Garvey smiled to himself. 'It all makes sense — the drugs liaison, the youth community work . . . He's trying to make amends.'

* * *

Later, in the abandoned trading quarter, a lone figure makes its way through the slush, slipping on the ice compacted by the police and journalists and friends and thrill-seekers who have made the pilgrimage to the site since Wednesday. He stops in front of the low terrace of artisans' cottages. Their mud-coloured bricks are crumbling now, the mortar ruined by damp.

He walks to the end house and listens to the blue-and-white police tape flutter and buzz in the bitter north-easterly wind. He looks up at the first-floor windows, remembering. Flowers have been placed in the doorway, still wrapped, frost-damaged, already faded and browning to become part of the litter on the narrow street.

He doesn't understand the urges that have brought him back here, but since he first brought Ryan to this place, he has gone over and over the events that followed in his mind, and it isn't only the sex that is a turn-on.

He won't go in. He wants to remember Ryan as he was, that final time.

Looking up at the soot-blackened window frame, he visualises Ryan, kneeling at his feet, and unthinking, closes his eyes and begins to masturbate.

* * *

Betty Mandel stood at the window looking out onto the street. She wrestled with feelings of irritation and disappointment. He was late. He promised he would come, and he was late.

It was bad enough having limited mobility, but this snow had made her a virtual prisoner in her own home. And Anthony never came — almost never — Sunday dinner once a month was all him and his stuck-up wife could manage. Picked up and dropped off like a package. She was just one of her son's responsibilities, a cross to bear.

Then she saw her grandson's head and shoulders above the hedge, and she felt a burst of pleasure. She made her way to the front door as quickly as her arthritic joints would allow, waiting in the hall as he let himself in with his latchkey.

'All right, Gran?' He closed the door softly. It was one of the things Betty loved about her Barry; he was so considerate. He didn't go banging about the place, shouting at the top of his voice, playing loud music. Her Barry was the quiet type.

She beamed at him, 'Thought you weren't coming.'

He slipped an arm around her shoulders and gave her the gentlest of squeezes. 'And let down my best girl?'

She gave him a shove. 'Get off with you! You could charm snakes with that tongue of yours.'

He laughed his soft, self-mocking laugh. 'Fancy a cuppa?' He went straight through to the kitchen and got the brew on while she followed more slowly, wincing a little at every step, too proud to use her walking frame while he was in the house, too crippled to move at more than a shuffle.

He had found the lemon cake and cut a couple of slices by the time she got to the door.

'I've been saving that,' she said, with a reproachful look.

He glanced up from stirring the teapot and grinned.

'For your favourite grandson.'

She wagged one twisted finger at him. 'There's a word for lads like you.'

'I know,' he said, happily filling his face with cake. 'Incorrigible.'

That was the difference between Barry and his dad. Barry would have a joke with her. Pass the time of day. He didn't make her feel like a nuisance. They sat and talked, supping their tea until nearly eleven, then he brushed the crumbs carefully from his hands onto the plate and stood up. 'I'll just check on things,' he said vaguely.

'Righto.' She began clearing away the plates and he disappeared. She heard him for ten or fifteen minutes, walking lightly about upstairs. He appeared at the kitchen door as she dried the last dish.

'All bedded down for the night,' he said. She gave his cheek a dry kiss and watched him leave, happy to let him go because she knew he would be back at the weekend for a cup of tea and a natter. If the snow was still lying, she would ask him to clear the path for her. And she'd need a bit of shopping doing.

* * *

As he walked home, Baz reflected on the turn of events that had given him his chance to grow his own quality dope in quantity. He considered expanding into the student pubs and clubs; demand already outstripped supply at school, but with the extra growing capacity he had set up over the last few weeks, he could be more ambitious. The arrogance of youth gave him the confidence that he could tackle the main dealer in the area — after all, he was in a vulnerable position, and all Baz need do was hint that he might mention what he knew in the right quarter.

If his biology teacher knew how much interest he was taking in botany, she'd be proud of him. The new set of clones was coming on nicely since he'd got the 1000W halide lamps and cooling fans, and the buds on the first cohort which he'd switched to a 12/12 diurnal cycle three weeks previously were fattening well. He did a mental calculation of growing times and predicted crop weights: six plants per cohort, a minimum of three quarters of an ounce per plant every eight or nine weeks. On a rotational basis, with three cohorts on the go, that made a minimum of three to four ounces every three weeks. Enough and plenty to spare.

12

The distant clatter of crockery and heavenly smells of bacon and toast woke Geri on Saturday morning. It was after eleven. She rolled out of bed and groaned at the ache in her calves and thighs. Nick had taken her dancing as the prescribed antidote to the gloom that had descended on her since her interview with Coral. All the resentment and cold distance he had put between them during the week was gone, and he was full of sparky energy and wit. Nick always was at his best when things were going badly for her, she reflected. The notion wasn't a comfortable one.

She groped her dressing gown from the door and stumbled downstairs. Nick was whistling out of tune to something on the radio. He looked up from buttering toast as she came in.

'Don't you look a picture!' he chuckled. 'Hang on a tick, I'll get my camera.'

'Sod off.' Geri was not in the mood for banter. She sat down with a grunt of pain and poured herself a coffee. Nick had propped the mail up against the milk bottle, and Geri sifted through it with a pang of anxiety: the habit of fear was quickly acquired. She hadn't yet got over the threatening note, even though there had been no repetition of it.

Nick scooped a couple of rashers of bacon out of the frying pan onto a plate and handed it to her with the toast.

'Fancy an egg?' he asked.

Geri shook her head. 'What's made you so bloody cheerful?' she demanded, making a sandwich of the bacon.

He leaned across the table and planted a kiss squarely in the middle of her forehead. 'You're always at your best in the morning, my sweet,' he said.

Geri invited him to sod off again. 'Anyway,' she added. '"Only dull people are brilliant at breakfast".'

He had long given up asking her who she was quoting, so he carried on: 'I've got a few bits to pick up for the bike, then I thought I'd do an hour or two at the gym. Fancy coming?'

Geri winced. 'I've got aches in places I didn't know had muscles,' she said.

'Do you good,' he said. 'Get some of that lactic acid metabolised.'

'It's too early in the morning for science,' Geri complained. 'I think I'll just have a soak in the bath.' She had already decided to call round and see Siân that afternoon. She knew Frank was hiding something, and if anyone knew what it was, Siân would.

Nick finished his breakfast on the hoof, ruffled her hair, dodged her fist lightly and, laughing, slammed out of the house.

It took her two hours to get herself together. She had looked up Siân's address in the school records before coming home on Friday. She lived in a cluster of new houses put up by a local builder when a row of terraces had been demolished. They huddled at the bottom of a hill, adjacent to the school playing fields.

Siân's mother was not pleased to see Geri.

'I was wondering how Siân is,' Geri said, feeling an unfamiliar nervousness.

'Right enough, given what happened.'

Mrs Walsh folded her arms and planted her feet apart. She was a tall woman, heavyset, with dark unruly eyebrows and a flat, broad face. Geri could only imagine that Siân got her fey, delicate looks from her father's side of the family.

'Could I see her, d'you think?'

'I'll tell you what I *think*—' She shoved her face into Geri's. 'I think she's in enough bother on account of you.'

'I think there's been a misunderstanding,' Geri began.

'That's the trouble with lasses like you — too much *thinking*, not enough common sense.'

'Mum!' It was Siân. Even in the shadows of the hallway, Geri could see she was ghostly pale. The girl hurried to the door, elbowing a place on the top step, clearly embarrassed by her mother's rudeness. The bruising on her face had turned greenish and the scratches were scabbed and beginning to heal, but if anything, she looked worse than she had done on Monday. 'It's not her fault!' she protested. 'She helped me sort it out!'

'Sort it? Bringing police to my door?'

Geri lost her patience. 'Would you prefer it if I'd left a man to die?'

'He attacked my daughter!'

'He was afraid — they both were. But I'd say he came off worse.'

'That what you *think* is it?' Mrs Walsh was red in the face. 'You want your head testing, you do. Taking a young lass to a place like that.'

Siân began protesting that she had gone on her own, and Geri interrupted. 'I'm leaving. I'm glad you're feeling better, Siân, and—' She touched the girl's hand briefly. 'I'm truly sorry about Ryan. He was a lovely lad. And I know he loved you.'

Siân's eyes filled with tears.

'Get that from your Ouija board, did you?' Mrs Walsh asked.

Geri turned and walked away, her nerves jangling; her limbs felt out of her control and she had to concentrate just to keep upright.

'Kids need protecting from the likes of you!' Mrs Walsh shouted. 'Call yourself a Catholic!'

Geri got to the car with Mrs Walsh's insults ringing in her ears; as she pulled away from the kerb a car horn blared and she slammed on the brakes, catapulting forward and hitting her head on the windscreen.

The driver of the other car tapped his temple and drove off, leaving her stalled. Her face burning, and her head beginning to throb, Geri willed herself not to look round at Mrs Walsh, but as she restarted the engine and drove off, she caught a glimpse of her in the mirror, meaty arms still folded across her chest, standing on the path outside her house, a look of gleeful malice on her face.

It hadn't taken long for word to get around about Mrs Connelly's visit to the spiritualist church. And it hadn't taken much persuasion for Mrs Walsh to label her irresponsible. She was sure that that, too, would soon be spread via the school grapevine. Rumours and gossip like these could finish her teaching career at St Michael's.

Dispirited, Geri returned home, vowing not to have anything to do with any controversy from that moment on. She was hoovering to keep herself from thinking, when she heard something above the insistent whine of the machine. The phone must have been ringing for some time. Geri dropped the vacuum-cleaner hose and ran to her study.

'Miss?' It was a girl's voice.

'Miss Simpson speaking,' Geri said, slightly out of breath.

'Will you meet me?'

'Is that Siân?'

'At the bus stop. Derby Street.'

'No!' Geri exclaimed. 'No way! Siân, you *can't* go there.'

'Okay,' the girl said, stubborn, perhaps a little fearful. 'I'll go on my own.'

Geri couldn't believe she was pulling the same stunt that she had on Monday. 'You heard what your mother said,' she protested. 'Anyway, it's getting dark. Leave it till tomorrow, then we'll talk about it.' No answer. Geri groaned. 'This is a bad idea.' *Bad idea? Geri Simpson, you've a genius for understatement.* But how could she leave Siân to do this alone? She spoke into the silence at the other end of the line: 'Derby Street . . . When?'

'Ten minutes. I'm on the bus, now.'

Geri ran out to her car still pulling on her coat. Siân was waiting for her when she arrived, hollow-eyed and sickly, wearing her uniform dark-coloured long dress and coat and carrying a bunch of flowers. She looked like a mourner at a funeral. In a sense, she was. The girl cut a macabre figure, standing by the deserted roadway. Her sombre clothing absorbed what little light there was, so that her body merged into the blank wall of the warehouse, and her face seemed to hover, disembodied in the darkness. If Geri hadn't been expecting to see her, Siân's sudden appearance out of the shadows would have given her a jolt.

Geri reached across and opened the passenger door.

'What changed your mind?' Geri asked as she moved away from the kerb.

Siân glanced at her, puzzled.

'You didn't intend to phone me, did you? You obviously left it till the last minute.'

She shrugged; what was the point in lying? 'I was going to go anyway,' she said. 'But I didn't want to give you the chance to change my mind.'

* * *

He had returned to the terrace again. The place drew him. *Bee to a honeypot*, he thought. His heart rate quickened; Ryan was so . . . beautiful. It was easier to remember what they had shared together when he was here, outside the place where it happened. He recalled running his fingers through the boy's hair — the silky sensation of those soft, glorious curls — the warmth of Ryan's scalp under his hands. Gently — he was always gentle, and even at the last, he made sure Ryan felt no pain — he showed the boy what he wanted, and Ryan, because he had no choice, had submitted. That was what he had relished most, the submission.

A car rumbled along the cobbled side street leading to the cul-de-sac where he stood.

'Shit!' He ran for cover, furious at the interruption, moving instinctively into the shadows. Police patrol? He thought they had packed up their little circus days ago. What then — ghouls?

* * *

Geri drew up outside the artisans' cottages and turned off the engine. A fleeting glimpse of something caught her eye, then was gone. The darkness, the silence and the dereliction of the streets seemed to crowd in on them and shroud the car in a sinister pall.

Siân looked at the flowers in her lap.

'Shall I come with you?' Her voice sounded too loud, unnatural after the silence, in which only the tick of the cooling engine could be heard.

Siân shook her head. 'I want to go alone.'

The interior light flashed on as she stepped out of the car, and the figure hiding behind a low wall had a clear view of the driver. *That bloody woman! What did he have to do to get her out of his life?*

13

Lauren was nearing the end of her Sunday shift. By rights she shouldn't have been on overnight duty, but one of her colleagues had called in sick, and she had got a call asking if she could fill in. She had been busy: a drugs overdose — this one had let them get an ambulance to her; a woman needing help to get away from her violent husband. Then an old man, worried he was wasting her time, sick with loneliness since the death of his wife. Four in the morning was the toughest time for dealing with the myriad ways in which humankind could be unhappy.

Someone handed her a coffee and she took it gratefully. Around her, their voices muted by the walls of the cubicles, rose the soft murmur of her colleagues, consoling, reassuring, gently probing, drawing out the misery of the callers, helping them to work out the next step, sometimes trying to persuade them that it needn't be suicide. There were no quick-fix solutions, no instant remedies, but for some a first step was an alternative to continuing terror, or guilt, or fear — of dying, or of living.

Her phone rang and she picked it up. 'Samaritans, can I help?'

Silence, then, 'Don't know why I'm phoning.'

Male? Teenage? He sounded truculent, tearful.

'Why don't you tell me what's bothering you, and we'll take it from there.'

'You won't be able to help.'

'Sometimes just talking helps.'

She heard a sigh at the other end of the line.

'My name is Lauren,' she said.

'I don't have to give you my name, do I?' He sounded panicked.

'You don't have to tell me anything, if you don't want to. But I'm here to listen.' She waited, not wanting to spook him again with the wrong question.

'I don't know what to do . . .' His voice rose, and she sensed he was fighting tears again. 'I think he killed Ryan.'

Lauren felt the hairs on the back of her neck prickle. 'Ryan . . .' she said, neutrally. She had seen the name in the logbook. An anonymous caller. *Ryan Connelly's death was no accident,* the caller had said. Ryan Connelly was the boy from Geri's school, the one who had died in a fire, stoned on solvents.

'It was in the papers,' the boy said.

'Ryan Connelly.'

'Yeah, Ryan. Only — I think he knows. He keeps looking at me like he knows.' He was slurring his words a little, perhaps because he was so upset, but Lauren thought it more likely he was drunk, or high on something.

'Someone knows that you suspect him?' she asked. She heard a whimper that could have been a yes. 'What makes you think he killed Ryan?'

'The stuff he's into. Look, I'm not making this up.'

'No,' Lauren agreed. 'I don't think you are.' She paused and when he didn't continue, she asked, 'Have you thought of taking this to the police?'

'No! You don't understand!'

She sensed she was losing him, that he would hang up at any moment. 'Perhaps you can help me to understand.'

She heard him breathing hard, trying to get himself under control. 'They wouldn't believe me. Not with him. The others'll back him up. They'll do whatever he says.'

'Are they afraid of him?'

'They should be. Bastard Georgie.' There was a lengthy pause. 'Look,' he went on at last. 'It's hard to explain. He comes over as okay most of the time, but he's got this way of looking at you . . .'

Lauren saw what he meant. He couldn't go to the police on the basis of an uncomfortable feeling and a funny look.

'What do you feel you should do?' she asked. Maybe he knew already but was afraid to go ahead and do it.

'I just needed to tell someone.' He hung up.

* * *

Lauren lay awake, staring at the ceiling. Nick and Geri had left for work an hour earlier. She had managed to avoid both of them, and had fallen into bed exhausted, but was unable to sleep. She tried telling herself that she was a professional, that she had done her best and she had to let it go, but that didn't help.

In her early days, just after her probationary period, she'd had a call from a woman — she called herself Vicky — who was convinced that her husband was sexually abusing her two little girls. She didn't know what to do.

Lauren wanted to scream at her, 'Get them out of there. Get them *away* from him!' Instead she had spoken calmly, rationally, in that neutral tone she had worked so hard to perfect. She drew Vicky out, got her to say how she felt about it, listening carefully and summarizing what she had told her, trying to help Vicky understand that what she had told Lauren in essence was that she wanted out.

They would get so far, Lauren would think that she had made the breakthrough, then Vicky would say, 'But he's a good man, really he is.' or, 'What would we do for money?' and the discussion would take a new turn.

Vicky would hang up when she least expected it, sometimes mid-sentence.

It went on like that for two or three months. Vicky refused any suggestion that she could talk to another Samaritan, that she could call any time — could even have a face-to-face interview: she only wanted to talk to Lauren. She phoned when Lauren was on duty, and Lauren spent the intervening hours and days with a burning dread in the pit of her stomach for the two girls. She would see children in the city centre, at the library, in the park. Walking with Daddy, holding his hand, and she would wonder is that them? She would look for signs, agonising, torturing herself with the notion that she might have walked past the two girls, might have stamped their books at the issues desk at the library, and never known. It would obsess her until the next telephone call.

Lauren began to suspect that Vicky was gaining some perverse pleasure from the situation, that she was enjoying her undivided attention, perhaps in some twisted way revelling in the drama of her predicament, in her status as the wronged wife. Then, without warning, the phone calls stopped. Lauren was almost mad with worry. She checked the log feverishly as soon as she got in each week for her stint on the phone lines, but there was no record of Vicky having spoken to anyone else. Lauren asked her mentor for help. She remembered pacing the floor of one of the private consultation rooms while Julia, her counsellor, tried to persuade her to sit down, to calm herself.

'How can I? How can I be calm? It's been weeks, Julia — what's happening to those little girls?'

'You can't think like that, Lauren. You'll never survive if you think like that.'

Lauren stopped and turned to Julia. 'I can't eat. I haven't had a decent night's sleep since she started calling. Why the *hell* doesn't she call?'

'Perhaps she's made her decision.'

Lauren clenched her fists in frustration. 'But what is it? Has she decided to stay with the bastard? Has she left? What's happening, Julia? I need to know.'

Julia was quiet, but firm. 'We have to hope that she's made the right decision.'

'But—'

'But it's not ours to make for her. And she doesn't owe us an explanation. We're not here to make *ourselves* feel better, Lauren.'

Lauren had used those same words in guiding new Samaritans. Sometimes they could stomach it, sometimes not. The impossibility of following through was the hardest thing for people to adjust to in their work as Samaritans.

A boy, probably one of Geri's pupils, was convinced that Ryan Connelly had been murdered; he was terrified that the killer would turn on him. And Lauren could do nothing about it. She couldn't even tell Geri. She had written up the call in the log, of course, and spoken to the duty manager, but when it came down to facts, all they had was a nameless boy who was making unsubstantiated claims. They could only hope he called back.

14

Few people at the spiritualist meeting would have recognized Agnes Hepple as she was dressed on Monday evening. She wore a low-cut burgundy dress, false nails painted a shade or two darker than the dress, and her eyes were subtly made up in the sludgy greens and greys she knew would not emphasise the fine lacework of wrinkles that had gathered on her upper eyelids in the last few years. Her lipstick was chosen to match her dress and applied to emphasise the fullness of her lips.

It had taken her just forty minutes to apply, file, varnish and buff her new nails when she had arrived home last Thursday, £250 better off than when she had walked into the musty hall in Erskine Street. It was good money, and worth the 'voluntary' £50 donation to the church, which she knew would guarantee her an invitation later in the year. Mediumship was her vocation, but there weren't many who made a living out of it, and she didn't get a booking every week, so she relied for her regular income on her work as a beautician.

Agnes could do anything from a manicure to a complete make-over, and she was equally at home with glamour or the natural look.

She finished the last coat of gloss on her client's right hand and splayed her fingers out under the drier.

'Your fella won't know you, chuck,' she said, smiling. Her voice was earthy, with a definite nasal Mancunian tone, quite unlike the high, childlike trill she adopted for psychic consultations.

The girl admired her long, painted fingernails under the infra-red lamp, comparing them with the finished and hardened left hand. Her real nails were weak and bitten to the quick, and Agnes knew that she'd need regular maintenance to keep them looking nice. This one would be one of her frequent fliers, she thought with satisfaction.

The little bell over the door tinkled merrily as someone came in. Agnes caught his reflection in the mirror but continued talking to the girl.

'You'll have to mind how you do things with them — 'specially things like getting your tights on.'

'I've always found getting them *off* is the hard bit,' the man said, with a wicked grin.

The girl blushed, not sure whether to feel insulted or flattered.

'You want to try a more subtle approach,' Agnes said. The girl glanced at the man in the mirror, then away, disconcerted by his appraising stare.

'Don't mind him,' she said, then after checking the positioning of her client's hand once more, she, swung her chair around to face the newcomer. 'What can I do for you, sweetheart?' she asked.

It was six short weeks since he had first come into her salon, introducing himself as a local businessman.

'Oh,' she had said, measuring him up. He didn't look like a hairdressing sales rep. 'What's your line?'

'Erotica.' It was the twinkle that had hooked her. That twinkle could win your heart or break it right in two.

Since then, he'd become a regular visitor. Agnes had to admit, he was easy on the eye, and she didn't pull away when he placed his hands on her upper arms and slid them slowly, sensuously up to her shoulders. He swivelled the chair so that she had her back to him, then began massaging her neck. Agnes stifled a groan of pleasure and her client stared hard at her hand under the lamp, willing the nails to dry.

Agnes closed her eyes, luxuriating in the feel of his strong hands loosening the tension in her shoulders.

He bent level to her ear and she felt his breath, warm on her neck as he whispered, 'The question is, what can *I* do for *you*, Agnes?'

She opened one eye. 'The name over the door is Angela.' Agnes was a good name for a psychic, but it didn't convey the sophistication people expected from a beautician.

'Ah,' he breathed, 'but I know you're no angel.'

She laughed lazily and slapped his hand. 'You're shocking this nice young lady.'

The girl tried to turn her head away from the two of them grinning at her in the mirror: a middle-aged woman and a twentysomething man. Without taking his eyes off Agnes, he raised his hand and clicked his fingers. The doorbell tinkled again. Both Agnes and her customer turned to look.

A girl of no more than fifteen stood in the doorway. She was pretty, if rather vacuous, and had the kind of complexion that looked best under the lightest touch of make-up, but Agnes sensed it wasn't the natural look he would want for this lass.

'Well,' he said impatiently, 'don't stand there letting the cold in. Close the door.'

He raised his eyebrows, then made the tiniest of head movements towards Agnes's client.

'You're done, lovey,' she said, switching off the lamp. She went to the till and took the girl's payment, helped her client into her coat and out of the door, changed the 'open' sign to 'closed', then slipped the snick on the lock and turned to face the pimp and his new girl.

This one, she recognized as one of Mikey's girls.

'Mikey won't like it,' she warned. 'He'll be out in a few months, and when he finds out you've moved in on his girls . . .'

He spread his hands. 'All I've done is pick up a few strays. I haven't touched his massage parlours, or his phone business. Just a few girls doing a bit of moonlighting on their days off.' He took the girl's hand and led her in front of him. 'Look at her. She's too young to be out on her own, eh, chick?'

'And what about the police?'

He laughed. 'They'll have to catch me first. And I'm light on my feet.'

She frowned, doubtful. She worried about him. He was a good-looking lad, and she wouldn't like to see him in trouble.

'Well?' he said.

Agnes tilted her head on one side, assessing the girl's fine blonde hair and china-blue eyes. She wore a short blue silk shift under a silver Puffa jacket.

'Let me guess,' Agnes said. 'The Baby Spice look.'

He laughed. 'You're a bit out of date, love. But aye, that's the general merchandising angle.'

'How long've I got?'

'An hour.' He ducked his head apologetically. 'I know, you need time to get your creative juices flowing, but I'm working to a tight schedule myself. Special order.'

Agnes pursed her lips in disapproval. 'Don't expect miracles, that's all.'

He grinned. 'I thought miracles was your speciality.'

'Don't make fun of my gift, love,' she warned.

'Would I?'

Agnes flushed angrily. She took her work seriously.

He made a placatory gesture. 'No,' he said, 'I'm serious.' He waited until Agnes began to settle her ruffled feathers. 'Anything that earns twenty-five quid for a half-hour session's got to be treated with respect, eh, pet?' He dropped a broad wink to the girl, who giggled and covered her mouth.

Agnes bristled. 'Right,' she said, marching up to the girl, who still hovered near the door. 'That's it.' She grabbed the girl by the wrist and spun her round. 'Out!' she said. 'The both of you.'

The girl balked. 'Hey!' she squirmed, looking back over her shoulder, dismayed.

Agnes shoved her to the door and began fiddling with the lock but was so angry she couldn't get the snick off.

'Woah!' he soothed. 'Come on, Agnes. Take it easy. Just a joke — you can take a joke, can't you?'

'I don't joke about my calling,' Agnes said, turning back to him, her eyes blazing, and her cheeks flushed. The girl wriggled, trying to get her to release her grip.

'You're hurting me!' she whined. 'She's hurting me!' Her voice rose to a screech.

'Shut up!' The words were as sudden and sharp as a slap, and the girl fell silent.

'Come on . . .' he repeated, cajoling. 'Don't be like that, Agnes, love. Look, I've been asking questions for you — I got some background.'

Agnes eyed him suspiciously. She had arranged a private session with Mrs Connelly, and although she regarded most of her talent as intuitive — a God-given gift — she saw no harm in doing a bit of research to augment her powers.

'I thought you said you didn't hold out much hope,' she said.

'I didn't,' he replied, 'but it's all over the street. He was in a terrible mess when they found him.'

Agnes led the girl to a chair and sat her down. She offered no more complaint than the odd snuffle.

'Go on,' Agnes said.

He nodded to the girl. 'I'll talk while you're working.'

15

Geri crept to the back of the church feeling like an interloper. As the other mourners came in, they genuflected and crossed themselves before shuffling sideways into the pews. The action was automatic, and Geri tried to remember a time when she had the same faith in the church's doctrine. Ryan's friends arrived. Siân stopped and seemed ready to turn and run, but Frank Traynor put his arm around her and guided her to a seat. She looked even thinner and frailer in the brightly lit church. She was wearing make-up to cover the bruises, but her eyes were red from crying.

Mrs Connelly came in, leaning on her sister for support. Dean followed behind, walking next to his father, who placed a protective hand on the boy's shoulder. They sat in the front pew, which had been reserved for them.

The school had paid for flowers and the altar was decorated with mixed sprays of lilies and large white chrysanthemums with waxy, reflexed petals. The triptych of Christ crucified, died and risen, above the tabernacle, gleamed in the light of a rack of votive candles, set up on the altar especially for the occasion.

By seven o'clock, the church was full. There was a shuffling and clearing of throats. Geri heard a baby's wail go up somewhere to her left, a sudden, frightened sound, quickly shushed by its mother, then the organist struck a chord and as one the congregation rose.

Geri sang with the rest, sharing a hymn sheet with an elderly woman who sang in a quavery soprano.

Surprised that the music still had the power to move her, Geri had to stop several times and close her eyes, her eyelashes moist, a lump in her throat, focusing on her breathing to try to avoid breaking down.

Father Rooney, the school chaplain, led the memorial service. He and the altar servers processed from the back of the church. One boy carried the processional crucifix, the other — Carl, from her own form — a thurible. Geri caught a whiff of incense as he passed. They made their way on to the altar; the crucifix was set in its stand and Carl handed the thurible to the other boy so that he could go down and lock the gates behind them. He turned and bowed to the centre of the altar, then took up his position to one side of the priest.

The second boy knelt beside Carl, closed the censer and set it down, lowering the chain gently to the ground so that it made no more than a faint rasp as it slipped through his fingers. He was wearing his school trousers and Nike trainers under his surplice.

Father Rooney opened his hands, palms upwards. 'Let us pray.'

There was a flutter as people placed their hymn sheets on the pews behind them, and then an uneven shuffle as the congregation knelt.

'We are here to remember a young man whom we all loved in our own ways: as a son, or a brother' — he glanced kindly in the direction of Ryan's family — 'as a friend, a pupil, a football coach, as a parishioner.' He smiled. 'Ryan Connelly meant so much to us in so many different ways.' Geri saw the slightest nod to somebody near the front of the church. 'Let us pray for his soul and for all the souls of the faithful departed.' He paused for breath.

'*Eternal rest give unto them O Lord . . .*'

Geri joined in, wishing with all her heart that Ryan was at peace. The prayer continued as Frank stood, hesitated, tripped and recovered, stepped into the aisle. He walked to the pulpit, a carved stone structure, attached to one of the pale lemon sandstone pillars. He waited, red-eyed and nervous, gripping the rail with both hands, waiting for the prayer to finish. Another nod from Father Rooney, and he began.

'Ryan was my mate,' he said. Feedback reverberated from one speaker to another and he jerked back, throwing the priest a frightened look.

'Just stand away from the mike,' Father Rooney said, giving him an encouraging smile.

Frank licked his lips and began again. 'He was good at everything, but he never made you feel like you weren't as good as him. He . . .' Someone started sobbing, and Frank looked across to where he had been seated. Poor Siân. Frank seemed on the verge of tears himself. He blinked rapidly, his gaze darting from one person to another. 'He was . . . okay, was Ryan. He . . . he never made you feel small. His brains — and he were a great striker.'

Geri wanted to rescue him but knew that her intervention would only make things worse. People were becoming uneasy, they were embarrassed, looking anxiously at each other and at Father Rooney. 'I think we all agree with those sentiments,' Father Rooney said. 'Ryan was a young man we all felt we could trust, who was a kind and generous friend.' He turned again to the congregation, drawing attention away from Frank's shambling attempt to negotiate the pulpit steps. 'The next hymn was one of Ryan's favourites,' he said, and the organist began the introductory bars of 'Make Me a Channel of Your Peace'.

Mr Ratchford, the headmaster, spoke. He began by describing Ryan's many achievements, his popularity within his own peer group, and his status as a role-model for the younger pupils. 'St Michael's has suffered a tragic loss,' he said. 'And the suddenness, the unexpected nature of his demise should give us all pause for thought. A life can be so easily snuffed out.

One mistake is all it takes, and it is irrevocable — we cannot take it back,' he added, for the benefit of the younger listeners. 'We must take comfort in our faith and in God's mercy. The terrible void caused by Ryan's death extends beyond the family and has touched the whole school community.' He paused and stared hard at the people below him. 'We *are* a community,' he said. 'The school is a part of the parish, as those of us here are part of the wider Church, and we must accept responsibility — each one of us — for every member of that community. We must be aware; we must look to our own.'

There was a hush as he stood for a few seconds more in the pulpit. His pupils, their younger brothers and sisters, their parents, all understood that he was asking them to share the burden of guilt for Ryan's death. For Siân it was too much. She fled down the aisle, sobbing, and after a moment Frank Traynor following her, looking tearful and wretched.

Geri felt the urge to say something. It didn't seem enough, this equivocating acknowledgement of Ryan's good qualities. It didn't do him justice.

* * *

Some of Geri's form kept her talking outside the church. It was cold, despite a slow thaw that had set in that afternoon. All that remained of the snow were a few grimy mounds and dirty puddles of water. Geri never believed that April was the cruellest month. February was the time of year she dreaded most. It was unforgiving, dark, cold and seemingly interminable. Her mother had died in February. She was about to move off when Mrs Connelly and her sister entered the porch. Mrs Connelly walked to the steps of the porch, while her sister, Una, thanked Father Rooney for the service. The children nudged each other and began whispering.

'Dean's been on tablets, since. That's why he's not been in.'

'He's never — he's looking after his mum, that's all.'

'Someone should go and talk to her. Look at her, poor thing . . .'

Geri wondered if Coral's moratorium on her talking to the Connellys extended to this evening. As she made up her mind to approach her, Mrs Connelly darted off to the left, to a cluster of Sixth-Form boys and girls. Frank Traynor stood with his arm around Siân, in a huddle with Barry Mandel.

As she drew close to the group, she saw Mrs Connelly place her hand on Frank's arm.

'You'd know, if anyone would. You were his friend, weren't you? Did he . . . ? I mean, was he . . . ?' She stared into their faces, pleading for an honest answer. 'Did he take drugs? Was my son into drugs?'

Barry Mandel seemed less self-satisfied than usual. In the light from the spotlamps over the church door he looked washed out, even sick, but he was still sufficiently in control to try to take charge of the situation.

'Mrs Connelly,' he said, his voice quiet, as always, but strangely penetrating, 'we don't know anything about Ryan's death.'

Siân looked up quickly, her eyes wide. The others shuffled uncomfortably, avoiding eye contact. The word 'death' seemed to make them uneasy; it was an affirmation that Ryan wasn't ever coming back.

Frank kept his eyes lowered, unable to look Mrs Connelly in the face. His eyelashes were wet. 'He said doing drugs was stupid,' he mumbled.

'Frank,' Barry warned. 'Don't make a bigger fool of yourself that you've done already.'

Frank reacted with shocking speed. He lunged at Barry, grabbing him by the lapels. Mrs Connelly released her grip on his arm but was flung off balance. Geri stepped up and steadied her as Frank launched into a tirade against Barry.

'He *told* us. He did! He'd never've, not on purpose. You stupid bastard, Baz! You think you can do what you like. You never think about what'll happen. You don't bloody *care*!'

Barry took hold of Frank's coat, and for one horrible moment Geri thought he was going to head-butt him. There were murmurs of dismay from the people who were leaving the church. Mrs Connelly was crying, and her sister hurried over from the porch.

'Come on now, lads, this's not the place.' Joe had appeared from a cluster of thirteen- and fourteen-year-olds. 'Think of the family, eh?' He put a hand on Barry's shoulder and instantly Frank let go and backed away, shaking and crying. Geri grabbed his coat sleeve and pulled him into the shadows at the side of the church.

'What the hell d'you think you're playing at?' she whispered. 'Isn't she upset enough?'

'I couldn't help it, Miss,' Frank muttered, wiping his eyes with his coat cuff. 'Ryan was my mate.'

'He was her son, and Siân's boyfriend. Other people have been hurt, too, Frank. Here—' She shoved a tissue at him. He took it and blew his nose. 'Go to the police,' she said. 'If you won't talk to me, bloody well go to the police!'

He shook his head in a wide, exaggerated movement. 'I can't . . . I can't, Miss!'

'You know Vince. You know you can trust him. It's not like you'd have to make a formal statement.'

He looked over at Vince, then back to her. 'You just don't get it, do you?' he said.

'No, I don't. Make me understand.'

'I don't want anyone to get hurt.'

'Too late for that,' she shot back.

'It's too dangerous,' he whispered.

'Look if it's Baz— If he had something to do with . . .' Her voice snagged and she couldn't go on.

Frank backed away from her, shaking his head, and shooting a look past her, as if afraid the others would overhear. Geri blinked away her tears, trying to see who it was in the knot of mourners by the porch that Frank was so frightened of.

When she turned back, Frank was heading for the far exit, near the church hall.

* * *

As Geri returned to the group, Baz shook off Joe's restraining hand and shoved him hard.

'Stay the *fuck* away from me,' he said. 'I mean it, Joe.'

Joe smiled. 'Oh, I'm on to you, lad. And I'm sticking like glue.'

'Insensitive choice of words, given the circumstances,' Barry said, recovering his composure, straightening the lapels of his coat.

Vince Beresford was hovering in the background, looking like he was wondering whether to muscle in. Geri caught his eye and gave a slight shake of her head. His eyes flickered in her direction, then he returned his attention to the exchange between the two men.

'You'll go too far,' Joe warned, and Geri felt that he was talking about more than Barry's cocky attitude and smart mouth.

Barry smirked. He was his old self again. 'Why don't you get back to sharing sweeties with the kiddies,' he said, nodding to the small knot of children who were watching, appalled and thrilled by the altercation. 'That lot like their M&Ms.'

Joe took a step forward, but Vince was in there first. He got between the two of them, towering over both. 'Not here,' he said. 'Not now.'

Dean stood in the porch, his hands bunched into fists. His heart and soul were filled with a hatred that would consign him to eternal damnation. *Baz,* he thought, grinding the damaged tooth until shafts of sharp pain shot through his skull. *He's gonna pay,* he thought. *I'll make him pay.* When Frank grabbed Baz, he had tried to go over to join his mother, but his dad had stopped him. He felt his father's hands on his shoulders, squeezing gently as he spoke to Mr Ratchford. He was stumbling over his thanks for the headteacher's speech, and Dean felt a confusing wave of embarrassment, resentment and pity.

16

Tuesday morning registration. Geri hadn't slept well. When Coral had seen her at the centre of the mêlée outside church, she had assumed Geri had been stirring up more doubts about how Ryan had died. Vince talked her round, explaining that she had stepped in to protect Mrs Connelly, but Geri fretted over the incident. What was Barry Mandel's involvement? Frank evidently thought he was accountable in some way for Ryan's death. Frank himself seemed to feel some share of blame.

She remembered the contemptuous look on Joe's face as he'd said *I'm on to you.* There had been rumours in school that Barry's circle of friends smoked a bit of weed, maybe dropped a few tabs of E, but if the statistics were to be believed, so did over half of all teenagers in Britain at some time. Was Barry supplying the stuff? Is that what Joe had meant?

Mr Ratchford had done a few random checks, but Barry had never been caught with anything even remotely incriminating on him. If he *was* selling drugs, however, it would explain the reaction of the children in the youth club. They seemed afraid of him. Joe was there every night; he was in a position to see things other people didn't. The children were more wary, more closed in front of their teachers, but Joe was accepted as one of the lads — they would be more open with him, talk to him without the worry of others accusing them of telling tales, confident that whatever they told Joe would go no further.

The internal reports had been reviewed by senior staff and pastoral tutors since they had been completed the previous Wednesday. Each form tutor was expected to go through the effort and achievement grades individually with the members of their form and discuss targets for the next four weeks. There were two interruptions — one to let children know that there was a choir practice after school on Thursday, and from Geri herself to call drama club pupils for a line-rehearsal that lunch time.

By the end of registration, she had got through only ten of her form. The rest would have to be fitted in on Wednesday. She dismissed her form and after cleaning the board, Geri began tidying her desk, ready for the start of the lesson. A movement at the back of the room caught her eye and she gasped, startled.

'Dean!'

He withdrew his gaze from the window with seeming reluctance. His eyes were deeply shadowed, and he looked gaunt.

* * *

'*Dean!*' The voice came from far off and it took a while for him to get her in focus. Miss Simpson.

'Are you all right?' Miss Simpson asked.

His tongue went to the hole in his lower molar. The pain shot through him like a knife when he sipped hot tea.

'We were going to go up on Rivvy again,' he said. 'Me and Ryan.' He closed his eyes. Sunlight glinted on water. They'd cycled up on their push-bikes, him and Ryan together. Rivington Pike for a spot of fishing. 'He said we'd take a boat out.'

Suddenly he was crying. He felt shocked — he hadn't cried, not once since that first day. He'd been strong for his mum and dad. And here he was, crying, screaming his grief, unable to stop. Miss Simpson put her arm around him. He felt a confused mixture of emotions: comforted by her touch but rejecting comfort: he had no right to it. He made a heroic effort to compose himself and then eased his shoulders out of her encircling arm.

He wiped his eyes on his sleeve. 'I'm okay.'

Miss Simpson handed him a tissue. 'It's all right to cry,' she said. 'It's normal to be upset.'

'Aye.' He blew his nose, stuffed the tissue in his pocket and took another from Geri. 'Only you'll not tell the others . . .'

'Of course not. Do you want to go down to Mrs Jackson's office? She'll make you a hot drink.'

He shrugged, his brow furrowing as he fought with a fresh wave of grief. 'I want our Ryan back.'

'I know,' she said, and he heard tears in her voice. 'We all do.'

* * *

Huddled at one end of the cab seat, Theresa Connelly wondered whether she could go through with it. She had spent the morning in church, praying for guidance, kneeling in the little chapel of the Virgin. She asked for Mary's intercession: she as a mother must understand. 'All I want is to know he's safe.'

Father O'Connor had heard her confession. She had poured out all her anger and bitterness, confessed every wicked thought, every murderous feeling in her heart. If she only knew who Ryan had been with that night . . . But she could not bring herself to tell the priest where she was going that morning. It was not shame, she told herself, but fear that her confessor would try to dissuade her from the only course of action she felt could give her some respite from the terrible emptiness she felt.

The taxi drew to a halt at the kerb and the engine turned over unevenly. Could this really be it? She checked the address on the embossed card: number seventy-seven. It had to be.

She paid the fare and stepped into the street. A gust of wind buffeted her, and she shivered. Her hand went automatically to her hair, reaching to tuck the wayward strands behind her ears, then, discovering how much the wind had tousled it, pulling out her hair tie altogether and fastening the ponytail again.

The house gleamed in the bright sunshine; the wood shingles cladding the brickwork of the upper floor looked newly varnished, and the lawn twinkled with the remnants of snow melt. She had expected something else — if not gloomier, then more atmospheric — more dramatic, perhaps. She tried not to feel disappointed.

A few cars stood at the kerbside, but the road was otherwise deserted. This was the commuter belt; the only people at home at midday would be the retired and mothers with babies. Stay or go? She couldn't make up her mind. It had taken all her energy just to get into a taxi and direct him here. She felt tears well up, and with it, a growing sense of alarm. What was she doing here? If John knew she was seeing a clairvoyant, he'd be furious. Vultures, he called them. Bloodsuckers who fed on other people's misery.

'God forgive me,' she murmured.

The pristine white front door blurred wetly and splintered into two and then four, and as she looked the door opened.

'Mrs Connelly?'

Theresa Connelly took a tissue from her pocket and wiped her nose. 'I'm sorry, Miss Hepple,' she said. 'I'm not sure if I can . . .' She swayed slightly, feeling dizzy and sick.

Agnes Hepple hurried down the path and put an arm around her. She had restyled her hair for the occasion. Modelled on Patricia Routledge: well groomed but comfortingly middle-aged. She wore a flowered frock with an elasticated waistband and a tie belt, and she had carefully removed her false nails. She intended no deceit in this, but she knew that people responded to a motherly quality in these situations. All she was doing was helping them to feel more relaxed and confident in her abilities.

Theresa Connelly followed her through to a large sitting room at the back of the house.

'Make yourself comfortable, dear,' Miss Hepple said. 'I'll make us a nice pot of tea.'

The room overlooked a lawn and wide borders, which retained odd patches of snow. Snowdrops pushed through the bare soil in places, their tiny flowers trembling in the breeze. Mrs Connelly calmed herself by looking at them for a few minutes, struck by their resilience despite their apparent frailty, then she sat on one of two brick-red sofas, set at right angles to each other. A long coffee table in pale ash held three jagged lumps of crystal: a pale pink, one she recognized as amethyst and another that was colourless, but which cast rainbow patterns in fleeting bursts as the sun came and went.

She heard a faint musical tinkling and looked towards the source of the noise. Miss Hepple had returned and was watching her. Above her head, wind chimes stirred slightly.

'You expected something . . . else, did you, love?'

Something else . . . Theresa Connelly realized she was staring. That was her very thought when she had first seen the house. 'No,' she said, giving herself a shake. 'It's very . . . nice.'

Miss Hepple smiled. 'I think so.' She put the tray down and set about pouring tea. 'I've never been one for all that hocus-pocus,' she said, handing a cup to her guest. 'Help yourself to milk and sugar.' She sat on the adjacent sofa.

As she added milk to her cup, Theresa found the courage to say, 'The thing is, you see, I'm a Catholic, and—'

'And your religion doesn't hold with . . .' Miss Hepple stopped and swept her arm to encompass the furniture, the glowing crystals, the watercolours on the walls. 'Doesn't hold with what, exactly? With talking to a friend who can give you news of a loved one?' She shook her head. 'You know why I don't go for darkened rooms and mystical symbolism?' She didn't wait for a reply but went on: 'I'll tell you. It's because that's what magicians use, to hide the truth.' She stirred her tea thoughtfully. 'I don't do magic, Theresa — it is Theresa, isn't it?' Mrs Connelly nodded. 'What I do is the most natural thing in the world.'

Theresa nodded, wondering why the church made out that it was so sinful.

'We all have it in us,' Miss Hepple went on, 'but not everyone has the gift to bring it out.'

Mrs Connelly stared intently at the psychic, thinking that her 'gift' must be the most wonderful thing anyone could possess.

'And if you've a talent, you've a responsibility to make good use of it,' Miss Hepple said, with a modest dip of her head. 'That's what I think, anyway.'

'Aye,' Mrs Connelly said. 'Like in the parable.'

Miss Hepple held her gaze. 'Like your Ryan.'

Theresa flushed at the mention of his name.

'With his football,' Miss Hepple explained. 'He went out and did his best. But more than that, he shared his talent with others — am I right?'

Theresa set down her cup, spilling tea into the saucer. 'He was team coach for the local youth club,' she said. 'That wasn't in the papers.'

Miss Hepple took a sip of tea before placing her cup on the coffee table and relaxing back on the sofa. 'Are you coming in, love?' she asked.

Theresa glanced nervously at the door.

Miss Hepple folded her hands in her lap. 'Come on, love,' she encouraged. 'Come and work with me.' She waited a moment, then nodded appreciatively. 'He's got lovely brown hair,' she remarked. 'A real looker, your Ryan. And freckles . . .'

Theresa frowned.

'No,' Miss Hepple said, 'not freckles . . . He's a bit faint, yet. But something . . . a dimple?'

Theresa felt a thrill run through her.

'He's a bit conscious of that dimple,' Miss Hepple added.

Theresa's hands went to her mouth. 'We'd make him laugh, just to see his cheeks dimple. He'd go mad, put out with us, but laughing at the same time.'

Miss Hepple leaned over, and without breaking her dialogue, passed her client a box of tissues from the shelf under the coffee table. 'He says you're not to worry. He's happy where he is.'

Theresa spoke, her breath hitching, her voice thick with emotion, 'How can he be, locked up in that awful place? In the cold, the dark.'

For a moment Miss Hepple's face was troubled. 'I thought you'd . . .' She tailed off, and then began again in a more confident voice, 'I'm getting a church, flowers . . . Big, white flowers . . .' She stared guilelessly into Theresa's eyes. 'Does that mean anything? D'you understand?'

'Memorial service, last night.'

Miss Hepple's face cleared, and she said, 'The dark, the cold — you mean the mortuary.'

'They won't let me bury him,' Theresa sobbed.

Miss Hepple placed a hand on hers. 'That's only his earthly form. Your Ryan has no use for that anymore. He's on a much higher spiritual plane. And Theresa . . .'

She waited and Theresa composed herself.

'He is not in the dark,' Miss Hepple said, emphasising every word. 'Ryan is in a place of light and warmth and colour.'

The band of tension around Theresa's chest eased a little.

'Can you ask him—' She broke off, unsure if she wanted to go any further. There were some things it was best not to know. But she had come all this way, and there were things that — no matter how terrible — a mother simply had to find out. 'I want to know how it happened,' she said at last.

Miss Hepple seemed to withdraw into herself. Her eyes became clouded, her face troubled. 'He won't talk to me, love . . . It's confused.' She flinched. 'But I'm getting flames. Heat—'

Theresa's heart contracted painfully. 'Ryan,' she said, then again, softly, 'Ryan . . .'

Miss Hepple gasped and seemed to come back to herself. Her upper lip was beaded with sweat. 'Best not go into that,' she whispered, slightly breathless.

'I've got to,' Theresa insisted. 'I must know!'

Miss Hepple shook her head. She looked pale, exhausted. 'It's too soon. The memory, it's too . . .' she struggled for the right word. 'Too *raw*.'

When Theresa's taxi arrived, Miss Hepple showed her to the door.

'Thank you,' Theresa said.

'I do what I can,' Miss Hepple replied. 'We don't always get the answers we want, or we're expecting, but it's wise to listen, all the same.'

Theresa stepped into the street. 'I feel so much better,' she said.

'You look it,' Miss Hepple said. 'I don't often see auras, but when I do . . . Yours was in a terrible turmoil when you first came — purples and reds and yellows all swirled up into a storm . . . and the grey, of course — that's the depression.'

'What's it like now?' Mrs Connelly asked, glancing up nervously.

Miss Hepple took her hand. 'Green and blue. A little yellow, for courage.' She smiled. 'You'll do just fine,' she said. 'He is worried about the others, though,' the psychic added.

'What do you mean?'

Miss Hepple looked astonished. 'I really don't know.'

Stepping into the cab, Theresa thought that she did know, and looking back at Miss Hepple, hugging herself against the cold in her doorstep, the idea filled her with cold dread: others were in danger.

17

Geri glanced at her watch. Jay was already ten minutes late. What had got into the boy? She had caught him trying to steal Carl's fountain pen. He even had the nerve to try to brazen it out. She finished checking through a stack of Year Eight classwork and went out into the corridor. Two Sixth-Form prefects were passing, doing a sweep of the school, rounding up anyone who had sneaked past the security system to get out of the cold.

She sent them to find Jay and went back to work on some A-level preparation. They arrived about ten minutes later with Jay in tow. Geri thanked them and they carried on with their rounds.

'Where were you?' Geri asked.

'Playground.'

'You should have been here twenty minutes ago.'

'Forgot.' He looked down at the floor.

'Sit down,' she said. 'Your work's on the front desk.'

She had provided him with a pencil to avoid any reference to the pen she had returned to Carl; he picked it up and began chewing on it as he read the exercise she had set him.

Geri went back to her work. After five minutes she was disturbed by a constant tap-tap-tap and looked up to find Jay staring at his pencil point while tapping on the paper with it.

'Get on with your work, please, Jay.' If he heard her, he gave no sign, but the pencil tapping got faster and harder and he stared intently at the point.

'Jay!'

He stopped, looking slightly dazed, but his hand trembled as if itching to begin again. He made eye contact for the first time, and Geri saw that his eyes were darting erratically from left to right in tiny, jerky, nystagmic movements. *What the hell is he on?* Geri got up from her desk.

''Kay,' he muttered. 'I'm doing it.' He looked at the paper but seemed to have trouble focusing.

Geri stood in front of him. 'Jay, look at me,' she said.

He got as far as her second shirt button, then his head dropped forward. With a rising sense of alarm, she bent down and looked into his face. There was a slight sheen of sweat on his skin and his pupils were dilated.

'What have you taken, Jay?' she asked.

'Nothin'. Just hungry, aren't I? Haven't had me dinner.'

'All right,' she said. 'Let's go.'

She saw panic in his face. 'What? I haven't took nothin', I'm just—'

'I know,' Geri reassured him, suppressing her own agitation, anxious that he might try to run off. 'You're hungry. Come on — you can get some lunch.'

He stood, shooting the table forward and sending his chair crashing into the second row. He had trouble negotiating the straight line to the door, slewing into the tables on the front row, overcompensating and careering off into the wall.

Geri caught him by the collar of his jacket, just saving him from going headfirst through the glass of the classroom door. She guided him down the corridor, talking lightly: half-term coming up; the prospect of more snow; the full rehearsals for the Easter play beginning after half-term, praying that she would see someone before he collapsed. There was no sign of the sixth-formers, and she grew increasingly desperate as his replies became more garbled.

She steered him ahead of her into the school office, where a Year Seven pupil was having her tears dried and a plaster put on her knee. The secretary, a trained first aider, saw the problem immediately and showed Geri through to the sick room.

'Shall I get him to lie down?' Geri asked.

'No. Talk to him. I'll bleep Mrs Golding and phone for an ambulance.'

* * *

The Sixth Form was housed in a separate block at the end of the school drive. Geri crossed the playground, hugging herself against the wind, and the furious shaking that had taken hold of her since the ambulance had come for Jay.

The common-room lights on the second floor were switched on against the grey oppressiveness of the day, and three figures were framed in the window, one of them lounging against the windowsill. Suddenly he pushed away, standing up straight, and spread his arms wide in a theatrical gesture. Baz.

She straight-armed the foyer door, startling two lovers engaged in extra-curricular activities, and ran up the stairs. The insistent thump of a techno-beat pulsed from behind the common-room door. Geri slammed it open and fifty heads turned.

Baz glanced at her, then coolly returned to his conversation. His two friends were less complacent and eyed her apprehensively as she approached.

'What was it, Barry?' she demanded, breathing heavily from the exertion and the fury she felt against Mandel. 'What did you give him?'

Baz stopped talking. He glanced briefly at the floor, then turned to look at Geri.

No, she thought, having difficulty controlling her rising anger. *You don't do that to me. You don't try intimidating me with your dead-eyed stare.*

‘I asked you a question,’ she said, holding his gaze.

‘I’ve forgotten what you said.’

‘What did you give him?’ Geri repeated, louder this time, enunciating every word.

‘Give who?’

‘Jay Davies.’ The fleeting alarm she saw on his face was quickly extinguished, and he shrugged, relaxing against the window ledge.

‘I don’t know what you’re on about.’

‘He’s in a state of collapse because of you.’

‘Because of me? You’re sure about that, are you?’ He made no attempt to hide his contempt for her. Geri subdued an impulse to take him by the lapels and shake him; she needed to know what Jay had taken.

‘He won’t tell us what he’s taken, Barry.’ She heard the plea in her voice, and knew that Barry would, too. Sod it, as long as she found out what poison he had fed Jay, she didn’t care.

‘I’d ring for an ambulance if I were you.’

You cold-hearted bastard! She tried again. ‘He’s on his way to hospital—’

‘Best place for him, if he’s feeling poorly.’

It was the smirk that did it. Jay might be dying, and he was prepared to make a joke of it, seeing how far he could push her.

‘I’d like a word with you, outside,’ she said, barely able to get the words past the rage that swelled inside her like a bubble in her chest. She was afraid it would burst, and she would not be responsible for her actions.

Baz looked like he was thinking about it.

‘Now,’ she added quietly.

Barry raised his eyebrows, inviting the others to share his astonishment, but nobody would meet his eye. Someone turned down the stereo and the techno-beat became no more than a tinny background rhythm. No one spoke.

Geri felt her cheeks flush at Barry’s unspoken challenge to her authority. She didn’t wait to see if he was following:

she knew he would take his time. She stood outside the door, trying to get herself under control. The shaking was worse. She had time for two deep breaths before he appeared.

'Well?' she said. 'You can tell me now. You don't have to play the part in front of your mates.'

'Tell you what?' He was calm, and if he resented being hauled out in front of the others, he didn't let it show.

'Don't mess me about. I know you're supplying.'

'You're talking to the wrong guy.'

The lie was so blatant she lost her temper and grabbed his coat by the lapels, flinging it open and groping for the pockets.

'Hey!' he shouted, his voice rising an octave. 'What the fuck?'

They struggled momentarily, then Coral appeared at the head of the stairs.

'Miss Simpson!' she boomed. Geri let go of Baz, and he straightened his coat. 'The registration bell has gone,' Coral said.

Geri stared at Baz, breathing hard, torn between a strong impulse to beat the shit out of him and an almost stronger urge to cry.

'I could have you done for assault.' It was said in a low growl — a threat — more evidence of Baz's coercive powers.

'I want him searched,' Geri said, turning at last to look at Coral. Alan Morgan was with her; Geri had avoided him since his outburst about Ryan. She couldn't look at him without wanting to take up where they had left off, to tell him that his view of the world was jaundiced, hard-hearted and cruel. He had not attended the memorial service on Monday — he had let it be known that he felt Christians should not endorse sinful acts by commemorating the sinner. She knew he was enjoying seeing her like this, and she knew that he would use this incident to remind her that everyone succumbed to his brand of realism sooner or later.

'It's best you go now,' Coral said, not unkindly. 'Mr Morgan and I will deal with this.'

Geri hesitated. Baz was getting away with it again. He would oil his way out of this situation like he did every other. She looked back at him. He was ruffled but defiant. He knew he was free and clear.

'You're the lowest form of pond life, Barry,' she said. 'You deal in death and you've no conscience about the people you hurt.'

Baz looked past her at Coral Jackson, and something made him drop his gaze. If he hadn't, Geri would have floored him, one way or another, and to hell with the consequences.

* * *

'How was Jay when he arrived for detention?' Coral asked.

'Truculent, but he seemed okay.'

Coral had sent for her after registration, and they were talking in the pastoral tutor's office, Geri standing, Coral seated at the far side of her desk.

'Any news? Geri asked. Her nerves were still tingling an hour after her confrontation with Baz. She experienced alternating waves of hot outrage at his response to her questions and cold dread at the possible consequences of her actions.

'He's adamant he hasn't taken anything. Mrs Golding will stay at the hospital until they're certain he's out of danger. You're sure he didn't take anything while he was with you?'

'Do me a favour, Coral!'

'All right. I had to ask.'

'He was late. I had to send for him. He had plenty of time to pop any pills he wanted to *before* he got to me.'

'All *right*. Nobody's accusing you.'

'Really?' Geri was beginning to feel more than a little beleaguered: first Mrs Connelly; then the scuffle after the memorial service; now this — and Barry's threat to prosecute for assault didn't make her feel any more secure.

It was evident Coral wasn't going to mention it, so Geri gritted her teeth and asked, 'Has Barry put in a complaint?'

Coral didn't answer immediately. She took a breath and glanced at the framed photograph of her family, on the wall behind Geri. 'He hasn't, and I don't think he will, but . . .'

'But what?'

'You cannot go about manhandling students, Geri.'

'Is this a verbal warning?'

Coral winced. 'There's really no need to take that attitude. I'm . . .' She searched for the right word. 'Concerned about you. It's not like you to react like this, and it just isn't *on*.'

'I'll consider myself ticked off, then, shall I?' It sounded petty, spiteful even, but she couldn't help herself. It was either that or break down in front of Coral, and she wasn't about to do that, not over Barry Mandel.

* * *

She tried talking to Nick about it when she got home. She sat next to him on the sofa in the TV room while he flicked through the channels with the sound turned down. She was still feeling bruised from her discussion with Coral, and although she tried, she couldn't keep the righteous indignation out of her voice.

'I don't know why she had to have a go at me. *I* didn't give him the damn stuff.'

Nick frowned, concentrating on the TV, glancing briefly across at her. 'You're being paranoid. She had to make sure, so if she was asked—'

'All right, smart arse.'

He ruffled her hair. 'You hate it when I'm right, don't you?'

'It's not *reason* I need, it's sympathy. And I wish you'd put that bloody thing down.'

He pressed the 'off' button on the remote control and tossed it onto the chair next to him.

'What did he take?'

She shrugged. 'They don't know. He's not admitting to anything. They sent him home after checking him over; he seems all right now.'

'So maybe he's telling the truth.'

'Yeah, and maybe the Pope's an atheist. He was off his *face*, Nick! I'm not stupid; and neither are the doctors in casualty.'

'Okay, okay,' he said. 'Did they search him?'

She nodded. 'We checked his school bag as well. Nothing. Why do they do it? Why do they protect Barry?'

He grinned. 'It's always worth protecting a good source.'

'He wants locking up!'

'Come on, Geri! We went to uni together, remember?'

'That was different.'

'Don't tell me — you didn't inhale.'

'We were nineteen, twenty. These are young kids. And it isn't just the odd spliff. He's giving, *selling,* them pills: Es, speed.'

Nick laughed. 'You haven't got his number, have you?'

Geri glared at him. 'Ryan died, Nick. He died in a filthy condemned building. Maybe he was conscious when he set fire to himself — they don't know for sure — but he was alive.'

Nick got out of his chair, scowling. 'You know, you're so up yourself, it's a miracle you don't come out the other end.'

'Is that it?' she demanded. 'Is that all you can say?'

He thought for a moment. 'No, you're right. There is something else. Fuck off.' He slammed the door behind him, leaving Geri blinking back tears.

* * *

Nick stamped upstairs. It didn't matter to her that he had spent the past three years in dead-end jobs, working forty hours a week for half her salary. When had she ever shown him any consideration? Kids, school, rehearsals, parents' evenings, marking, marking, marking. *Too tired to go out, too shagged to fuck*, he thought.

It was Geri who had encouraged him to go for the job at the research facility. She just couldn't stand to see him doing nothing. Something — anything — was always preferable to doing nothing in Geri's eyes.

* * *

What had happened to them? Geri wondered. What had changed since Nick had so gently brought her back to the world after the death of her mother?

The day after her mother died, Geri had woken to find fronds of frost on the inside of the windows. She had forgotten to set the central heating, and the house shivered, preternaturally silent, as if in sympathy with her numbed sorrow.

She lay awake in bed for hours, listening to the creak and sigh of the woodwork, straining for the sound of her mother busying herself in the kitchen, although it had been many months since she had heard the chink of crockery as her mother set out the breakfast things. Once or twice she almost convinced herself, but then the silence would reassert its presence and she was forced to acknowledge that the only sounds her mother had been capable of making of late were the sounds of the sickroom: a cough, a groan, the querulous demands for attention. Sporadically, the phone would ring, on and on shattering the stillness, but she could not find the energy to answer it. How could she? If she answered, she would have to say that her mother was dead, and for now there was a perverse comfort in pretending that she might come into her room, demanding to know why Geri was lying in bed so late on a working day.

She tried not to think of the night before, of how her mother had died. She did not 'go gentle into that good night' — God, no — and Geri had been powerless to help. Powerless and appalled by her mother's ravings, and — though it shamed her to admit it — even afraid.

Nick had rescued her, hammering on the front door until she answered, sullen, red-eyed, still in her dressing gown. Without fuss he led her through to the sitting room and switched on the gas fire, then he vanished into the kitchen. Moments later she heard the gurgle of water in the pipes as the central heating came to life again. He cooked her breakfast at two in the afternoon, the smell of bacon and mushrooms provoking a fresh wave of weeping.

He sat and watched as she tried to eat, struggling against the unbearable constriction in her throat, gently urging her on, passing no comment when she pushed the food away uneaten, but listening patiently as she told him over and over how it had been. What had happened to Nick since then? Had she used up all his reserves of patience, all his quiet consideration?

* * *

Since they found Ryan's body, Frank had become more and more shrill — making accusations, talking to all the wrong people, stirring things up. He found the pathetic whiner plodding to school, the day after the service.

'Get in.' That's all it took. He just drew up alongside Frank and said those two words. An order, given in a tone of voice that brooked no argument. It still surprised him that it was so easy. You said, 'Do this', 'Give me that', and they did. They gave it to you, they did it for you, to you, with you. It was a question of faith, except the belief wasn't in a God who looked down and wept over his creation; this was self-belief. Hesitate, look over your shoulder to check if the sheep were following, and you were sunk. The illusion was shattered, and they saw you were just another human being, like them, that they didn't have to do what you told them to. Keep faith with yourself, and the sheep recognized your authority. They respected it — and that meant they respected you.

He wondered if Frank had known when he got into the car what was going to happen to him. Perhaps he suspected, but still he did as he was told.

Frank wasn't attractive — not like Ryan. Frank was skinny and gawky; his Adam's apple jumped up and down as he swallowed. A startling revelation burst upon him: the very fact of Frank's physical unattractiveness gave him licence to go further than he had with Ryan. Because although Ryan had been just as compliant, with the persuasive assistance of the cocktail of drugs in his veins, he had been to some extent inhibited, in awe of Ryan's beauty.

Now, seeing Frank on his knees, begging to be allowed to leave, he was aroused by him; he even felt a certain tenderness for the lad. He would maybe keep him a little longer than he'd kept Ryan. They would talk, and he would make Frank tell him everyone *he* had talked to. Then he could assess the danger.

* * *

Frank was coming round enough to be able to wonder if he had a future. He still had enough of the chemicals in his system for this to be an academic question; one which didn't frighten him, but which nevertheless perplexed him.

He tried to move, but he was cocooned inside a sleeping bag, and it seemed to be sealed around his neck with something. He struggled momentarily, then gave up. It wasn't worth breaking into a sweat. Was it? He couldn't answer the question and gave a mental shrug: he couldn't be bothered pondering over it. He nodded, waking, dreaming — sometimes the dreams were so real, so filled with light and warmth, that it was a surprise to wake up in the damp, echoing chamber, dripping with snowmelt.

It was pleasant for him to drift in this way, thinking on things he hadn't dared remember from his early school days: the bullies, the beatings, missed meals because someone had threatened to thump him if he didn't give up his lunch money. Until he'd met Ryan, he couldn't remember a day he hadn't been scared. But he wasn't scared now. Rats squeaked in the far corners, and he was unable to move, to defend himself. *He* would return soon, as he always did when Frank started to make sense of things, to be able to think, but Frank didn't care. While there was enough of this kindly stuff in his veins, he was afraid of nothing.

18

'Another one down, eh, Vince?' Garvey's voice carried from the far end of the corridor.

Vince Beresford stopped, one hand on the door. 'What?'

'Just saying — another kid's gone missing.'

Even with his back turned, Vince could tell that Garvey was grinning.

'So it seems.' He pushed the door open.

'They drop like flies around you, don't they?'

Vince let the door go and turned to face Garvey; by now, he was just a few feet away. 'Look, Garvey, if you've got something to say—'

Garvey raised his eyebrows. 'I just said it.' He walked past Vince, smirking.

His pupils were dilated, his eyes darted back and forth, not quite fixing on anything. Vince edged forward, talking all the time, talking over the babble of the boy's wild ramblings. His raised his hands slowly, waiting for his chance to strike.

'You all right, Sarge?'

WPC Dhar was staring up at him.

Vince shook himself, tried to raise a smile. 'Fine,' he said, holding the door for her. But it wasn't fine. Garvey knew. It was stupidity, thinking he could escape his past. The past was something you carried with you. Everywhere.

* * *

One moment Geri was standing, the next she was sitting. Between the two, there was a blank of a fraction of a second — not much, but enough to confuse and disorientate her.

'Frank?' she echoed sickly. Coral had called her into her office after Thursday morning registration. Geri had braced herself for an announcement that Barry Mandel had decided to press charges. Nothing could have shored her up against this news.

'He left for school on Tuesday and hasn't been seen since.'

'*Tuesday?* Why didn't his parents report it before now?'

'His mother,' Coral corrected. 'His parents are separated. Apparently, he's done this sort of thing before. Run off. He usually heads for his dad's place, in Lancaster.'

'Has his dad heard anything?'

Coral shook her head.

Geri groaned. 'Oh, Coral, it's happened again, hasn't it?'

'He just didn't go home, Geri. I don't think we should panic.'

'It's been two days already, Coral. Wouldn't he have been in touch with someone by now?' She swallowed. 'I spoke to him after the service . . . I wasn't very kind to him. He was frightened. Frightened enough to run?' she added, half to herself. 'God, I hope he did, I hope he did run.'

'Frightened of what?' Coral asked, intrigued now.

Geri looked down at her hands. They were shaking. 'He wouldn't tell me.' She recalled his nervous glance in Barry's direction. 'Barry Mandel, maybe?'

'Oh, now Geri.' Coral half rose from her seat. 'You got to give up on this . . .'

'You think I'm victimizing him. Ask Siân what she thinks of that. Or Jay.' *Jay! What if he'd deliberately given Jay an overdose? Tried to shut him up because he knew too much.* She couldn't say this to Coral — she already thought her paranoid. But it might be worth talking to Jay's friends.

At the end of school, Geri sought them out. Nobody wanted to talk to her. As two boys hurried away, she saw Barry Mandel leaning against a wall of the playground, coolly watching her.

She walked up to him, determined this time to keep her temper. 'You've got them scared, Barry,' she said. 'But you don't frighten me.'

'Good thing too,' Barry said. 'A teacher who loses her nerve might as well give it up.'

She returned, shivering, to her classroom to do some work before going home, and by the time she left, the school was in darkness. She flicked on the corridor lights as she left her classroom and waited while a couple of reluctant tubes flickered and buzzed, shedding no more than a grey glimmer. The distance between her room and the lights on the main passage seemed filled with dark threat.

'Sod it,' she muttered, clasping her briefcase more tightly and marching down the centre of the corridor, while the lights crackled and fizzed overhead. A chair scraped loudly in the room to her right and Geri jumped. The room was in darkness, but for a spectral blue light that seemed to flit across the walls. Abruptly, the light went out, and Geri hurried on, anxious to make it to the main corridor. The door opened and she heard a footstep behind her. She tensed, turning to face her assailant.

'Are you all right?' It was Coral. 'You look like you've seen a ghost.'

Geri let her breath out in a rush. 'Jesus, Coral! What were you doing in the dark?'

'Sorting through some slides for a PSE lesson.'

Coral was wearing a rather extravagantly fringed purple cape, evidently ready to leave. She quickly caught up with Geri and they walked on together. 'Interesting how lapsed Catholics are still moved to profanity in moments of stress,' she said, sliding a sly look at Geri.

'I'm an *atheist*, and it's just a turn of phrase.'

'Oh,' Coral nodded solemnly. 'Feeling a bit jumpy?' The question was asked mischievously, but beneath it there was concern.

Coral didn't know about the incident with the blood-filled syringe the previous week, and Geri wasn't about to fill her in on her adventures with Siân. Nor would Coral approve of her questioning children about Barry Mandel, so she simply shrugged. 'Just tired. I've not slept well since . . .'

Coral nodded. 'Get an early night, eh? And stop obsessing about Barry Mandel. If he is mixed up in this, let the police sort it out.'

Geri rubbed her eye tiredly. 'I don't know how they can, while they believe Ryan's death was misadventure.'

'And you don't.'

'Ryan's dead. Frank's gone. There are a lot of frightened children who won't talk to me.'

'Of course they're frightened. For most of them, it's the first time in their lives they've had to face death. You're misreading the signs, Geri.'

'I hope so,' Geri said fervently. 'I really do.' They went through a fire exit out into the rear car park, and Coral rattled the door after it clicked shut, checking it had locked properly. Geri pressed the remote button on her keyring and her alarm chirruped. She opened the boot and dumped her briefcase.

'An early night, and you'll feel differently,' Coral repeated, talking to her from over the top of her own car.

'You're probably r—' Geri stopped and stared at the bonnet of her car. It seemed to be swathed in mist. She actually shook her head and looked again. It occurred to her that the engine had overheated, but that didn't make sense since it had been sitting in a freezing car park all day.

'Geri?' She heard Coral's voice as from a distance. Then, 'What the hell . . . ?'

Geri took a step closer and immediately began coughing. The 'mist' was acrid, it caught in her throat and sent her lungs into spasm. She turned away, coughing and choking, as Coral reached her. The older woman took her arm and looked at the car, keeping her distance, wary of the fumes.

The paint had bubbled, and the liquid had run, but the image was just discernible: two bulbous lips with a huge tongue sticking out, apparently in the act of licking something.

'Acid,' Geri spluttered.

'I can see that, but why?'

'No,' she coughed, trying to get her breath. 'The symbol . . . for acid . . . blotter-art . . . LSD.'

* * *

She told the police everything. Her hunt for Ryan, the note tacked to her front door, the row between Baz and Frank after the memorial service, Jay being rushed to hospital, her argument with Baz; she even admitted to questioning the children that afternoon.

DCI Thomas sat in on the interview, listening courteously. 'You're convinced this Barry Mandel is at the root of it,' he said.

'Who else?' Geri asked, looking into the inspector's sorrowful eyes. 'Frank was terrified when I spoke to him on Monday night. I've had no trouble since last week, but as soon as I start talking to children again, this happens.'

'Has he threatened you?'

'Not actually threatened,' she admitted. 'Baz is more subtle than that. He could make an *apology* seem like a threat.'

'We'll bring him in for questioning,' he said. 'But from what you've said, it could be anyone who damaged your car.'

'Who else would know that I'd been—' She stopped. She had spoken to the boys at three thirty, just as school finished. She'd worked until about four thirty, which gave the lads she'd spoken to an hour to spread the word that Miss Simpson had been nosing around, asking questions about drugs. He was right. It could have been anybody, but it *was* Baz, who else?

The police dusted for fingerprints. There were two sets. Hers were quickly eliminated, Siân's could be checked out the next day. Geri dreaded Mrs Walsh getting a second visit from the police, and she persuaded them to wait so that she could warn Siân's mother. They washed the remainder of the acid off the car — it was nitric — and sent her home, by which time it was late.

The house was warm, and the smell of cooking greeted her. Nick, however, did not. Hardly surprising after their row over Barry Mandel. She dumped her coat and briefcase, left a stack of exercise books on the window ledge and went through to the kitchen.

The table was laid. A posy of anemones sat in the centre, in a small glass vase. Two candles, now almost burned down, stood at either end of the table. Nick sat at one place setting.

Shit! She had completely forgotten. 'Nick, I'm sorry.' She sat opposite him. 'I was on my way home, when—'

'Five o'clock, you said. It's now nearly seven.'

'I know, but . . .'

Nick stared at her with such dislike that the words of explanation dried in her mouth.

'You want to eat?' He grabbed a tea towel, went to the oven and flung open the door. He slid the tray onto the table with such force that one of the potatoes, blackened and hard, rolled off and Geri had to stand up to avoid it landing in her lap. Two brown lumps that may have been chicken were stuck to the tray.

'You didn't have to leave it to ossify!' she said angrily. 'We could've warmed them through in the microwave.'

'And you could've made the effort to get home on time.' He shrugged. 'I guess neither of us could be bothered.'

* * *

Lauren came into the kitchen as Geri was scraping the carbonised remains of the meal into the bin.

'That looks yummy.' Geri shot her a look. 'Ouch,' she said.

'Did you see Nick on your way in?' Geri asked.

'Saw him, heard him — he was on his way out.' Geri's shoulders slumped. 'Want to talk to Auntie Lauren about it?'

'Oh, I don't know what's the matter with him,' Geri said, throwing the baking tray into the sink and tossing the tea towel onto the table. 'One minute he's thoughtful and supportive, the next he's acting like a boorish slob, slamming about the place and sulking because things haven't gone as planned.'

'Hormones,' Lauren said.

'What?'

'Think about it. We only have to deal with a burst of male hormones once a month, he's got them zinging around his system all the time.' Geri fixed her with a baleful stare, but Lauren wasn't so easily intimidated. 'Cheer up,' she said. 'Get something out of the freezer and we'll crack open a bottle of wine.'

'I'm not hungry.'

'Okay, skip the food and move straight to the wine . . .' She stopped, distracted, and peered at something off to her right.

Geri tensed. 'If it's a spider, don't tell me, just stamp on the damn thing.'

Lauren continued staring. 'I wouldn't stamp on something this size — it might take my foot off.' She advanced cautiously and prodded the object with her toe, then smiled, relaxing and bent down.

'What is it?' Geri asked.

Lauren picked it up and placed it carefully in front of Geri. 'Sure you're not hungry?' It was the potato that had nearly ended up in her lap earlier.

Geri looked into her friend's face. Lauren's puzzled amusement was enough to start her laughing, but once she started, she found she couldn't stop. She was overtaken by waves of hysterical giggling, that soon turned to tears.

Alarmed, Lauren sat next to her and put an arm around her. 'God, Geri, it wasn't *that* funny.'

Geri elbowed her. 'You never are,' she said, then: 'Shit, my nose is running.'

Lauren fetched her a piece of kitchen roll and Geri began to explain.

'It's the same thing all over again, Lauren. First Ryan, now Frank. And someone . . .' She shook her head, couldn't bring herself to talk about the damage to her car, not just yet.

Lauren stared at Geri. 'What about Frank?'

'He's vanished.'

Geri felt a pressure under her friend's stare, which built became unbearable. As she was about to frame a question, Lauren broke eye contact.

'Let's open that wine,' she said briskly, leaning on the kitchen table, ready to stand, but Geri put a restraining hand on her arm.

'Did I say something?' Geri asked.

Lauren forced a smile. 'Nothing.' She stood and went to the fridge. 'This calls for strong and sweet,' she said, bringing out the bottle with the highest alcohol content.

An hour later, Lauren said she was going to fetch one of her quilted cushion covers to work on. She took the phone from the hall into the sitting room and dialled Meredith, her day leader on the Sunday that she'd received Frank's call and recounted her earlier conversation with Geri.

'What are you saying?' Meredith asked.

'He's missing!' Lauren repeated. 'He told me he was frightened of someone, and now he's missing.' She was avoiding saying what they both knew she was driving at, because she knew, in the end, that it was impossible.

'Assuming your caller is the same person, he may have gone away for a while. He may need time to think.'

'I'm living in the same house as her, Meredith! She's worried sick.'

'And if you told her, what would that achieve?'

'I didn't say I wanted to tell her.'

'No . . .' She let the silence hang for a few seconds. 'But if the caller had wanted you to tell anyone else, he'd have said so.'

'He hung up before I had a chance to ask him.'

'His choice. We have to wait until he calls again.'

'*If* he does.'

'And whether he does or not, he has a right to expect complete confidentiality. He may have changed his mind. If he was distressed and confused by events, he may have been looking for someone to blame. None of us wants to believe that someone we love has killed themselves, whether deliberately or by a reckless act.'

It made sense, but Lauren could not let go of this so easily. But she had to live with her knowledge, not Meredith, and she had to face Geri every day, knowing what she knew and saying nothing.

'He may need time to come to terms with Ryan's death,' Meredith went on.

'I feel terrible, listening to her talk about him, sympathizing with her and pretending I don't know anything about it.'

'This isn't about how you feel, Lauren. I'm sorry, I know that sounds harsh, and I know it's difficult for you, but we have to respect Frank's wishes. And this is about more than one individual. It's about the integrity of the entire organisation.'

How many times had Lauren delivered that lecture to fellow Samaritans? She knew she couldn't tell Geri, and she had telephoned Meredith wanting to hear that she was doing the right thing. Well, now she had heard it. But it was cold comfort.

19

Word got around that Barry's house had been raided by the police. Geri couldn't believe it seemed to have raised his status even further with the younger children. She'd had to move on a crowd of Year Nines she had found clustered around Barry at lunch time.

'Saints preserve us!' Coral said. 'He wasn't passing anything to them, was he?'

'Even Barry isn't that brazen,' Geri replied. They were closeted in Coral's office for privacy, the staffroom being too open and too full of eavesdroppers.

'I can't understand it,' Coral said. 'The whole school knows he's supplying drugs and yet the police found nothing, you say?' She had been more sympathetic to Geri's opinion of him since the acid attack, and Geri's edited highlights of the events leading to it.

Geri shook her head. Vince had rung her after the raid. DCI Thomas had questioned Barry, but he had remained imperturbable.

'If he gets other kids to carry the stuff, maybe he's got it stashed at a friend's house.'

Coral snorted. 'That boy doesn't have friends; he has business associates.' She sucked her teeth. 'Did Sergeant Beresford say what they're doing to find Frank?'

'He's not officially supposed to be doing anything. But he said he'd have a quiet word with some of Frank's friends if he got the chance today.'

'*Someone* must know where he is!' Coral burst out.

'I tried last night, I tried to find out, but the kids won't talk to me and—' She shuddered, remembering the wisps of poisonous vapour curling, *crawling* over the bonnet of her car.

'What do the police say — about the damage to your car, I mean?'

'Same as last time: drug dealer, warning me to stay off his turf; a pupil with a grudge. But it wasn't like that, Coral. All I did was I ask a few kids some questions—' Suddenly she was shaking. What was there to stop him going for her instead of her car, next time? An HIV-infected needle in the neck, acid in the face?

'Oh, God,' she groaned, covering her mouth with her hand.

Coral enfolded her in her arms. She smelled of Opium perfume. Her bangles clacked as she smoothed Geri's hair, comforting her. After a couple of minutes the shaking subsided and Geri drew on her reserves of strength and stood.

'You stay away from trouble, y'hear? Keep your head down and stay well out of it, and everything will be just fine.'

'Yeah,' Geri said, wishing she could believe it. She had her hand on the door handle, ready to leave, when Coral added:

'Before you go — what exactly do you mean by "Same as last time"?'

* * *

Geri decided to go into the city centre on her way home to talk to Adèle. It wasn't as if there was anything to rush home for, since Nick still wasn't speaking to her — she had heard him come in at two a.m., but he had slept downstairs, and he had stayed out of her way as she got ready for work. She was still too angry with him to tell him why she had been so late.

Adèle's usual pitch had been taken by a man. At first, Geri was wary of approaching him. She no longer knew who it was safe to talk to — who she was *allowed* to talk to. But he was friendly: he and Adèle had done a swap, he told her, and Adèle was outside Waterstones. Adèle smiled over at her, as she crossed the road. ''Lo, stranger,' Adèle said, as she came closer. She looked tired and very pale. Geri stood to one side so that she could carry on selling her magazines.

'I heard about the lad,' Adèle said.

'You did?' Geri felt a surge of optimism. If Adèle had heard, it meant that Frank had been seen about. 'Can I buy you a meal?' she asked. 'I'd like to talk about him.'

Adèle stopped her plaintive chant, 'Buy a *Big Issue*, help the homeless!', and gave Geri a curious look. She shrugged. 'Okay. Half an hour. Pizza Hut.'

Geri went into Waterstones determined only to browse and came out with a study guide to *Romeo and Juliet* and two paperbacks. Adèle was still selling, so she went to the Pizza Hut and waited. When Adèle arrived fifteen minutes later, Geri was absorbed in *Behind the Scenes at the Museum*.

'Sold the lot,' Adèle said, when she came in. ''S funny, right? Windy days you'll hardly get a sideways glance — people are too busy rushing to get out of the cold. But a still day, like this . . .' She grinned and jingled the coins in her pocket.

'So, what're you having?' Geri asked.

Adèle shot her a shy look. 'You're buying?'

She had the Four Seasons with extra cheese and pepperoni.

'Any news from the housing trust?' Geri asked.

Adèle grimaced. 'Takes time,' she said.

'How did you manage in all that snow?'

'Emergency shelter.'

'Still, you'll be back in your warehouse by now.'

Adèle picked up a slice of pizza and took a bite. 'Moved out,' she mumbled through a mouthful.

'I thought you liked it there.'

Adèle shrugged.

'Have you found somewhere else?'

'I'm gonna move into a hostel, when a place comes up.'

'I thought you hated hostels.'

Another shrug. *This is like pulling teeth*, Geri thought.

Adèle seemed to sense her exasperation and added, 'Lost all my stuff.'

'Lost? How?'

She didn't answer.

Geri could see she would get no further with this line of conversation and gave up, talking instead about Adèle's plans for her new flat, when she eventually had one allocated. Adèle had saved up from her social security, and she had a few hundred in the bank ready to furnish and decorate her new home. She waited until Adèle had nearly finished her meal before bringing up the subject of Frank's disappearance.

Adèle licked her fingers and took a pull on her beer. 'Who's Frank?'

'The lad who's gone missing — that's his name.'

'I thought it was Ryan.'

Geri's heart sank. She was hoping that Adèle would have news of Frank, but if she hadn't heard of him, it could mean he wasn't on the streets, or it could have another, far more sinister meaning.

'I think I remember Ryan,' Adèle went on. 'He was in the year below me. Drop dead gorgeous.' She stopped, colouring slowly from her neck to the roots of her hair. 'Sorry, I wasn't thinking.'

'That was the first boy, the one who was found in a burnt-out terrace. This is someone else . . . A friend of Ryan's. I thought you might—' She broke off. Adèle had stopped eating and was staring at her.

'Adèle?' she said.

Adèle blinked and swallowed with difficulty. 'When did he . . . ?'

'He was at the memorial service on Monday night, but he didn't turn up for school on Tuesday and no one has seen him since.'

Adèle blanched, then flushed.

'Could you ask about?' She hardly believed she was breaking her promise to herself and to Coral so soon after making it. 'See if any of your mates have—'

'Mates? What mates?' Adèle cut in sharply.

'People on the street . . .'

'I'm trying to break with my street "mates",' Adèle said. 'They're what got me into trouble in the first place.' She seemed angry, frightened.

'I'm sorry,' Geri said. 'I didn't mean to put you on the spot. It's just that I'm really worried about him, and I don't know who else to ask.'

'Yeah, well . . .'

They sank into an uneasy silence for a few minutes. Adèle ate steadily, while Geri toyed miserably with her food.

'I don't know what you think I can do,' Adèle said, at length. Geri looked up, hopeful, but not daring to speak in case Adèle changed her mind. 'But I'll talk to some people.' She shrugged.

'Thanks,' Geri said. 'Thanks, Adèle. Any news, anything at all. Just so we know he's all right.'

As Adèle left the pizza parlour, she shivered.

A sudden flare of light, then screams, an explosion. No connection, she told herself. But Ryan was found in a burnt-out terrace. And Frank was Ryan's friend. *Forget it*, she told herself. Arsonists are always wrecking old buildings. You're not even sure what you saw. None of your business. Keep your nose out, stay safe.

* * *

Friday, and there was still no sign of Frank. Night fell, closing the library inside its own walls. Lauren collected a stack of books and arranged them on the trolley for shelving. The boy had called her on Sunday, afraid for his life, then Ryan's friend, Frank, had disappeared. It had to be the same boy.

She wheeled the trolley from behind the counter and started with the fiction titles. Where was he? Why hadn't he called back? She had checked with the day leader on Wednesday, after her talk with Meredith — Frank hadn't been in touch. Perhaps he would call today. If he would only telephone someone could help him. If he spoke to someone else, she felt her burden would be reduced.

* * *

The church smelled of incense. The altar boys were clearing away after six o' clock Mass, and the congregation had gone home. He felt a quiver of emotion he couldn't identify, looking at the waxy flowers and votive candles shimmering below the triptych.

Sometimes, he could see the attraction of religion. Frank's confession had put him in a state of agitation. Trust Frank to off-load his problems onto someone else — the *Samaritans*, for Christ's sake! Now, sitting in the contemplative stillness and gloom of the church, he realized there was a way out. He had a name — Lauren — which meant she was traceable. *And the Samaritans are here twenty-four hours a day*, he thought. All he had to do was call, then watch and wait.

20

Vince watched the passengers alight from the London train. Commuters, day trippers, students back from a few days playing hooky. They'd discovered that Frank had left a note — he had to get away for a while — London, maybe — didn't matter, as long as it was away.

'He's not gonna be amongst this lot.'

Vince turned to Sam Mayhew. He was in civvies — they both were — the boys on the concourse weren't going to stick around to chat if they saw uniforms about. Mayhew was wearing a grey-brown mackintosh with a broad cape-effect across the shoulders; it made him look like a football manager, or CID.

'He hasn't been seen since Tuesday. He's long gone,' Mayhew added, thrusting his hands deep into his pockets and hunching his shoulders against the cold. 'This is a waste of bloody time.'

'If he took a day or two thinking about it, making up his mind where to go, the lads will have seen him.' Vince jerked his head in the direction of two boys sharing a cigarette by the vending machine.

Mayhew shrugged. 'Let's get to it, then.'

Vince put a hand on his arm. 'You try the ramp,' he said. 'I'll do the concourse.'

Mayhew shot him a deeply antagonistic look and wandered off muttering about freezing his balls off. DCI Thomas had told him to keep it low-key, and Mayhew's style did not lend itself to discretion. They didn't want to fuel press speculation on a possible connection between the two disappearances, but they did want to show willing as far as the local community was concerned.

Vince shivered. His leather jacket wasn't enough protection from the intense cold. The snow had all but gone, leaving only a few dirty wedges in the darker corners of the narrow backstreets of the city. The rain earlier in the week had given way to sharp, bright days of dazzling sun, and black nights of severe frost.

He walked from the platform to the concourse. Cream marble floor tiles and a high, vaulted roof did nothing to provide shelter from the freezing air. There were only two likely candidates: the lads got moved on periodically by security, concerned that they might offend the sensibilities of genuine travellers.

He wandered over to one of the lads. From ten feet away he saw panic in the boy's eyes. He was preparing to bolt. Vince shook his head and raised his hands, palms down in a placatory gesture. The lad stood his ground but kept an eye on the escape routes.

'I'm not here to hassle you,' Vince said, when he'd got within a few feet of the boy. The lad's stance changed subtly from anxiety to cagey mistrust. He didn't speak, but leaned back against the wall, one foot flat against it, and hung his head, pouting a little.

Rebel Without a Cause, Vince thought, reminded of posters of James Dean. The boy's face was too plump to be a good likeness, but he had the hair, and the sullen good looks.

'I'm looking for a lad,' Vince began.

The boy gave him the once-over.

'He's gone missing,' Vince went on, ignoring the boy's provocative glance. He held out a photograph of Frank. The boy bided his time, taking it only after Vince shoved it at him.

'Looks pissed.' It was a recent picture — Frank was smiling, a bit the worse for wear at one of the half-dozen millennium parties he had attended.

'D'you know him?'

The boy shrugged. A negative. He pushed the picture back at Vince.

'Keep it,' Vince said. 'If you see him, call the number on the back.'

The boy raised his eyebrows. *As if.*

'There's a reward.' Frank's parents had put it up.

The amusement in the lad's eyes was partly displaced by avarice. 'How much?'

'Ring that number with the info, you'll find out.'

The second boy had slunk off while Vince was talking to James Dean. Vince walked to the side of the station, to the exit ramp from the car park. It was a good place to pick up passing trade, and if they couldn't stake their pitch on the concourse, the lads invariably ended up out here.

He started the climb up to the car park; so far there was no sign of Mayhew, then, halfway up the ramp, he heard shouting. Mayhew was struggling with the boy who had left the concourse. He was about fifteen, small for his age, and he squirmed and protested as Mayhew slapped him around the head.

Vince yelled Mayhew's name and he stopped, one hand raised, the other gripping the collar of the boy's leather jacket.

The boy swung at Mayhew, but the constable caught him by the wrist and twisted his arm up his back, forcing him against the wall. He screamed.

'Let go of him!' Vince roared.

Mayhew looked startled. He eased his grip but kept hold of the boy who by now had stopped struggling and was crying with pain.

Vince strode up to Mayhew and grabbed him by the shoulder.

'I said let him go!' His eyes blazed with anger.

The lad started squealing and Mayhew gave him a shove that made him yell for real, then he released him. The boy turned around, eyeing both men malevolently while he rubbed his sore arm. The contact with the wall had grazed his face slightly and one or two pinpricks of blood appeared on his cheek.

'Do him!' the lad shouted, sensing that the junior officer was already in trouble. 'He assaulted me!'

Vince switched his attention from Mayhew to the boy. 'How old are you?' he demanded.

'Old enough.' He had startlingly blue eyes — the kind that could glow with aching vulnerability or glaze with icy contempt.

'How old?'

'Eighteen.'

'No, you're not.' He was barely five foot two, and he looked underfed.

'Got any ID?' He began checking the boy's pockets, and the kid started shrieking.

'Get off me you fag — you perv!'

Vince stopped, shaken by the ferocity of the boy's response.

'Want me to do it?' Mayhew asked.

A muscle jumped in Vince's jaw. 'Have you shown him the picture?'

'Oh, yeah,' Mayhew said. 'That.' He took out a copy of the photograph. 'Seen him?'

'Nah.'

He grabbed the boy by the neck, but Vince's warning glance made him let go. 'Look at it,' he said.

The lad flipped a look in the general direction, just to avoid being roughed up again. His ears were red from the mashing Mayhew had given them, and the graze on his face was oozing. Vince handed him a clean handkerchief and the boy dabbed at his cheek. 'I don't know him,' he said, truculently.

Mayhew stuffed the photograph inside the boy's jacket. 'There's a number on the back,' he said. 'If you change your mind.' He swaggered off, leaving Vince alone with the boy.

'What's your name?' he asked.

'What's it to you?'

'I could take you in.'

There was a spark of anxiety, then he seemed to sense that the risk was small. 'Take me in? What for?' he demanded. 'Being out past me bedtime?'

Vince didn't reply, and the boy, gaining confidence, looked him in the eye. His expression changed from aggression to amusement. Vince took him by the arm and began leading him down the ramp.

'Where're we going?' the boy demanded.

'I'm taking you home.'

He pulled away, smirking. 'I don't do freebies.'

'Don't try to be funny,' Vince said. 'You're underage. What you're doing is dangerous.' He reached again for the boy's arm.

'Touch me again,' the boy said quietly, 'and I'll scream rape.' His pale blue eyes were cold, calculating. He knew exactly what he was saying.

Vince hesitated. His mouth was dry, and his heart pounded. He reached out again. Nimble, evasive, the boy moved just out of range.

'I'll tell them you tried to bumfuck me.'

Vince held his gaze, uncertain what to do. There were no witnesses, but if the lad started screaming . . . The boy stared back at him, unafraid. 'Clear off,' Vince said at last. 'Get out of my sight.'

The boy ran, laughing, back up the ramp, disappearing into the darkness.

When he reached the roadway, Mayhew was showing the photograph to another lad. He hadn't seen Frank either; Vince had to admit to himself that he hadn't expected anything useful from the exercise. They were going through the motions, doing what was expected of them.

As they walked back down to their car, parked outside the concourse, a high, clear voice carried to them on the thin night air. 'Arse bandit! Perv!'

Mayhew laughed. 'Nice to be popular,' he said.

Vince wasn't laughing.

21

'Lauren?' Meredith Carter stopped and put her head round the door of the main office to check she hadn't been mistaken. Phones were ringing, but the two Samaritans on duty were already busy. After a couple of rings, the calls were re-routed. 'What on earth are you doing here? You should have gone home hours ago.'

Lauren shot her a guilty look. 'I did, but I couldn't settle . . .'

Meredith held the office door open. 'You and I need to talk,' she said.

Lauren closed the logbook which she had been scanning for news of Frank. After a moment's hesitation she took it with her, following the supervisor into the private consultation room. It was plainly furnished: oatmeal carpet, terracotta-coloured upholstered chairs, a small, square table with a box of tissues in the centre. Lauren went to one of the chairs and sat down, expecting Meredith to follow, but she stood at the door, holding the handle as if to prevent anyone coming in.

'You can't do this, Lauren,' she said. 'You know you can't do this.'

Lauren opened the logbook. 'Look.' She riffled quickly through the pages. 'Half a dozen calls since Frank disappeared. Thursday, Friday, Saturday, all asking for me.'

'I've seen the logbook. Let someone else deal with it.'

'He won't *talk* to anyone else! He asked for me.' She looked back at one of the entries. '*Caller hung up when I told him Lauren wasn't working this evening*,' she read. 'And here, on Friday, he asked when Lauren was on duty. He wouldn't be persuaded to talk to anyone else. *Caller sounded desperate*.' She looked up from the log. 'He might do something stupid, Meredith.'

Meredith took her hand from the door handle and folded her arms across her chest. She was a gaunt, severe-looking woman with straight, dark grey hair cut in a short bob. Her large, slightly bent nose added to her acetic appearance, and gave her glance a piercing quality. Lauren was spared her shrewd appraisal for the moment: Meredith's eyes were fixed on the floor. Although Meredith could compartmentalise her work, shutting off the often-traumatic conversations she had with callers, locking them away from her everyday life, Lauren knew she was capable of great compassion and deep intuitive insight.

'We aren't a suicide prevention society,' Meredith said, after a long pause. The sentiment was harsh, but her voice was gentle, warm. She had used it to almost magical effect in her seventeen years as a Samaritan.

'But if we can prevent a suicide, we do, right?'

Meredith tilted her head, conceding the point. There was an implacable quality to her stillness.

'If I can persuade him to talk to someone else, I will,' Lauren tried again.

'And what makes you think he'll call?'

'He has done, at least once a day since Thursday. He's not likely to give up now, is he?' Meredith pursed her lips. 'Let me do a couple of hours,' Lauren begged. 'If he does call, I'll be here. If not, there's no harm done.'

'You've already done an extra session.'

'That was a favour,' Lauren explained. 'When Rick was ill.'

'And now you want a return of the favour, is that it?'

Lauren looked up into Meredith's face. Her sombre expression seemed to have lightened a little; there was a twinkle of amusement in her eyes and a smile flickered around her mouth.

'I'll take the next two months off, if it makes you happy,' Lauren begged.

'It would make me happy if you'd go home,' Meredith said.

'But it'd make me miserable.' She smiled. 'Go on, Meredith — you know you could use the help . . .'

Meredith considered. 'If I let you stay,' she began. Lauren leaned forward eagerly, but Meredith shook her head. 'I said *if*. You're to try to pass him on.'

'Yes.' In truth, she would have acceded to any stipulation.

'And I'll listen in,' Meredith finished.

'All right,' Lauren agreed, but this time with some reluctance. She was used to supervising others, not having her own calls monitored. 'Okay.'

Since Geri had told her about Frank's disappearance, Lauren had felt sick with apprehension. Each day she scanned the newspaper headlines and listened to the radio with a confused mixture of eagerness and dread. There was no news of Frank.

She had worked at the library until eight on Saturday night, and during a quiet spell she had found Thursday's issue of *The Tribune*. The front cover carried a slightly blurred photograph of Frank Traynor. The caption read simply *Missing from home*. There was background information on Ryan's death — Ryan was described as a glue-sniffer — and the fact that Frank and Ryan were school friends was taken as some kind of indication that Frank was also involved in what the paper described as the 'drugs culture' at St Michael's. A plea followed from his parents, begging him to get in touch.

Lauren had made an effort to be rational: there were plenty of highly competent staff who could take Frank's call. She had to maintain professional objectivity. Geri was evidently puzzled by her reserve, when Frank's name came up at home, and she felt constantly anxious that seeing Geri worried about the boy, listening to her concerns for his safety, she would be unable to stop the words bubbling up like spring water. It was easier to avoid Geri, and when contact was unavoidable, to speak only about trivial matters.

So, the two of them had made awkward conversation while Nick seemed to relish the apparent cooling of their normally warm relationship. On Saturday night she had telephoned the Samaritans office to ask someone to check the log. They had told her that a youth had been trying to contact her all week; she would have gone there and then and waited for his call, if the supervisor would allow it, but she was told that the boy had already telephoned. Perhaps because of Geri's involvement, Frank had become someone who impinged on her life; he couldn't be put in a box when her voluntary stint had finished. In the normal run of things, there was a small part of her mind that read each new scenario as an interesting puzzle. Although she cared about the callers, and she wanted to help them resolve their difficulties, there was that sliver of cool detachment that occasionally worried her, but which, in the main, served her well as a Samaritan.

She slept badly that night and had counted the hours until her shift started on Sunday. Call after call had been logged, all from the same person, described as male, young, distressed. He had given his name on Thursday — just 'Frank' — as if he wanted her to know that it really was important, that he *had* to speak to Lauren.

She sat in her booth feeling exhilarated that he would call and that she would be there to speak to him, but at ten o'clock when the overnight shift had arrived, she had been forced to go home. She picked up her needlework, then tried reading a book, only to throw it down minutes later. She had returned to the Samaritans office at just after midnight and was relieved to see that he hadn't yet phoned the switchboard.

Within the sound-damped confines of her cubicle, she felt at once cocooned from the world and immersed in the harrowing stories of the callers. In the quiet minutes, between the calls, she kept hearing Frank's voice, muffled with tears: *I think he killed Ryan. He keeps looking at me, like he knows.*

If he did get in touch, she would have to be careful not to reveal that she knew more about the situation — about him — than she should in her role of Samaritan. But he didn't phone, and by four a.m. Lauren had all but given up.

When she picked up the receiver as the phone rang for perhaps the twentieth time that night, there was none of the anticipation she had felt with her earlier calls.

'I want to speak to Lauren.' He sounded despondent, as if he expected to be told that Lauren wasn't available.

'I'm Lauren,' she said.

She heard him breathing at the other end of the line, but he didn't speak. Meredith was in the consultation room, dealing with a woman who had turned up with two children, terrified to go home because her husband had threatened her with a knife.

The silence stretched for perhaps half a minute, until Lauren, unable to wait any longer, asked, 'Can I help?'

'I doubt it.'

He said no more; he didn't seem in a hurry to talk, but he didn't seem about to hang up, either.

'Why don't you tell me about it?' she asked.

'How do I know you're Lauren?' The voice was quieter, more controlled than when she had last heard it.

'You don't. Not for sure. But that doesn't matter. What matters is that I'm here, and I'm listening. You're Frank, right?' she said.

'You see? Names *are* important, aren't they?' He was mocking her.

'You don't have to say your name, I only meant that it's easier talking to someone with a name,' she said.

‘The name doesn’t make the person.’

‘No, of course not. But I’ve been getting calls, and I want to be clear who the calls have come from. You *are* Frank, aren’t you?’

‘Might be. And you might be Lauren.’

Lauren spoke to hundreds of people during the course of a week, answering the telephone at work, talking to library users. She couldn’t say she remembered his voice, but she was sure that it was Frank, nevertheless. Certain that she was speaking to the phantom caller, Lauren stood and waved to the other Samaritan on duty, then handed her a hastily scribbled note to take to Meredith. She decided not to address Frank’s implied question, but to pose one of her own.

‘Why did you run away?’

‘If you *are* Lauren, you’d know why.’

‘You said you were frightened,’ Lauren said.

‘You don’t know how much! I phoned you I don’t know how many times. But you weren’t there.’ He seemed bitter, angry with her.

‘I shouldn’t be here now. I’m breaking all the rules talking to you, Frank. I should hand you over to somebody else.’

‘No!’ He seemed to catch himself, then he repeated, ‘No . . . please, don’t do that.’

‘You said the others are scared of him as well. Couldn’t you get them to help? I mean if you all stuck together—’

‘Fat chance!’ he interrupted.

‘You say he watches you. Is it someone you see every day?’

‘Yeah, every day.’

‘Have you thought about what you should do?’ Lauren asked.

‘You mean going to the police?’

‘It’s one possibility.’

‘No,’ he said, this time quite calm, in control. ‘I won’t do that.’

‘Your friends are worried. Your parents are frantic.’ Lauren took a breath. She glanced towards the office door, willing Meredith to come in. The door remained firmly closed, and she gave a mental shrug. 'What will you do?'

'Meet me.'

The question was so sudden, so unexpected, that Lauren was momentarily taken aback. 'You could come here,' she suggested. 'We have a private consultation room where we could talk.'

'No. I . . . I'm too scared. He might find out.' For a short while, she heard only his ragged breathing. Then: 'Meet me,' he said again.

'I can't do that,' Lauren replied. 'I'm sorry . . . But you've nothing to be afraid of. Who would know you're here?'

'He knows,' the boy said. 'He knows everything.'

'If you're still in the city, wouldn't it be better to be under the protection of the police? I mean, isn't it risky—'

'Risky?' he interrupted. 'You make it sound like a dodgy bet.'

'I'm not trivializing it, Frank. I know you've good reason to be scared.' He grunted an acknowledgement and she went on, 'So wouldn't it be better to come in, make a statement—'

'Look!' he yelled. 'It's not going to happen, right?'

'I'm sorry, I know you're under pressure.'

He wasn't listening. 'I thought I could trust you!' he shouted. 'I thought you weren't supposed to push people into doing stuff they didn't want—' He broke off, and Lauren listened in silence as he fought to calm himself. 'I knew this was a mistake,' he said, at last. 'I don't know why I bothered.'

'You've called every day now for nearly a week,' Lauren said. 'You asked for me. There must have been a reason.'

'There's no one I can trust.'

'You can trust me,' she said without hesitation.

'I hope so.' It was said softly, without inflection, neither plea nor threat. Lauren shivered.

'Frank,' she said. 'I won't be here if you call again. Like I told you, I shouldn't be here today.'

'Doesn't matter.'

'If you call again, you'll have to talk to someone else. That's the way it works.'

'I don't need to talk to anyone else.'

'But if you do—'

'I won't.'

The silence lengthened, then, just as Lauren roused herself to say something, she heard a click and the line went dead.

* * *

Lauren was the last to leave the office at seven fifteen on Monday morning. Meredith should have to kick her out earlier, immediately after Frank's telephone call, but Lauren guessed she was glad of the extra help. February was a miserable month for most people: the winter stretched interminably, and by now it was clear that the promise of a new beginning — the excitement of a new start — was nothing more than an illusion, left over with the Christmas tinsel. The millennial New Year had failed to deliver in spectacular style for some of the callers, and the failure seemed more depressing, more devastating simply because this one was so rare.

Meredith had requested a debriefing on the telephone call and Lauren had given a full and honest account, including her stipulation that she would not be available to take any more calls.

'It's for the best, Lauren,' Meredith assured her.

'I know,' Lauren said, still wondering how Frank would survive alone on the streets, still anxious to know who he was so afraid of. 'But I don't think he'll call again.'

'What makes you so sure?'

'I don't know.' Was it the way he said it didn't matter that she wouldn't be there? 'It was as if . . .' she began, trying to make sense of her instincts, '. . . as if he'd got what he wanted — the reassurance he needed, I suppose.'

She couldn't help thinking, as she walked to her car, that she had done little to help Frank. There were times when she felt that she had given out more on a call than she had discovered about the caller, and when she analysed the conversation, she felt that this was one of those times.

She never walked home from the Samaritans office — a precaution only, but she saw no point in taking unnecessary risks: the people who phoned the Samaritans were often desperate, sometimes disturbed, and the office was in a prominent position in the high street — easy to find, and it would be easy to pinpoint a particular Samaritan.

Lauren shivered and turned up the collar of her coat. A cutting wind was swirling the dust and sending chip wrappers cavorting along the street. She would be glad to get home and a have few hours in bed, but she suspected that sleep would elude her, even now.

22

He watched. Three people had gone into the office just before seven a.m. Change of shift.

The first of the night shift left at 7.05. A man. That simplified things. The second he discounted also: Lauren sounded young, although it could be difficult to judge age over the phone, but she was certainly younger than this fifty-something sexless old maid. Another woman came out a few minutes later. This must be her. She wasn't bad looking, either. Long legs, nice bone structure. She hesitated a moment, then set off down the hill. He would have to follow on foot: he had left his car in a side street at the top of the hill, and it looked like she was heading in the opposite direction, towards the car park in Minshull Street, he guessed.

He vaulted over the barrier and ran across the road. Traffic was light, and the dawn still came late, offering him cover. The darkness, the woman's figure disappearing around the corner, the thrill of needing to hurry but also keep his distance was an aphrodisiac. He hadn't had a hard-on like this since . . . Well, since Frank — and that was, what? He shied away from working it out, unwilling to admit to himself that he was losing track of time. He kept well back and walked softly.

He felt a pull of something he could not quite identify at the thought of Frank — shame, perhaps — not at what he had done, but at the compulsion that made him do it. More than anything, he feared discovery. He told himself that he had no choice. Frank knew what he'd done; he had protected himself. It was that simple.

With Ryan, it had been different. there was a genuine attraction, and if he had been willing, *compliant* — without the added persuasion of the drugs, that is — none of the rest need ever have happened. It didn't occur to him to blame himself. Ryan had struggled and cried, which made him angry, and then he had begged, which made him *horny*. He didn't pretend to understand these feelings, but he couldn't deny them either: they were urgent, demanding, throbbing in his groin and pounding in his head until it was all he could feel, all he could hear, and he had to — *had to* — find release.

The boys at the railway station were one form of release, but he didn't like the knowing looks they gave him, the cheap way they flirted — anyway, they were chancy, now he was getting better known. All they had to do was drop his name in the right place, and everything he had built up over the past year would fall. He'd had a close call the other night, and he didn't intend putting himself in that kind of danger again.

Lauren was thirty or forty metres ahead of him; her shoes rang out on the cold pavement, and the sound carried to him in bursts as the wind backed and turned in his direction. There were only two cars on the car park, and she stopped at a battered, pale blue Fiesta. He couldn't read the licence plate, and he didn't want to alert her by hurrying after her, but the car park exit would take her into Alderney Road, a one-way street. He cut through a back alley onto Alderney, turning now towards the car park. A moment later, the blue Fiesta turned out and he had plenty of time to note the licence number and get another look at her face as she passed him. He would get her address from the index number without too much trouble.

He walked to his own car and got it started. He knew all the backstreets and rat runs around the city centre and used his knowledge to get onto the dual carriageway without having to backtrack a mile to the nearest roundabout, in order to head back in the right direction. As he waited at the lights, he saw the Fiesta drive past, farting blue smoke from its exhaust. Apparently, Lauren had taken the long route.

A sensation of pins and needles in his scalp left him feeling light-headed. It was as if every nerve was firing at once. He slowed his breath and forced himself to wait. The traffic was building steadily now, and there were cars queuing to his left and right. He was positioned for the outside lane, and a right turn at the fountains roundabout, but as the lights changed to amber, he screeched through, cutting into the inside lane to follow Lauren; two cars separated him from the Fiesta, which was just enough to camouflage him, but when a yellow Fiat tried to ease into the gap in front of him at the roundabout, he speeded up, giving the driver a look of such savage fury that she braked and dropped back. The shock on her face made him laugh out loud.

The blue Fiesta accelerated onto the roundabout and he fumed as she disappeared from sight. It didn't matter, when it came right down to it — he had her index number and could get her address and call round at his leisure, but the adrenaline was screaming through his veins and he couldn't stop now. He gunned the engine, bullying the car ahead into squeezing onto the roundabout and forcing the cars already on it to slow down. He pulled out, giving the irate motorists a maniacal grin, in case they were considering complaining.

Lauren had passed the first and second exits. The fourth would take her back into the city, which seemed unlikely, so he took the third and accelerated into the outer lane. He almost missed her — even drew level with her — as she began slowing for a left turn, but he managed to slot in behind her, staying closer this time, but hanging back on the quieter stretches of road.

She rarely checked her mirror, but when she did, he had to resist a reflex to duck down behind the steering wheel; she evidently hadn't seen him, but nevertheless, he felt a bond between them. Around him, the city was building to its frantic morning pace, but it was as if he and Lauren were sealed in a bubble. There was excitement, hunger, that growling sexual urge which confused and thrilled him, but also a kind of reverence for her, a respect, which he imagined the predator feels for its prey.

She turned into a side street, and unease began to stir in the pit of his stomach. She took a left, up Gresford Avenue. This was too weird! He drew up behind a Nissan as Lauren's Fiesta slowed near the top of the hill and kept the motor running, just in case she carried on. She parked and let herself into the house.

Geri Simpson's house. *Oh, fuck!* Lauren lived with Geri Simpson. The fact stupefied him. Her car was parked outside. Still with his artwork adorning it. He felt a stab of icy fear. He waited five minutes, then walked from his car to the gate. A couple of schoolgirls gave him the eye as they passed him, hitching their bags higher on their shoulders and sticking out their tits. Under normal circumstances, he would flash them one of his looks, maybe drop them a wink, just out of habit — he was always on the lookout for new talent — but today he didn't want to draw attention, so he walked past the house without a backward glance. Over the brow of the hill, he slowed, carrying on a little distance until he calculated it was safe to turn back.

The front gate was open, and he slid through. The curtains were drawn at both bays, and after checking no one was about, he crept down the side of the house to the rear. There was a sudden clatter and he whirled, ready to run. A big tortoiseshell cat had knocked a plant pot off a low wooden bench under the kitchen window. It yowled and ran, flinging itself at the wall between Lauren's and the house next door, and disappearing from sight.

'Bloody cats!'

He heard it distinctly, coming from the open kitchen window. Keeping near the corner of the window frame, and moving slowly, ready to dart out of sight in a moment, he peeped over the edge, into the kitchen.

Lauren stood side on to him. He could see her in profile, standing at the table, pouring cereal into a bowl. It gave him a towering sense of power that he possessed this knowledge, but she knew nothing about him — not even that he was watching her at this moment.

She pulled out a chair and sat with her back to him. On impulse he stretched to his full height and leaned against the ledge, reaching forward to kiss the window. His eyes were open, and he watched her as his lips made contact with the freezing glass.

He would go to the front of the house and watch for a while. See if Simpson went out. When he was sure she was alone, he would knock at the front door and take it from there.

'I thought you were on a late today.' This was Geri. 'Couldn't you sleep?'

'Haven't been to bed.' Lauren's voice. 'I went back to the Samaritans last night.'

'I thought you'd already done your overnight stint.'

'. . . 'flu bug doing the rounds,' he heard Lauren say. 'I couldn't leave them in the lurch.'

He crouched below the window ledge, with his back to the wall, listening, forcing himself to be still and assess the risk that Lauren would tell her about his phone call. Simpson might make connections. Bloody Geri Simpson again!

'. . . fairly quiet, really,' he heard, tuning back into the conversation.

Lauren was lying, first saying she was on duty because of illness among the staff, now making out that nothing out of the ordinary had happened. It seemed that she didn't want to talk about his call to the Samaritans. Professionalism, was it? He'd never really believed all that shit about confidentiality — people liked having hold of information — the more shocking the better. They couldn't wait to pass it on. Look at Agnes, with her spirit guides — it was just a more novel line in street gossip. He gave her the juicy details; she passed them on them to her clients.

The conversation went back and forth for a couple of minutes. Lauren suggested spraying the acid-damaged car with primer to keep out the rust; Simpson said she'd get around to it. Did Lauren know her theory as to the culprit?

He heard the gaps, in which the silence was broken only by the clink of Lauren's spoon against her breakfast bowl. Things were strained between these two. Perhaps they didn't know each other well. Or they had argued.

Lauren's promise not to go to the police bought him some time, but she wasn't going to leave anything to chance. While they weren't communicating, he was safe, but they would doubtless talk again, and he knew from past experience that getting the answers you needed was only a matter of asking the right questions with the right inducements.

23

The atmosphere in the interview room was charged with emotion. DCI Thomas had called in WPC Dhar to act as witness and chaperone. She was unhappy with the duty and had even wondered aloud why a WDC couldn't be found. But to her credit, she had done her best to make Mrs Connelly comfortable, bringing her a cup of tea and sitting next to her to make the exchange less formal.

Mrs Connelly had demanded to speak to DCI Thomas, saying that she had information that would help the investigation. She had spent the first ten minutes complaining that she had not been kept informed. Thomas had taken her through the various stages: their interviews of friends and family; trying to establish Ryan's last few hours. Privately, he believed that Ryan had not been alone in the warehouse, but he had no proof, and until he did, he could not follow that line of enquiry.

DCI Thomas had a kind, rumpled face and curly hair, thinning a little, but still black. When he shaved, he saw a tired man he hardly recognized, and he wore an air of sadness about him from having seen too much tragedy in his work. He wished he could shake it off like some of his colleagues did, metamorphosing into husbands and dads and grandfathers, weekend gardeners and DIY hobbyists at the end of the working day, but he'd never acquired the knack.

He was a tactful, considerate man, and it pained him to have to talk to Mrs Connelly in the drab, functional setting of an interview room, but there was nowhere else that was suitable, his own office being a glass cubicle facing onto the open-plan incident room, where a whiteboard catalogued contacts, details of the death scene and photographs of Ryan's body.

Mrs Connelly listened with an intensity that disconcerted him. It was as if she expected him to give out encrypted information which, if only she could decipher it, would unravel the mystery of why her son had died so horribly.

'I can tell you,' he told Mrs Connelly, 'that we haven't closed our minds to any line of enquiry. We will keep this investigation open until we are satisfied as to precisely how your son died.'

'What does that mean?' she asked. 'That you haven't a clue what happened, or you can't make up your minds?'

'It means we're continuing with our investigation.'

'Until you're satisfied.'

'Yes.'

'And what about his family? What if we're not satisfied? What comeback have we got?'

'Why not wait until we've completed our enquiries, Mrs Connelly,' he said, gently. 'You might find—'

Mrs Connelly shook her head angrily. 'You trot out the official line and expect me to run along like a good girl. I want answers, Mr Thomas, not reassurances.'

'We don't have any answers yet.'

'I wouldn't worry,' she said, the bitterness and hurt making her voice harsh. 'The papers think they've got the lot. They've made up their minds. You know they're saying my Ryan was a druggy, a waster?' Her voice rose in her distress. 'A lad who was respected and loved by everyone who knew him. He spoke *out* against drugs!'

DCI Thomas had children of his own. He knew the worries and pressures of being a parent. He knew the difficulty in keeping them on the right path, and he sympathized with Mrs Connelly. She was a decent woman, trying to bring up her boys according to her moral and religious beliefs. Seventeen years of hard graft, of never taking the easy way out, destroyed in just a couple of weeks by press speculation.

'I know it's hard to take, Mrs Connelly,' he said. 'But there's nothing we can do to stop the press theorizing on the facts.'

'What facts?' she demanded angrily. '*You* don't even know how he died.'

'The bod— Ryan,' he corrected himself. 'Ryan was very badly burned.'

She shuddered and he paused for a moment, wondering if he should go on. 'It's been difficult to establish the cause of death.'

A creeping horror of realization showed in her face. 'You mean . . . Oh, dear God, no! You think Ryan could have been *alive* when—' She broke off, clasping a hand to her mouth.

DCI Thomas spoke gently. 'Do you need to take a break?'

'Don't you *dare* try and slide out of this,' she said.

'Mrs Connelly,' he protested, 'I'm not trying to—'

'Two weeks!' The exclamation was almost a plea. 'You've done nothing! And now his friend is missing.'

'We're treating Ryan's death very seriously,' he assured her.

'Two weeks,' she repeated. 'And you still don't know what he was doing in that godforsaken place.' Her face took on a look of anguish, as if she could see in her mind's eye the crumbling terrace where they had found her son.

'The initial lab reports show that he did have inhalants in his system.' He was expecting further results through any day, but he didn't tell her: mothers don't like to think of their children in terms of body fluids and forensic tests.

'I don't care *what* your bloody tests show. My Ryan *did not do drugs*! You should've talked to Frank. He knew. He *knew* what had happened. But you left it too late, and now he's gone as well.'

'We are doing everything we can to trace Frank Traynor,' Thomas said. 'But if he doesn't want to be found . . .'

Mrs Connelly snorted dismissively. 'You'll find him, like you found my Ryan, too late to save him. Too late for his poor mother. Too damned *late*, Inspector!'

He saw the pain behind her red-hot rage and wished there was something he could say which didn't sound like a platitude. But he knew there was nothing, so he brought her back to the reason for her visit.

'Mrs Connelly, you said you had information . . . If you have any idea of Frank's whereabouts—'

'Why d'you think I'm here?' she demanded. 'I've come to help. Much good it'll do the poor lad.'

Thomas glanced at WPC Dhar and saw that she was as puzzled as he.

'He's in a warehouse. In the east of the city.' She frowned, evidently trying to remember the details. 'It's flooded. There's a steel door. He's . . .' She swallowed, closing her eyes. 'He's badly disfigured. She said campfire or bonfire is significant.'

'She?'

Mrs Connelly opened her eyes and the room swam into focus. DCI Thomas looked tense. 'What?' she asked.

Thomas leaned forward. 'You said, "*She* said campfire was significant."'

'Or bonfire,' Mrs Connelly corrected. 'She wasn't sure which.'

'Mrs Connelly, who told you this?'

She blinked. 'Miss Hepple,' she said.

Mr Thomas jotted down the name. 'And she is . . . ?'

'A psychic.'

He looked up, a question half-formed on his lips.

'She makes contact with the spirit world,' Mrs Connelly said, as if he hadn't grasped her meaning.

Dhar shifted uncomfortably.

'I see,' Thomas said.

Mrs Connelly fixed him with a quiet, calm look that said she knew he didn't believe her, that she had expected it, but it didn't matter, because *she* believed. 'She's never been wrong, Inspector.'

'We'll look into it,' he said.

She didn't take her eyes off him. 'No,' she said, after a few moments. 'You won't. It doesn't matter to Frank now, he's beyond hurt and fear. He's safe in the arms of the Blessed Virgin, but it does matter to his mother. She has a right to know what's happened to her son.' She looked away, tears filling her eyes at her own loss. 'A right to give him a Christian burial.'

'I don't think it would be wise to upset Mrs Traynor with ideas like—'

She puffed air between her lips. 'It's not for me to tell her,' she said. 'That's your job. Find him. Find the poor boy's body, then tell his mother — explain to her why he had to die.'

The chief inspector took a breath. 'It's possible Frank is living rough, here or in London.'

'Do you really believe that?' She watched him in that strange, intense way for a second or two longer, then she gathered up her handbag and stood. 'I hope you'll be able to live with yourself when you're proved wrong.'

24

Geri dumped her briefcase and an armful of books in the hall and hung up her coat. It was Monday, the last week of half-term, and Year Nine lessons five and six had proved hard work: Valentine's Day was guaranteed to create tensions. The girls giggled and the boys pretended to ignore them. Notes were passed across the classroom. Geri had confiscated a couple, but she hadn't caught them all, and the swing from high spirits to bad temper among some of the children had sapped her.

She trudged down to the kitchen, with the intention of making coffee while she made up her mind if she could be bothered to cook something for dinner. The light was on. Nick sat at the table, reading the evening newspaper.

'Oh,' Geri said. Nick had been avoiding her since the previous Wednesday, almost a week of sleeping on the sofa in the sitting room, waiting until she had left for work before getting up. He was invariably out before she got home, so Geri had assumed he must be on the two-ten shift.

'I'm on twelve-hour nights this week,' Nick said, as if answering a question. 'I'll have to be out by half-six.'

Geri said, 'Oh,' again, then, aware that Nick was making an effort and that she wasn't meeting him halfway, she added, 'Have you eaten?'

'We could have an omelette, if you fancy.' He got up, folding the paper carefully.

'Sure.' Geri stepped towards the fridge.

'No.' He guided her to a chair. 'I'll do it.'

She watched as he chopped and fried onions and peppers, whisked eggs, grated cheese and buttered bread. He took care over it — the closest Nick would ever come to making an apology for having deliberately ruined their previous dinner together. His culinary repertoire was limited, but what he did, he did well. He had even mixed a green salad which he placed on the table with a flourish as they sat down to eat.

'I'll sort out the damage to your car when I've finished this stint of nights.' He muttered this with his back turned to her, but it was the first time he had referred to the acid attack on her car, and this, too, was a tacit admission that he could have behaved better the night it happened.

Geri felt a flood of emotion she couldn't quite understand; relief, but also hurt and resentment that it had taken him so long. She had spent the intervening days nervous each time she answered the doorbell or turned a corner. At night, she left school always in the company of one or two others, and she would have cried off youth-club duty on Thursday had it not been for Joe offering to pick her up and drop her off afterwards.

Her conversation with Nick was not easy or fluid, but it came as a huge relief to have one source of tension removed from the household, and Geri made an effort to be friendly. Relations with Lauren were still strained, though, and that troubled her.

She got up from the table with a sigh, and Nick caught her hand. 'We'll work it out,' he said, which made Geri feel even worse: while Nick was doing his best to repair some of the damage caused by the rows and silences of the past two weeks, she was worrying about what Lauren thought of her.

* * *

Nick took the bus to work. The horticultural research station where he worked was only a couple of miles out of the city centre, but the urban sprawl extended mainly southwards and he was heading north, so the built-up areas thinned rapidly, and with it the traffic.

Soon, all that was visible beyond the ghost of his own reflection was the string of orange lights along the road as it twisted up and out of the city. Sleet spattered the bus, sticking for a second or two, then melting in viscous streaks down the windows.

When they first met, he and Geri had been special. He had fascinated her — she admired his refusal to conform, his unpredictability. When had it started, this decline? They had been close; he understood her, took care of her when her mother died, protected her from shocks, from anything — anyone — who might harm her.

In their final year, anything had seemed possible — until the results were posted and he lost his chance of a job at ICI. He'd been awarded an ordinary degree. He had never been *ordinary* in his life! She had tried to comfort him, but how could she with her 2:1 honours?

He had seen something new in her eyes in the weeks that followed. He was no longer exceptional, wild, unconventional. He was *ordinary*.

He had seen that look each time he had taken a new job: meat packer; security guard, petrol station clerk, tele-sales rep — horticultural research technician? Perhaps not then. He thought perhaps he had seen something else in her eyes then, which was why he had stuck this job for so much longer than any of the others. What had he seen? A faint glimmer of hope in her eyes, perhaps.

But he sensed that change had come too late. She was distant, vague; he felt as if he was constantly intruding on her thoughts.

We'll work it out, he had said, and she had looked at him as if to say, 'Work *what* out?'

They had gone too far, he and Geri; they wouldn't come out of this together.

* * *

Geri worked until 8 p.m. Lauren still hadn't come home, and the silence in the house oppressed her. She found herself listening to every creak and groan of the old place, imagining bumps and footfalls and softly closing doors.

'Sod it!' she muttered, marking the last book on the pile, then went upstairs and got changed into jeans and a sweater. She would go for a brisk walk, maybe try to find Adèle — see if she'd had any word on Frank.

She walked fast, blinking against the keen wind blowing sleet into her face, using the exercise to put distance between her and the empty house, loud with accusing silence. But she was also trying to escape the clamouring voices in her head: Frank, missing, lonely, afraid, each passing day making her more anxious for his safety; Lauren, evasive, withdrawn; her own confused feelings about Nick — at least he had broken his silence, but could they really work it out, as he'd said?

Dread settled like a solid mass in the pit of her stomach. It had been two years since their relationship had been on an even keel.

She stopped, breathless and freezing. When she had finally admitted to herself that her mother was dying, she had experienced a terrible ambivalence: desperately wanting and needing her, while yearning for her release. Although she couldn't admit it to herself at the time, nor for months and years after, she had begun gently breaking the bonds between them, quietly taking her leave of her mother long before her physical death.

Hadn't she begun this same distancing process with Nick over the past few months? Nick had sensed it too. Otherwise, why had he made sporadic attempts at romance:

the cosy meals for two; candlelight and flowers? She pushed the thought away. She could not think about life without Nick — not now, not in the middle of all this.

Instead, she looked about her and took in her surroundings. She had skirted the edge of town and ended up on the east side; it would be pointless going back into the city centre at this hour — Adèle rarely worked past seven o'clock and it was now eight fifteen. She was five minutes' walk from the youth club; there was still time to talk to a few people. If she could just get the kids to *talk*.

Two of the younger girls hurried over, smiling when they saw Geri. They wanted to show off their glitter nail polish and tell her about the valentine cards they had received. Valentine's Day! Usually, Nick bought her flowers and sent her the biggest, tackiest card he could find. So that was why he'd had a sudden change of heart — guilt had driven him to making the small concession of rousing himself from his sulk and cooking her an omelette.

It was an unkind thought, but Nick had put her through the silent treatment for six days, and although she didn't want to prolong the argument, she couldn't simply forget what she had gone through this last week.

'Well, look what the wind blew in,' Joe said. 'We don't often see you on a Monday, Miss Simpson.' He always used her surname when kids were close by — children often had difficulty making the distinction between the rules at school and the informality of the youth club, so it was easier to stick with her formal title. He grinned over at Geri and she returned the smile, grateful, almost, for the friendly contact. S Club 7 were blasting out "Bring It All Back" with unrelenting cheerfulness on the jukebox.

'I . . . was just passing,' she said, feeling suddenly awkward.

'Well, you're very welcome.'

His North-East accent added warmth to his words, and Geri felt tears prick at the back of her eyes. *Ridiculous!* she told herself. *Stop this!*

'Time to start the washing-up, is it?' she joked, struggling out of her overcoat.

'Funny you should say that . . .' He tossed her a tea towel and she caught it with one hand, the other still tangled in the sleeve of her coat. Mari and another girl stood at the kitchen counter, ogling her.

'What's the matter, Mari?' Geri asked. 'Never seen a teacher in jeans before?'

Mari blushed. 'Miss, yeah.' But she seemed doubtful, nevertheless. She offered to help with the washing-up, which Geri took to be penance for her rudeness.

'Has Vince been in?'

Joe jerked his head in the direction of the café area, beyond Geri's line of sight. 'Been interviewing suspects all night.'

'He's trying to help, Joe,' Geri said.

'Aye, so you keep saying. Me, I'm not so sure.' Joe walked away and entered into a boisterous exchange with a group of boys at the jukebox. A moment later, "Careless Whisper" began playing, and there was a burst of laughter from the boys. Joe threw Geri a mischievous grin, but she shook her head in disapproval.

The atmosphere in the club was edgy; there was a charge of nervous energy, perhaps even of defiance. The last time Vince had come in to talk to them, many of the boys and girls — those Geri thought of as Baz's followers — had left, but tonight, it seemed they would not be driven out. Geri felt they were showing solidarity. Was it for each other? For Joe? She couldn't say. Perhaps for Frank. Perhaps they really did want to help find him.

She sat with a group from her form and chatted — about valentine cards mostly — it seemed that some of the lads had borrowed heavily from Romeo and Juliet in their romantic scribblings.

'Beats "Roses are red, violets are blue",' Geri commented.

This prompted a competition for the silliest rhyme. Liam topped the others with, 'So is your nose, but you *have* got the 'flu.'

As the laughter and groans of protest died down, a quiet voice asserted itself.

'You're likely to snuff it, if you sniff too much glue.'

Geri turned. 'Barry.' *Callous, cold-hearted bastard!*

'Miss Simpson.' When he said her name, it always sounded like insolence.

'Nobody's laughing,' Geri said.

He gave her one of his dead-eyed stares. 'Who says I'm joking? I'm delivering an important message, Miss Simpson.' He raised an admonishing finger at the subdued group around the table. 'Don't do drugs.' Carl glared angrily at him, but he looked away after a moment or two.

During the last week, Geri had seen Barry saunter around school like some New York gangster. Long overcoat, dark glasses, that arrogant swagger. He was playing a part — Geri had directed enough theatre to see that — and he was hamming it up. The trouble was, the children, at least the younger ones, couldn't see through his little act. For them, Barry Mandel was the man.

'Go home, Barry,' she said, trying to quell the rage fizzing through her bloodstream. 'You're not wanted here.'

He raised both eyebrows. 'I don't think that's unanimous,' he said.

He was right, she realized, and the thought depressed her: not all of the children wanted rid of him. There seemed to be a division between those who despised Barry, and those who feared, or even respected him.

From the corner of her eye, Geri saw a movement: one of the boys trying to sneak past unnoticed, had brushed against the coat rack, knocking her coat to the floor.

'Leaving so soon?' Barry said.

The boy froze. Geri glanced at him, a sturdy-looking lad with a skinhead haircut. She did a double take. '*Jay?*' He had been off school for the remainder of the previous week — a suspension, in all but name.

'Barely recognizable, is he?'

‘What on earth possessed you?’ Geri demanded. His blond curls had been cut off, his head shaved to the bone.

‘Tell Miss Simpson what possessed you, Jay,’ Barry said.

‘Lay off, Baz.’ Joe had come over from the jukebox and stood at the edge of the group.

Barry was about to say something else when Joe spoke again. ‘Lay off and piss off.’

Jay stood between the two of them, hanging his head. Barry seemed to consider, then his eyes flickered in the direction of Vince. Joe had replaced the overhead strip lights in the café area with low-wattage coloured bulbs and glass shades, and the lighting in that part of the room was murky, but when Vince stood, anticipating trouble, he was hard to miss.

Geri took a step forward, and Baz recoiled, almost jumping back in an exaggerated theatrical movement.

‘Watch it,’ he warned. ‘We’ve got a police witness this time.’

Geri flushed angrily. ‘You’re a bad influence, Barry,’ she said. ‘You’re banned. I don’t want to see your face in here again — ever.’

Baz looked from Geri to Joe, then across to Vince, who took a step forward. Baz laughed and turned away. ‘Coming, Jay?’ he said over his shoulder.

For one awful moment, Geri thought that she would see a replay of the last time Frank had been into the club, and she expected Jay to shuffle meekly after him. Then Jay threw a frightened look in Joe’s direction. Joe stepped up and clasped one hand on the back of the boy’s neck.

‘He’s staying,’ Joe said.

Barry turned back. ‘Funny,’ he said, drawing down the corners of his mouth. ‘A minute ago, I thought he was leaving.’ He shrugged and continued to the door. ‘Suit yourself.’

While Vince bent to pick up her coat, Geri looked over at Joe. Both he and Jay were staring at the door as if they could see Barry’s retreating figure through it. Joe seemed to register her curiosity and broke into a rueful smile, and Geri felt the tension flow out of her. It was a relief to know that she wasn't the only one Baz had such a profound effect upon. She returned Joe's smile.

'Why *did* you shave your head?' Geri asked Jay, lowering her voice. 'You know you'll be suspended as soon as you go in tomorrow.'

Jay shrugged and flushed right into the pale, smooth skin of his naked scalp. He kept his gaze on the floor, but Geri thought his eyelashes were wet.

'Ne'er mind,' Joe said, running his hand over the boy's shining pate. 'It'll soon grow.'

25

The music was an insistent pulse, a throb of pure sexual energy. Vince moved a little to the rhythm, scanning the dance floor as he took a pull on his beer, eyeing the talent. He had been here an hour and the music, the mindless power of the beat, had worked its charm; this was better than booze, better than drugs for euphoric oblivion.

At a diagonal he noticed somebody watching him: beautiful body, red Lycra top and leather pants, platinum hair. Vince smiled, nodded in the direction of the dance floor. The leather pants walked towards him, already moving to the insinuating beat of the music. They met halfway. Those eyes! Green, luminous, long-lashed.

'You're gorgeous,' Vince said, bringing his mouth close to one small, delicately furzed earlobe. A nod — compliment accepted — no more than expected.

'And you're Vince.' A smile at Vince's surprise. 'Saw you in here the other night. I've had my eye on you.'

Vince wasn't sure how to take this. 'And you are?' he asked, cursing himself for sounding like a copper.

'Chris.' The name was mouthed, finished with a pout that made Vince want to kiss those lips.

They danced. A full hour of substitute sex.

‘I need food,’ Chris said, in a lull between tracks.

‘Let’s find somewhere,’ Vince said. ‘Or we could go back to my place.’ He was astounded at his own audacity, but knew he wanted more than vicarious sex with this fabulous creature.

The green eyes shone from beneath the lashes, amused. Vince’s heart skipped a beat. ‘Your place, then.’

They walked to the door together and Chris’s arm slipped around Vince’s waist. Vince forgot Ryan, forgot Frank, right now, there was only this feeling, and the feeling was fine.

The steps up from the club were narrow and Vince went ahead, stepping up onto the cobbles and gratefully breathing fresh cold air.

‘Oh, *shit*!’ DS Garvey and a few of his cronies. Vince turned to go back down the steps, but his dancing partner barred the way.

‘Oy, Vince!’ They had seen him.

He turned to face them, trying to look unconcerned.

‘Wouldn’t go in there, mate,’ Garvey said. ‘It’s full of queers.’

Chris stood beside him now, looking puzzled. ‘Mates of yours?’ he asked.

Garvey was drunk, and his reactions were slow. He looked at the two men, focusing with some difficulty on Chris’s hand, which was now resting on Vince’s shoulder. There was a silence, in which the cogs and wheels of his sodden brain could be seen turning, then a broad, uneven grin spread over his face.

‘Bloody hell, Vince!’

Vince stared stupidly at his colleagues. He felt sick and cold to the very core of his being. All he had worked for, his elaborate efforts to keep his personal life private, wiped out in an instant. He had always been so careful, checking and double-checking when entering or leaving a club or a gay bar, making sure there were no patrols about, people who might know him. But Chris was special, wasn’t he? Instant pyrotechnics. Christ! he thought savagely, how special can a fuck be?

He shrugged Chris's hand from his shoulder, reading the end of his career in the gleeful look on Garvey's face. The end of twelve years' hard graft. What kind of respect could he command when his team were sniggering at him behind their hands?

'Have a nice night, girls,' Garvey said. His mates dragged him away. 'Don't do anything I wouldn't do.' This brought guffaws from the others.

'Tourists!' Chris exclaimed. He turned to face Vince, and there was a moment of awful realization. 'Oh, God! You poor bastard — you've just been outed, haven't you?'

Vince stared after Garvey. One of his mates was humping a bollard while the others cheered him on.

'Ey, mate!' Garvey shouted.

Chris looked at Vince and rolled his eyes.

'You into bondage?' A few people turned to see who the drunk was talking to.

'Come on,' Chris said, taking Vince by the elbow. 'Ignore the twat.' Vince lifted his arm, breaking his grip.

''S your lucky day,' Garvey bellowed. 'Ask him to get the handcuffs out.' As if on cue, all five men dipped into their trouser pockets, brought out a set of keys and jangled them in unison, laughing like they had made some hysterically funny joke.

Chris stared at him. 'You're a copper?' he said.

Vince turned abruptly and started walking. He could barely feel his limbs and one or twice he stumbled. He got as far as the high street and then he ran. He ran until his lungs and throat burned and his legs began to cramp. When he stopped, he was in among the run-down warehouses and empty mills on the east side of the city. He leaned against a wall and threw up.

* * *

Pale sunlight, filtered by a high layer of cloud, gave a metallic cast to the faces of Metropolitan Police officers converging on the four-storey building. It was cold, and a sharp wind whipped up dust-devils on the road.

Their target was Anthony Barton-Willis, who owned the third-floor loft apartment in Chelsea. He was dealing cocaine and heroin to children as young as twelve. But this was no backstreet dealer — Barton-Willis supplied quality to quality; his customers were monied, and his parties were notorious throughout the city.

Vince had gone to the back of the building, as instructed, and climbed the fire escape, creeping past the long, plate-glass window and positioning himself just above the doorway. His task was to stop anyone going up onto the flat roof.

Seconds later, all hell broke loose. Screams tore the air, sounds of fighting. A small wooden casket was thrown through the window, showering glass onto the two officers stationed at the foot of the fire escape. The casket shattered on the ground, sending up a puff of white powder.

A man came out onto the fire escape. He ran down the steps, taking the last few at a leap, and was tackled to the ground, beads of glass and bright red blood mingled on the grey flags as he fought the arresting officers.

There was a movement to his left and Vince turned. A window swung open at the corner of the building and a boy climbed out. Standing on the ledge, he reached across to the drainpipe.

'Don't do it!' Vince yelled. 'You'll kill yourself!'

The boy laughed, slipped, screamed, grabbed the drainpipe with hands, knees and feet and laughed again. He was out of reach of the fire escape, but Vince shadowed him as he shinned up the drainpipe with the agility of a squirrel. He gained the rooftop in half a minute and ran to the edge.

Vince yelled, holding up his hand, and the boy turned, giggling. His pupils were dilated, and his eyes danced back and forth, as if he could see something flickering at the edges of his vision.

'You look a bit tense, Vinnie.' He hopped onto the low ridge at the extreme edge of the rooftop, his arms spread wide. 'A bit on edge.'

Vince recognized him. A sweat broke out on his forehead, thinking about the terrible consequences of a wrong move — a wrong word. 'Kyle,' he said. 'Come down.' His voice was no more than a croak.

'Why would I want to come down? I'm high, man! Try it, you'll buy it. I'm high as the Eye, sky-scraper high — sky-high. I can *fly*!' He pirouetted, wobbled, pinwheeled his arms and somehow regained his balance, then walked back along the ridge the way he had come.

'Come down? It would be a come-down if I came down now. If I do, my dad'll kill me. I'll be grounded for good. Grounded for *bad*. You know Dad, Vince — he's the man who kills the thrills when you pop the pills.' He babbled on non-stop, some of it making sense, some not.

'Just step off the ridge. We'll talk about it. I promise, I'll do what I can to help you.'

The boy's eyes changed, from hazel to icy blue. 'You queer or something? Hey mate!' he called down to the officers below. 'He's a fag. An arse bandit!'

Vince took a step forward, raising his hands to quiet the boy.

'Hey! Vince is gay!'

'Stop it!' Vince warned. 'Stop this, Kyle.'

'Stop it!' the boy mimicked, lisping. 'Stop it, I like it.'

Vince took one more step and pushed. One light tap, no more than a fingertip's pressure.

The boy that was no longer Kyle flailed, trying to take hold of Vince, but Vince stood back. His mouth opened in a silent scream, and then he fell — no sound, then the dull thud of impact.

Vince woke with a shout. His heart was hammering. It was pitch-dark, but he could still see the look of horror on the boy's face as he gave him the gentle tap that sent him into oblivion. It was look on the face of the boy at the railway station, the same look on the face of the boy Mayhew had roughed up — and the boy who had screamed abuse after him from the station car park. Horror and fear and hate all rolled into one.

* * *

He waited for her. All night, he waited. Watching the moon, reflected from the slate of the roofs opposite, gleaming like fish-scales. He noted its passage over the sleeping houses, remained watchful as its pale blue light slipped over the rooftops and was lost to darkness. Still Lauren does not come.

It's Ryan he thinks about, mostly. He wishes he had taken photographs — maybe even a video. Next time . . . The thought startles him and he sits for several minutes, breathing hard, his nostrils flared, nausea threatening and then subsiding again.

After a few short minutes the idea has become an embryonic plan. *Next time* . . . Such potent words. *Next time* he'll find somewhere quiet, isolated where they'll have time to . . . To what? To develop a relationship that isn't dependent on a chemical cosh. *Next time.* He savours the notion that there will be a next time, and the thought returns unbidden at unexpected moments during the day.

He sees Ryan on his knees, tears coursing down his face and that is the turn-on: the fact that he doesn't want to do it, but he's doing it anyway. It isn't just the sex — he can have that any night of the week with the lads on the station, or casual pick-ups in the bars and night clubs in the city centre.

He doesn't want consensual sex. It's *submission* he wants. The feeling of superhuman power he experienced as he stood over Ryan. That was better than sex.

26

Dean switched the cricket stump from his right to his left hand to wipe his palm on his trousers. He had waited all day for this, stealing the stump during PE and hiding it in his locker, avoiding Miss Simpson's eye at registration, unable to bear her concern for him.

Baz often went home across the field; he would meet one of his carriers, reclaim his stash and do a bit of dealing if there were any punters hanging around at the back of the sub-station. Its distance from the main building, and its secluded position facing onto the blank walls of the PE block, made it a safe meeting point.

He tensed: Baz was coming! He could hear his long, loping stride on the wet grass. Dean took the stump in a two-handed grip. First the shins, then the head. His heart thudded dully, and he was sweating, despite the thin rain soaking through his jacket. The hole in his tooth gave sharp, stabbing reminders of its presence each time he sucked in air.

He crouched at the side of the low building, out of sight. On the other side of the fence he heard voices — two women — and the rattle of pram wheels.

'What you doin', man?'

Beefy, one of the Year Tens — Dean didn't know his real name — had come around the side of the sub-station.

'Fuck off, Beefy. This's got nothing to do with you, right?'

'If you're after Baz, it bloody has.'

Dean eyed him with sullen dislike, and Beefy laughed, astonished. 'You are, aren't you? Get real! Size of you, he'll mash you to a pulp!' He made a grab at Dean's arm, but Dean pulled free, breaking cover, rushing at Baz and swinging the cricket stump.

Baz's eyes widened. His mouth dropped open, then he fell, yelling as Dean made contact with his knee.

'Don't be stupid, Dean,' Beefy shouted, keeping out of range of the flailing stump.

Dean laid into Baz. Arms, body, back, screaming all the time: 'Bastard! Murdering bloody bastard!'

Baz rolled back and forth, using his arms to protect his face and head. 'Get him off me!' he yelled.

Beefy lunged and caught Dean's weapon arm, twisting the cricket stump from his hand. A small group of boys had already gathered, and now more were running from all over the field, slipping back from the street into the school grounds between broken railings, running across from the top gate to get a better look.

As Baz began to get up, Dean threw himself at him, his fists bunched. Baz fell back, winded.

'Fight . . . fight . . . fight . . . fight!' The chant started slowly, gathering pace as more and more joined the crowd. 'Fight-fight-fight-fight!'

Dean was crying, blinded by tears, throwing punches wildly, but one or two made contact, and Baz's nose dripped blood. Baz suddenly seemed to collect himself and lashed out with a back-handed slap that sent Dean tumbling off him.

Baz struggled to his feet, still winded by his fall. His coat flapped about him, muddied and wet, tangling about his legs. The chants of 'fight-fight-fight' were quieter now, more speculative, as the crowd, mainly boys, watched to see what would happen. Dean dived at him, knocking him over, and the crowd yelled their excitement.

'I'll throttle you, you little bastard,' Baz gasped.

The boys whooped and whistled their approval, then the sudden, sharp trill of a sports whistle cut through the noise, and someone shouted, 'Teacher!'

The majority of spectators ran off, heading for the fence, or the top gate, leaving only a few of the more brazen, who stood a little way off, their hands in their pockets.

'It's Killer,' someone muttered.

Mr Killroy, the PE teacher, stormed over to the two boys, ludicrously mismatched in size, who were still brawling on the mud on the pitch. 'What the hell are you two playing at?' he demanded.

Baz got the better of Dean and held him face down on the grass, while Dean, crying and struggling, tried to kick him.

'He went ape!' Baz exclaimed. 'He's off his head!'

'You given him summat, have you?' Killroy said, seizing Dean by the collar of his jacket and setting him on his feet. He continued to struggle until Killroy gave him a shake that rattled his teeth. 'Stand still, lad,' Killroy warned him.

Baz wiped his nose with the back of his hand. He was panting, but his control was returning. 'Given him something?' he repeated, glancing quickly at Beefy, who wormed his way to the back of the loose knot of onlookers and slipped out of sight behind the sub-station.

'Empty your pockets!' Killroy ordered.

'Oh, *what*?' Baz shook his head in exasperation. '*He* went for *me*!'

'Aye,' Killroy said. 'And we know why.'

'I'll *kill* him!' Dean yelled, making a futile lunge for Baz.

'Inside,' Killroy said. 'And walk ahead of me, where I can see what you're up to.' He glared at the other boys. 'You lot — disappear.' They did, reluctantly, but without complaint, because Killroy picked the teams, and football was about all that inspired the remaining spectators of this particular sport.

Besides which, Killer Killroy wasn't past inflicting a bruises-in-footie training that you couldn't complain about without looking like a girl.

Killroy watched Baz like a hawk to make sure he didn't drop anything on the way back into school. They passed some staff, on their way out at the end of the day, Geri among them. Baz, limping and bloody, was trying to look moody, but actually seemed upset. Dean had stopped crying, but struggled ineffectually, his feet barely touching the ground, as Mr Killroy frogmarched him into the building.

Geri hurriedly finished packing her briefcase into the boot of her car and then followed them inside, catching up with them at the headmaster's office.

'What happened?' she asked.

'That's what we're about to find out, eh, lads?' Killroy knocked at the door and opened it without waiting for a reply. He shoved Baz ahead of him, still holding Dean firmly by the collar. Geri heard Mr Ratchford exclaim, and then Killroy was closing the door on her. She stopped him.

'Dean is in my form,' she said firmly.

Killroy lowered Dean to the floor, letting go of his jacket cautiously, ready to seize hold of him again if he made a move for Baz. Geri edged around the back of the group and slipped Dean a couple of tissues. He dried his eyes and blew his nose while Mr Killroy gave his account of what had happened.

'Well?' Mr Ratchford said. 'Barry?'

Baz dabbed his nose carefully with a handkerchief. 'We were messing about,' he said coolly. 'It got a bit out of hand.'

Dean clenched his fists and made a slight movement which was quickly checked by Killroy.

'Dean?'

Dean scowled at the floor and said nothing.

'This one,' Killroy said, tapping Dean on the crown of his head, 'was threatening to kill Mandel, here.'

'What have you got to say?' Ratchford asked.

Dean merely hunched himself smaller, refusing to answer.

'What were you doing on the top field?' Ratchford asked Baz. 'The front entrance is your quickest way home.'

Baz shrugged. 'It was such a lovely evening, I fancied a walk.'

'It's pi— pouring down out there!' Killroy objected. 'He was off up to the 'leccy station. There's a gap in the fence up there, and plenty of cover, eh, Barry?'

'You have a suspicious mind, Mr Killroy.'

Ratchford sighed. 'If he has, it's not without cause, Barry,' he said. He seemed to consider for a moment. 'You say you were just taking a walk?'

Baz tilted his head in acknowledgement.

'Then you won't mind emptying your pockets.'

Baz met him eye to eye. 'In principle, yeah, I mind, Mr Ratchford.' He seemed to savour the headmaster's irritation, then added, 'But if it'll clear the air . . .' He began unloading his belongings onto the headmaster's desk.

'And the rest,' Killroy said.

Baz looked at him in mock surprise, and Killroy dragged open the skirt of his coat, feeling in the deep pockets of the lining. Baz submitted to the search without comment, but he gave Killroy an icy stare as he stood back, angry and disappointed at having found nothing.

'What was the fight about?' Ratchford repeated. 'Who started it?'

There was a pause, then Baz said, 'Like I told Mr Killroy, we were messing about — right, Dean?'

'Don't talk rubbish!' Killroy exclaimed. 'You're twice his size and look at the state of you.'

Baz gave a rueful grin. 'David and Goliath, eh, Dean?'

'Well, Dean?' Ratchford demanded sharply.

'Yeah,' Dean said, staring straight ahead, gritting his teeth. 'It just went a bit far.'

They all knew it was a lie, and Dean put no effort in to trying to convince the adults in the room — Geri could see it that was all he could do just to keep from going for Baz again.

Mr Ratchford turned his full attention on Dean. 'I know you've been through a lot this last two weeks,' he said. 'And I sympathize. We all do. But your mother's got enough to deal with, enough to worry about, without you adding to her problems.'

Dean nodded, blinking and chewing at the side of his cheek.

'I want you to shake hands and settle your differences.'

Dean's head snapped up so fast that Geri heard his neck crack. He stared at Ratchford, then at Baz. Baz looked away.

'Dean?'

'Forget it.' He continued staring at Baz.

'You'll do as you're told.'

He turned back to Ratchford. 'No way.'

Ratchford was shocked. 'I *beg* your pardon?'

'You can suspend me, if you like. I'm not shaking his hand.'

'Sir, it doesn't matter.' There was a note of pleading in Baz's voice.

'Don't do me no favours,' Dean snarled. Killroy put a steadying hand on his shoulder.

Ratchford could see he wouldn't win this one. 'Very well,' he said. 'You'd better go home and think this over. I'll be in touch with your parents. Miss Simpson—'

'I'll take him home,' Geri offered, anxious to get him out of harm's way before he said anything that would really enrage Mr Ratchford.

* * *

'Why did he stand up for you, Dean?' Geri asked.

'Nobody asked him to.'

'That's not what I asked.'

They were easing out onto the main road; Dean was slumped in the passenger seat, wet and muddy, shivering with cold and suppressed rage.

He didn't reply, and she tried again. 'Is it because he feels guilty?'

'He should do.'

'About Ryan?'

No answer.

'Or about drugs in general?'

Dean stirred but didn't reply. He was evidently uncomfortable refusing to answer her questions, but for his own reasons, he didn't want to tell her what he knew.

Geri's frustration at his sullen refusal to talk to her was tempered with an intense sympathy for him. Dean had been in her form since he first came up to senior school, in Year Seven. That was when she was a newly qualified teacher, so they had been newcomers together, had learned the ropes together, and since Ryan's death, she felt an extra responsibility for the boy.

'There's a lot of rumours going around about what happened the Saturday Ryan disappeared,' she began again.

'He never did drugs, right? Never.'

'No,' Geri said. 'I don't believe he did.' He turned to look at her, but glanced quickly away, blinking back tears, when she took her eyes off the road for an instant to look at him. 'But the fact is, Ryan was found in that house surrounded by solvents,' she went on.

He sighed.

'If you know something about that, Dean, you should tell someone. You shouldn't try to deal with it yourself.'

He sat stony-faced, emanating fury and despair in equal measure, but she couldn't get another word out of him. He must have some reason for thinking that Barry Mandel had caused Ryan's death, but exasperated though she was by his refusal to talk to her, she couldn't feel anything but pity for Dean.

He went straight upstairs when his mother opened the door, walking past her without even acknowledging her and leaving Geri to explain why she was there.

* * *

Dean went to his bedroom and opened and closed the door, then crept back along the landing to listen. If he'd done what he set out to do, he'd be in the cop shop by now, not sitting at the top of the stairs, waiting to see what punishment he'd get for giving that bastard Baz a bloody nose.

He quivered with impotent rage. 'I should've kicked his head in,' he whispered. 'Should've kicked his bastard head in.' He ran back to his room and slammed the door, clenching his fists and punching the wall until four round dabs of blood appeared on his knuckles.

He drove his thumbs into his eyes until green spots danced on the back of his eyelids and he felt faint. He went through the fight, from the first badly aimed blow with the cricket stump, to his pathetic attempts to pummel Baz with his fists. What made him think he could finish Baz with his fists? He was too big, too strong.

He heard the front door close, and then the sound of Miss Simpson's car firing up. His mother called, and Dean jumped up and quickly dragged the chest of drawers — Ryan's chest of drawers — in front of the door. Then he remembered. He opened each drawer in turn, ignoring his mother's calls, searching under the T-shirts and jeans, sweatshirts and combat trousers. He finally found it in the bottom drawer: Ryan's fishing knife in its leather sheath. He slid it out and held it up, catching the finely ground cutting edge in the lamplight.

His mother knocked softly at the door and tried the handle. 'Dean,' she said. 'It's all right, love. I just want to talk to you.'

Dean rolled up his sleeve and drew the blade across the meagre flesh of his forearm, making a neat, diagonal slash. He bled, while his mother wept outside the door.

* * *

Geri couldn't bear to go home to an empty house. It was Lauren's day off, and she had gone out. By now, Nick would be on his way to work. Geri went into the city centre, intending to get a bite to eat and then go to the theatre and see a play. Outside the theatre, she heard the plaintive call, 'Buy a *Big Issue*, help the homeless.'

'Adèle?' She was standing outside the main foyer, shuffling from one foot to the other, looking nervy and excitable.

Geri walked over. 'What are you doing here? Why aren't you at your usual pitch?' she asked.

Adèle glanced past her, her eyes darting around the square. 'Can't talk,' she said.

'Adèle . . .'

'I'm busy, right.'

'You look ill — is something wrong?'

Adèle seemed to flinch at the suggestion. 'No,' she said, her anxiety giving the lie to her words. 'A bit a trouble with the Taxman, that's all.' She gave a nervous smile.

Geri had read somewhere that *Big Issue* vendors were responsible for their own tax affairs, but she had always thought it was a joke — an ironic comment on their earnings. 'Look, Adèle, if there's anything I can do . . . D'you need money?' She reached into her handbag, but Adèle grabbed her hand and pushed it away.

'No, don't,' she begged.

Geri caught herself glancing about in the same furtive way. 'You can't talk here, right?'

'Right.'

'Are you still at the shelter?'

'Yeah, yeah . . . All right?' She hopped about on the balls of her feet.

'I'll be in touch, then.'

Adèle's relief at her going was palpable, and Geri spent much of the first act of the play worrying about it. Was she being watched? She hadn't wanted Geri to get her purse out — was that because she was afraid Geri would become a target? Adèle said she hated hostels, that they were full of weirdos and psychos . . . and drugs. Had Geri put her in danger by persuading her to ask questions on the street? It was bad enough for her, and she could go home and lock her door against the lunatic who had poured acid over her car. Adèle had nowhere to retreat, safe from threat.

Unable to contain herself, Geri stood up, excusing herself to an irritated row of people. She hurried outside, but Adèle had gone.

27

Geri gave up on sleep at around five a.m. and was showered and dressed by the time Nick got home from his night shift. She prepared breakfast for him, then, at a loss for something to do, decided to mend the tear in the lining of her coat. The small rip along the seam had become a gaping hole, and she wouldn't be able to afford a new one before the next January sales.

She sat at the kitchen table and spread the coat out, lining-side up. With Radio 4's *Today* programme providing discreet background noise, she smoothed the lining but it wouldn't lie flat. She slid the skirt of the coat onto the table, running her hands over the silk.

'That's funny,' she muttered.

Nick grunted from behind his newspaper.

There was a lump in the bottom seam. Small, shaped like a cigar stub. She worked it up to the hole in the lining between her finger and thumb.

'Oh, shit,' she breathed.

Nick flicked down one corner of his paper. 'Shit is right! Where d'you get that?'

'It was . . .' She indicated her coat, too bewildered to speak for the moment.

He took the package from her and broke it open.

'What the hell are you doing?' Geri demanded angrily.

He sniffed the fibrous contents of the package. 'That's good-quality hash you've got there, Ger. Somebody out there likes you.'

She took the pellet of hash from his hand. 'Somebody out there is trying to get me in serious trouble,' she corrected. 'If this had been found on me . . .' She tried to think how it could have got there. She kept her coat locked in her stock-room at school.

Oh, God. The youth club! She remembered Jay brushing past the coat rack on Monday night, her coat falling to the floor. Baz! *We've got a police witness,* he'd said. If Joe hadn't seen him off, would he have persuaded Vince to search her coat lining? She shivered, remembering that Vince had picked the coat up from the floor.

'Bastard! The vindictive bloody bastard!' She squeezed the pellet in her hand and ran upstairs.

'Whoa!' Nick called, racing after her, grabbing her hand. She twisted free and ran to the bathroom. The pellet wouldn't flush.

'Are you crazy?' he demanded, pulling her away from the toilet cistern. 'You're flushing fifty quid's worth of MJ down the bog!'

She shoved him hard, and he cracked his elbow on the towel rail.

'Bloody hell!'

She tore off a strip of toilet paper and stuffed it down the pan, flushing again. This time it went.

'What the fuck?'

She rounded angrily on Nick. 'If I'm found with drugs on me, after the hell I've raised over Barry Mandel, I will — no question about it — *will* lose my job.'

Nick stared at her for a few seconds before turning away. 'You're paranoid,' he said. 'I mean you are losing it completely.'

28

A fine drizzle was falling. It coated DCI Thomas's hair like a thin net as he stood shivering outside a canal-side warehouse. Red and blue lights shimmered through the mist of rain. Police, fire service.

'They've declared the building safe,' DS Garvey informed him. 'The pathologist is in there now.'

'Drayton?' Thomas asked. Garvey nodded. Drayton had performed the PM on Ryan Connelly. 'How sure are we it's Frank?'

'He's wearing a trench coat, and he's got one of those death's-head badges on the lapel.'

'As per his parents' description,' Thomas added, his heart sinking. 'I suppose we'll have to get suited up.'

'The forensics team gave me a couple of spares. I've got them in the boot of the car.'

'Who's the informant?' Thomas asked.

'Security firm. New bloke, a bit keen, by all accounts. Mostly, they don't much bother with these properties — they're falling down anyway. The guards are told to concentrate on the occupied premises. He found a side door open and went to investigate.' He nodded in the direction of one of the division cars. A pale shocked face stared out at them.

'Poor sod,' Thomas commented. 'Where's these suits, then?'

'Mr Drayton said to wait till he gave the word, Boss.'

'Did he?' Thomas strode to Garvey's car and pulled a thin white overall from the boot. He sighed. 'I feel like Andy Pandy in these things,' he said, sitting on the boot rim to get his feet into the leg holes.

Garvey took the second suit. 'It's a bit wet underfoot, at least on the ground floor, so . . .'

'Save the overshoes for indoors. Right,' Thomas said. He went ahead of Garvey, nodding to the PC guarding the mesh gate into the passage at the side of the warehouse. He used a flashlight to pick a safe course through the rubbish and slime in the narrow passage. The beam picked out the blackened and rotting corpse of a rat, and Thomas gave an utterance of disgust.

'How the hell did that get there?' he demanded.

Garvey peered over his shoulder. 'Ran out after the fire?' he suggested.

They went inside, Thomas first, stepping too heavily over the threshold and splashing icy water into his shoes.

'It's fairly deep in places, Boss.'

Thomas, resisting the temptation to make a sarcastic remark, sighed and went on, taking more care, heading for the ghostly light which flared from the direction of the concrete steps up to the first floor. Arc lamps had been set up to aid the pathologist's preliminary examination. Occasional flashes and the whirr of an electric motor informed Thomas that the SOCOs were also at work; the soft murmur of their voices carried down to them. Thomas paddled over to the staircase.

'Is that you, Chief Inspector Thomas?'

Thomas recognized the gravelly voice of the Home Office pathologist, Timothy Drayton. Thomas identified himself.

'You can come up, if you're properly attired.'

'Left my dicky-bow at home.'

He heard a dry chuckle, reminiscent of rocks skittering down a mountainside.

'Don't forget the overshoes,' Drayton said.

At the top of the steps, Thomas and Garvey stood blinking in the light. The floor was littered with splinters of wood, some blackened by the fire, as well as fragments of fabric and tufts of some sort of fibrous material. In addition to taking photographs, the SOCOs were videotaping the scene, holding tape measures next to various items and giving details of their position in relation to the body.

The air reeked of accelerants, charred wood and the sweet smell of burnt pork — except Thomas realized, with a sickening jolt, that it wasn't pork.

'Inspector!' Dayton's appearance matched the voice: he was craggy-featured, and his skin had a desiccated look. He shooed a couple of the crime scene team to one side, and Thomas resisted — just — the impulse to close his eyes and turn away.

'Not pretty, I'm afraid.'

Thomas cleared his throat. 'How long?'

'Difficult to say, but more than a few days. You will have noticed this poor chap isn't as badly burned as the first. But only because of the blast.'

'Blast?' Thomas echoed.

'Much of the debris you see was, we believe, originally here.' He indicated a pile of rubbish near the body. 'Our friend here was probably lying face down on top of what appears to have been a bonfire.'

Thomas's neck bristled and he felt a chill of recognition.

'The body took the main force of the blast. If you'd care to come around here, you'll see what I mean.'

'I'll take your word for it.'

Drayton smiled sympathetically. 'There was a container of camping gas under this pile of junk,' he went on. 'It exploded when the fire got going and more or less put out the blaze.'

'So you could get more forensic evidence from this boy?'

Drayton looked at the corpse. 'We'll see,' he said. 'But there is extensive soft-tissue damage.'

'Boss,' Garvey said excitedly, catching up with Thomas at the bottom of the steps. 'Didn't Mrs Connelly say something about a bonfire?' Thomas slipped off his overshoes and stepped into the inky water on the ground floor.

'She also said something about the place being flooded,' Thomas said. 'The significance hadn't escaped me.'

DCI Thomas called an early morning briefing on Thursday. The main office was packed: CID and uniformed officers sat at or on desks, a few stood at the back of the room, or leaned against filing cabinets. Thomas turned his sad gaze on them, and the room fell silent.

'The body discovered last night at Norton's warehouse has been identified as Frank Traynor.' There was a murmur of surprise from the few officers who had got in too late to hear the news in the staff canteen.

'We haven't had the PM results, but the body was burned, and it was also—' he searched for the right word — 'damaged as a result of an explosion. There were accelerants at the scene, and the explosion was almost certainly caused by a full bottle of camping gas.'

'Was he sniffing that an' all?' PC Mayhew asked.

There was a ripple of laughter, and Thomas fixed him with a rheumy eye. 'Was that a serious question?'

Mayhew straightened up. 'Yeah, Boss, I mean, these kids'll sniff anything to get high, won't they?'

Thomas stared until Mayhew blushed.

'Likely not, in this case. Forensics think it was buried under a pile of junk. We've got a batch number on the bottle — I'll need someone to check with the manufacturers — find out which retailer it went to — see if we can trace the purchaser.'

Nita Dhar volunteered, and he moved on. 'Now, it was wet in that warehouse, swimming, you might say. So maybe the lad climbed on top of the rubbish to keep out of the damp, but the injuries—' He pointed to a photograph of the body, pinned to one of the noticeboards. 'The injuries are mainly to his chest, so he must've been lying face down when it went off. I don't see it myself. He might lie on his side, or curl up to keep warm, but lying face down like that . . .'

'You think he was put there?' Vince asked.

'Of course, we have to wait for Dr Drayton's findings, but for now . . . The official line is we're treating this death as suspicious. Garvey, see if we can hurry up the tox reports on Ryan Connelly, will you? Remind them we've been waiting two weeks, and now that we've got Frank as well, they might like to treat this as urgent.' He returned his attention to Vince. 'Have you okayed the interviews at St Michael's?'

Vince nodded. 'The headmaster's having the assembly hall set up with desks so we can interview as many as possible at once.'

'Start with the Sixth Form,' Thomas said. 'I want to know if Frank's been in touch with anyone since he disappeared last Tuesday. Has anyone been acting strangely? Anyone been off sick, whatever. Anything out of the ordinary.'

Garvey spoke up. 'Should I get on to *The Tribune*, see if they'll run an appeal for information?'

'It can't hurt, but I don't want any hint that we're treating this any differently to the first death. We're not sure it *is* any different, and if there are other people involved, I'd like to keep them feeling complacent about the investigation.

'Vince,' he said. 'You were trawling the railway station a couple of days back, weren't you?'

Mayhew stifled a snigger.

'Did you get anything useful out of the lads?'

'Not as much as she would've liked.' It was said in a low growl, but the officers around Garvey heard it and a couple of them laughed. He had seated himself a little in front of Vince, and he now turned back, trying to catch his eye. Thomas made a mental note to have a word with Garvey after the briefing.

Vince looked past Garvey as if he were invisible. 'Nothing useful, Boss,' he said. 'We left a contact number with some of the lads.'

'I bet you did.'

Thomas lost his temper. 'Have you got something to say, Garvey, or is that just flatulence I hear?'

There was general laughter at this, and Garvey said, 'No, Boss.'

'No, you've got nothing to say, or no, it wasn't flatulence?'

'Neither. I mean, no to both.'

Thomas let his gaze rest on Garvey's shining face, until he squirmed uncomfortably and added, 'Sorry, Boss.'

'You want me to go back — talk to them again?' Vince asked.

Thomas shook his head. 'You know the St Michael's kids better than any of us,' he said. 'Let's take advantage of that special relationship. You'll lead the interview team at the school.'

Ten minutes later, tasks assigned, the office emptied. Vince found that a way parted for him as he walked down the stairs, some of the non-uniformed officers pressed back against the wall to let him pass. 'Vince thinks he's in heaven,' he heard from behind him. Garvey.

'Why's that, John?' an obliging crony asked.

'Being *ordered* to take advantage of his "special relationship" with the kids.'

Vince swung round, nearly bumping into WPC Dhar. She shot him a sympathetic glance and then hurried on.

'What the hell are you driving at?'

'Just making an observation.'

'You can take your observations and shove them where the sun don't shine.'

'Not my bag,' Garvey said, camping it up. 'Shows how wrong you can be, though,' he went on, looking at Vince, but addressing the others who were enjoying the entertainment. 'Here's me, thinking it was guilt made you volunteer for drugs liaison officer at St Michael's, when you had different reasons altogether.'

Vince blanched, seeing in a vivid flash the boy in his dream tumbling backwards.

The door opened and DCI Thomas stepped through. Onlookers started to shuffle past the two men. Thomas didn't have to speak. He looked from Garvey to Vince. Vince was the first to move; Garvey held his ground, only following a few seconds afterwards, and Vince knew that he would see it as a victory in what was beginning to look like a campaign.

29

It was a toss-up between driving and going by bus. The car was almost out of petrol, and she didn't fancy queuing to get on and off the petrol station forecourt on her way to work. The weather forecast was for rain later, which made getting the bus a less attractive prospect, but for now it was dry, and Lauren decided to take a chance.

She was feeling more relaxed and optimistic than she had been for weeks. She had visited her mother on her day off, and the trip home to Frodsham had helped her to recover her sense of proportion in a way that her counsellor and her own endless inner arguments could not.

'Work, a man, or that voluntary stint you do?' It was said out of the blue, as they shared the washing-up in her mother's narrow kitchen after lunch.

'Samaritans,' Lauren said, feeling a little sheepish. She thought she had put in a convincing performance of ease and jollity during the morning.

'Well, I won't ask 'cos you'll not tell me. I don't need the details, but you've said it often enough yourself, Lauren: do your best, then walk away.'

'I've tried, Mum . . .'

'It's not your problem, love. It's someone else's that they've brought to you. They've talked it over, you've given what help you can, now it's up to them.'

Lauren had thought about that a lot since her mother had said it, knowing it to be true, and wondering why she found it so hard, in Frank's case, to let go. It was partly because he kept telephoning, asking for her, and partly because he was one of Geri's pupils — and knowing what had happened to Ryan didn't help. But Frank was *not* her responsibility, and however painful that knowledge was, she had to accept it.

She turned right at the bottom of Gresford Avenue, in the direction of the main road. It was tough on Geri, she knew, but she couldn't tell her friend even that she'd spoken to Frank last weekend. How could she? Apart from breaking the confidentiality of the caller, she would be putting Geri in the invidious position of knowing that he was alive and well, but unable to tell anybody.

As she paid for a newspaper at the newsagent's next to the bus stop, she decided she would talk to Geri that night, tell her that she couldn't say any more about Frank, but she hoped it wouldn't drive a wedge between them.

She leafed through the paper, thinking about her day ahead. Thursday was busy for her: a school party was due in from ten until eleven-thirty for a session on using the library for research, then the University of the Third Age were having a guest speaker to talk about exercise and joint pain. They would need access to tea- and coffee-making facilities, but they organised themselves and always cleared up afterwards — Lauren would only have to make sure the chairs were set out in the meeting room on the ground floor. The bus arrived, and she folded her newspaper and got on board, still planning her day.

* * *

He had watched her go down the hill, holding back until she turned the corner before gunning the engine and following.

He pulled up at the junction with the main road and waited to see if she would cross over. When she went into the newsagent's, he had to signal a car to pass him while he watched to see where she would go. Satisfied that she was staying at the bus stop on the near side of the road, he turned into the main road and switched off the engine.

She queued with her back to him, reading her newspaper. Not so much as a twitch of the shoulder blades to hint that she sensed his presence. He felt mildly disappointed: he felt that his commitment to her deserved some degree of recognition.

Following the bus was more of a problem than he had expected. The bus lanes weren't available to him at this time of day, although he risked using them once or twice when the traffic was badly snarled, and he was in danger of losing the bus.

He decided to take a chance on being stopped by the police, and followed the files of buses into the new bus station, waiting until he saw her get off, then he zipped out into the traffic and took the next road left, where he parked the car. She couldn't be going far, and he would be less conspicuous on foot. He ran back to the corner and almost bumped into her coming the other way. He carried on for a few yards, then doubled back, and watched her cross the road and walk up the steps into the memorial gardens. She didn't seem to be in a hurry, and even paused for a few minutes to look at the snowdrops that were just beginning to flower. Museum, library, or art gallery?

He amused himself for a moment or two guessing her occupation. When she went into the library, he was surprised. She looked too classy to fit his idea of a librarian — he had half convinced himself she was the arty type, expecting her to trot up the steps of the art gallery. He waited a few minutes: she might be returning overdue books, after all — then he used his mobile phone to call the library.

'Hi, I'm over at Lauren's place. I thought she wasn't working today, but I must've got the days mixed up.'

The woman who had picked up the phone said, 'I saw her come in a few minutes ago. I'll try to find her for you.'

'No! No . . . I hate to bother her at work.' He lowered his voice conspiratorially. 'Thing is, I wanted it to be a surprise. When does she get off?'

'She's working late tonight, love,' the woman said, sorry to disappoint him. 'She won't finish till nine. But she's off at five o'clock on Friday and Saturday, if that's any good.'

'Thanks,' he said. 'Thanks, you've been a great help.'

He punched the disconnect button. It was tempting to go in and see her. Watch her going about her work, see how she dealt with the public, but he didn't want to alert her — if she saw him here, and then again near her house, she might make the connection; it could spook her, and he didn't want her to be forewarned.

30

The mist and drizzle of the previous night had dispersed after sunrise, but the early part of the day had been grey and overcast and Adèle had done little trade during the morning and early afternoon. Then a short cloudburst was followed by an unexpected parting of the clouds, and the sun twinkling on the puddled pavement seemed to prompt a change in mood — the crowds became more cheerful, and individuals more generous. She sold four magazines in half an hour to office workers on their way home — more than she had sold all day.

Since the Taxman had first put the squeeze on her she had been careful, moving about, selling at different times of day, making it harder for him to creep up on her. She hadn't seen him in four days, and that was just fine by her. Today she was outside Marks & Sparks, and at the rate she was going, she'd be finished in less than an hour.

The sky was beginning to tinge with red, and here and there streetlights flickered into life. A woman came over, her pound coin ready; it was still warm to the touch. Adèle wished her a pleasant evening, and she rolled her eyes. 'You don't know my lot,' she said. Simple contact like this, a brief exchange with someone who had a normal family, a normal life, was what gave Adèle confidence that she did have something to offer. There had been times when she thought she was marked in some way — like the man in the Bible, cursed to wander the world, branded with his sins, but since she'd started selling the *Big Issue*, she had recovered some of her self-respect, and there were times when she actually enjoyed the work.

'You seem to be doing a brisk trade.'

Adèle turned, smiling, taking the coin offered by her next customer, another woman, and handed her a copy of the magazine. 'At this rate, I'll be able to retire to my mansion in Cheshire by the end of the month,' she said.

Only two more to sell. She dropped the coins into the deep pockets of her waterproof and heard the satisfying jingle as they made contact with the others.

A hand gripped her arm, just above the elbow.

'Hey!' She half-turned, ready to lash out, then let out a little scream of surprise.

'I haven't seen you in a few days,' he said.

'I've been sick,' she replied, fear rising like vomit in her gullet.

'I'd be really upset if I thought you'd been avoiding me.'

'No, no . . . I've been really bad.'

He held her at arms' length, and she winced at the pressure of his thumb digging into the flesh of her inner arm. 'You do look a bit peaky,' he said. 'I'm willing to give you the benefit of the doubt, providing—'

Adèle glanced past him at the shoppers and office workers making their way home.

'Look at me,' he ordered, and although he spoke quietly and calmly, Adèle flinched.

She felt helpless. When he looked at her, it was as if she was nothing, nobody, and in her state of terror it seemed as though she had become invisible. He gave her a shake and she whimpered.

'Like I say, I'll let you off, providing you compensate me for all that wasted time.'

He rummaged through her pockets with his free hand and came out with the coins she had worked all day to earn.

'Is that it?'

Adèle nodded wordlessly. She became aware that people were avoiding them, giving them a wide berth, but she daren't look away from him until he gave her permission.

He let go of her arm and she felt it throbbing as blood began to return, then he was behind her, his mouth next to her ear, his breath warm on her neck.

He handed back three pounds. 'That'll pay for tomorrow's magazines,' he said. 'I'm not out to ruin you.'

She thanked him, her lips numb with fear.

'You're doing the right thing,' he told her. 'Best to pay up and stay on the right side of the Taxman.'

She nodded, fighting back tears. He had her money, why wouldn't he let her go? He carried on, talking in a low, almost intimate tone.

'I know a bloke said he wanted to keep his cash. After all, he'd earned it . . . Taxman bit his ear clean off. Got it in his teeth and worried it like a terrier with a rag. Took some of the flesh over his left eye, an' all. Bloke wears his hair long, now.' He snapped his teeth together and Adèle darted forward with a yelp. He laughed, and she recognized him in an instant of terrible clarity: a dark alleyway, a spurt of flame dripping gold, the nauseating stench of burnt flesh and hair, and the dreadful screams of a rat.

She jostled though the crowds, dropping her last two magazines in her urgency. She ran and ran, up the hill, away from the awful sound of his laughter. Heedless of the traffic, she blundered into the road. A car horn blared, and she leapt like a startled cat, then bolted blindly into the night.

* * *

Nick was in a rush — people to see before work — somebody who could get him a mint-condition Triumph insignia for the petrol tank. The bike renovations were nearing completion.

He still hadn't forgiven Geri for flushing the hash down the toilet, and the nearest she got to a greeting was a scowl, then he grabbed his jacket and ran, slamming the front door, leaving a silence that was all the more intense for having been preceded by so much activity.

Still holding her briefcase, Geri stared at the door feeling abandoned, bereft. She set down her briefcase and took off her coat, then went to each room, peering in as if hoping to find companionship within.

'Almost identical,' Vince had said. Frank's body had been found in almost identical circumstances as Ryan.

The police had interviewed children all day, and the fevered excitement their presence caused had been hard to contain. She was exhausted and depressed.

'Oh, for heaven's sake — stop it!' Geri said aloud. She wouldn't allow herself to think about it. Not while she was alone, not while she had no one else to share in the horror of it.

She checked the time — five thirty — enough time for a light meal before going to the youth club. She busied herself in the kitchen, preparing something to eat. Tuna, rice, fried vegetables. She spooned them onto a plate and poured herself a glass of wine, then left the food to go cold while she wondered how Frank had come to be in that awful place. He had told Siân that he had to get away. Why, then had he stayed? Stayed and died?

She got up and scraped the remains of her dinner into the bin, washed up and wiped down, moving spice jars and utensils, cleaning with a ferocity that banished thought.

An hour and a half later, the cupboards had been cleaned and tidied, old tins, past their sell-by date, thrown out, mail sorted, and the kitchen floor washed. She looked at her handiwork and thought, *what good did that do?*

It was time to leave; Joe would expect her at the youth club, but she put it off. Another evening trying to explain to the children something she couldn't understand herself — trying to tell them why people their age died. And so horribly . . . She couldn't face it. She went to the sitting room and picked up her address book. Twice she dialled and hung up before the connection was made. On the third attempt, she let it ring.

She could hear music and lively conversation as the phone was picked up.

'Turn that thing *down*!' Coral commanded. 'I can't hear myself *think*!' Her accent seemed more decidedly Caribbean; her voice more richly musical than it sounded at school.

'Hold on a second,' she said. 'I'll take it in the hall.' There was a pause, then the voices and music were abruptly cut off. 'Better,' Coral said. 'You know, I love my sons, and I'm flattered they want to live at home at their age, but you never get a minute's peace!'

Geri didn't know what to say, so she remained silent.

'Are you all right, love?'

'I can't settle, Coral. I still can't believe . . .'

'I know, I know. I spoke to his mother earlier. She kept asking "Why?"' She sighed. 'What could I tell her? There is no reason, no logic to all this.'

'He should never have been in that place. He was leaving the city. Siân said.'

'He must have changed his mind. Didn't Vince say he had camping gear?'

'They found his body near a pile of rubbish. That doesn't mean it was his.'

'Sleeping bag, plastic sheeting, rucksack, billy cans, a gas canister. Who else's? He was lying low, Geri, waiting for all the fuss to die down.'

'I suppose . . .' A tiny alarm bell started chiming, not loud enough to make her stop and think what was causing her disquiet, but enough to make her feel uneasy, dissatisfied with the police explanation.

'I suppose . . .' she repeated, almost decided that she would tell Coral about the drugs she had found in the lining of her coat. 'Coral, d'you think Barry—'

'*Look* nuh,' Coral interrupted, her West Indian accent more pronounced as she lost patience. 'The police know of our concerns about that young man. They're not stupid. Leave them to get on with their job.'

'I would, if they'd do it,' Geri said tartly.

'What you saying?'

'If they think Frank died alone—'

'We don't know what they think.'

'No,' Geri said. 'We don't.' She heard the irritation in Coral's voice. She liked Coral and valued her good opinion. Where some staff viewed Geri's vigilance as a form tutor as excessive, her defence of her pastoral charges irksome and naive, Coral encouraged her commitment. But even Coral had her limits, it seemed.

'So, you'll let it be?' Coral said.

'It's a police matter, right?'

'Right . . .' Coral didn't sound convinced, but she let it go, and they agreed to talk about it again on Friday.

* * *

Geri went into the hall and dragged on her coat, snagging the lining and tearing the hole wider — after her argument with Nick, she hadn't felt like completing the repair. 'Shit!' she hissed.

A sound from the kitchen startled her; she hadn't heard anyone come in.

'Lauren?' she called. There was no reply.

Geri crept down the hallway. Her heart thudding dully, she trod carefully on the boards nearest the skirting, unconsciously holding her breath. The kitchen light was on. She pushed the door open and saw Lauren sitting at the table.

'Lauren?' she said. 'Are you all right?'

'Fine.' Lauren wiped her eyes and picked up a bundle of papers and books from the tables and walked out.

'Is there anything I can—'

The door closed behind her.

'—do?' Geri finished. 'What the hell is the *matter* with everyone?' she asked the empty room.

In her own room, Lauren spread the newspaper out on her bed. The front-page headline of *The Tribune* read, *SENSELESS*, and beneath it was a picture of Frank with the caption, *Second tragic death in glue-sniffing craze.*

* * *

Adèle concentrated on the interlocking diamonds of the wire-mesh base of the bunk bed above her. She didn't owe Frank Traynor a thing. She didn't even remember him from school. But every time she closed her eyes, she saw a thin stream of liquid flame, heard the screams of the rat and the horrible cruel laughter. It had haunted her dreams and echoed in every alleyway since that night, just over a week ago, when she had first heard it. She couldn't even go in to suss out a new doss anymore — didn't have the courage. She hated the shelter, but the Taxman had made her too afraid to live on the streets.

The night it had happened, she'd returned to her doss buoyant, after the thaw, glad to be free of the shelter at last. The drizzle that had fallen earlier in the day had exhausted itself leaving a misty pall that threatened to turn to fog, creeping up, it seemed, from the dirty gutters. The rain had melted the last remnants of snow, and with mixed feelings of relief and apprehension, she had quit the emergency shelter for the last time, moving her gear back to the warehouse that afternoon, stopping to buy a new gas canister for the primus stove, grateful to leave the fetid air of the shelter but not entirely thrilled with the prospect of rebuilding her bivvy.

She had postponed the rebuilding, deciding it made more sense to try to sell a few magazines before the shops shut and get down to the hard work later. Now, in the mist and the dark, she wondered if she had made the right decision.

The mist was denser in the deep shadows of the warehouses. It lay in milky pools in the hollows at ground level, and in the windowless upper storeys it drifted like spiders' webs, floating out on the breeze. Its cover made her feel secret, invisible, and she began to relax a little. She could still hear the whizzes and bangs of the Chinese New Year celebrations, but the sounds were muffled by the gathering mist, and the flashes were muted, distant, like sheet lightning.

She stopped outside her warehouse. The downpipes had been ripped out long ago for scrap and what was left of them spattered dirty water onto her head. She ducked and shivered as an icy drop found its way down the back of her neck. Nobody ever came this way anymore, but she always approached the building with the same caution. She listened, but there was only the rush and boom of the fireworks a mile away in the city, and the gurgle and splash of water in the drains.

She picked her way through the rubbish in the side passage; the carpet, which had been moulded into a fantastic sculpture by the frost, lay flattened, sodden on the ground. Her heart missed a beat. *Flattened* . . . She fumbled in her pocket for her torch. Yes, it was definitely there: a boot print, trampled into the pile. Had it been there that afternoon? She didn't think so, and anyway, wouldn't the rain have washed it away?

Her heart pounded and she felt a tingling in her scalp. She leaned against the wall for support and tried to decide what to do. Everything she owned was in there: sleeping bag, change of clothes, the lot. Even the refill for the primus stove, hidden it with the rest of her gear under the display boards.

Adèle forced herself to breathe normally. Whoever it was, likely he'd come down the side passage and maybe had a squint through the door. The ground floor was under half an inch of muddy water after the thaw. He'd probably seen the state of the place and buggered off.

She stood upright, still feeling a little light-headed, but now able to go on.

A flash of light, and she flinched, her heart racing, until she realized it was her own torch. She thrust it into her pocket, flicking the switch: if there was someone inside, she didn't want to alert them to her presence. She waited until her eyes were fully adjusted to the dark before going in through the narrow gap in the doorway. It was wider. She had been unable to shift the metal door on the occasions she had tried, which meant someone bigger and stronger had been through here, and recently.

Inside the building, the mist was thicker. Wisps swirled and danced on the surface of the water, filling her nose with the reek of damp brickwork and moss . . . and something else. Something elusive, which sparked emotion: excitement and fear. She knew that smell, but as the air currents changed, she lost it, and focused instead on the steady splash of water, like the click of a scolding tongue. She listened. Below it, the intestinal gurgle of broken water pipes. Then, a rustle. A movement. She held her breath.

A high squeak, almost out of her range of hearing, then another, answering call — rats. She let the air out of her lungs gently and moved to the staircase, placing her feet with slow care, to avoid splashing.

On the steps she paused, angling her head to catch any sound. Nothing. For ten seconds, twenty, thirty . . . Nothing. She took one step at a time, and as she peered over the last, she kept low, lying almost full-length on the staircase.

Her gear was a formless hump in the darkness at the far side of the floor, fading in and out of focus in the thickening vapour that penetrated the building.

She froze. A shape stepped out from behind one of the pillars and she flattened herself against the steps. He gasped; for a moment she thought he had seen her, and she tensed herself ready to run. Then he repeated the sound and she thought it was like a sob, or a wordless exclamation.

He turned and disappeared into the darkness, then she heard a heavy dragging, and he was back again. He dumped his burden on top of her gear.

My, God, she thought. My God, what's he doing?

She heard a familiar rattle, then a flash of flame, and Adèle got another whiff of that elusive smell. Solvent. With his back to her, he flicked the match and a sheet of flame exploded. He stepped back, cursing, and she saw, horrified, the outline of a body on the bonfire.

She covered her mouth with both hands to stifle a whimper that threatened to become a scream. *Go, no! Please, God, no* . . . she prayed inarticulately as she backed away down the steps, trying not to make a noise. Halfway across the uneven concrete of the ground floor she stumbled and fell with a splash. The man shouted and she leapt to her feet, running for the door.

He would expect her to run for the street. If she did, he would catch her. She dived right instead and ran into the gloom at the far end of the passageway. It was a dead end. She hid behind a sheet of corrugated iron and hoped he wouldn't come and investigate.

She heard him splashing about in the water inside the building, then saw the flash of a powerful torchlight in the passage, shining in her direction. The mist had thickened to a fog, and he cursed as the saturated air reflected the light back at him, then the torch went out. Adèle closed her eyes. Her heart pounded so loudly in her throat she thought it would give her away. She heard the man's boot crunch on the grit underfoot. He was waiting. She pressed herself against the wall, shifting one foot carefully, and came in contact with something soft. It squealed and shot out from under her — a rat as big as a cat.

She couldn't see the man in the milky air, but she heard the snick of a cigarette lighter, and then a narrow shaft of flame shot towards her, dripping fire. Then the rat was screaming, splashing in the puddles of black water, leaping and squirming. Coming towards her.

His aim was good; he kept the flame-thrower on the creature no matter how it leapt and twisted. And all the time he was laughing. Laughing like he thought it was really funny. Laughing as the animal flailed and screamed, its fur blackening and its skin sizzling, and when it stopped struggling, not dead, but too shocked to offer any resistance, he stood in the dark and watched it twitch and shiver for a full five minutes.

Adèle tried to keep her breathing even and silent. Would he come and check there was nothing, *no one*, else in the alley?

A huge crash overhead made the man shout. The gas refill! It had exploded.

She heard him mutter, '*What the fuck?*' then the crunch of his boots as he turned to go back inside. She waited until she heard him splashing across the floor towards the staircase before making her escape.

Adèle felt a sudden icy chill — did he *know*? Had he seen her running away that night? Was that why he was hounding her? She forced herself to slow her breathing, made it keep time with the light snore of the woman in the upper bunk. Gradually she became calmer, more able to think. *If he knew, I'd be dead already*. Small consolation. Then the chilling thought: *And if he finds out, he'll do me for certain. He knows street people. He knows the places to hide, the dosshouses, the shelters, squats, hostels . . .*

Her stomach gave a sickening lurch. Her choice was a stark one: stay at the shelter and wait for him to come for her or leave and face the terrors of the street once more. Less than a fortnight ago she wouldn't have hesitated: the shelters were full of the crazies and druggies she had spent the last six months trying to avoid. But now she would rather face a crack addict than the Taxman, with his quiet voice and his terrifying laugh. The Taxman didn't hurt people because he was mad or desperate or stoned — he did it because he *liked* doing it. And he knew how to get away with it.

31

Vince arrived back at the station after lunch time on Friday. He had spent the morning finishing the interviews at St Michael's. The uniformed officers on his team had returned to normal duties, and the CID members had been reassigned other tasks. Garvey looked up from his desk as two DCs came into the incident room.

'School finished for the day, has it?'

Winters, the taller of the two men answered, 'We're all done over there, Sarge.'

'Good. You can join the grown-ups and get some real police work done.'

Vince ignored the jibe and headed for DCI Thomas's office.

Garvey tossed a slip of paper across his desk to Winters without looking at him. 'Someone was asking for you earlier,' he said to Vince. He waited until Vince turned to him before going on. 'One of the lads selling his plump little rump on the railway station. Asked for you 'specially.' He affected a camp little lisp on the last word. 'Called himself Alex — said you'd know him.'

Ice-blue eyes and a vicious tongue. The boy had occupied his dreams for the past week. Vince knew him all right. He saw Winters and his partner exchange an amused glance.

'There's half a dozen lads working Handley Street,' Vince said.

'He said he's the one you wanted to take home.'

Winters had a choking fit and turned away.

'Information on Frank Traynor?' Vince asked.

Garvey didn't answer immediately, but stared at Vince, who returned the stare. Eventually Garvey shrugged. 'Says he saw our lad on the station the Tuesday he disappeared.'

'D'you think he was telling the truth?'

'Lying little toe-rag wouldn't recognize the truth if it leapt up and bit him on the arse — he kept asking about the reward,' Garvey sneered. 'Well, playtime's over, boys,' he said, looking from Winters to Vince Beresford. 'You waiting for your dinner money or something?'

'A name, Sarge,' Winters said with heavy emphasis. 'There's just an address on here.'

'Agnes Hepple,' Garvey said. 'Boss wants to find out how she knew so much about how Frank Traynor died.'

Vince knocked and went into Thomas's office. The DCI looked haggard. 'Vince,' he said, indicating the one upholstered chair in front of his desk. 'Anything?'

Vince shook his head. 'No one saw him or heard from him after he disappeared.'

'What about the drugs connection?'

'The kids're still saying Ryan didn't touch drugs. Frank dabbled. Recreational drugs — E, a bit of dope, sometimes speed, if he had a lot of partying to do.'

'Nothing heavier?'

'No.'

'What about solvents?'

'No chance. It's considered uncool, and Frank worked hard not to appear uncool.'

Thomas sighed. 'Well, it was worth a try.'

'There was an incident on Wednesday of this week,' Vince went on. 'Ryan's younger brother attacked Barry Mandel.'

'That name does keep cropping up, doesn't it?' he mused. 'Did you interview the two scrappers?'

'They're singing from the same hymn sheet: it was a bit of horseplay that turned nasty. I don't get it — why would Dean protect Mandel if he thinks he was responsible for his brother's death?'

Thomas rubbed a hand over his face. 'Have you got kids, Vince?' He coloured slightly and gave an apologetic smile. 'They have a code of silence stronger than any you'll see in the criminal world,' he went on. 'You just don't grass.'

Vince sensed the interview was over, but that the DCI had something more to say. The chief inspector shuffled uncomfortably in his chair, and Vince realized suddenly what was coming. He tried to forestall it with, 'If that's all, guv?'

But Thomas waved him back to his seat. 'Um . . .' he began. 'About your personal situation . . .'

Vince felt a rising sense of panic, 'Sir—'

'I want you to know I'm right behind you.' He winced. 'I mean, you have my support.' He stood and leaned across his desk, offering Vince his hand. Vince got to his feet and they shook, making eye contact briefly.

'Thanks, sir,' Vince said, unexpectedly touched by the gesture.

As Vince made his way out through the main office, DC Quinn burst in.

'Got them!' he announced, holding up a handful of videotapes. 'Midnight Monday to midnight Wednesday last week: the sleazy underbelly of city life as lived on Handley Street station.'

Vince paused. 'You've got the CCTV tapes?' he asked. 'I wouldn't mind a look at those.'

Quinn looked at Garvey, who held out his hand for the tapes.

'What's up, Vince,' Garvey said. 'Hoping to do a bit of window shopping?'

'I knew Frank,' Vince said, evenly. 'I know the people he hung out with — I might recognize someone.'

Garvey put his feet up on his desk and jerked his head at Vince. 'Give them a proper job for a day, they think they're Inspector bleeding Morse,' he sneered. 'Get back in your box, Vince.'

Vince was ready to go over and punch him in his shiny, red face. Then Quinn smirked and he knew he had missed his chance.

He decided to go to the canteen and get a bite to eat before tackling the paperwork that had mounted up over the past two days. He picked up a sandwich and a plate of chips and carried his meal to an empty table.

At the next table, a few of his interview team were finishing a late lunch and were talking over the case.

'Thomas is bringing in the psychic,' PC Mayhew said.

'He doesn't believe that stuff, does he?' PC Porter asked. Porter was about the same age as Mayhew, bull-necked and broad chested.

Mayhew shrugged. 'She got a few of the details right.'

Porter smirked. 'And she's gonna solve the case for him, is she?'

Mayhew chortled. 'Thomas should've asked Beresford to look in his crystal ball — he'd've got the whole story.'

Shouts of laughter, then Vince leaned forward and stared into Mayhew's face. An embarrassed silence fell.

* * *

Agnes Hepple wasn't quite sure how to play the situation: for one thing, the police had called for her at her salon, so she wasn't properly got up to be Miss Hepple, and for another, she'd had to leave instructions with her assistant, Pearl — who was anything but — to cancel her afternoon appointments, which had put her very much out of sorts.

She looked at the baggy-eyed policeman opposite and considered demanding just who the hell he thought he was, dragging her away from her business without so much as an apology, but the truth was that, technically at least, she had come voluntarily and she could see that if she wanted to impress this fellow, it would have to be by more subtle means.

She took a breath and closed her eyes, seeking out her special place. The conditions weren't exactly conducive, but she'd played worse venues and left with the audience eating out of the palm of her hand.

Another breath . . . She found it; a green, open landscape and her above it, on a mountain top, in the sunshine. She opened her eyes, focusing on the inspector's weary face, distancing herself from the mundane actions: the starting of the tape, giving her name, listening to the caution and responding to his question, '. . . Do you understand?' with a smile and a nod.

'For the tape, Miss Hepple.'

She kept the smile, suppressing a prickle of annoyance and sending out love to this sad-faced man. 'Yes,' she said. 'I understand.'

'You seem very well informed about our investigation,' he began.

'I'm sure I haven't the faintest idea what you mean, love.'

'You gave Mrs Connelly certain . . . details about Frank Traynor's death.'

'Oh . . .' Mrs Connelly had telephoned her to warn her of her visit to DCI Thomas. It had happened before, on other occasions when she had helped the families of victims of crime. Those times, there had been no follow-up. The police generally dismissed spiritualists as cranks — so although she had been irritated that Mrs Connelly had gone to the police before discussing it with her, she had dismissed the matter as unimportant.

'And now can you tell me how you came by such detailed information?'

'Well, where do I begin?' This was difficult. It didn't feel right, being Miss Hepple in her salon get-up. Purple nails and a matching two-piece didn't suit the persona. There was a lot of hostility in the room — some from the inspector, who evidently thought her a liar and a con-artist, some from the Asian girl who was sitting in on the interview.

She had a message for Constable Dhar, but now was not the time to deliver it. She gathered her thoughts, making an effort to create a positive aura around herself.

'The spirits are my messengers,' she said.

'Miss Hepple, you gave specific information about how Frank Traynor died, and where he would be found.'

'Not me,' she said. 'The spirits. I am only a conduit. I pass on the information they give me.'

'I don't believe in ghosts—'

'Spirits,' Miss Hepple corrected. 'They don't need you to believe in them, Inspector.'

He sat up straight, exhaling loudly. 'Tell me, exactly, how you discovered the particulars of Mr Traynor's death.'

She thought for a moment. She couldn't very well tell him that her friendly local pimp had found out from his contacts on the streets — anyway, some of it really had come from her spirit messengers. 'You want to know how the spirits speak to me?' she asked.

'I want to know how you came by the information you passed on to Mrs Connelly,' he replied. 'A warehouse, you said. Flooded. And campfire or bonfire was significant.'

She felt a warm rush of spiritual energy. 'And it *was*, wasn't it?'

DCI Thomas's face was grim. 'Miss Hepple.' It was said as an admonishment and a warning.

She regarded him closely for a few seconds. 'I see cracks in your aura, where dark light escapes.' She said it to shake him. She couldn't see his aura at all, but she could sense his anger clearly enough, and his contempt for her and her beliefs.

'Answer the question, please, Miss Hepple,' he said.

'He wanted to be found,' she said, having let enough time elapse to show she would not be intimidated. 'He wanted his mother to know what had happened to him. You see, the spirits don't care about their physical bodies, but they care about justice, and they watch over those they've left behind on the earthly plane.'

'Spare me the lecture,' he said.

She was stung by his hostility. 'I'm not looking to make a conversion, Inspector,' she said.

'Just as well.' He drew his chair closer to the table and leaned on his forearms. 'Now let me tell you how I think you got your facts. You knew about the warehouse, the flooding, the bonfire, because you're involved in some way in Frank Traynor's death.'

Their eyes met and locked and Agnes sighed inwardly. This was going to be a long session.

32

The sky was beginning to darken, and a waning crescent of moon showed as a thin creamy sliver above the chimney pots and aerials of the narrow street. Baz walked quickly to keep warm; in the gutters, cracked sheets of glassy ice had already begun to form — there would be a hard frost tonight.

Gran would be surprised to see him so early on a Friday night, but since Dean had freaked on Tuesday, Mr Ratchford had posted teachers at the school gates and at likely dealing places around the perimeter fence at the beginning and end of the school day. All of which meant that he had been forced to find new venues, and to lay off having the younger kids carry his stash around school for him, at least until things cooled off. He would pop in, make her night, chat for a while — maybe even stay for his tea — then get off to the city to see if he could make a few quid selling in the city-centre pubs.

He knew his gran would be standing at the window, as she always did, watching the comings and goings of the street from behind her polished oak table, her Zimmer close by in the unlikely event that someone would call, sitting down every once in a while, or going off to make a cup of tea, but essentially watching until it was too dark to see.

It pained him to see her excited wave when she caught a glimpse of him over the privet hedge, the way she would hurry into the hall, with that agonising shuffle, leaving her frame, so he didn't think her an invalid. He despised his parents' easy dismissal of her loneliness — Dad had seen to it that she had a downstairs shower and loo installed when she could no longer manage the stairs; he had even helped to move her bed and wardrobes down into the back room, but that done, he had left her to it.

Baz avoided looking into the front parlour, as his gran called it, and so he didn't see her initial surprise, that little wave, nor her more frantic gestures as he put the key in the door, otherwise he would have seen what was coming.

Two men, both in ski masks, both heavyset. The first one — the one in the blue mask — grabbed him by the scruff of the neck and slammed him into the doorpost. His lip split. A burst of pain flared in his nose, then it spouted blood.

They threw him inside. He could hear his gran's high, cracked screams and he tried to get to his knees and crawl to her. He had to tell her to be quiet or they would—

A boot in the ribs and he crumpled, gasping and retching.

'Where is it?' the blue mask screamed. 'Where's the gear?'

He wanted to tell, but he couldn't get his breath. He was lifted by the hair, caught a glimpse of his gran in the parlour doorway, wide-eyed, screaming for them to leave her grandson be. He couldn't see straight: his right eye was swelling, already closing up, and both eyes streamed.

He tried to say, 'Upstairs', but his mouth, full of blood, wouldn't form the word. His face was slammed into the carpet. He groaned and choked, gagging on the blood.

His gran was still screaming. The black mask rushed past, into the parlour. Baz heard a dull thud and her cries were suddenly cut off. Black mask yelled at her. 'Where does he keep his stuff?'

His gran whimpered.

'Please,' he mumbled through swollen lips.

They didn't hear him. The first man had gone to the back of the house. He heard furniture being overturned, drawers emptied. Then he was back, his face in Baz's, his eyes — all that Baz could see of his face — glittering, mad. He was high on something, and through his pain, Baz felt a plummeting sense of terror. They were going to kill them both.

'Where?' blue mask screamed.

Baz pointed upstairs.

'Take anything portable and smash the rest, he said,' Black mask reminded the blue.

'I know what I'm doing. You watch them,' Blue mask ordered. Gran was crying. Baz heard the sound of a slap, and the second man told her to shut her noise. There was a moment's silence when all Baz could hear was the sound of his own laboured breathing, then there was a crash, and he knew his cloning cupboard had been emptied.

A few minutes later blue mask returned, carrying paper bags of hash and plastic bags full of pills.

'Right little pharmacy, aren't you?' he said.

Baz had struggled to a sitting position, propped up against the wall next to the staircase. His breath whistled — they'd a cracked rib.

The man stuffed the bags into his pockets and leaned over him, lifting him easily by his lapels. 'Where's the rest?'

Baz's good eye widened. 'That's it,' he spluttered, spattering blood on the mask. 'That's all of it, I swear.'

The man looked past him, and Baz saw a movement, no more than a slight lift of the head, then he groaned as the first punch to his kidneys winded him afresh. Again and again he was punched and kicked, shoved backwards and forwards between the two of them until he collapsed, curling himself into a ball, trying to protect his vital organs, his head. Then suddenly it was over. He felt his coat ripped open, his pockets checked, money taken. He lay passively, praying that his gran wouldn't start screaming again.

The first man took his hand, turned it over gently, then grabbed his thumb and bent it back until he heard it crack. He heard screaming — deep howls of pain — his own screams, but he could feel himself retreating, and the sounds seemed far away.

The blue mask stood over him. 'Are you listening?' he asked. A pause, then, 'I can't hear you.'

'Yes! Yes!' His voice a high-pitched scream.

'The Taxman doesn't like competition,' he said. 'Stay off his turf.'

He heard a wail of dismay from his gran. Then blue mask lifted his foot and stamped on Baz's groin, and finally, blessedly, he blacked out.

* * *

Vince was checking duty rotas, filing paper, typing up reports — doing the admin tasks he hated when the phone rang. The superintendent wanted to see him. Immediately. PC Porter stopped him in the corridor.

'Word just in, Sarge. Barry Mandel's been beaten up.'

'Dean Connelly again?'

Porter shrugged massively. 'He's unconscious, and his gran isn't making much sense. He was at her house when it happened. The place has been smashed up. The gran's in shock.'

'How bad is he?'

'Looks pretty bad.'

Vince ran up the stairs to the superintendent's office. DCI Thomas stood beside Allan's desk, looking uncomfortable.

'Close the door, Sergeant,' Superintendent Allan said.

'Sir, can this wait? There's been a development. Barry Mandel. Looks like he's upset one of his drugs associates.'

Allan picked up a remote control and pointed it at the TV and video in the corner of the room. Vince turned around. A slightly blurred image appeared of the interior of Handley Street station. Victorian tiling, modern marble flooring. The image jumped, then came back into focus. A tall, dark-haired man in a leather jacket entered the concourse and approached a boy near the entrance. It was the boy Mayhew had roughed up during their visit to the railway station the previous week. The boy who had haunted his dreams since. *Alex*, he thought. *His name is Alex.*

'Can you explain why you were trawling the station on Tuesday the eighth — the night that Frank Traynor disappeared?'

Vince shot him an angry look. The choice of verb hadn't escaped him. 'I was trying to find out where he'd gone.'

'I didn't authorize that line of enquiry until the Friday,' Allan said. 'And you're not in uniform.'

'It was on my own time.'

'You do know what this looks like?'

Vince met his stare. 'I suppose it depends what you're looking for.'

'Insolence won't help you, Sergeant Beresford.'

He thought for a moment. 'I knew Ryan,' he said. 'I knew Frank. I wanted to find him before he ended up in a mortuary, on a slab. If my concern was unauthorized, I'm sorry.'

Superintendent Allan looked ready to launch into a tirade, but DCI Thomas intervened. 'Your actions were ill-judged, Vince.'

'My timing was certainly off,' he muttered.

'Why?' Allan asked sharply. 'Because you got caught on tape?'

Vince bit back a reply. 'Is there anything else, sir? I'd like to find out what's happening to Mandel.'

Allan checked his watch. 'Your shift finished ten minutes ago,' he said. 'Go home. Mandel will be interviewed by CID.'

The office was empty when Vince returned. He bundled together the papers he had been working on and reached for a folder to file them into temporarily. As he did so, the top page caught his eye: the *n* of his first name had been carefully Tippexed out, so that it read 'Vice Beresford'. He dumped the documents and stormed out into the corridor. Nobody. The communications room was quiet.

* * *

Alex was working the concourse. Vince saw him exchange a glance with James Dean, then he turned his back and dropped a couple of coins into the vending machine. As Vince approached, he bent down to retrieve his sweets, pushing out his buttocks in a manner reminiscent of street girls negotiating a trick with a punter in a car.

'Pastilles,' he said. 'I love 'em.' He popped one in his mouth. 'I can suck 'em down to a sliver, me.'

'Save it for the punters, Alex. What have you got for me?'

The boy turned his startling blue eyes on Vince. 'Depends what you want to pay.'

'You said you had info on Frank Traynor.'

'You said there was a reward.'

'For information leading to an arrest.'

'I need some up front.'

Vince handed him a five-pound note.

'You're joking me!'

'Another fifteen if I'm satisfied.'

Alex arched an eyebrow. 'I've never had no complaints.'

'Stop pissing me about,' Vince warned.

Alex pouted. 'He was here. Tuesday.'

'Frank Traynor? You're sure it was him?'

Alex looked in the direction of James Dean. Vince followed his line of sight, but the boy avoided his eye, and Vince formed the impression that Alex was talking on James Dean's behalf. Alex fished in his pocket and drew out a crumpled photograph of Frank. 'Him,' he said. 'That's the one I saw.'

Vince gave him the rest of the money.

'Surprised you didn't see him yourself.'

Vince held his breath for a moment.

'Well you *were* here. I seen you.'

'I didn't see you,' Vince replied.

'You weren't looking for *me*.'

A silence stretched between them. Vince could almost see the cogs turning as Alex calculated how much he could make out of the knowledge he possessed. The boy could do a lot of damage with what he knew.

'Another fifty and I'll likely forget you was ever here.'

Vince hauled him up to eye level by his jacket front.

'Fuck with me, little boy,' he snarled, 'you're going to get hurt.'

Alex squeaked and Vince let go, dropping him to the ground. He fell awkwardly, landing on his backside in a greasy puddle on the marble tiles. For a few moments he seemed unable to catch his breath, then he spat out the pastille he had been sucking and began screaming at Vince's back as he walked away. 'Bastard! Bastard fag!'

Vince glanced over to where James Dean had been standing. His pitch beneath the poster advertising vodka was empty.

33

Dean woke in the dark. His room was stiflingly warm; he had fallen asleep fully dressed, on top of the bedclothes. He hadn't been getting much sleep over the last two weeks, and for once he had been undisturbed by dreams. He looked across at Ryan's bed. There was a hump, a clear outline of a human form, lying under the bedclothes.

'The stupid bastard,' he breathed. Then he was on the floor — four, maybe five steps, grabbing Ryan by the shoulder—

The bed was empty. There was nothing. Nothing at all. Nothing that could have made him think it was his big brother lying under the covers, waiting for him to say 'Wake up, dickhead! We've all be worried sick about you.'

A trick of the light, of the mind. Ryan's bed was empty.

Every night, sometimes three or four times a night, he would dream: the bedroom door opened and Ryan walked in and flopped onto his bed. He carried a magazine in his hand, or sometimes textbooks.

Dean glanced up, then back to his own reading; Ryan was going through a familiar routine, there was no reason to take special note of it. After a while, Ryan said, 'Gotta go, bro.' A phrase he often used. A second or two of dreadful recognition, when Dean would realize he had missed his chance again.

He would jump out of bed, yelling, 'No! No! Stay!'

He always woke at this moment, sobbing. The terrible, terrible anguish, the awful sense of loss was just as strong as on that first day, in Mrs Golding's office, when they had told him Ryan was dead.

He sat on Ryan's bed and wept until his head ached. The sudden electric bolts of pain in his broken tooth, reactions to hot and cold, had abated, replaced by a dull feverish ache that played along the length of his jaw. But it wasn't enough. In RE they had learned the word *atonement*. He wanted to atone for his sins, for not making enough of his time with Ryan, for not saving him.

He carried Ryan's knife with him always — even in school — hidden in his sports bag, up the sleeve of his jacket, its steel cool against the hot, stinging pain of the thin score marks on his arm. Three now. One for every day since he'd failed to get Baz. Since he'd failed to atone. He would make a tally, marking time until he did what he'd set out to do.

It took a little while for him to register that the banging wasn't in his head. His dad was at the bedroom door, his voice now raised, panicky.

'Dean, son. Open the door.'

'All right.' He didn't mean to sound nowty, but somehow everything he said lately seemed bad-tempered and sulky.

He slid the chest of drawers away from the door, feeling a mixture of self-pity and angry satisfaction as the effort pulled at the healing tissue of the cuts on his arm.

'What?' he said, staring sullenly at his father's shirt front. He couldn't bring himself to look into those horrified eyes, red-rimmed with sleeplessness and unshed tears.

'Come downstairs, son. The police want a word.'

They were waiting in the front room, an Indian woman and a man. They looked too big for the room, seemed to make it shrink. The man was standing next to the mantelpiece when they came in, looking at a family photo: Mum and Dad,

Ryan with his hands around Dean's neck, like he was about to throttle him, both of them laughing. He wanted to tell the copper to put it down, that he had no right, touching their things, but he just stood there, glaring at him. The man put the picture back, and the woman got up from the sofa.

'Hello, Dean,' she said. 'I'm Constable Dhar, and this is Constable Mayhew. I hope we didn't get you out of bed.'

'It's only eight o'clock.' People always did that. Treated him like a baby, just because he was small. He saw a look pass over his head, between the policewoman and his dad. They were 'making allowances', because of what he'd been through. It pigged him off, that — the sympathetic looks, the way they talked to him like he was thick or something. Although he didn't realize it, their compassion only made him behave more badly.

'Dean,' the woman said. 'We've come to ask you about Barry Mandel — Baz.'

'Sod *him*!' He turned, ready to walk out, but his father barred his way. He placed both hands on his shoulders and turned him back to face the two police officers.

'Show some respect, lad,' he said under his breath.

'Don't see why I should.'

'Now look—'

'They never even started looking for Ryan till it was too late.'

His dad sighed. A silence followed. The heat of his dad's hands burned through the fabric of his shirt, his sadness like a heavy weight, so that Dean felt as if he were holding his father up, that if he moved, his father would fall.

Dhar tried again. 'I understand you being upset,' she said. 'I would be, if it was me.'

'Yeah, well it wasn't, was it?'

'Dean!' His father gripped his shoulders more tightly and Dean blushed a little for having shamed him.

'Baz is seriously ill in hospital,' WPC Dhar told him.

'Good.'

'He was attacked earlier this evening.'

'Dean's been home since a quarter to four,' his dad said.

Dhar smiled. 'We don't think Dean was there,' she said. 'The neighbours saw two men.'

Dean threw her a hot, resentful look. Like it couldn't be him because he was just a short arse.

'I'm nearly fourteen,' he said, then felt an idiot for having said it.

She didn't laugh. 'Do you know anything about it?' she asked.

Dean shrugged.

'He's badly hurt, Dean.'

'Hope he dies. Hope he bloody dies!' A tear spilt onto his cheek and he wiped it away, furious in case they thought he was crying for Barry.

His dad spoke, talking down at the top of his head, pressing firmly on his shoulders. 'Answer the lady. Do you know anything about it?'

'They hurt his grandma as well,' Dhar said. 'Pushed her around. Hit her.'

Dean frowned at the floor.

'She's just an old lady, Dean.'

The furrow between his eyebrows grew deeper. Why should he feel guilty? It was Barry he wanted, not his grandma.

'I wish I'd been there.'

'Dean!' His father spun him around, bent down to his eye level. 'God forgive you!' he demanded. 'That's a wicked thing to say!'

He couldn't help himself, couldn't bear to have people think so badly of him. 'Not her,' he said. 'Not his gran. *Him*. Baz. I wish it could've been me with Baz.'

His dad shook his head. Tears trembled on the raw rims of his eyelids. Dean couldn't take his eyes off them, fascinated and horrified by the possibility of his father breaking down. He stared full into his father's face for the first time since Ryan's death, wanting to comfort him, but not knowing how.

* * *

Before he finished up for the night, Garvey called in at DCI Thomas's office. He stood across from Thomas, who was working in a pool of lamplight, which when he sat up, lit the lower half of his face, putting his eyes in sinister shadow.

'I hope it's good news, John,' Thomas said. 'Because so far, today's been a complete wash-out.'

'You had to let the psychic go?'

'What can you do with someone like that?' Thomas asked. 'Tell her she knows more than she should, and she says she got it from the "other side".'

'She didn't give you anything useful, then?'

'Not unless you count a few bland statements about Frank being safe in the light, and the spirit world taking special care of the young when they pass over. The man we're looking for hates all mankind, apparently. What he can't control, he wants to destroy.'

'There may be something in that.'

'Doesn't help us find him, though, does it?'

'This might,' Garvey said. 'Frank Traynor is on the railway-station security videotapes. The video timer puts it at 9.12 p.m., Tuesday.'

'Was he with anyone?'

Garvey shook his head. 'He didn't stop long, either. Got frightened off by station security. I'll get some stills made up from the tape and send someone over tomorrow, see if we can get anything out of the guard who moved him on.'

'Good. Thanks, John.'

Garvey hovered by the door, undecided whether to say what was on his mind.

'Was there something else?'

'Yeah, Boss. Vince Beresford.'

Thomas's eyes narrowed. 'What about him?'

'I was wondering what was going to happen — you know, about the evidence on tape.'

'Evidence?'

Aware that he sounded defensive, but determined to make his point now he'd stuck his neck out, Garvey went on: 'Him hanging around the station. Talking to the rent boys.'

'*Interviewing* them,' Thomas corrected him. 'He was looking for information on Frank Traynor.'

Garvey gave a short laugh. 'Is that what he said?'

Thomas returned a blank stare. 'His explanation satisfied both me and Superintendent Allan.'

Garvey, hearing the implied reprimand, drew himself up, almost standing to attention. 'Right, Boss, but—'

'But what?'

'You know about Beresford's history — the kid who fell off the roof?'

'Yes,' Thomas said. 'I know about that. What's your point?'

Garvey wanted to yell 'similar fact evidence' at him, but this was his boss, so he remained polite.

'There's the drugs link, for a start, then there's the fact that boys are involved, and given his sexual orientation—'

'Oh, for God's sake!'

'And he knew the house — the place where the first lad was found.' Garvey had been building up to this all day, and he wasn't going to be put off. It was the railway-station security tapes got him thinking. 'Said he was interested in local history. I'll bet *Vince* knows every empty old building on the canal side of town.'

'That's *enough*,' Thomas interrupted angrily. 'You'd better drop this vendetta against Sergeant Beresford. You made the error of judgement. You got kicked up the backside for it. Accept it.'

Garvey took a breath and held it.

Thomas stared at him for a few seconds, then, satisfied that Garvey understood his position on the matter, he went on in a more even tone.

'I don't want to hear any further reference to the videotape in the office, the canteen, or on the station grapevine — do I make myself clear?'

‘Sir.’

Bloody typical! Folk were too easily impressed by the glamour of a cockney accent. Still, Garvey thought, as he took out his car keys, there was one small consolation — it was a bit late to scotch rumours about Vince cruising Handley Street for something warm to cuddle up to.

34

Geri watched TV without really taking anything in. She sat on the floor with a cushion behind her, while Lauren stretched out on the sofa with her feet up. From time to time they exchanged the odd word. One or other of them would get up to make coffee in the programme breaks but for most of the night they simply watched, trying to anaesthetise themselves with banality. Neither of them could bear to watch anything that might contain violence, or even conflict, which left them with a choice of nature programmes and quiz shows.

'God, this is depressing!' Lauren said at last. 'Mind if I turn it off?'

'I want to listen to the local news,' Geri said. 'See if anything . . .' She left the rest unsaid.

Lauren flipped channels and they caught the end of the national news. The first item on the regional bulletin was a shooting in a pub not far from them. The next made Geri sit bolt upright.

'Bloody hell!'

'What?'

Geri shushed her, while they listened to an account of the attack on Barry Mandel.

'There is a suspected drugs connection,' the newsreader said. 'But police are refusing to speculate on a possible link with the death of a second pupil at St Michael's school in what was thought to be a glue-sniffing experiment.'

The camera cut to a shot of DCI Thomas standing outside a derelict warehouse.

'We're anxious to trace a young woman who purchased a gas canister at Great Outdoors in Dean Street on Tuesday, February the eighth,' he said. 'She could have vital information about Frank Traynor's death — even if she can't help us, we need to eliminate her from our enquiries.'

Adèle! No wonder she was so cagey about what had happened to her gear. Geri's stomach did a sickening roll — if Adèle had seen something, she was in terrible danger.

She scrambled to her feet and Lauren followed into the hallway and started pulling on layers of clothing.

'Where are you going?' Geri asked.

'Depends where *you're* going.'

'The shelter on Fairview.'

'I'm coming with you.' Lauren stuffed one cardiganed arm into her coat sleeve.

'There's no need.'

'I think there is,' Lauren said. 'And there's safety in numbers.'

'I'm going to see a five-foot-three skinny girl. Where's the danger in that?'

'I'm going, and that's that,' Lauren insisted. 'We could take separate cars, but it makes better sense to go together.' She picked up Geri's car keys from the hall stand. 'I'll drive.'

Geri reached her own coat down. 'Why my car?'

'I'm almost out of petrol again.'

Geri was dazed with tiredness and too much TV. 'Then why don't I drive?' she protested, following Lauren out of the house.

'You'll need your wits about you to explain what you're so het up about.' Lauren wrapped a scarf around her neck and hurried to Geri's car, hunching her shoulders against the cold.

* * *

The shelter was twenty minutes' drive away in a shabby pocket of urban decay, rimmed by reclaimed mills and warehouses. The streets surrounding it had mostly been bought up by property developers and several rows of terraces were in the process of being demolished.

St Charles's stood on the side of a hill, black and crumbling, towering defiantly over the squat, red-brick houses of the two remaining streets which flanked it on two sides. The church had been deconsecrated long ago, but it still cast its pious shadow over the area.

A group of men stood in a huddle ten or fifteen yards from the entrance. They stopped talking and turned to look at the two women as they got out of the car. Lauren locked up and glanced doubtfully up and down the street.

'Are you sure it'll be safe here?' she asked.

Geri appraised the scabrous paintwork and acid-damaged front bumper. 'They're welcome to it.'

They went to the broad steps of the shelter and were stopped by a man with dirty blond hair twisted into matted dreadlocks.

'Got any change, love?'

Geri gave him a pound. 'Have you seen Adèle tonight?' she asked.

'What's she look like?'

'Long, fair hair, about five foot three. She usually wears a woolly hat.' He shook his head doubtfully. 'She's a *Big Issue* vendor.'

'Oh, her . . .' He nodded, pleased to have remembered.

'So, is she . . . ?' Lauren prompted.

He snapped out of his reverie. 'No, haven't seen her.' He paused, trying to remember. 'Not tonight.'

The interior of the building was noisy and smelly. The high walls and open-plan design meant that sounds bounced about, echoing and redoubling. The floor space had been partitioned off with plywood, painted pastel yellows and greens, but it did little to muffle the noise. A reception desk and further panelling had been constructed across the back of the church, and a circle of pale stone marked where the font had once stood. The panels blocked the view to the interior of the building, and Geri's eye searched upwards. A narrow balcony fringed the central aisle, and halfway down on the western side of the church stood a woman, or perhaps it was a girl — it was difficult to tell at that distance. She stared intently at Geri, continuing her disconcerting scrutiny even after it was plain that Geri was aware of her presence.

'Can I help you?'

Geri turned gratefully to the woman who had appeared from behind the partition and now stood at the reception desk. She was tall, solid and meaty, with frizzy gold hair and a broad, amiable face.

'We're looking for Adèle . . .' She searched her memory for a surname. 'Adèle Moorcroft.'

The woman gazed at them, the bland expression on her face masking a careful assessment of them both.

'I'm a friend,' Geri went on. 'I haven't seen her around for a few days, and I was worried.'

'A friend.' The woman's tone was neutral.

Geri was aware that someone had joined them — one of the men from the huddle standing outside. 'I said I'd come and see her. She seemed anxious about something.'

The man behind her laughed.

'D'you want to come in, Drew, or are you just getting a warm?' the woman asked.

He shrugged. He was clean-shaven, but his chin had a bluish shadow that wasn't all dirt. He wore a grey overcoat and a red baseball cap over long, black hair. His eyes slid away from eye contact, but Geri felt he was curious about her. The woman at the counter recalled her attention and the man slunk out of the door. Lauren touched Geri's elbow to let her know she was following him.

'Look,' Geri said. 'I'm not police or social security. I used to teach Adèle. I just want to know that she's all right.'

The woman stared back. 'I'm sorry,' she said at last. 'She isn't here.'

'Are you expecting her?'

She chuckled. 'This isn't a hotel. Our guests don't make reservations.'

'But you must have some idea.'

'I'm sorry.' She wore an implacable, complacent look that made Geri want to shake her. She turned on her heel and left.

Lauren was waiting for her outside.

'No luck?'

Geri shook her head. 'You?'

'I gave him a couple of quid. He said she left yesterday, or the day before. Sometime in the last couple of days. He was a bit confused about time . . .' She paused, frowning.

'What?'

She shrugged. 'Doesn't make sense, really. He said something about avoiding the taxman. Adèle isn't likely to be paying tax, is she?'

'The taxman . . .' Geri echoed.

'Does that mean something?'

'I don't know. Adèle told me she was in trouble with the taxman just before she disappeared.' Geri looked up and down the street, but there was no sign of the man. 'Where'd he go?'

'He got a bit nervous when I asked him why Adèle would owe taxes. Said it was a joke and cleared off.'

'So, we've got nothing. She's disappeared, could have gone anywhere, and we don't even know where to start. Shit!' She pushed a hand through her hair. 'I should've come earlier. I should've *done* something. I knew something was bothering her and I did bugger all!'

'Hey . . .' Lauren touched her lightly on the shoulder. 'You're only human. Come on,' she said. 'There's nothing more we can do tonight.'

As they turned to walk down the steps, they saw someone watching them. Geri recognized the woman from the balcony. She was small and painfully thin, and her skin had an unhealthy grey pallor.

At first, she didn't speak, merely staring at Geri with her big, frightened eyes. She stood slightly hunched and her eyes seemed to flare occasionally as if she was in pain — not physical pain, but a deep, tormenting sorrow, or regret.

'Can you help us?' Geri asked.

The woman didn't answer, but a shiver ran through her as she stared at them.

'Do you know where Adèle is?'

Silence.

'Can you get a message to her?' She had to thrust her hands into her pockets to prevent herself seizing the woman by the shoulders and shaking her.

'What d'you want her for?' She spoke reluctantly; her voice had a damaged, cracked quality, and she seemed to have trouble with her breathing.

Geri decided to come clean. 'I know she was bothered about something. I saw her on Wednesday. I said I'd come and see her.'

'Took your time.'

'I know,' Geri said, feeling her eyes water suddenly. 'I wish I'd—'

'She went on Thursday.'

'Why? Do you know?'

The woman flashed her a frightened look. 'You won't find her,' she said, after a moment or two.

'Is she safe?' Lauren asked. 'You can at least tell us that.'

'I don't have to tell you nothing.' She stared at Geri, sizing her up. 'You her teacher?'

'I was,' Geri said.

The woman frowned slightly, then nodded. 'She said to tell you she was sorry.'

'Sorry? What for?'

She shrugged. 'That was the message. I've give it.' She began to walk up the steps.

'Is that it?' Geri demanded, angry and frustrated. 'Duty done, now you can just forget about her?'

The woman turned on them, her eyes blazing. 'How many times did you remember her, eh? Once a week when you got your *Big Issue* and felt all holy for parting with a quid?' She turned away from them, heading for the church doors.

'You're right,' Geri called after her. 'I didn't do enough. But I'm trying to put it right now.'

The woman's expression was one of frank astonishment. 'Just what d'you think you can do?'

Geri found it hard to answer. What *could* she do to set right whatever it was that had put Adèle on the streets and kept her there for two years?

'I don't know,' she said at last. 'I was hoping maybe you'd tell me.'

The woman seemed to relent; she even smiled a little. 'You've got to watch your own back on the street, love,' she said. 'No one's gonna do it for you.'

'Was it something to do with owing tax?' Geri asked. 'Is that why she left?'

The woman took a sharp breath and shook her head.

'Look,' Geri said. 'I've got ten . . . fifteen pounds. It's yours.' The woman hesitated. 'I just want to know what's got her so frightened.'

She plucked the money from Geri's hand. 'She's running from the Taxman,' she said in a low voice, glancing cautiously past them at the group of men further down the street. 'He doesn't bother the lads. He goes after the nice-looking girls like Adèle. If they can't pay him, he lets them do sex work.'

'*Lets* them—' Geri clamped down hard on her anger. 'How do I find him?'

The woman shook her head in disbelief. 'You suicidal, or what? You don't go looking for the Taxman. Not if you want to stay healthy.'

They were caught in a hail shower going from the car to the house. Geri jiggled the key in the lock as hailstones rattled on the pavement and stung their cheeks.

'Come *on*!' Lauren shouted, hopping from one foot to the other to keep warm.

Geri took the key out of the lock and tried again. 'It's jammed,' she said. 'The key won't turn.'

'Bloody Nick!' Lauren grumbled.

'No, he's at work.'

A crash at the back of the house startled them both. Lauren looked at her wide-eyed. Geri started down the steps, but Lauren snatched at her coat sleeve. 'Call the police,' she whispered.

'What, because we've locked ourselves out?'

Lauren jabbed a finger in the direction of the back garden.

'Probably just that bloody cat again,' Geri said. But the woman's words rang in her ears: *You don't go looking for the Taxman!* Had he been here before? Was the note, the syringe, the acid attack on the car all down to the Taxman?

To hell with him! He had bullied and terrorized her for long enough. She pulled free, tiptoed down the steps and up the side path to the back of the house. She sensed Lauren at her back, which gave her the courage to go on, although her heart hammered in her chest. The back door stood open, and the kitchen light was on. They both stood at the corner of the house, Lauren clutching Geri's shoulder as if to prevent her going any further. They listened for a full half-minute, but all they could hear was the clatter of hailstones and the odd musical *ping* as a stone hit something resonant.

'I'm going in,' Geri breathed.

'Don't!'

Geri gritted her teeth and walked to the house, side-stepping a plant pot that had fallen from the bench beneath the kitchen window. The kitchen seemed unnaturally quiet after the clamour of the hailstorm; she could see nothing in the shadows of the hallway beyond the kitchen lights. The house seemed almost to be waiting, holding its breath.

Geri felt for the light switch just outside the kitchen door, hugely relieved to find that the hall was empty. The snick was on the front door Yale lock. A sharp hiss behind her made her jump and turn.

'Lauren!'

'The top bolt,' Lauren said, nodding at the door. The bolt had been drawn across. Geri grabbed an umbrella from the rack next to the hall stand.

They searched every room, every cupboard, under beds, behind doors. There was no sign that anybody had been there. Nothing had been moved, nothing taken, just the front door locked, and the back door left open.

* * *

He watched from behind the fence at the far end of the garden. They looked comical, the two of them, creeping up the side of the house, jostling forward, then pulling back. They left the back door open and he wondered if he should follow them — do them both, while he had the chance.

Separate, they were harmless, but put the two of them together and it was like paraquat and sugar: potentially explosive.

Lauren had information that could finish him. Frank had given the name Georgie, and the longer she was about, the more likely she would tell Geri Simpson. He stood, ready to vault back over the fence, but checked halfway. The lads had been stoned, easy to control, easy to dispose of. Control was the key: of the individual, and therefore the situation. It wasn't enough to put the fear of God into Lauren and hope she kept quiet. Once he started on this, he had to follow through, he had to be sure he could finish her. Her silence had to be guaranteed. But two was more difficult than one. More unpredictable. And he'd never done a woman before.

There was only the one car outside when he arrived. Lauren's. Go in, do the job and get out again. That was the plan. But she wasn't home, and when they came back together, he'd thought, *if she sees me . . .*

He'd panicked and run for it, right across the lawn, without thinking. Footprints all over. Hopefully they'd go as the hailstones melted. As he watched, the lights went on in an upstairs room and Lauren moved across the window.

He gripped the fence, still undecided, then an idea came to him and he smiled. Simple. He'd find out from Lauren what she'd told Geri, *then* he'd do her . . . And then he'd know what to do about Geri.

* * *

The police sent out a lone WPC. She gave them a reference number.

'You'll need it for insurance.'

'Nothing's been taken,' Geri said.

'In case you find anything missing.'

'Aren't you going to take fingerprints or something?' Lauren demanded.

'We're short of resources. And you said yourself you've had nothing stolen. You probably disturbed them. They often lock the front to give themselves a bit of extra time if the owners come back unexpected.'

'And what if *they* come back?'

'Not likely. You might consider having a mortise fitted. Or a Yale deadlock — these old ones are so easy to open. All you need is a wire hook, in through the letter box and Bob's your uncle.'

'I'll get it done tomorrow,' Geri said.

'Meantime keep them bolted. Front and back,' she advised.

'As if we needed telling,' Lauren muttered as she closed the door after her.

* * *

Geri woke with a violent start. The doorbell was ringing, and someone was hammering at the door. She peered at the green LED of her alarm clock. Seven thirty-five. She groaned. 'Nick!' It was still dark, and very cold. She struggled into her dressing gown and jammed her feet into her slippers.

'All right,' she grumbled, stumbling down the stairs. 'I'm *coming*!' She hadn't slept well and in her few snatches of sleep had dreamt that the catch on the front door was faulty and the door kept blowing open in the wind.

She drew back the bolts and Nick stormed in, furious. 'What the fuck's all this about? Locking me out of my own house.'

'Before you start,' Geri interrupted sharply, 'we were burgled last night.'

'*Burgled?*' He looked past her as if searching for signs of the break-in.

'Nothing was taken. I'm going to get someone to fit a new lock.'

'Oh, great — there goes my sleep for the day.'

'Thanks for your concern,' Geri said, ladling on the sarcasm, 'We're a bit shaken up, but we'll get over it.'

Nick glared at her, a muscle in his jaw jumping. 'I've just finished a twelve-hour shift,' he said. 'I'd like to get a bit of kip.'

'Who's stopping you?'

'If you've got some locksmith banging and hammering—'

'I'll get him to come later, all right?'

He didn't answer. His eyes widened suddenly, and he paled so dramatically that Geri actually looked over her shoulder expecting to see the burglar returned, axe in hand.

'What about my workshop?' he demanded.

'What about it?'

'Oh, you bloody idiot!' He pushed past her, running down the steps and around to the side of the house, returning a few moments later. 'Sorry,' he said. 'I overreacted. I thought—'

'You thought your bike had been stolen. Now I know where I come on your list of priorities.'

'No,' he said. 'I—'

'You're a self-obsessed, selfish bastard, Nick.'

There was a finality in her voice that she had never heard before, in all their arguments, and reading the look on his face, Geri realized Nick had heard it, too. They both knew what it meant, but neither was ready to acknowledge it. Not yet. For a moment, they just looked at each other, then Nick stalked past her and went straight upstairs.

Lauren waited until Nick had gone to bed before venturing downstairs. Geri had showered and dressed, but she still felt fragile. 'You look a hundred,' Lauren remarked.

'That's a comfort,' she shot back. 'At least I don't look as old as I feel.'

'I know what you mean.' Lauren ran a hand over her face. 'Tell me I look human,' she said.

Geri glanced up from buttering a piece of toast. Lauren's complexion glowed with good health and her eyes sparkled as if she'd had eight hours of dreamless sleep. 'I'm too good a friend to lie to you,' she said. Then, 'Could you do me a favour? Phone a locksmith and get something fitted that might keep out a determined five-year-old for more than two seconds.'

'Where will you be?'

'*Big Issue* office.'

Lauren considered for a moment. 'On condition you report back.' Geri nodded. '*And*, if you're going to do any manhunting, you'll let me tag along.'

'I thought you were working today.'

'I'm too shaken up by the burglary,' she said, flashing her a wide-eyed, wounded look.

'Yeah,' Geri said, a little sourly, 'I can see that.'

'Am I to give Nick a key?'

Geri looked up and saw the teasing glint in her friend's eye. 'Don't tempt me,' she said. 'Just don't bloody tempt me.'

35

The *Big Issue* office was closed when she arrived, so Geri walked into the shopping centre and window-shopped for an hour. She got back just after ten and joined a queue of three men who were picking up their morning's quota of magazines. The office was divided into two: the counter, which was slightly raised above floor level, and a glass-fronted interview room, which was furnished with comfortable chairs and a coffee table.

Geri asked to speak to the manager while the men stood to one side, sipping tea from plastic cups, apparently in no hurry to leave, and evidently curious about her.

The manager, a lean, angular man of about thirty-five, came out of a room at the back of the premises. He raised the flap at the end of the counter and stepped into the main foyer.

'Paul Watling,' he said, offering his hand. He greeted the three men who were making slow progress with their tea, and they replied warmly. Geri felt a surge of optimism — this was a man who might be prepared to listen.

He showed her into the interview room and shut the door.

'Bit of a goldfish bowl, but at least it's private,' he said. 'Excuse the smell.' There was a musty odour, like damp cardboard. 'We had a load of new clothes donated recently and some of the lads left their old stuff for disposal; haven't been able to get the smell out since.'

It was said to disarm, but Geri's encounter at the hostel had made her wary, and she determined to keep her distance. She apologized for taking up his time, but he dismissed it lightly.

'You saved me from a shitload of paperwork,' he said, sitting opposite her in one of the chairs. He leaned forward slightly and made eye contact. Geri was struck by the iridescence of his eyes; their colour seemed to shift from time to time, like light reflected from brown silk. There was intelligence and a huge charge of energy that seemed to spark about him, appearing almost to make him crackle as he moved. He held her gaze with such intensity that she had to look away, unable to bear his steady, open appraisal of her.

'You know Adèle Moorcroft? Adèle N218,' she added, giving Adèle's badge number.

'I know her.'

She was grateful, when she glanced up into his face that the question hadn't put him on his guard, that it hadn't made him suspicious of her.

'She's vanished. I've looked everywhere for her — she's not at her usual pitch and she's left the shelter. She been acting strangely this last week; something was bothering her, and now—' Her shoulders slumped. 'I'm really worried.' It had come tumbling out, despite her original resolve to test the water, see how far she could trust this man.

He sat cross-legged on the chair, his hands gripping his ankles. 'She hasn't been into the office since Thursday,' he said. 'It happens. People have good intentions, big dreams, but reality sometimes gets in the way. It takes a hell of a lot of will-power to get off the street.'

'When I talked to her last week, she was full of plans for her flat. She told me she wanted to train as a hairdresser. Adèle isn't stupid. She was getting herself together, saving up . . .' Her voice trailed off. *It's impossible*, she thought, crushed by the enormity of the task. She would never find Adèle.

'The longer you're on the streets, the harder it is to get off them,' Paul said in answer. 'The skills that help you survive on the street are the skills that keep you there.' He frowned. 'But you're right. Adèle was getting herself straight. She's off drugs, stopped doing sex work months ago, and she's coming to the top of the list for supported accommodation.' He shrugged, unwrapped one ankle and stretched out his leg.

'I saw her on Wednesday,' Geri explained. 'She seemed frightened. She refused money from me.'

'Refused money?' He seemed incredulous.

'I got the feeling she was being watched and didn't want to get me involved.'

He was still for a moment or two, and his gaze drifted slightly to Geri's left. 'Shit,' he said quietly and unemphatically.

'One of the men at the shelter said she owed taxes. Could that have anything to do with it?'

He glanced up. 'Is that what he said — that she owed taxes?'

Geri tried to remember the phrase the woman at the shelter had used. 'Someone told me she was "running from the Taxman".' Something like that. It's street slang, isn't it?'

Paul nodded. In one fluid movement he climbed up onto the chair, crouching like a gargoyle and staring at the floor. '"Taxing" is another word for thieving,' he said. 'Sometimes gangs, sometimes individuals. They prey on beggars, *Big Issue* vendors, whoever they think won't fight back. Sometimes they take a percentage, sometimes the lot.'

'Taking a percentage?' Geri said. 'Of *what*?'

'It's easy money,' Paul said, with a shrug. 'And it builds their rep. as hard men.' He moved again to a sitting position. Geri was fascinated by his sheer physical energy.

'If Adèle was being taxed, maybe she decided it was safer to move on.'

'Don't you know?' She glanced apologetically at him. 'I mean, wouldn't she tell you?'

'Sometimes it's easier to pay up and keep *shtum*. Hope they get fed up or move onto bigger prey.' He frowned, tugging at his lower lip. 'You're right, though — normally I get to hear about it. Either he's got them badly scared, or he's new. Maybe he's only just moved in on them.'

Geri considered for a moment. Paul had been straight with her, but she didn't want word getting out that Adèle might know something about Frank's death. 'There was something else,' she said, choosing her words carefully. 'Something that made her frightened to sleep on the streets.'

'Yeah. I was surprised she went into a shelter.'

'She *hates* those places,' Geri agreed.

'If she thought this Taxman would find her at her squat, it could explain why she plumped for the emergency shelter.'

'Maybe,' Geri said.

He regarded her steadily for a few moments, the colours in his irises shifting and swirling. 'But you think that's why she moved *out* of the shelter, don't you?'

Geri nodded. 'I don't think she feels safe anywhere.' She hesitated, then decided to ask, 'I was wondering . . . If she gets in touch, or if anyone hears anything, could you give her my number? Tell her to call any time.' She rummaged in her handbag for a scrap of paper and wrote her name and number on it. 'Any time,' she repeated, handing him the slip.

He tucked it in his shirt pocket. 'You a relative?'

'A friend.'

He smiled. 'It's nice to have a good friend.'

Geri felt sick to the core. If she was such a good friend, why hadn't Adèle come to her — told her what she was frightened of?

* * *

Self-preservation was a large part of Adèle's reason for keeping quiet about what she had seen, but a concern for her friend's safety was also a factor. Geri was more than just another punter, and when she was properly straight, and off the street for good, she would make Geri proud to be called her friend.

She shivered and curled up tighter in her layers of cardboard. One damp old building was much like another, but in this new city, where everything was unfamiliar to her, the shadows seemed deeper and the emptiness bigger and lonelier and far, far more dangerous than ever they did at home.

She felt homesick for her warehouse, her own things around her, the bivvy she had spent so much time gathering together. A shudder racked her like a convulsion; it was nearly two weeks since she had made that final journey to the warehouse, seen what she had seen — but his laughter had rattled around in her head, replaying that fearful night over and over.

When she heard that laugh again, on Thursday night, it was as if a monster had stepped right out of her nightmares. Even here, a hundred or more miles away, faceless and nameless, she was afraid.

36

PC Mayhew snaffled a mug of tea and some beans on toast from the food counter and hurried over to the group sitting in the centre of the canteen. They were taking a lunch break and catching up on the latest on the glue-sniffing case.

Mayhew slid his tray onto the table and dragged out the middle chair of three. 'Have you heard?'

'Heard what?' Dhar asked.

'Beresford, on the CCTV videotapes. Mincing around, chatting up them lads on the concourse.'

'Old news, Sam. He was asking around for information on Frank Traynor,' Dhar said.

'So *he* says. Only he wasn't told to question the rent boys until three days later.'

'He's—'

'Keen?' Mayhew laughed. 'We all know what he's keen on. He can't stay away from the place.'

'I was going to say concerned. What *is* your problem?' Dhar demanded.

Mayhew stared at her, astonished. 'He's bent, a shirt-lifter—'

'You always said Sergeant Beresford was all right.'

'That was before.'

'*Before?* He was gay "before". You just didn't know it.'

'Well, now I do.' Mayhew was enjoying himself: he hadn't forgiven Beresford for dragging him off the squealing little fucker at the railway station earlier in the week. He took another mouthful of beans and toast and chewed as he spoke. 'Me, I like to see what I'm up against.'

'That why you and me got on so well when I first came here?' Dhar saw the others look at her as if to remind themselves of the colour of her skin. They looked away as she caught their eye — even Mayhew looked a little abashed.

'That was a misunderstanding, Nita,' he said, blushing slightly. 'We got off on the wrong foot. Beresford has been sharing a locker room with us lads.' He shuddered at the thought. 'How can you trust a guy like that? He could've lied about all kinds of stuff.'

Dhar sighed. 'We all lie, all the time. Place like this, if you're honest, you're asking for trouble.'

'All I'm saying is he's been warned off cruising the station and there he is, back again.'

Dhar exclaimed in exasperation at the word 'cruising'.

'He was *seen*,' Mayhew insisted. 'Talking to the lads again. That sulky-looking one — the one on the tape.'

'If he was, he must've had good reason.'

Mayhew looked around the table at the others, raised his eyebrows and pursed his lips. It was enough. The others started laughing and Dhar knew the argument was lost.

She was on her way out through the door when Beresford came in. She blushed guiltily for having been talking about him, even if it was in his defence. The laughter died down at her back as the others noticed the sergeant at the door.

'Go up to the incident room, will you?' he said. 'DCI Thomas wants to see everyone.'

'Has something happened?' she asked.

He shrugged. 'I know he's had those lab results back.' He seemed to hesitate, looking past her to the group she had just left.

'I'll tell the others, shall I?' she suggested.

There was no mistaking his relief. 'Five minutes,' he said.

As he left, the laughter broke out again.

Not everyone was available to attend the briefing. Some of the uniformed officers were out on patrol, and a few of the CID team working on the case were off duty, but the incident room was still fairly packed. Files, reports and photographs were stacked on desks and filing cabinets, jumbled with crisp and sweet wrappers and empty paper cups. The mess would build up until someone lost patience with it and swept a load of the detritus into the nearest bin. Thomas came out of his office and crossed the room to stand in front of the whiteboards.

'Until now, we've been treating these deaths as suspicious. We hadn't ruled out the possibility that others were involved, but we didn't have proof they were, either. Well,' he gazed into their faces, his eyes glittering with excitement, 'now we've got it.' He nodded to DI Hesketh, who stood up and faced the gathering.

'The boss has been mithering scientific support for reports on blood and stomach contents,' he said. 'They've been slow, as ever, but they came back today with details on Frank Traynor.'

'I requested a more thorough analysis of his stomach contents,' Thomas explained, 'because the pathologist was fairly sure that Frank's body had been moved after death. It was possible, therefore, that the fire was intended to destroy evidence.'

There were a few nods around the room. The team looked tired, but they were keyed up, sensing his excitement at this new development. He went on, 'I was particularly interested to know if semen was present in the stomach.'

'It was,' Hesketh said, answering the unspoken question of the fifteen or so officers present. 'Which means we're now looking at sexual assault and murder.'

Thomas silenced a rumble of concern with a wave of his hand. 'We couldn't have treated these cases any other way — there simply wasn't enough evidence to confirm or completely rule out strangulation in either of the lads, and there was a strong chance they'd been experimenting with drugs. There still is.'

He scanned the room; some of these men and women had children of their own — some of them about the same age as the two dead boys. 'Blood analysis confirms inhalants in the lads' bloodstreams.' He paused, his brow furrowed. 'And morphiates.'

'Smack?' Mayhew murmured, almost to himself.

'Right now, we don't know what was forced on them, and what they did willingly, so we take the approach that there have been new developments, but the investigation is ongoing.'

'Is that the official line, Boss?' someone asked.

Thomas nodded. 'We all know how long it takes for lab tests to come through. And it was pure fluke that the semen was intact — forensics say stomach acid normally destroys it.'

'What about Ryan?' Garvey asked. 'Is the pathologist going to check him out for sexual assault an' all?'

'He's collecting samples now,' Thomas said. 'There'll be a press conference at one this afternoon. Meanwhile, we start looking for a male homosexual.' There was an uncomfortable silence as everyone made an effort not to look at Vince.

'Will they be able to get a DNA match from the semen?' DC Winter asked.

'We don't know yet. For now, we need to check any registered paedophiles in the area and ask the public to come forward with information — sightings of either of the lads with an older man, anyone who's been behaving strangely — the usual.'

'Any sick bastard who like little boys for company,' Garvey muttered.

Thomas saw Vince tense. 'Sick bastard he may be,' he agreed. 'But he's also cool and calculating. And he seems to have some knowledge of forensic procedure — enough anyway to obliterate most of the evidence. These boys were supplied with heroin. Maybe they wanted it, or maybe it was used to subdue them. Either way, someone provided it.'

'So, we interview known dealers — ruffle a few feathers,' Hesketh said.

There were a few mutters of complaint at this, finding and talking to all of the dealers and drug pushers, even in their small patch of the city, was a tall order.

'What about the possible witness?' Dhar asked. 'The girl who bought the gas canister from Great Outdoors?'

'Nothing so far. If she was homeless, she might have moved on, but a description has been circulated to the emergency shelters and hostels.'

'I wouldn't mind talking to a few street people — see if they recognize the description.'

Thomas nodded. 'Good idea. But take someone with you.' His eyes skimmed the room, demanding their full attention. 'This guy could have previous form; he may have done this elsewhere in the country. I'm having a HOLMES room set up,' he went on. 'From now on, I want every enquiry, every phone call logged on the proper forms.' He glanced at Hesketh.

'There's a stack on their way up to us now, Boss.'

'Good. No exceptions,' he warned. 'I want the operatives to be able to get to work on the backlog as soon as they're up and running.

'But until we get some feedback from the database, we'll have to do this by hard slog. Garvey — anything on the security guard on the video tape?'

Garvey grimaced. 'The teams change over at the weekend, Boss, and they have a high staff turnover anyway — new faces coming and going all the time. No one recognized him. But I'll talk to the supervisor when he gets back off holiday on Monday.'

Thomas wasn't happy with the delay, but nothing could be done about it. 'Make it a priority,' he said. 'If the guard saw whatever it was that scared Frank off, we might get a description of the killer.'

Teams were set up to question known paedophiles and a couple of DCs were sent to talk to the boys on the station concourse to see if they had any ideas. Within minutes the room was empty, and Thomas turned his attention to what he would tell the journalists later that day.

* * *

The press conference was noisy and difficult. A briefing room was cleared of rubbish and folding chairs were set out for the gathered media. Blue pinboards were set against the wall to provide a backdrop for the cameras. The table at which DCI Thomas and DI Hesketh sat had been borrowed from a conference room on the top floor and getting it down three flights of stairs had been no easy task.

Cameras began flashing and whirring as the men took their seats. Thomas made a simple statement, explaining that 'new evidence' had come to light, and that the two deaths were now being treated as murder. The questions began immediately:

'Why has it taken so long to discover that the boys had been murdered?'

'What "new evidence" has been uncovered?'

'Were the boys sexually assaulted?'

'What are you doing to put right your earlier mistakes?'

'How many officers have been assigned to the investigation?'

Then, 'What have you to say to the parents? Their sons' characters have been dragged through the mud.'

'Not by me,' Thomas growled, his voice cutting through the hubbub.

The gathered TV, press and radio journalists fell silent, and he realized that he had committed an unforgivable gaff: reminding them of the consequences of irresponsible reporting. He needed their co-operation, and was anxious not to alienate them, so he went on in a more conciliatory tone, 'The men and women on my team have great sympathy for what the families are going through, and we are doing everything we can to find out how Ryan and Frank died.'

He knew that Frank had died, as Ryan had, retching and vomiting, humiliated beyond anything he had ever feared at the hands of the playground bullies.

* * *

Five hours later, some of the team were watching the press conference on a TV in the incident room. The registered paedophiles had been rounded up and questioned; all but two had consented to blood samples being taken for DNA typing; the other two could be matched using samples already on record. It would take time to access the records, but the process had already been put in train.

Garvey glanced over as Vince Beresford came into the room. Thomas was appealing for information: '. . . anyone who is concerned about an older man associating with younger boys . . .'

'He should ask Vince,' Garvey said. 'Get him to put out a few feelers.'

'Get stuffed, Garvey,' Vince said, cutting off the laughter before it really got started.

Garvey turned, his arm stretched across the back of the chair. 'Sorry, Vince, didn't see you there. I was just saying you'd be best placed to get inside information on the gay scene.'

'Yeah? All I heard was a cheap joke made to raise a cheap laugh.'

Garvey smiled. 'What's up, Vince, not getting enough?'

Vince lunged at him, and Garvey jumped to his feet, but Mayhew got between them. 'Come on, Sarge,' he said. 'We've got overtime to earn.' He may have had his differences with Beresford, but when it came to a ruck between uniform and CID, he knew where his loyalties lay.

Vince stood for a moment or two, breathing hard, staring at Garvey, wondering if the satisfaction of punching his fat mouth would be worth the resulting fallout.

Mayhew looked embarrassed and a little nervous.

'I'll meet you downstairs — five minutes,' Vince said.

Mayhew hesitated, but Vince glared at him until he gave way. Garvey sat down again, and the remaining CID officers settled to listen to the rest of the news. As Vince turned to leave, something on the noticeboard near the door caught his eye: a picture of Julian Clary in sequinned pink. A photograph of Vince had been pasted over his face. Vince tore down the picture and took a few steps towards Garvey. He was apparently absorbed in the TV news. Vince changed his mind and went instead to a stack of videos piled on a table near the whiteboards. The railway-station tapes. They were clearly labelled by time and date. He chose one and slipped it inside his tunic.

37

He waited outside the library until five twenty. The woman he had spoken to on Thursday said that Lauren finished at five on Saturday. Where the hell was she? Thirty-five minutes freezing his balls off in the worst downpour since the pigging flood!

He was drenched and in a foul temper. He should be checking on his girls: he liked them to think he could turn up any time, and he didn't want them skiving off into pubs and caffs just because of a shower of rain.

A steady stream of people had left the building from five until a quarter past, but Lauren was not among them. He waited, standing in the shadow of the stone gate into the gardens opposite the library until the main lights went out and a small, balding man in a belted overcoat came out. He pulled the great wooden door closed, locked it and, dropping his keys into his briefcase, put up his umbrella and trotted off towards the bus station.

He felt cheated. Betrayed. She should have been here. For a few minutes he continued standing in the gateway. How could one stupid bitch prove so elusive when the lads had been so easy?

* * *

It was dark. Headlamps froze the raindrops in their glare and dazzled off the wet tarmac. A changeable wind goaded the rain in icy bursts, spattering pavements and pedestrians, driving even the more determined shoppers indoors.

Lauren seized Geri's arm and pulled her inside Dixons. 'Look!' she exclaimed.

Ryan's photograph smiled out at them from a TV screen. They huddled close to the set, listening to the muted commentary. '. . . treating the two deaths as murder . . .' They heard. The news item went on to DCI Thomas's appeal for help from the public, and he asked again for the woman who bought the gas canister at Great Outdoors to come forward.

Geri stood in front of the TV set staring stupidly at it, even though the presenter had gone on to the sports news.

A salesman approached them. 'Can I help you at all?' he asked.

'No,' Geri said, with a finality that was more than a simple answer to his question.

'Only we're about to close . . .'

They stepped back onto the pavement. The possibility had always been there, but Geri had held it at arm's-length, listening to the arguments of those around her, trying to convince herself, at least in part, that it was a vicious prank that had gone wrong. Now she had to face the fact that both Ryan and Frank had been murdered.

'Murder,' Geri said.

'And Adèle probably disappeared because she saw what happened to Frank,' Lauren said. 'Maybe it's time to go to the police — tell them about her. If she *is* the woman who bought the gas canister, she might've seen—'

'I'll go to the police when I find her,' Geri interrupted. 'She's frightened, terrified, and I won't have them hunting her down like a criminal.'

'*Witness*. They didn't imply she was involved, they're asking her to come forward as a witness.'

'It's all the same to Adèle.'

They left the store and walked on. They had been looking for hours, asking street people, trying the theatres, shops, the arcades, even the library. No one had seen Adèle since Thursday, when someone had seen her selling magazines outside Marks & Spencer. They arrived outside the storefront in another burst of heavy rain. The security staff were guarding the doors, preventing any last-minute hopefuls from gate-crashing, shepherding the few remaining shoppers out into the rain and wind. There was no sign of Adèle.

'I give up,' Geri said. 'Let's go home.' She ducked under the umbrella and they began the climb up the hill towards her car. Fifteen yards ahead, a man stood with his back to them, hair flattened, his overcoat streaked by the rain. He seemed to be looking for someone. Geri steered Lauren towards him.

'Joe?'

He turned and for a fraction of a second it seemed he didn't recognize her, then his face lit up.

'Geri!'

'You look lost,' Geri commented, smiling despite the cold, despite their absolute failure in their search for Adèle, despite everything, simply because Joe looked so pleased to see her.

Joe waved a hand in front of his face. 'Got stood up, didn't I? How about you? Out shopping?' He glanced down at their hands.

'No, we're . . .' She hesitated, unsure how to explain. Joe gave Lauren a curious look and Geri realized she hadn't introduced them. 'Oh, sorry,' she said. This is Lauren — Lauren, Joe. He—'

'Helps out at the youth club. I know.' Lauren offered her hand. 'She's told me all about you.'

He took her hand, smiling slowly.

The rain was getting heavier, buffeting the umbrella, threatening to turn it inside-out, but Joe seemed reluctant to leave them and Geri asked, 'Are you going to wait for your friend, or can I offer you a lift anywhere?'

He checked his watch. 'Might as well give up on her,' he said. 'I'm working later and I'll be wanting me tea soon.'

'You're a security guard, aren't you? Lauren asked.

'Aye.'

'And you patrol warehouses and such around the city centre.'

'So?' She had put him on the defensive.

Lauren squeezed Geri's arm. 'Tell him, Geri.'

Geri balked at the idea.

'You said yourself we can't go around these places on our own, not after what happened last time.'

'What places?' Joe asked.

'Derelict places,' Geri said.

He shot her a pained look. 'You were lucky it was me found you last time, and not some druggy or drunk.'

Geri shrugged. She felt uncomfortable talking to Joe about it — after all, he was supposed to kick people out if he found them dossing on premises protected by his firm. But if Adèle *was* in trouble, if she had seen something in the warehouse where Frank was killed, they had to find her, persuade her to go to the police.

'Have you seen the news today?' Geri asked.

'Aye.' He searched her face. 'Is it something to do with the killings? Is that it? You know they're saying it's murder, now?'

Geri shivered as an icy raindrop fell from the umbrella onto the back of her neck. 'Look,' she said. 'Can we go somewhere where we can talk?'

He led the way, showing them to a dingy pub frontage in a narrow street around the corner. Geri must have walked past it a thousand times and never noticed it. The interior was cosy and warm and the atmosphere friendly. By the time they had got the second round in, the story was told.

Joe sipped his beer, pinched the froth off his upper lip and thought for a moment. 'Why don't you two go home, get yourselves warm and dry and let me do a bit of poking about?' he suggested. 'If I can't find her, there's people I know who can.'

Geri felt a surge of excitement. Joe would find Adèle, she was sure of it. 'I would be glad of a hot shower and a change of clothing . . .'

'Go home and get some rest,' Joe advised. 'It might take a while, mind. If she did see the bloke, she won't want to be found. And she'll know all the places to hide.'

'But she's our best chance of finding the bastard who killed Ryan and Frank.' Geri said. 'And anyway, the longer she stays out there, the greater the danger.'

'You're right there,' Joe said, with feeling.

'He's bound to find out about Adèle sooner or later, and when he does, he'll go looking for her.'

Joe took a breath and exhaled explosively; he seemed to be struggling with himself. Geri gave him a questioning look and he shrugged. 'I think you should be careful who you talk to,' he said, with apparent reluctance. 'I don't want to be overdramatic, but this bloke must be someone the kids trust. Ryan was no fool. He wouldn't go with just anyone.'

Geri digested the full implications of the statement: if the kids trusted him, so did she, which meant it was someone close to her — someone she dealt with on a day-to-day basis.

'What about Barry?' Lauren asked. Geri and Joe looked at her blankly. 'I mean, is it just coincidence he got beaten up around the time Adèle disappeared?'

Joe took another swallow of beer and shot a glance at Geri. 'Baz Mandel's so full of shite, he was bound to have it kicked out of him sooner or later.'

Geri was shocked: it sounded callous, cruel. She was about to reply, but checked herself — hadn't her first reaction been to think that he'd had it coming? People like Barry wrecked lives. He didn't care who he sold to, and he revelled in the power it gave him, revelled in his ability to sell drugs right under their noses knowing they couldn't catch him. But an unsettling idea kept needling away at her: whoever attacked Barry must be worse than him, and if *he* started supplying kids, where would it end?

38

'The police are saying it's murder,' Agnes said. It was after closing time and she was snipping and trimming a new girl's hair. Pearl had left a pile of sweepings in the corner by the back room; she really would have to talk to that little slattern.

She assessed the new girl in the mirror — a pale redhead, gorgeous rich auburn hair, and no make-up. Barely sixteen. Another 'special order' no doubt. 'I'll layer it to give it a bit of lift — it's a bit heavy in the fringe the way she's got it now.'

He shrugged. 'Whatever. Only get a move on — I'm in a hurry.' He sat down and watched her work. 'What makes them think it's murder?'

'You tell me.' She was angry, but there was still time for him to redeem himself.

He turned down the corners of his mouth. 'I give up.'

'I've been telling that poor woman it was a terrible accident,' she said. 'But it was murder all along.'

'Which are you worried about — her feelings, or missing the chance of some amateur dramatics?'

'I've been misleading her.'

He raised his eyebrows. 'You said it.'

She gestured with the scissors. 'I feel such a fool! You're supposed to know that sort of thing — you're *supposed* to have contacts.'

'I thought you were the one with the hot-line to God.'

'The spirit world,' she corrected him. 'What am I going to *say* to her?'

'You'll think of something.'

'I shouldn't have to,' she snapped, already thinking how she would frame her excuse to Mrs Connelly: Ryan had been protecting his mother, hiding things from her, not wanting to upset her.

'You've had some good intelligence from me.'

She snorted derisively. 'Thirty quid's worth? That's what this cut and style'd cost you anywhere else. And what about the make-over I did on the blonde lass?'

'How many sessions have you done with the grieving mother?' he shot back. 'What is it, twenty-five quid a throw? I'd say you've had your money's worth.'

She missed the threat in his voice, or she wouldn't have carried on. 'Bits and bobs, I've had. About as much use as all this dead hair.' She snipped away at the girl's head.

'Don't take it out on me,' the girl protested, pulling away from her.

Agnes took a handful of hair and gave it a tug. 'Hold still,' she warned. 'I know what I'm about.'

'Meaning I don't?' He had settled into his chair, adopting a lazy, almost sleepy pose. Agnes had seen it before, and it usually meant trouble, but she'd been embarrassed, professionally, and she felt for Mrs Connelly.

'What happened to those boys?' she demanded. 'Surely you can find out?'

'Maybe they got too lippy,' he said quietly.

He leaned forward in his chair, a slow, sinuous movement — Agnes got the impression he was *uncoiling*, and she sensed the true danger of her situation.

Agnes busied herself, feeling his gaze on her face, trying to avoid looking at the girl in the mirror, because the redhead had sensed it too — her eyes were wide and filled with dark fear.

She finished the job in silence, drying and primping until the girl looked the right side of presentable.

'So,' she said, brightly. 'What do you think?'

He took a long time to answer. Standing the girl up and turning her around, pinching her chin between his thumb and forefinger and tilting her head this way and that while Agnes looked on with a nervous smile.

'She'll do,' he said at last.

Agnes's smile broadened and she patted the girl on the shoulder. 'Off you go, chick, and get your coat.' The girl went obediently to the coat rail and Agnes turned back to the Taxman.

Two rabbit punches, one to her eye, the other to her mouth as she dropped. The girl shrieked in dismay as Agnes fell. He bent over her, hauled her up by the front of her dress.

'Not the face!' she pleaded.

He grinned — or rather he bared his teeth, and Agnes quailed.

'I only wanted a bit of inside information,' she wailed.

He dropped her and she banged her head on the floor. She saw him take the girl by the elbow and steer her out of the shop, but as the door swung to, he stopped it with his hand and turned back to her. She cowered, and he laughed.

'Your spirit messengers didn't see that coming, did they?'

* * *

Fucking Agnes! Talking to him like that in front of one of his girls. Talking him *down*. He slipped the car into first and screamed away from the kerb, enjoying the slight hiss of alarm from his passenger. One word — just one word of complaint, anything to justify giving her a slap. But she kept her head down and avoided his eye.

'She should be grateful,' he said. 'Gems I've fed her.'

'I know.'

This was enough. 'You *know*? What the fuck do you *know*?'

The girl gulped audibly. If she could've bitten her tongue off, she would have. 'I'm agreeing with you.'

He tapped her across the mouth with the back of his hand. He didn't even need to look to gauge the distance; it was a reflex. Her teeth scraped his knuckles and he had to suppress an urge to slap her again for the discomfort.

'I'll tell you what you'd better *know*,' he said. 'You'd better know when to open your legs and when to shut your mouth.' He glanced across at her. She was staring at her hands.

'Don't you *dare* fuck up your face with crying. You've got twenty minutes. Mr Alman asked for a pretty, freckled redhead, not a frog-faced cunt with a fat lip and red blotches all over her face.'

She sniffed, swallowed, blinked, stared hard at her fingernails.

He pulled up outside the hotel and looked at her properly. 'You'd better not be sulking.'

Her eyes flew wide. 'No! I swear — I'm . . . I'm just keeping my mouth shut, like you said.'

Was she throwing his words back at him? He was about to give her a dig, just in case, when he saw the punter go in. It would have to wait.

'Know who you're looking for?' he asked.

She nodded and got out, moving slowly towards the revolving doors of the hotel. Dozy bitch! He got as far as opening the window to shout after her to shift her arse but managed to stop himself in time. He'd give himself away if he wasn't careful. He ran a hand over his face and took some calming breaths.

Looking for your special place, Agnes called it. If she knew where his special place was, maybe she wouldn't be so keen to encourage him to go there.

Images of Ryan flashed through his mind, and he moaned softly. He was beginning to realize that this need in him, now awakened, would never be satisfied. He wanted to experience more, to do more. That phrase, *next time,* had rattled around in his head until it became a background noise, like city traffic.

He thought he had found someone. Purely by chance: he was getting out of his car after work, and almost bumped into him. About sixteen, smooth skin, with that healthy blush of colour you only ever see on middle-class kids. He was delivering newspapers.

When he'd sorted Lauren, he would find out the lad's name, his school, where he lived. Snatch him on neutral territory. He had already given some thought to finding a suitable place. Somewhere with a few home comforts this time; if he couldn't find an empty place, he would maybe go for rental. Somewhere nice, but private, where they wouldn't be disturbed.

* * *

Dean left the house at seven forty-five, using the latchkey to close the door silently. Since Ryan's death, he always barred his bedroom door with the chest of drawers, and his mum had given up trying, so he knew she wouldn't notice him gone. He had left his bike in the back entry earlier in the evening — a risk, given the crime rate in the area, but he expected to do a lot of travelling that night, and he couldn't afford bus fares.

He retrieved the bike, wheeled it to the far end of the smelly passage, avoiding the dog turds and split rubbish bags that disgorged their contents onto the ground. He emerged at the end of the street and mounted up out of sight of home.

Visiting time had just finished; the car parks were emptying, and he was the only person waiting to go up in the lifts on the ground floor. He waited for what seemed an age, clutching a box of Maltesers he had bought at the petrol station opposite the hospital. He had to wait for fifteen or more people to get out before he could step inside, and as the doors closed, a man in a white coat rushed up and jammed a hand in the gap. The doors shuddered, then opened.

The doctor stood next to Dean, towering over him and occasionally glancing down. Dean expected at any moment to be challenged. Sweat broke out on his upper lip; he had stuffed Ryan's knife in the back of his waistband, and it chafed his buttocks.

He began to think he was mad to have come here, but the feverish pain in his tooth and the constant tugging sensation of the cuts on his arms were a reminder: he had a debt to repay.

He stepped out of the lift into a large, grey-tiled lobby. The wards ran in opposite directions on either side of it. He went to the door marked 3B, and went in. The ward was L-shaped, divided off into rooms around the nurses' offices. Handwritten labels slotted into metal runners held the patients' names.

Dean got as far as the second door before a nurse stopped him.

'Hello,' she said, using that voice adults put on for kids much younger than him. Normally it pissed him off, but this time he decided to use it.

'Hiya.' He gazed up at her.

'Are you lost, pet?'

He shook his head. 'Come to see our Barry.'

She glanced back at one of the doors further up the corridor. 'He's tired now, pet. Why didn't you come in with your mum and dad — they've not long since gone.'

'I did,' Dean said. 'But I . . .' He wriggled his shoulders, frowning. 'I got upset and . . .' He hung his head.

She patted his shoulder. 'I know it looks bad, but he'll soon be on his feet,' she said.

Dean sniffed a bit, refusing to be comforted. Somewhere a buzzer sounded, and she glanced round, distracted.

'Can I see him?' Dean pleaded. 'Just for a minute? I bought him some chocolates.'

'He'll not be wanting those, pet,' she said gently. 'His mouth's too sore for the minute.'

Dean offered them to her. 'You have them,' he said.

The nurse blushed. She was nice, and he felt a bit mean, fooling her like this, but he shoved the Maltesers at her and said, 'Mum says you deserve a medal, the way you've looked after our Barry.'

He couldn't know that Mrs Mandel had complained long and hard that her son wasn't getting enough attention, that he needed stronger painkillers, that he shouldn't be stuck in a side ward with a lot of incontinent geriatrics. He did notice the surprise on the nurse's face, however, and added, 'Well, that's what she said . . .'

'It's after time, love. We don't allow visitors on the ward this late.'

Rapid footsteps from somewhere around the corner, then, 'Carla?'

'Just coming,' the nurse called. She looked down at Dean and chewed her lower lip. 'I suppose a few minutes won't hurt — only you will keep the noise down, won't you? There's a chap just come up from the operating room.'

Dean nodded, copying the wide-eyed innocent look he'd seen in nine- and ten-year-olds.

The buzzer sounded again, and he pushed the chocolates into her hands, giving her a happy grin before he turned and padded down the corridor. Baz's bed was furthest from the door. All three patients were asleep, but Baz started and groaned as Dean pulled the curtain around his bed, for privacy.

A drip fed into his arm, while another tube emerged from under the bedclothes and trickled yellow liquid into a container on the floor. His face was swollen, mottled purple and black with bruising, and his skin looked stretched and full, like an overripe pear. His right eye, as big as a golf ball, was closed. His lip had shrunk to almost normal size, but it was disfigured with stitches.

It made Dean sick to look at him, and for a minute or two he stared instead at the steady drip-drip-drip of liquid from the bag above the bed. When he looked down again, Baz's one good eye was open.

'Come to gloat?' His voice was hoarse, barely more than a whisper.

'You should've got worse.'

The eye closed and Baz's head sank into the pillow. 'What d'you want, Dean?'

'A name.'

'Sheryl Crow — will that do?'

'Who did it? Who turned over your gran's?'

Baz's mouth twitched — the closest he could manage to a smile. 'Think I've got a death wish?'

'I don't know, have you?'

'Give over, Dean. I've been threatened by professionals.'

'You were with him,' Dean said. 'That night. You know what happened.'

Baz sighed. 'I didn't kill him.'

'I'm listening,' Dean said. He didn't want to make a mistake. What he was planning was a mortal sin. Not even an eternity in purgatory could wipe a mortal sin from your soul. He felt the knife slip a little and reached back to reposition it in his waistband.

'He said he felt sick,' Baz told him. 'Got off the bus. That's the last I saw of him.'

'Yeah? And why was he sick?'

Baz didn't answer.

Dean reached back and unclipped the catch on the leather sheath of Ryan's knife. 'I asked you a question.'

'I don't know, maybe he had a bad pint.'

'He was in training. Ryan never touched booze when he was in training.'

'Well he did that night.'

'You're a bloody liar.'

'Maybe he did and maybe he didn't. I wasn't watching. I'm not his *mother*.'

'You were supposed to be his mate. You're supposed to look after your mates.' Dean felt tears well up but was unable to stop them.

Baz looked away.

'You gave him something, didn't you? You slipped him a Mickey. Look at me.' Baz shook his head, staring at the drawn curtains. 'Look at me, you bastard!' Dean hit him once in the chest. Baz groaned and coughed, his chest making alarming liquid gurglings. Dean stood back from the bed, frightened, wondering if he should call the nurse. At last, the coughing subsided, and Baz looked at him. He was crying.

'Tell me,' Dean said.

Baz began to talk in a slow, laboured whisper, stopping every few words to catch his breath.

'I spiked his drink . . . Just for a laugh. He got high . . . Relaxed, for once in his . . . life . . .'

Dean wanted to hit him again, but he controlled his anger because he needed to hear the rest. 'We were going to this pub I know . . . but Ryan . . . got sick.' Baz stopped. 'I didn't mean for him to . . . It was a joke . . . A giggle.' The tears were streaming down his face. 'He was mad at me. Knew what I'd done . . . He . . . got off the bus. I don't know . . . what happened after that — I swear . . . I swear I don't.'

Dean stood at the window, watching the lights of the city swim in and out of focus. His shoulders heaved and he shook all over, but he couldn't cry. He thought he'd had it all worked out: Barry had killed Ryan because Ryan was going to turn him in. It was simple, straight-forward: he would repay his debt to Ryan. He couldn't think of it as it really was, even though he was carrying Ryan's fishing knife around with him, knowing what he intended to do with it. Baz was the cause of Ryan's death. He had a picture in his head: the Montagues and the Capulets fighting it out in a town square; he cast himself in the role of Mercutio. If he got rid of Baz, then perhaps he would have earned some peace — but Mercutio had died, hadn't he? What had the Prince said at the end? 'All are punished.' Now he saw that his guilt and Baz's were alike. Theirs were both sins of omission.

The door opened and the nurse came in, rattling the curtain back on its rail. 'How're you two getting on?' she asked.

Dean turned and ran from the room.

39

Nick was home when Geri and Lauren got back, sitting in the TV room, looking sorry for himself.

'I thought you were working tonight,' Geri said, being careful to keep her tone neutral.

'I'm not feeling too good,' he said, avoiding eye contact. 'I might go back to bed.' He looked up at her, a swift, furtive glance, then away again.

Geri glanced at him, suspecting that he was spoiling for a row over the locksmith, but he seemed fretful rather than irritable.

'I'll probably be up late,' she said. 'I'll maybe sleep on the sofa.'

He stared dully at her for a few seconds, then looked away. 'Might be for the best,' he said. 'If I've got a virus . . .' He stopped mid-sentence as if going on with the lie was too much effort.

'You got your keys?' Geri was aware that they were talking to each other with the polite distance of mere acquaintances, and she felt an ache just below her sternum. Since their argument that morning, she had tried not to think of his easy dismissal of the possible danger she and Lauren were in the previous night. She didn't want to believe that he was more concerned about his bike than her safety. Now, seeing him unrepentant, perhaps even resentful, she found the hurt of his indifference almost unbearable. *It's over*, she thought, and her heart contracted. *It really is over.*

Nick shot her a look of — of what? Reproach? Regret? As he walked away and she heard his slow tread on the stairs, she almost called him back, but what would be the point? Another brief reconciliation, then a downward spiral into bitter rows?

The television had been turned down low, and Geri watched the actors grind their way through an aimless plot, delivering meaningless dialogue, and saw in their earnest posturing the futility of her own interactions with Nick. She fixed her gaze on a biking magazine Nick had left on the arm of a chair. Suddenly she was crying.

Lauren sat and put her arm around her.

Geri wiped her eyes. 'I've made such an unholy mess of things.'

'No, you haven't.'

'I *have*! I should've talked to Frank earlier. I knew he was upset. I just left it till it was too late. If only he'd *talked* to someone . . . I should've found out what was bothering Adèle and I didn't. I should've told the police what I knew, and I didn't. And now I've sent Joe out looking for Adèle and I might have put him in danger.'

Lauren stiffened and Geri faltered, looking into her friend's face. 'Lauren, are you ill? You're as pale as plaster.'

Lauren gave her a squeeze, then let go. 'I'll make us some tea, shall I?' she said. 'I'm just cold, Geri. You know what I'm like in the cold.'

She started for the door, but Geri said, 'You had a call, didn't you? Frank rang you.'

Lauren changed course and went to the window, hugging her elbows. 'I can't talk about it, Geri. You know I can't.'

'What did he say?'

Lauren shook her head.

'That's why you were upset on Thursday, isn't it?' She stared at Lauren's back. 'You could have saved him, and you said nothing.'

Lauren spun round, her eyes glittering with tears. 'I couldn't, Geri. I couldn't break his confidence. He asked me not to—' She broke off. 'I shouldn't even be telling you this.' She strode to the door.

'At least tell me when! When did you speak to him?'

'Last Sunday, all right?' She was out in the hall before Geri could react.

She blinked, then ran to the door. '*Sunday*?' she called after Lauren, who was already halfway up the stairs. 'It can't have been Sunday.'

'All right, early hours of Monday.'

No!' Geri followed Lauren up the stairs. 'He was *dead* last Sunday. He died—' She took a breath. 'They're not sure exactly when he died, but they think he was . . .' For a moment she couldn't go on. 'He'd been there several days,' she finished, her voice hoarse and choked.

Lauren turned to face her. 'I spoke to him!' she insisted.

'To someone,' Geri answered. 'But not to Frank.'

A breathless silence. Then Lauren came down a few steps and looked into Geri's eyes.

'Oh, God,' she said, grasping Geri's hand. 'He wanted me to meet him. He wanted to be sure he'd got the right person.'

A more sinister meaning to the phrase suggested itself. Geri squeezed her hand, and Lauren began shaking. Geri put her arms around her and held her until she was calmer, then she drew her down to sit next to her on the stairs.

'It was definitely Frank the first time,' Lauren said at last. 'I'm sure it was.'

'He called more than once?'

'He was so frightened.'

'What did he say?'

Lauren made a move to get up, but Geri restrained her. 'You have to protect yourself, Lauren. What if the break-in was—'

'Oh, Jesus,' Lauren whispered, then slowly, reluctantly, 'He gave me a name. I wasn't sure if I'd heard him right.'

She remembered that last call, the unnerving way in which she felt that he was running the show, that *he* was the one in control of the situation.

'What was the name?' Geri asked. 'Who was Frank so frightened of?'

'He was upset,' Lauren said. 'It was difficult to make it out.'

'*Lauren!*'

She took a breath. 'Georgie,' she said. 'I think he said Georgie.'

'We've got to call the police — tell them what you know.'

Lauren shook her head. 'I should talk to someone — get advice.'

'If that's what you feel you have to do,' Geri said, exasperated by Lauren's insistence on viewing the situation from the Samaritans' perspective. 'In the meantime, I'm calling the police.'

'And what will you tell them?' Lauren demanded, returning to her old self for a moment. 'I don't *know* anything. "I got a call two weeks ago from someone who refused to give a name — but it might have been Frank Traynor, you understand, officer — and he said the guy he was scared of was called . . . Well, I'm not quite sure, but he might've said Georgie."' She shook her head. 'They'll think I'm barmy!'

Geri thought for a moment. Lauren was right, it did sound preposterous. 'Okay,' she said, determined not to be put off. 'I'll talk to Vince.'

She rang his number, but it was constantly engaged. 'I'll go round,' she said. 'You stay here and wait for word from Joe, I'll try to get Vince to come over.'

* * *

Dean stood outside an ordinary-looking suburban house, looking up at the light in one of the bedroom windows. He couldn't go home, not until he knew who to blame — apart from himself — because with blame came punishment. Dean was already being punished. The fact of Ryan's death was constant punishment, but he had made other acts of contrition: the cuts on his arms, and the throbbing pain in his damaged tooth bore testament to his willingness to make reparation. Baz had been punished, too, but the one person who truly deserved to suffer was still free, and Dean could not rest until he was found and punished.

His religious interpretation was simple: sins must be paid for, you must atone, but Dean's understanding of atonement owed less to the Christian doctrine of the New Testament than to the Old Testament's edicts of bloody retribution.

He had cycled for an hour or so after leaving the hospital and ended up outside this perfectly ordinary house in a quiet street. He watched the house for fifteen minutes, trying to decide what to do, then a car swished up the road towards him, slowing as it came closer, and to avoid being seen, he wheeled his bike up the drive and rang the bell.

It took a long time, but eventually the hall light went on and a shape appeared behind the frosted glass of the front door.

She was taller than his mum, and older. One side of her face was swollen and puffy, and even his untrained eye could that see she was wearing a lot of make-up.

'I'm Dean,' he said. 'It's about our Ryan.'

Agnes Hepple gasped, all suspicion fled. 'Oh, love!' she exclaimed. 'You're soaked through. Come in!'

He propped his bike against the wall and stepped inside, wiping his feet carefully on the doormat. She walked ahead of him, but turned when she realized he wasn't following.

'I'll drip on your carpet,' he said, suddenly distressed.

'Not a bit of it! Here—' She stripped him of his coat and he hissed as she caught the red lines of punishment on his arms. She bustled into the kitchen, shoving him ahead of her, and found a fresh towel for him to dry his hair. He rubbed it while he looked around him. It was twice the size of their kitchen at home and had a big pine table in the centre. No proper fitted units, only a Welsh dresser and pine cupboards, but nice, all the same.

'You must be perished,' she said. 'Sit down, love. Sit down.' When she had fed him tea and biscuits and satisfied herself that he was warm and dry, she sat opposite him at the table.

'Now,' she said. 'You've come about your Ryan.' She placed both hands palms down on the scuffed surface of the table and closed her eyes, drawing in a deep breath.

'He's worried about you.' Her voice had changed subtly; it was higher and lighter. It made Dean think of birds fluttering. 'He says you're acting wild.'

'Tell him I can take care of myself,' he replied ungraciously. 'It's him I've come about, not me.'

'Tell him yourself,' Miss Hepple said.

Dean looked over his shoulder, taking it slowly, not wanting any unpleasant surprises. 'You mean . . . ?'

'The other shoulder,' she said. 'And he's smiling.'

He whipped round, his eyes wide. 'I can't see nothing.'

She laughed. 'Isn't that why you've come to me?' She patted his hand. 'Not everyone's got the gift.'

'Where is he?' he asked, frightened, despite his attempt to appear cool.

Miss Hepple indicated a spot to his left. 'He says if you've got something to say, you might as well come right out with it.'

'All right,' he said, turning around in his chair and resting one arm along the top. 'Okay, you asked for it . . . You're a daft bloody twat — sorry miss, but he is. If I got off the bus in the middle of bloody nowhere, what would you say to me — eh, Ryan? "Stick with your mates", you always said. "They look out for you, you look out for them." What the *hell* did you think you were playing at?'

He stopped, breathless and tearful and, stared at the blank space next to him until Miss Hepple spoke.

'He says he's sorry for putting you through all that. He says it's not your fault — you've to stop blaming yourself.'

'It's too bloody late for that.'

'He was tricked. He says he felt weird.'

'Baz slipped him a Mickey.'

'He felt sick . . .'

Dean nodded. 'I already know all that.' He eyed Miss Hepple hungrily, waiting for her to tell him what he had come to find out.

She closed her eyes again. The voice she heard was clear and strong, as real as the voices on the radio she had left on in her bedroom. She felt faint; a tremor of fear ran through her as she said, 'It was someone he trusted.'

An icy chill coursed through Dean and he shuddered violently.

'Someone everyone trusts . . .' she went on. '*I thought he'd help*.' She relayed the words she heard in her head directly to the boy. '*He knows the area, he'll get me home all right*.' She paused, opening her eyes and blinking in the light, then she said in a small, shocked voice, 'But he didn't.'

A spark of anger kindled and began to glow in Dean's gut. For the first time in weeks there was hope — a perverse, twisted kind of hope, but it was better than the cold emptiness he had felt, the bitter recriminations against himself since that day in Mrs Golding's office.

'Who is it?' Dean asked. 'Where is he?'

Miss Hepple touched the swelling beneath her eyes and ran her tongue around the inside of her lip. The teeth had mashed the soft tissues when he had hit her.

Until now, she hadn't known it herself; but she had experienced one of her blinding intuitions, a spiritual epiphany, when she truly felt in touch with the spirit world. It made perfect sense on a purely practical level, too — how else could he have known so much? How else had he been able to tell her precisely how Ryan and Frank died? Why shouldn't she tell the boy? He had a right to know. A right to see justice done.

She put from her mind the notion that what she wanted was revenge, not justice. She was helping Mrs Connelly's child — both her children — to find peace.

* * *

Vince sat within three feet of the TV screen. He had skimmed through the first hour of video tape and had reached the crucial point. The last couple of hours at work he had spent waiting for Garvey to tap him on the shoulder and demand what he had done with the missing videotape, but its absence had not been noticed — at least not yet — the CID having run through it and presumably got what they needed, including the incriminating footage of him talking to the rent boys.

The concourse was almost empty. The boy he thought of as James Dean was standing alone, leaning against a wall below the poster advertising vodka. For several minutes the boy stood against the wall, shifting position, slumping into a moodier pose when a crowd of commuters got off a train and swept through the concourse on the way out. Then a tall, nervous-looking youth came into shot from the direction of the main entrance. Frank. He hesitated, his eyes darting anxiously about him, then he went over to the boy. Vince leaned closer.

The doorbell rang.

'*Shit!*' He had taken the phone off the hook, but the curtains stood open and his sitting room looked out onto the street. He fumbled the video control unit, first pressing *Pause* instead of *Stop*, finally managing to eject the tape as the bell rang a second time. They weren't going to go away.

Geri had her finger poised to ring again when he opened the door. She apologized immediately.

'No,' he said. 'It's okay. Come in.' He held the door for her, directing her through to the sitting room on the right of the hallway.

He saw her take in the length of shelving he'd built along one wall, stacked with videos, books and CDs; the sofa bed near the door and his large-screen TV, set into one of the alcoves at the side of the fireplace.

'Sit down,' he said, then hearing the peremptory tone in his own voice, added, 'Please.'

Geri went to the sofa. He turned off the TV, now broadcasting a static snowstorm, but he didn't sit with her; instead he stood with his back to the door, his arms folded.

* * *

He looked handsome in an understated way, Geri thought. Black jeans and a crew-neck sweater, watching her closely with his blue-grey eyes.

'I've interrupted your evening,' she began.

'I wasn't doing much,' he said, but his edgy manner told her otherwise.

'I've come to ask for your help,' she said simply. She told him everything that had happened since the previous day, culminating in the name Frank had given Lauren.

Vince seemed distracted. He didn't respond at first, and Geri wondered if he had been listening. Then he broke the silence.

'We're already looking for the girl,' he said. 'But it's useful to have a name. Taxing's a problem that waxes and wanes — we had problems eight or nine months ago, but we stamped on the culprits and they went away for a while. They're small-time criminals, hard to pin down. If the *Big Issue* manager hadn't heard about it, we certainly wouldn't. I'll talk to him on Monday — see what I can do.'

'What about the name — Georgie?'

'Your friend isn't sure it was Frank Traynor who called her,' he said doubtfully. 'And she can't be sure about the name he gave her, either . . .'

'She's sure it was Frank,' Geri said growing increasingly desperate. If she couldn't persuade Vince to help them, how could she hope to convince CID? 'Come and talk to Lauren,' she pleaded. 'Let her explain.'

He shook his head slowly. 'I can't do that.'

'You said you weren't busy. *Please*, Vince.'

'I've just finished a double shift, and I'm on again at eight tomorrow morning,' he said. 'Besides, there's no point. I'll pass on the info to DCI Thomas and he'll be in touch.'

Geri realized she was being dismissed.

'I'm sorry to have taken up your time,' she said, bitterly disappointed.

'I'm just tired, Geri.' He passed a hand over his face. 'Why don't you have a coffee? Or I think I've got some beer in the fridge.'

'No,' Geri said. 'Thanks, but I promised I'd be back.'

He moved out of her way and showed her to the front door. As she slid behind the wheel of her car, she saw him watching her from the doorway and she felt a sudden spasm of uneasiness. She put her foot down and pulled away too fast, skidding on the wet surface.

Vince shut the door and went back into his sitting room. He pushed the tape back into the machine and pressed *Play*.

Frank stood next to James Dean. A third figure came into camera shot, dressed in uniform, watching them both. As he approached, Frank backed away.

Vince was out of the house before the tape had ejected. He ran a couple of red lights on his way to the railway station. If he was stopped, he wasn't likely to get a sympathetic hearing, but the way he saw it, he could risk a fine for speeding or miss his chance altogether. There had been two witnesses at the station that night: Frank and James Dean. Now there was just James Dean.

He parked on double yellow lines in Handley Street, leaving his hazard lights on. On the concourse, he scanned the faces. It was a bit early, but he was confident he'd find him there: Jimmy Dean was keen.

The boy saw Vince first. Vince saw him check that his jacket collar was up and adjust his pose slightly to cast shadows on one side of his face.

Vince walked towards him, picking up the pace as he got closer. The sullen pout turned to a confused frown, then the boy pushed himself away from the wall and his eyes opened wide. By then it was too late — Vince was on him.

He took him by the elbow and started steering him towards the entrance.

'Hey! What the fuck, man?' The boy struggled, tugging, twisting, trying to get away. His voice rose to a shout, then cracked, and he was screaming.

Two of the boy's co-workers came at him from the right, looking wary, but willing to have a go.

'He's a pervert!' the boy screamed. 'I'm being abducted!'

People were turning to see what the noise was about. There was a danger that someone would try to stop him. Vince dipped into his inside pocket as a security guard approached him, hands raised, palms down, placatory.

'Police officer,' Vince yelled, showing his warrant card. 'He's under arrest.'

'I haven't *done* nothing!' The boy's voice had risen to a squeak: he was scared, close to tears, and people began to gather, moving in behind the security guard.

Vince had to get the boy out of there before someone got heroic.

'Done nothing?' He held the boy one-handed while he checked through his pockets. He came out with a plastic wrap. It contained a white crystalline powder. He held up the packet for the crowd to see and felt the boy physically slump: all the fight had gone out of him.

'Now back off,' Vince shouted, 'or I'll do you for obstruction!' The crowd parted reluctantly, and he hustled the boy out of the station and into his car.

For a while he sat with the packet dangling between his index and middle fingers. The boy slouched low in his seat. 'What's your name?' Vince asked, after a long silence.

No reply. Vince grunted. 'I'll call you James,' he said.

The boy's head jerked up. 'Jamie.'

'What?'

'My name's Jamie, not James.'

Vince grinned. 'You're kidding me.' He saw that the boy was serious. 'Okay — Jamie, what's in the packet?'

The boy shrugged.

'Let me guess.' He tilted the packet to catch the light from the streetlamps. The crystals glittered in the pink-tinged glow. 'Crank?'

The boy shifted uncomfortably.

'Working nights can be tough going for a lad your age. Crank would keep you going, though, wouldn't it?'

The boy looked out of the window, refusing to answer.

'Methamphetamine,' Vince said. 'Better than speed. Some like it more than coke — and it's certainly cheaper, isn't it?'

'I wouldn't know.'

'This your first time, is it?'

'It's a plant, and you know it.'

'You've never seen it before.'

'Not until you took it out of my pocket.'

'Oh . . . you're saying *I* put it there.'

The boy rolled his eyes and said, 'Duh . . .'

'Well, since you've never taken it before, let me tell you about crank, Jamie.' He looked down at the boy, and reassessed his age, revising his estimate downwards by a couple of years.

'Crank makes you feel like Superman. You can do anything, be anything, take on anyone. I tried to arrest a lad who'd been smoking crank. Want to know what happened?'

Jamie shrugged.

'Go on, your turn to guess.'

Jamie looked straight ahead. 'Bet he left you flat-footed.'

'You might say that.' Vince thought about it for a few moments. 'You might say he did . . .'

He stared at the packet of sugary crystals for a few seconds, then turned his gaze, cold and hard, on the boy. 'He walked off a roof.'

Jamie gasped.

'Straight off.' For a fraction of a second the air seemed to lift him up — it just held him there, then—' Vince brought his hands together with a *crack!* 'Piss, blood and brains all over the pavement.'

Jamie scrabbled at the door, trying to get out, but the handle was missing. Vince took hold of him by the lapels and shoved him back in the seat.

'Think you're Superman, Jamie? Well this—' He held the packet centimetres from the boy's nose. 'This is kryptonite.'

40

The bike's kick-start cranked and coughed twice, then the engine caught, and the Bonny rumbled and growled as Nick backed it out of the workshop. Lauren looked out of the sitting room window onto the street. He was fully kitted out: leathers, boots and helmet. Seemed he had fought off the 'flu. Once on the street, he flicked a switch and the taillights flared. A bag was strapped to the pannier.

'Oh, God,' Lauren sighed. Poor Geri.

He checked over his shoulder, then roared off into the night, leaving an echo, and a faint shimmer of light behind him.

Lauren had come to a decision: she would telephone Meredith and tell her everything. She wasn't relishing explaining how she came to tell Geri about Frank's call to the Samaritans; she should have spoken to her supervisor before saying anything, but the revelation that Frank was already dead when she'd got taken a phone call from him the previous Sunday had come as a shock, to put it mildly. Still, Lauren thought, feeling an uncomfortable warmth in her cheeks, it was unprofessional of her to have blurted it all out like that.

She got as far as lifting the receiver when the doorbell rang. She hesitated, then, with a shrug, she replaced the handset in its cradle and went to the door.

'Joe!' She stepped back to let him in, but he remained on the doorstep.

'Tell Geri,' he said. 'I'll wait in the car.'

'She's not here.'

'Shit! I can't guarantee she'll stay put.' He half-turned, looking back towards the car.

'Adèle? You've found her?'

'Aye.' He glanced over his shoulder to his car, idling at the kerb. 'Look, what d'you want to do?'

Lauren considered: if they waited for Geri to get back, they might lose Adèle again. But Adèle trusted Geri, and she didn't even know her or Joe . . .

'Where is she?' she asked. 'I'll leave Geri a note.'

'Hard to explain. It's an old storehouse near the docks. We'll phone her when we get there.'

Lauren dashed back inside and grabbed her bag and coat.

The warehouse was in a part of town Lauren had never ventured into before. The buildings had a greasy, glistening sheen in the continuing rain. It was darker on this side of the city; there were fewer streetlamps, and the damaged ones hadn't been repaired — and of course there was no light in the blank, mournful windows of the deserted buildings.

Joe drove off the main road, down a series of potholed and ruined cobbled side streets. Brown tufts of last summer's weed growth colonised the cracks in the paving stones. Joe cut the engine and lights and they coasted the last twenty-five yards down a slight incline, coming to a halt outside a two-storey building with a flat roof.

He took a torch from the boot of his car, shining the beam along the side of the building to indicate the path.

'Mind you don't trip,' he cautioned. The gap between this and the next building was wide enough to take a car, but the cobbles had been torn up in places and bricks and rubble were strewn about.

'See that door?' He spoke softly, keeping close to Lauren, catching her by the elbow once, when she stumbled.

The lock on the door had been broken and it swung inwards to her touch. The air inside was freezing, and although the windows were intact, they had been boarded over so that the darkness was an almost tangible thing, with texture and substance. Joe swung the torch in an arc, and Lauren saw that the ground floor was a vast open space, empty except for old packing material and small piles of rubbish. The light glanced off the panes of glass in the windows, and Lauren saw her own ghostly reflection, looking cold and anxious: she hadn't had time to put on her usual extra couple of layers against the cold.

'Where is she?' she whispered.

'This way.' He went to a staircase in the centre of the floor space which led to an office mezzanine which took up one third of the building's length and seemed to be little more than a wooden box on stilts. 'Keep to the sides — the wood's a bit soggy in the middle.'

'Okay,'

'No need to whisper now,' he said in his normal voice. 'There's only one way out of here, and that's it.' He nodded to the door they had just come through.

Lauren saw a faint glow on the landing as she mounted the steps. The air smelled of damp plaster; she could taste it on her tongue, and it caught at the back of her throat.

Wood-framed partitions in painted pine planking divided off the area up to a height of about four feet. The upper sections of the partitions consisted of window panels, about nine inches square.

'She's using one of the offices.' Joe gestured for Lauren to go forward while he guarded the stairs. She went to the office at the end of the row, where there was as faint glimmer of light through the windows. She hesitated, then knocked softly before turning the door handle.

A single candle stood on the floor beside a sleeping bag and bedroll.

'She's gone.'

'Shit!' Joe worked towards her, checking each office on either side of the corridor before moving on. 'Here.' He beckoned her to follow him to the far end of the room, which lacked a window panel and where they would be invisible from outside.

'We'll wait for a bit — see if she comes back. Maybe she went for a pee or something.'

* * *

Geri was gripped by a paralysing fear. She stood in the porch, listening. Waiting to hear the sound of someone ransacking the house. Where the hell was Nick? His workshop was open, and the bike gone. *Oh, God! No! No! No!*

'Lauren?' Her voice echoed faintly through the hall. why had she involved Lauren? She had gone on, asking questions, making waves, not stopping to think of the danger. She grabbed the door frame for support; she had never been so frightened. Fighting an impulse to run, she ventured inside. Concern for her friend gave her the courage to continue. She closed the front door and ventured further into the house. It was like a repeat of the previous night, except this time, the house seemed secure. Even so, Geri felt the same gut-wrenching terror.

She ran to the kitchen, the sitting room, the TV room, checked Lauren's bedroom, the bathroom, even the spare rooms — Lauren was not home. A terrible premonitory dread gripped her, and she became convinced that the man who had telephoned the Samaritans on Sunday had taken her.

She rang Vince but his line was still engaged. She hung up immediately and began dialling 999 but disconnected when she recalled how reluctant the police had been to search for Ryan, and he had already been missing for twelve hours when his parents first called.

She put her head in her hands, ready to abandon herself to her terror, berating herself for having left Lauren alone, then her head came up and she ran from the TV room to the sitting room. Joe! He must have found Adèle. She riffled the pages of her address book, almost ripping them in her haste to find Joe's mobile number.

* * *

Lauren and Joe crouched side by side.

'Oh, hell,' Joe stood up and started pacing. 'She's not coming back, is she? She must've heard me, earlier.'

'We should give her a few more minutes.'

'What's the point? She's long gone.' He kicked a ball of paper and sent it skittering across the floor. 'I wanted to get this bastard, Lauren. I've watched the kids, looking over their shoulders, the fear in their eyes . . .'

Lauren got up, easing the pins and needles out of her feet. As Joe paced, the candle guttered, its yellow light giving his skin a waxy cast, the unsteady flickering mirroring his agitation. He stopped and turned abruptly to face her. The candlelight shimmered behind him like a halo, but he was a black, solid mass at the far end of the room. 'They'll never catch him now, will they?'

The misery, frustration, and regret in his voice invoked her own anguish in not be able to do more to help. 'They might . . .' she said.

His face was no more than a dark oval, but she sensed his interest: she had his full attention.

'Frank gave me a name.'

'And?'

She shook her head. 'I'm not sure if I heard it right.'

'What was it?'

'Georgie.'

'What do the police say?'

'I haven't told them, yet. Geri—'

'So, you've told *her* . . .'

He moved, no more than a shifting of his weight from one foot to the other; she heard it scrape on the gritty floor, and his shadow touched Lauren's face. She sensed danger as a tangible presence. 'Geri?' she said. 'No. I — I meant—'

Hearing the rising panic in her voice, powerless to control it. 'What would be the point? I'm — I'm probably wrong anyway. Forget I said anything.'

'Sorry, pet,' Joe said. 'No can do.'

* * *

Geri misdialled and made an effort to slow down on her second attempt. It was answered on the fifth ring.

'Joe!'

'I was just about to ring you.' He sounded out of breath.

'Lauren — she's not here. Have you seen her? Is she with you?'

'She's here,' he soothed, 'With Adèle.' He lowered his voice. 'She's a bit hysterical, but Lauren's been great.'

'Christ, Joe! I've been worried sick!'

'My fault. Lauren wanted to leave a note, but I was that worried Adèle'd do a bunk again . . .'

'Where are you?' Geri demanded.

'Northwaite's Storehouse. You want to come? I'll give you directions — Adèle'd be happier with a familiar face.' His voice grew fainter, as if he was holding the receiver away from his mouth. 'Geri,' he said. 'She's on her way.'

41

Sirens howled in the distance as Geri pulled up outside Northwaite's Storehouse. Chinese New Year celebrations got out of hand, Geri speculated.

Joe's car was parked outside the front entrance. A helicopter buzzed overhead, somewhere near the waterfront, she guessed, and getting nearer. She looked up but could see nothing in the narrow slats of sky visible between the warehouses. The wind had abated somewhat, but the rain continued to fall implacably, and she was drenched before she had finished locking the car.

The front of the building had been ostentatiously secured: there was steel cladding over the double doors, riveted and bolted in place, and boards over the windows. To the right, the storehouse was attached to a much taller building — an old grain store — to the left was a cobbled access road. She walked to the left of the building, taking it slowly because the darkness and the unevenness of the road surface made the going hazardous.

She found the side door and went in. It was inky black and intensely cold. She sensed a large, open space, but could hear nothing over the persistent thrum of rain in the street behind her. She stood near the door, allowing her eyes time to adapt.

'Lauren?' she called. 'Joe?'

'Over here.'

A faint outline drifted into her vision, but it disappeared when she turned to look at it. Smells of damp concrete and mould mingled with a sharper, coppery smell which made her stomach do a slow roll. Joe didn't speak again, so she walked forward, sliding her feet along the floor and stretching her arms out in front of her.

About five yards in she stumbled over an obstacle and put her hands down to save herself. It was soft and yielded to her touch. She bent cautiously and felt the object. It was warm. Her breath came in short gasps as she explored the still form, her hands moving more and more frantically upwards: arms, shoulders, neck. She looked to her left, trying to catch the face in her more sensitive peripheral vision.

A torch beam shone with pitiless precision and she could see. It was Lauren. She was bleeding. Frighteningly still, very pale. A sticky red pool surrounded her head. Geri wanted to close her eyes, to shut out the terrible image, but she couldn't look away, couldn't even blink. She knelt beside her friend and the torch light flashed in her eyes. Geri shielded them with her hand and peered into the glare.

'It's all right, it's me.'

'Joe! What happened? She's hurt!'

'Adèle . . .' He moved closer and the light wobbled and jerked wildly about the room. 'She went berserk.'

As he drew closer, she saw that he was injured, too. His face was bruised, and he had a cut over his right eye.

'Give me your mobile,' she said. 'I'll call for help.'

'I was looking for it,' he said. 'Must've dropped it in the struggle.'

He stood over them now and shone the torch into Lauren's face. She did not flinch.

'I think she's—'

'No!' Geri couldn't let him say it, couldn't even think it. 'She'll be fine. But we have to get *help*!'

She sobbed, trying frantically to find a pulse, and thought she could feel a flutter in Lauren's neck. Her skin felt clammy and so very cold.

Geri stood, almost knocking Joe over, and began stripping off her jacket.

'What're you doing?'

'She's cold,' Geri said. 'Lauren hates the cold.' Tears streamed down her face as she covered Lauren with her jacket, tucking it gently in around her neck and shoulders. She stood and wiped her face with the heel of her hand, then turned to the door.

Joe caught her arm. 'You can't leave.'

He had a strange light in his eye, and Geri thought that perhaps he was concussed. She tugged away from him, but he held her fast.

'Joe, you aren't up to driving, and we need to get an ambulance for Lauren — for both of you.'

'Let go of her.' They both looked towards the door. It was Vince.

Joe didn't budge. Geri felt the pressure of his fingers increase. 'It's him,' he hissed. 'He did Ryan and Frank.'

Vince took a step into the room. 'Geri,' he said. 'Walk towards me.'

Geri held back.

'You must be joking,' Joe said, pinning him in the beam of his torch. 'Adèle told us all about you. She saw you in the warehouse . . . He set fire to Frank.'

Geri felt as if she had been kicked in the stomach.

'Listen to me, Geri,' Vince said. 'Joe was on security on Handley Street station the night Frank disappeared, covering the concourse at chucking-out time.'

Geri felt Joe shake his head. 'Yep, I was on duty. What were *you* doing there that night?' He grunted at Vince's expression of surprise. 'Oh, aye, I saw you.' He lowered his voice. 'He was cruising the concourse, looking for underage talent. Paying for it with drugs.'

Cruising? What was he saying? That Vince was some kind of paedophile? *The hash she had found in the lining of her coat!* Geri had blamed Jay. After all, he had knocked the coat to the floor the night she had banned Baz from the youth club. But now she saw it with stark clarity: Vince picking the coat up, dusting it off, hanging it back on the rail.

'We've got you on tape,' Vince went on. 'You and Frank together. Frank looks terrified.'

Geri looked from one to the other, confused, frightened, desperate to get help for Lauren. These were both men she trusted — *had* trusted — and now she couldn't read either of them.

'Frank talked to one of the lads on the concourse,' Vince was saying. 'He's in protective custody. And he's confirmed that Joe followed Frank out of the railway station — except he knows Joe as the Taxman.'

Geri started. *The Taxman!* The same man who had frightened Adèle into hiding?

'Joe, let *go* of me!' she shouted. 'Let me go, I need to think!' His grip tightened.

'Got your finger in a lot of pies, haven't you, Joe?' Vince said.

'He's lying,' Joe licked his lips. 'He's making it up.'

'What did Frank say, Geri?' Vince asked. 'What was the name he gave Lauren?'

'Georgie,' Geri said, not understanding.

'It *sounded* like Georgie. He was upset, remember. Maybe even drunk. It was *Geordie* he said, not Georgie . . . "Bastard Geordie".'

Geri gasped and pulled away, but Joe held on, grabbing a handful of hair and inadvertently cuffing her with the torch which was still in his hand. Geri swung out with her free hand, but he caught her off balance, switched his grip and got his right arm around her neck. His coat was still wet, and the thick, animal smell of damp wool nauseated her. He tightened his grip on her arm and she cried out in pain.

'Listen,' Vince said. The buzz of the helicopter had become a clatter and the sirens were almost upon them.

'You've got nothing to hide any more, Joe.'

They heard the slamming of doors outside, and seconds later half a dozen uniformed police piled in, behind Vince. Beams of torchlight danced in all directions, fracturing the scene like pictures refracted through a prism. Vince held up his hand and the men came to a halt.

'Everyone knows,' Vince said.

'They don't know fuck all,' Joe said. 'Adèle attacked us — the lass you've been looking for. She knocked Lauren down the stairs, then turned on me.'

'You don't know when to give up, do you?' Vince said. 'I think you believe half the crap you come out with.' He took a step towards them, but Joe increased the pressure on Geri's windpipe, choking her. Vince raised both hands. 'All right,' he said. 'But look at it sensibly, Joe. You're not getting out of here.'

'You've got nothing against me.' He looked at the police standing behind Vince, tense, ready to fight. 'You know what he is, don't you? He's trying to implicate me, but—'

Vince laughed. 'They know, Joe. They know about me, and they know about you.'

Joe hesitated, unsure of himself.

'You weren't thorough enough,' Vince said softly. 'The bodies got burned, but you didn't destroy everything. There was semen in Frank's stomach. We'll be able to cross-type the DNA.'

Joe slowly released the pressure on Geri's throat and pushed her away from him and, holding her at arm's length, stared into her face as if trying to gauge her reaction.

'Joe?' she said.

He raised one shoulder and gave her that lopsided grin that said *Hey, I'm only human.*

Geri saw with perfect recall the youth club, Jay, his head shaved, trying to sneak past Barry unnoticed. Barry tormenting him, echoing her question, *What on earth possessed you?* Joe had intervened, Geri thought to protect Jay, but she now remembered how cowed Jay seemed: Joe had shaved off Jay's hair as a punishment, and as a warning to the others not to defect to Barry. She remembered Joe's hand on the back of Jay's neck, the fear in Jay's face.

'You planted the drugs on me,' she said. 'Not Barry, *you*. It was you the kids were afraid of. It was you who gave Jay the drugs that nearly put him in a coma,' she said. 'Christ! If I hadn't gone looking for him . . .'

'There's no loyalty cards in my business,' he said. 'But there's penalties for *dis*loyalty.'

* * *

Dean had cycled the length and breadth of the docks, looking for Joe. When Miss Hepple told him, he realized how stupid he had been not to have seen it before. He must have thought he was really clever, being with them every day, talking to them, pretending sympathy, shaking his head and asking, 'What sort of person . . .' and no one suspecting him.

He had seen Miss Simpson's car, surrounded by police cars and, fearing the worst, had crept up the side of the building and through the door. Unnoticed, he had edged his way to the side of the knot of policemen.

Joe let Miss Simpson go. She stumbled forward, then turned again to face him as two constables stepped up and grabbed him.

Miss Simpson spoke: "Someone the kids trust," you said. We *all* trusted you, Joe. Why? What made you do it?'

Joe shrugged. 'He was already high on something when I found him. I was on mobile patrol, rattling padlocks, moving the drunks on.'

Dean stood a little to the side, wanting and dreading to hear the truth, needing some sign that Joe regretted what he had done. But Joe's face was set — hard and cold.

'I never made him do anything,' he said.

Dean sobbed. A few heads turned in his direction, but their attention was drawn back to Joe; it was him they were interested in.

Joe stared directly at Dean. 'It was his idea.'

'No.' Dean's mouth contorted in pain.

'What did you expect, Dean? A confession?'

He had. When you got caught, you were supposed to own up, take your punishment, 'cos it was the right thing to do. For a few seconds, the only sound in the dark, empty warehouse was Dean's tortured sobs. If he had expected a confession, so had they all.

Joe looked around at them and began again. 'Ryan wanted some dope. Said he'd suck me off for it. Well, I'm no shirt-lifter, but I'm not gonna turn down an offer like that, now, am I?'

Joe's eyes burned into Dean's and the boy knew that he was saying these things deliberately to hurt.

'He did the biz, I gave him the dope, he left — licking his lips.'

Fury raged like hot oil in Dean's veins. 'Liar!' he screamed.

He rushed at Joe and punched him hard in the belly.

Vince stepped up and dragged him away. He didn't resist. For the first time since Ryan had disappeared, Dean was completely calm. He had done his duty; now it was in God's hands. He strained against Vince, dwarfed by the policeman — not struggling — but leaning forward on the balls of his feet, waiting.

Joe folded; the torch dropped from his hand and shattered on the floor. His escorts fought with him briefly, thinking he was trying to break free, then he fell. It was only then that they saw the knife, buried to the hilt in Joe's stomach.

Dean relaxed. 'You're a bastard liar, Joe,' he said quietly.

42

They worked on Lauren in the ambulance for fifteen long minutes. Geri sat in her car, trembling convulsively. She felt cold to the centre of her being. Lauren was the closest she had to family, and she had put her in mortal danger. She stared at the closed ambulance doors, willing her friend to live, wishing she could take her place.

Senior officers arrived just after the SOCOs. Geri recognized DCI Thomas. Tape was stretched across the access road at the side of the building to keep out the press, who had somehow got word of the stabbing.

The ambulance moved off slowly and Geri gave a cry. No light — no siren! She fumbled in her pocket for her keys, sobbing, then blue light filled the car, washing over it and she gasped, feeling an overwhelming sense of relief as the siren began its insistent banshee wail.

She dropped her keys trying to get them into the ignition, and as she retrieved them, the passenger door opened and Vince folded himself into the seat next to her.

'You're in shock. You shouldn't be driving.'

'I can't leave her on her own.'

He held out his hand; she gave him the keys and they swapped places.

'Was there any sign of Adèle?' she asked. 'He said she was here.'

'A sleeping bag on the first floor, but I think we'll find it was his.'

'Will you go on looking for her?'

'Sure. She might come out of the woodwork when word gets around on the street telegraph.'

It would take three more weeks, and a personal assurance from Paul Watling at the city's *Big Issue* office before Adèle would feel safe enough to come home. And when she did, Paul was able to tell her that he'd kept her name on the accommodation list in the hope that she would return, and that she would be in her own place by Easter.

'What about Joe?' Geri asked.

'He's gone.'

Neither spoke for some minutes, until, unable to endure the thoughts that crowded her mind, Geri broke the silence. 'He was so . . . charming. So damn *plausible*. What made you suspect him?'

'The memorial service, when he had that stand-off with Barry. Baz implied that Joe was giving the kids M&Ms. It's a street name for E.'

'I found some hash in the lining of my coat.'

'Oh, Geri . . .' He touched her hand lightly. 'I wish you'd told me.'

'I know, I should have, but I was terrified school would find out. I was already in trouble — so bloody worried about my reputation,' she added bitterly. 'I thought Baz had put Jay up to it.' She shook her head in disbelief. 'I never once suspected Joe.'

Vince ran a hand through his hair. 'If I'd been allowed to see the security video earlier . . .' His voice was husky with emotion.

'He said he worked the railway station from time to time,' Geri said, 'but I was so sure Barry had something to do with the deaths.' She sighed.

He turned right, tailing the ambulance towards the city centre. 'Baz gave us a statement this evening.' He checked the rear-view mirror with elaborate care before indicating to follow the ambulance into the outside lane.

'And?'

'He's admitted supplying. He said the men who attacked him were sent by Joe.'

'Did he recognize them?'

Vince shook his head. 'Hired thugs, but they made it clear that Joe didn't welcome his entrepreneurial forays into his empire.'

They parked and went through the door marked Ambulance Admissions. They were going to have to wait some time — the neurosurgeon had been called and he had asked for a brain scan. Geri telephoned Lauren's mother and they went through to the main reception.

After a few minutes' silence, Vince said, 'I'm sorry. You don't deserve this.'

'Well, people don't always get what they deserve, do they?' she said bitterly.

'Joe might take issue with that.'

She had meant Ryan and Frank, their families. She snagged a tissue from her pocket and wiped her eyes.

'What Joe said earlier . . .' She left the question unsaid.

'Yeah,' he said. 'It's true. Not about me cruising for kids, but yeah, I'm gay.' He shrugged.

She waited for him to go on, and when he didn't, she said. 'Okay.'

He turned to face her. 'Is it?'

'Why wouldn't it be? Although you might have given a girl a hint — saved her from falling . . .'

She looked up at him and he blushed. They both smiled, then Geri looked away, feeling suddenly shy.

'What will happen to Dean?' she asked.

'That'll be for the juvenile courts to decide.'

'That's a bit harsh,' she remarked.

He looked down at her. 'I know,' he said, his face lined with exhaustion. 'I know. The kid's been through a lot, but it's not going to look good, a death in custody.'

'He's been out of his mind since Ryan died, Vince. He can't be held responsible.'

'You'll get your chance to vouch for him, I'll make sure.'

They both looked up as a white coat approached them. Geri, her heart pounding, tried to read his expression.

'Miss Simpson,' he said. 'If you'd like to come through.'

Vince helped her to her feet, otherwise she would have sat, unmoving, in her moulded plastic chair. They trailed behind him, through reception, through the swing doors, and into the imperturbable chaos of the accident and emergency department.

Geri walked ever more slowly until she felt Vince's arm around her shoulders, a gentle pressure at her back.

'It's all right,' he said. 'Whatever happens, I'll be with you.'

She wanted to tell him that she didn't want to go any further, with or without him; wanted to explain to him that until you opened the envelope, anything was possible: triple grade As in your exams; a monstrous win on the pools. Until you heard the words, everything was fine: your father was sober, coherent, carrying a birthday present to you; your mother was still doggedly fighting the cancer that struck her down at the age of forty; Lauren was recovering, waking from her coma as from a diffuse dream, complaining of the cold and demanding to know where Geri had skived off to. She reflected that perhaps only Dean could really understand her feelings at this moment.

She stood at the threshold of the private waiting room, looking at the surgeon, knowing that she would have to go in after all, but delaying the moment for as long as possible; for here, where hope and dread were balanced equally, despair could not send its shockwaves to shatter her world.

THE END

ACKNOWLEDGEMENTS

Writing this book under the scrutiny of fellow writers at Liverpool John Moores University was both a trial and a privilege. Their comments and feedback, though tough and uncompromising, were invaluable.

For background research, I am grateful to Pat Riordan at the *Big Issue* office in Liverpool for his wisdom and insight into homelessness. He was generous with both his time and the wealth of information he was willing to impart, and I hope that the resulting portrayal of life on the streets is fair and realistic.

I would also like to thank Dr Eric Robinson of UCL for some fascinating information about the geology of the Thames Valley — his input ensured that Ryan's essay on fossil evidence was factually correct.

Finally, thanks to Rinty, whose recommendation of pub therapy helped me to sort out a troublesome plot line.

ALSO BY MARGARET MURPHY

CLARA PASCAL SERIES
Book 1: DARKNESS FALLS
Book 2: WEAVING SHADOWS

DETECTIVE JEFF RICKMAN SERIES
Book 1: SEE HER BURN
Book 2: SEE HER DIE
Book 3: DON'T SCREAM

DETECTIVE CASSIE ROWAN SERIES
Book 1: BEFORE HE KILLS AGAIN

STANDALONE NOVELS
DEAR MUM
HER HUSBAND'S KILLER
THE LOST BOY
DYING EMBERS

FREE KINDLE BOOKS

Do you love mysteries, historical fiction and romance? Join thousands of readers enjoying great books through our mailing list. You'll get new releases and great deals every week from one of the UK's leading independent publishers.

Join today, and you'll get your first bargain book this month!

www.joffebooks.com/contact

Follow us on Facebook, Twitter and Instagram

@joffebooks

Thank you for reading this book.

If you enjoyed it please leave feedback on Amazon or Goodreads, and if there is anything we missed or you have a question about, then please get in touch. The author and publishing team appreciate your feedback and time reading this book.

www.joffebooks.com

We're very grateful to eagle-eyed readers who take the time to contact us. Please send any errors you find to corrections@joffebooks.com. We'll get them fixed ASAP.

Printed in Great Britain
by Amazon

56782887R00203